THE GOLDEN TREASURY

OF STORIES FOR BOYS & GIRLS

THE GOLDEN TREASURY

OF STORIES FOR
BOYS & GIRLS

ANNA SEWELL   EDWARD LEAR
HILAIRE BELLOC   W. M. THACKERAY
ROBERT BROWNING
LORD MACAULAY
HANS ANDERSEN   GRIMM
WILLIAM COWPER
LEWIS CARROLL
ETC & ETC

LONDON
VICTOR GOLLANCZ LTD

First published in 1959
Revised and reissued 1975
Second impression November 1975
Third impression March 1979

ISBN 0 575 02025 3

In 1932 THE same publishers issued *The Children's Omnibus*. It was edited by Sylvia Lynd, who dedicated it to her two daughters, Shelia and B.J. *The Golden Treasury* is a new form of substantially the same book. The publishers expressed their thanks to the following authors and publishers for permitting their books or portions of their books to be included in this volume: to Mr. Ernest Rhys, and Messrs. Dent for the version of Æsop's fables, from the Everyman Library; to Mr. Hilaire Belloc and Messrs. Duckworth for "Matilda" and "Franklin Hyde," from *Cautionary Tales*; to Messrs. Frederick Warne for Lear's *Nonsense Songs and Stories*, for Mrs. Paull's translation of Andersen's "The Snow Queen," and for some of the Nursery Rhymes collected by Andrew Lang; to Messrs. Harrap for the sentences quoted from *A Little Book of Eastern Wisdom*.

Printed in Great Britain by
Lowe & Brydone Printers Ltd, Thetford, Norfolk

CONTENTS

N.B. Everything in this book is complete and unabridged except *The Travels of Baron Munchausen* and *Æsop's Fables*.

CONTENTS

BLACK BEAUTY

by ANNA SEWELL

CHAPTER I

My Early Home

THE FIRST place that I can well remember was a large pleasant meadow with a pond of clear water in it. Some trees overshadowed the pond, and rushes and water-lilies grew at the deep end. Over the hedge on one side we looked into a ploughed field ; and on the other, we looked over a gate at our master's house which stood by the roadside. At the top of the meadow was a plantation of fir-trees ; and at the bottom, a running brook overhung by a steep bank.

Whilst I was young I lived upon my mother's milk, as I could not eat grass. In the daytime I ran by her side, and at night I lay down close by her. When it was hot, we used to stand by the pond in the shade of the trees ; and when it was cold, we had a nice warm shed near the plantation.

As soon as I was old enough to eat grass, my mother used to go out to work in the daytime, and to come back in the evening.

There were six young colts in the meadow besides me. They were older than I was ; some were nearly as large as grown-up horses. I used to run with them, and have great fun. We used to gallop all together round and round the field, as hard as we could go. Sometimes we had rather rough play, for they would frequently bite and kick as well as gallop.

One day, when there was a good deal of kicking, my mother whinnied to me to come to her ; and then she said : " I wish you to pay attention to what I am going to say to you. The colts who live here are very good colts, but they

A*

are cart-horse colts, and, of course, they have not learned good manners.

"You have been well bred and well born; your father had a great name in these parts, and your grandfather twice won the Cup at the Newmarket races; your grand-mother had the sweetest temper of any horse I ever knew, and I think you have never seen me kick or bite.

"I hope you will grow up gentle and good, and never learn bad ways. Do your work with a good will; lift up your feet well when you trot, and never bite or kick even in play."

I have never forgotten my mother's advice; I knew she was a wise old horse, and our master thought a great deal of her. Her name was Duchess, but he often called her Pet.

Our master was a good, kind man. He gave us good food, good lodging, and kind words; and he spoke as kindly to us as he did to his little children. We were all fond of him, and my mother loved him very much. When she saw him at the gate, she would neigh with joy, and trot up to him. He would pat and stroke her and say, "Well, old Pet! How is your little Darkie?" I was a dull black, so he called me Darkie.

Then he would give me a piece of bread, which was very good, and sometimes he brought a carrot for my mother. All the horses would come to him, but I think we were his favourites. My mother always took him to the town on a market day in a light gig.

There was a ploughboy, Dick, who sometimes came into our field to pluck blackberries from the hedge. When he had eaten all he wanted, he would have, what he called, fun with the colts, throwing sticks and stones at them to make them gallop. We did not much mind him, for we could gallop off; but sometimes a stone would hit and hurt us.

One day he was at this game, and did not know that the master was in the next field; but he was there, watching what was going on. Over the hedge he jumped in a moment, and catching Dick by the arm, gave him such a box on the ear as made him roar with pain. As soon as we saw the master, we trotted up nearer to see what was going on.

" Bad boy ! " he said, " bad boy ! to chase the colts. This is not the first time nor the second, but it shall be the last. There, take your money and go home ; I shall not want you on my farm again." So we never saw Dick again. Old Daniel, the man who looked after the horses, was just as gentle as our master, so we were well off.

CHAPTER II

The Hunt

BEFORE I was two years old, a circumstance happened which I have never forgotten.

It was early in the spring ; there had been a little frost in the night, and a light mist still hung over the plantations and meadows.

The other colts and I were feeding in the lower part of the field when we heard, quite in the distance, what sounded like the cry of dogs.

The oldest of the colts raised his head, pricked up his ears, and said, " There are the hounds ! " and immediately cantered off, followed by the rest of us, to the upper part of the field, where we could look over the hedge and see several fields beyond. My mother and an old riding horse of our master were also standing near, and seemed to know all about it.

" They have found a hare," said my mother, " and if they come this way, we shall see the hunt."

Soon the dogs were all tearing down the field of young wheat next to our meadow. I never heard such a noise as they made. They did not bark, nor howl, nor whine, but kept up a " Yo ! yo, o, o ! Yo ! yo, o, o ! " at the top of their voices. After them came a number of men on horse-back, some of them in green coats, all galloping as fast as they could. The old horse snorted and looked eagerly after them ; and we young colts wanted to be galloping with them, but they were soon away into the fields lower down. Here it seemed as if they had come to a stand ; the dogs left off barking, and ran about in every direction with their noses to the ground.

" They have lost the scent," said the old horse ; " perhaps the hare will get off."

" What hare ? " I said.

" Oh ! I don't know *what* hare ; possibly it may be one of our own hares out of the plantation. Any hare they can find will do for the dogs and men to run after."

Before long the dogs began their " Yo ! yo, o, o ! " again ; and back they came all together at full speed, making straight for our meadow at the part where the high bank and hedge overhung the brook.

" Now we shall see the hare," said my mother ; and just then a hare, wild with fright, rushed by, and made for the plantation. On came the dogs, followed by the huntsmen. The dogs burst through the bank, leaped the stream, and came dashing across the field. Six or eight men leaped their horses clean over the hedge and stream, following close upon the dogs. The hare tried to get through the fence ; but it was too thick, and she turned sharp round to make for the road.

Alas ! it was too late ; the dogs were upon her with their wild cries. We heard one shriek, and that was the end of her. One of the huntsmen rode up and whipped off the dogs, who would soon have torn her to pieces. He held her up by the leg, torn and bleeding ; and all the gentlemen seemed well pleased.

As for me, I was so astonished that I did not at first see what was going on by the brook ; but when I did look, there was a sad sight. Two fine horses were down ; one was struggling in the stream, and the other was groaning on the grass. One of the riders, covered with mud, was getting out of the water ; the other lay quite still.

" His neck is broken," said my mother.

" And serve him right, too," said one of the colts.
I thought the same, but my mother did not join with us.

" Well, no," said she, " you must not say that. But
though I am an old horse, and have seen and heard a
great deal, I never yet could make out why men are so fond
of this sport. They often hurt themselves, spoil good horses,
and tear up the fields ; and all this for a hare, a fox, or a
stag, that they could get more easily some other way. But
we are only horses, and don't understand."

Whilst my mother was saying this, we stood and looked
on. Many of the riders had gone to the young man ; but my
master, who had been watching what was going on, was
the first to raise him. His head fell back and his arms hung
down, and everyone looked very serious.

There was no noise now ; even the dogs were quiet, and
seemed to know that something was wrong. They carried
him to our master's house. I heard afterwards that the
young fellow was George Gordon, the Squire's only son,
a fine, tall young man, and the pride of his family.

People were now riding off in all directions, to the
doctor's, to the farrier's, and no doubt to Squire Gordon,
to let him know about his son.

When Mr. Bond, the farrier, came to look at the black
horse that lay groaning on the grass, he felt him all over
and shook his head ; one of the horse's legs was broken.
Then some one ran to our master's house and came back
with a gun. Presently there was a loud bang and a dreadful
shriek, and then all was still ; the black horse moved no more.

My mother seemed much troubled. She said she had
known that horse for years. His name was Rob Roy ; a
good bold horse with no vice in him. Afterwards she never
would go to that part of the field.

Not many days after, we heard the church bell tolling
for a long time ; and looking over the gate we saw a long,
strange, black coach covered with black cloth and drawn
by black horses. After that came another, and another, and
another ; and all were black. Meanwhile the bell kept

tolling, tolling. They were carrying young Gordon to the churchyard to bury him. He would never ride again. What they did with Rob Roy I never knew ; but 'twas all for one little hare.

CHAPTER III

My Breaking In

I WAS now beginning to grow handsome ; my coat had grown fine and soft, and was glossy black. I had one white foot, and a pretty white star on my forehead. People thought me very handsome. My master would not sell me till I was four years old ; he said lads ought not to work like men, and colts ought not to work like horses till they were quite grown up.

When I was four years old, Squire Gordon came to look at me. He examined my eyes and my mouth, and felt my legs all down. Then I had to walk, trot, and gallop before him. He seemed to like me, and said, " When he has been well broken in, he will do very well." My master promised to break me in himself as he would not like me to be frightened or hurt ; and he lost no time about it, for the next day the breaking in began.

Every one may not know what breaking in is, so I will describe it. To break in a horse is to teach it to wear a saddle and bridle, and to carry on its back a man, woman, or child ; to go just the way the rider wishes, and to do so quietly. Besides this, the horse has to learn to wear a collar, a crupper, and a breeching ; and he must learn to stand still whilst these are put on. Then he must be taught to have a cart or a chaise fixed behind him, so that he cannot walk or trot without dragging it after him ; and he must learn to go quickly or slowly, just as his driver wishes.

He must never start at what he sees, speak to other horses, bite, kick, or have any will of his own ; but must always do his master's will, even though he may be very tired or hungry.

But the worst of all is that when his harness is once on, he may neither jump for joy nor lie down for weariness. So you see this breaking in is a great thing.

Of course I had long been used to a halter and a headstall, and to be led about in the fields and lanes quietly, but now I was to have a bit and a bridle.

My master gave me some oats as usual, and after a good deal of coaxing, he got the bit into my mouth and fixed the bridle. What a nasty thing the bit was ! Those who have never had one in their mouth cannot think how bad it feels. A great piece of cold, hard steel as thick as a man's finger is pushed between your teeth and over your tongue, with the ends coming out at the corners of your mouth, and is held fast there by straps over your head, under your throat, round your nose, and under your chin ; so that no way in the world can you get rid of the nasty hard thing. Bad ! bad ! Yes, very bad ! At least, I thought so ; but I knew my mother always wore one when she went out, and that all horses did when they were grown up. And so, what with the nice oats, and what with my master's pats, kind words, and gentle ways, I got to wear my bit and bridle.

Next came the saddle, but that was not half so bad. My master put it on my back very gently, whilst old Daniel held my head. Then, patting and talking to me all the time, he made the girths fast under my body. I had a few oats, then I was led about for a little while ; and this went on every day till I began to look for the oats and the saddle.

At length, one morning my master got on my back and rode me round the meadow on the soft grass. It certainly did feel queer ; but I must say I felt rather proud to carry my master ; and, as he continued to ride me a little every day, I soon became accustomed to it.

The next unpleasant business was putting on the iron shoes ; that too was very hard at first. My master went with me to the smith's forge to see that I was not hurt or frightened. The blacksmith took my feet in his hand, one after the other, and cut away some of the hoof. It did not pain me, so I stood still on three legs till he had done them all. Then he took a piece of iron the shape of my foot, clapped it on, and drove some nails through the shoe quite into my hoof, so that the shoe was firmly held. My feet were very stiff and heavy, but in time I got used to it.

And now having got so far, my master went on to break me to harness ; for this there were more new things to wear. First, they placed a stiff, heavy collar just on my neck, and a bridle with great side-pieces, called blinkers, against my eyes. And blinkers indeed they were, for I could not see on either side, but only straight in front of me. Next there was a small saddle with a nasty stiff strap that went right under my tail ; that was the crupper. I hated the crupper— to have my long tail doubled up and poked through that strap was almost as bad as the bit. I never felt more like kicking, but of course I could not kick such a good master ; and so in time I got used to everything, and could do my work as well as my mother.

I must not forget to mention one part of my training which I have always considered a very great advantage. My master sent me for a fortnight to a neighbouring farmer who had a meadow which was skirted on one side by the railway. Here were some sheep and cows, and I was turned in amongst them.

I shall never forget the first train that ran by. I was feeding quietly near the pales which separated the meadow from the railway, when I heard a strange sound at a distance ; and before I knew whence it came—with a rush and a clatter, and a puffing out of smoke—a long black train of something flew by, and was gone almost before I could draw my breath. I turned, and galloped to the further side of the meadow as fast as I could go ; and there I stood snorting with astonishment and fear.

In the course of the day many other trains went by, some more slowly ; these drew up at the station close by, and sometimes made an awful shriek and groan before they stopped. I thought it very dreadful, but the cows went on eating very quietly, and hardly raised their heads as the black, frightful thing came puffing and grinding past.

For the first few days I could not feed at peace ; but as I found that this terrible creature never came into the field nor did me any harm, I began to disregard it ; and very soon I cared as little about the passing of a train as the cows and sheep did.

Since then I have seen many horses much alarmed and restive at the sight or sound of a steam-engine ; but thanks to my good master's care, I am as fearless at railway stations as in my own stable.

Now if anyone wants to break in a young horse well, that is the way to do it.

My master often drove me in double harness with my mother because she was steady, and could teach me how to go better than a strange horse. She told me the better I behaved, the better I should be treated, and that it was wisest always to do my best to please my master. " But," said she, " there are a great many kinds of men : there are good, thoughtful men like our master, that any horse may be proud to serve ; but there are bad, cruel men, who never ought to have a horse or a dog to call their own. Besides these, there are a great many men foolish, vain, ignorant, and careless, who never trouble themselves to think ; these spoil more horses than anyone, just for want of sense. They don't mean it, but they do it for all that. I hope you will fall into good hands ; but a horse never knows who may buy him, or who may drive him. It is all a chance ; but still I say, Do your best wherever you are, and keep up your good name."

CHAPTER IV
Birtwick Park

AT THIS time I used to stand in the stable, and my coat was brushed every day till it shone like a rook's wing. Early in May there came a man from Squire Gordon's who took me away to the Hall. My master said, " Goodbye, Darkie ; be a good horse, and always do your best." I could not say " Good-bye," so I put my nose into his hand ; he patted me kindly, and then I left my first home. As I lived some years with Squire Gordon, I may as well tell you something about the place.

Squire Gordon's park skirted the village of Birtwick. It was entered by a large iron gate, at which stood the first lodge ; and then you trotted along on a smooth road between clumps of large, old trees. Soon you passed another lodge and another gate, which brought you to the house and the gardens. Beyond this lay the home paddock, the old orchard, and the stables. There was accommodation for many horses and carriages ; but I need only describe the stable into which I was taken. This was very roomy, with four good stalls. A large swinging window opened into the yard ; this made it pleasant and airy.

The first stall was a large, square one, shut in behind with a wooden gate ; the others were common stalls—good stalls, but not nearly so large. My stall had a low rack for hay and a low manger for corn ; it was called a loose box, because the horse that was put into it was not tied up, but left loose to do as he liked. It is a great thing to have a loose box.

Into this fine box, clean, sweet, and airy, the groom put me. I never in my life was in a better box, and the sides were not so high but that I could see through the iron rails at the top all that went on.

The man gave me some very nice oats, patted me, spoke kindly, and then went away.

When I had eaten my corn, I looked round. In the stall next to mine stood a little fat grey pony, with a thick mane and tail, a very pretty head, and a pert little nose.

Putting my head up to the iron rails at the top of my box, I said, " How do you do ? What is your name ? "

He turned round as far as his halter would allow, held up his head, and said : " My name is Merrylegs. I am very handsome. I carry the young ladies on my back, and sometimes I take our mistress out in the low chair. They think a great deal of me, and so does James. Are you going to live next door to me in the box ? "

" Yes," I replied.

" Well, then," he said, " I hope you are good-tempered ; next door to me I do not like anyone who bites."

Just then a horse's head looked over from the stall beyond. The ears were laid back, and the eye looked rather ill-tempered. This tall chestnut mare, with a long, handsome neck, looked across to me and said, " So it is you who have turned me out of my box. Is it not a very strange thing for a colt like you to come and turn a lady out of her own home ? "

" I beg your pardon," I said, " I have turned no one out. The man who brought me put me here, and I had nothing to do with it. And as to my being a colt, I am turned four years old, and am a grown-up horse. I never yet had words with horse or mare, and it is my wish to live at peace."

" Well," she said, " we shall see. Of course I do not want to have words with a young thing like you."

I said no more.

In the afternoon, when she went out, Merrylegs told me all about the mare.

" The thing is this," said Merrylegs. " Ginger has a bad habit of biting and snapping : that is why she is called Ginger. When she was in the loose box, she used to snap very much. One day she bit James in the arm and made it bleed, and so Miss Flora and Miss Jessie, who are very fond of me, were afraid to come into the stable. They used to bring me nice things to eat—an apple, or a carrot, or a piece of bread ; but after Ginger stood in that box, they dare not come, and I miss them very much. I hope, if you do not bite or snap, that they will now come again."

I told him I never bit anything but grass, hay, and corn, and could not think what pleasure Ginger found in it.

" Well, I don't think she does find pleasure in it," said Merrylegs ; " it is just a bad habit. She says no one was ever kind to her, and so why should she not bite ? Of course it is a very bad habit ; but I am sure, if all she says be true, she must have been very ill-used before she came here. John and James do all they can to please her, and our master never uses a whip if a horse behaves himself ; so I think she might be good-tempered here.

" You see," he said with a wise look, " I am twelve years old ; I know a great deal and I can tell you there is not a better place for a horse all round the country than this. John is the best groom that ever was ; he has been here fourteen years ; and you never saw such a kind boy as James is. So it is all Ginger's own fault that she did not stay in that box."

CHAPTER V

A Fair Start

THE NAME of the coachman was John Manly. He had a wife and one little child, and they lived in the coachman's cottage very near the stables.

The next morning he took me into the yard and gave me a good grooming. Just as I was going into my box with my coat soft and bright, the Squire came in to look at me, and seemed pleased.

" John," he said, " I meant to have tried the new horse this morning, but I have other business. You may as well take him for a round after breakfast. Go by the common and the Highwood, and come back by the water-mill and the river ; that will show his paces."

" I will, sir," said John.

After breakfast he came and fitted me with a bridle. He was very particular in letting out and taking in the straps, to fit my head comfortably. Then he brought the saddle, but it was not broad enough for my back ; he saw this in a moment, and went for another, which fitted nicely. He rode me at first slowly, then at a trot, and afterwards at a canter ; and when we were on the common he gave me a light touch with his whip, and we had a splendid gallop.

" Ho, ho ! my boy," he said, as he pulled me up, " you would like to follow the hounds, I think."

As we came back through the park, we met the Squire and Mrs. Gordon walking. They stopped, and John jumped off.

" Well, John, how does he go ? "

" First-rate, sir," answered John. " He is as fleet as a deer, and has a fine spirit, too ; but the lightest touch of the rein will guide him. Down at the end of the common we met one of those travelling carts hung all over with baskets, rugs, and such like. You know, sir, many horses will not pass these carts quietly ; but he just took a good look at it, and then went on as quietly and pleasantly as could be.

" Some men were shooting rabbits near the Highwood, and a gun went off close by : he pulled up a little and looked, but did not stir a step to right or left. I just held the rein steady and did not hurry him ; it's my opinion he has not been frightened or ill-used while he was young."

" That's well," said the Squire. " I will try him myself to-morrow."

The next day I was brought up for my master. I remembered my mother's counsel and my good old master's, and I tried to do exactly what the Squire wanted me to do. I found he was a very good rider, and thoughtful for his horse, too. When we came home, the lady was at the hall door as he rode up.

" Well, my dear," she said, " how do you like him ? "

" He is exactly what John said, my dear. A pleasanter creature I never wish to mount. What shall we call him ? "

" Would you like Ebony ? " said she ; " he is as black as ebony."

" No ; not Ebony."

" Will you call him Blackbird, like your uncle's old horse ? "

" No ; he is far handsomer than old Blackbird ever was."

" Yes," she said, " he is really quite a beauty, and he has such a sweet, good-tempered face and such a fine, intelligent eye—what do you say to calling him Black Beauty ? "

" Black Beauty—why, yes, I think that is a very good name. If you like, it shall be so " ; and that is how I got my name.

When John went into the stable, he told James that master and mistress had chosen a good sensible English name for me that meant something ; not like Marengo, or Pegasus, or Abdallah. They both laughed, and James said : " If it were not for bringing back the past, I should have named him Rob Roy, for I never saw two horses more alike."

" That's no wonder," said John. " Didn't you know that Farmer Grey's old Duchess was the mother of them both ? "

I had never heard that before. So poor Rob Roy who was killed at that hunt was my brother ! I do not wonder that my mother was so troubled. It seems that horses have no relations ; at least, they never know each other after they are sold.

John seemed very proud of me : he used to make my mane and tail almost as smooth as a lady's hair, and he would talk to me a great deal. Of course I did not understand all he said, but I learned more and more to know what he *meant*, and what he wanted me to do. I grew very fond of him, because he was so gentle and kind, and seemed to know just how a horse feels ; and when he cleaned me, he knew the tender places and the ticklish places ; and when he brushed my head, he went as carefully over my eyes as if they were his own, and never stirred up any ill-temper.

James Howard, the stable boy, was just as gentle and pleasant in his way ; so I thought myself well off. There was another man who helped in the yard, but he had very little to do with Ginger and me.

A few days after this I had to go in the carriage with Ginger. I wondered how we should get on together ; but except laying her ears back when I was led up to her, she behaved very well. She did her work honestly, and did her full share ; and I never wish to have a better partner in double harness.

When we came to a hill, instead of slackening her pace, she would throw her weight right into the collar, and pull away straight up. We had both the same sort of courage at our work ; and John had more often to hold us in than to urge us forward. He never had to use the whip with either of us. Then our paces were much the same, and I found it very easy to keep step with her when trotting. This made it pleasant, and master always liked us to keep step well, and so did John. After we had been out two or three times together, we grew quite friendly and sociable ; this made me feel very much at home.

As for Merrylegs, he and I soon became great friends. He was such a cheerful, plucky, good-tempered little fellow that he was a favourite with every one, and especially with Miss Jessie and Flora, who used to ride him about in the orchard and have fine games with him and their little dog Frisky.

Our master had two other horses that stood in another stable. One was Justice, a roan cob, used for riding, or for the luggage cart ; the other was an old brown hunter, named Sir Oliver ; he was past work now, but he was a great favourite with the master, who gave him the run of the park ; he sometimes did a little light carting on the estate, or carried one of the young ladies when they rode out with their father ; for he was very gentle, and could be trusted with a child as well as Merrylegs. The cob was a strong, well-made, good-tempered horse, and we sometimes had a little chat in the paddock, but of course I could not be so intimate with him as with Ginger, who stood in the same stable.

CHAPTER VI

Liberty

I WAS quite happy in my new place, and if there was one thing that I missed, it must not be thought I was discontented. All who had to do with me were good, and I had a light, airy stable and the best of food.

What more could I want ? Why, liberty ! For three years and a half of my life I had had all the liberty I could wish for ; but now, week after week, month after month, and no doubt year after year, I must stand up in a stable night and day except when I am wanted ; and then I must be just as steady and quiet as any old horse who has worked twenty years. I must wear straps here and straps there, a bit in my mouth, and blinkers over my eyes.

Now, I am not complaining, for I know it must be so. I mean only to say that for a young horse, full of strength and spirits, who has been used to some large field or plain where he can fling up his head, toss up his tail, gallop away at full speed, and then go round and back again with a snort to his companions—I say it is hard never now to have a bit more liberty to do as he likes.

Sometimes, when I have had less exercise than usual, I have felt so full of life and spring that when John has taken me out to exercise, I really could not keep quiet. Do what I would, it seemed as if I must jump, dance, or prance ; and many a good shake I know I must have given him, especially at the first, but he was always good and patient.

" Steady, steady, my boy," he would say ; " wait a while, and we'll have a good swing, and soon get the tickle out of your feet." Then as soon as we were out of the village, he would give me a few miles at a spanking trot, and bring me back as fresh as before, only clear of the fidgets, as he called them.

Spirited horses, when not enough exercised, are often called skittish, when in fact it is only play ; and some grooms will punish them, but our John did not ; he knew it was only high spirits. Still, he had his own ways of making me understand by the tone of his voice or the touch of the rein. If he was very serious and quite determined, I always knew it by his voice, and that had more power over me than any-thing else, for I was very fond of him.

I ought to say that sometimes we had our liberty for a few hours ; this used to be on fine Sundays in the summer-time. The carriage never went out on Sundays, because the church was not far off.

It was a great treat to us to be turned out into the home paddock or the old orchard ; the grass was so cool and soft to our feet ; the air was so sweet, and the freedom to do as we liked—to gallop, lie down, roll over on our backs, or nibble the sweet grass—was so pleasant. Then, as we stood together under the shade of the large chestnut-tree, was a very good time for talking.

CHAPTER VII

Ginger

ONE DAY, when Ginger and I were standing alone in the shade, we had a long talk. She wanted to know all about my bringing up and breaking in ; so I told her.

" Well," said she, " if I had had your bringing up I might have as good a temper as you ; but now I don't believe I ever shall."

" Why not ? " I said.

" Because it has been all so different with me," she re-plied. " I never had anyone, horse or man, that was kind to me, or that I cared to please ; for in the first place I was taken from my mother as soon as I was weaned, and put with a lot of other young colts ; none of them cared for me, and I cared for none of them. There was no kind master like yours to look after me, talk to me, and bring me nice things to eat.

" The man that had the care of us never gave me a kind word in my life. I do not mean that he ill-used me, but he did not care for us more than to see that we had plenty to eat and were sheltered in the winter.

" A footpath ran through our field, and very often the big boys passing through would fling stones to make us gallop. I was never hit, but one fine young colt was badly cut in the face, and I should think it would leave a scar for life. We did not mind the boys, but of course it made us more wild, and we settled it in our minds that boys were our enemies. We had very good fun in the meadows, either galloping up and down and chasing each other round and round the field, or standing still under the shade of the trees.

" But when it came to breaking in, that was a bad time for me. Several men came to catch me ; and when at last they closed me in at one corner of the field, one caught me by the forelock, another took me by the nose, holding it so tight I could hardly draw my breath, and a third, grasping my under jaw in his hard hand, wrenched my mouth open ; and so by force they got on the halter and put the bar into my mouth.

" Then one dragged me along by the halter, and another flogged me behind. This was the first experience I had of man's kindness : it was all force. They did not give me a chance to know what they wanted. I was high bred, with a great deal of spirit, and no doubt was very wild, and gave them plenty of trouble ; but then it was dreadful to be shut up in a stall, day after day, instead of having my liberty. I fretted and pined and wanted to get loose. You know yourself, it's bad enough when you have a kind master and plenty of coaxing ; but there was nothing of that sort for me.

" There was one—the old master, Mr. Ryder—who, I think, could soon have brought me round, and have done anything with me ; but he had given up all the hard part of the trade to his son and to another experienced man. My master came only at times to oversee.

" His son was a strong, tall, bold man called Samson ; and he used to boast that he had never found a horse that could throw him. There was no gentleness in him as there was in his father, but only hardness : a hard voice, a hard eye, and a hard hand. I felt from the first that what he wanted was to wear all the spirit out of me, and just make me into a quiet, humble, obedient piece of horse-flesh. ' Horse-flesh ! ' Yes, that is all that he thought about " ; and Ginger stamped her foot as if the very thought of him made her angry.

Then she went on : " If I did not do exactly what he wanted, he would get put out, and make me run round with that long rein in the training field till he had tired me out. I think he drank a good deal, and I am quite sure that the oftener he drank the worse it was for me.

" One day he had worked me hard in every way he could, and when I lay down I was tired, miserable, and angry ; it all seemed so hard. The next morning he came for me early, and ran me round again for a long time. I had scarcely had an hour's rest when he came again for me with a saddle and bridle and a new kind of bit.

" I could never quite tell how it came about. He had only just mounted me on the training ground, when something I did put him out of temper, and he jerked me hard with the rein. The new bit was very painful, and I reared up suddenly ; this angered him still more, and he began to flog me.

" I felt my whole spirit set against him, and I began to kick, and plunge, and rear as I had never done before ; we had a regular fight. For a long time he stuck to the saddle and punished me cruelly with his whip and spurs ; but my blood was thoroughly up, and I cared for nothing he could do if only I could get him off.

" At last, after a terrible struggle, I threw him off backwards. I heard him fall heavily upon the turf, and without looking behind me, galloped off to the other end of the field ; there I turned round and saw my persecutor slowly rise from the ground and go into the stable. I stood under an oak-tree and watched, but no one came to catch me.

" Time passed ; the sun was very hot, the flies swarmed round me and settled on my bleeding flanks where the spurs had dug in. I felt hungry, for I had not eaten since the early morning ; but there was not enough grass in that meadow for a goose to live on. I wanted to lie down and rest, but with the saddle strapped tightly on my back there was no comfort, nor was there a drop of water to drink. The afternoon wore on, and the sun got low. I saw the other colts led in, and I knew they were having a good feed.

" At last, just as the sun went down, I saw the old master come out with a sieve in his hand. He was a very fine old gentleman with quite white hair, but I should know him by his voice amongst a thousand. It was not high, nor yet low, but full, clear, and kind ; and when he gave orders it was so steady and decided that every one, both horses and men, knew that he expected to be obeyed.

" He came quietly along, now and then shaking about the oats that he had in the sieve, speaking cheerfully and gently to me : ' Come along, lassie, come along, lassie ; come along, come along.' I stood still and let him come up.

" He held the oats towards me and I began to eat without fear ; his voice took all my fear away. He stood by, patting and stroking me whilst I was eating, and seeing the clots of blood on my side he seemed very vexed. ' Poor lassie ! it was a bad business, a bad business ! ' Then he quietly took the rein and led me to the stable.

" Just at the door stood Samson. I laid my ears back and snapped at him. ' Stand back,' said the master, ' and keep out of her way ; you've done a bad day's work for this filly.' He growled out something about a vicious brute. ' Hark ye,' said his father, ' a bad-tempered man will never make a good-tempered horse. You've not learned your trade yet, Samson.'

" Then he led me into my box, took off the saddle and bridle with his own hands, and tied me up. Calling for a pail of warm water and a sponge, he took off his coat, and while the stable-man held the pail, he sponged my sides for some time so tenderly that I was sure he knew how sore and bruised they were. ' Whoa ! my pretty one,' he said ; ' stand still, stand still.' His very voice did me good, and the bathing was very comforting.

" The skin was so broken at the corners of my mouth that I could not eat the hay, for the stalks hurt me. He looked closely at my mouth, shook his head, and told the man to fetch me a good bran mash and put some meal into it. How good that mash was ! so soft and healing to my mouth. He stood by, stroking me and talking to the man all the time I was eating. ' If a high-mettled creature like this,' said he, ' can't be broken in by fair means, she never will be good for anything.'

" After that he often came to see me, and when my mouth was healed, the other breaker, Job, went on training me. As he was steady and thoughtful, I soon learned what he wanted."

CHAPTER VIII

Ginger's Story Continued

THE NEXT time that Ginger and I were together in the paddock, she told me about her first place.

" After my breaking in," she said, " I was bought by a dealer to match another chestnut horse. For some weeks he drove us together, and then we were sold to a fashionable gentleman, and were sent up to London. I had been driven with a bearing-rein by the dealer, and I hated it worse than anything else ; but in this place we were reined far tighter, the coachman and his master thinking in this way we looked more stylish. We were often driven about in the Park and other fashionable places. You, who never had a bearing-rein on, don't know what it is ; but I can tell you it is dreadful.

" I like to toss my head about, and hold it as high as any horse ; but you can fancy how it would feel if you tossed your head up high and were obliged to hold it there for hours together, not able to move it at all, except with a jerk still higher ; and all this time your neck was aching till you did not know how to bear it.

" Besides this, you have two bits instead of one ; and mine was a sharp one. It hurt my tongue and my jaw, and the blood from my tongue coloured the froth that kept flying from my lips, as I chafed and fretted at the bits and rein. It was worse when we had to stand by the hour waiting for our mistress at some grand party or entertainment ; and if I fretted or stamped with impatience, the whip was laid on. It was enough to drive one mad."

" Did not your master take any thought for you? " I said.

" No," said she, " he cared only to have a stylish turn-out, as they call it. I think he knew very little about horses ; he left that to his coachman, who told him that I was of an irritable temper, and that I had not been well broken to the bearing-rein, but that I should soon get used to it.

" However, he was not the man to do it ; for when I was in the stable, miserable and angry, instead of being soothed and quieted by kindness, I only got a surly word or a blow. If he had been civil, I would have tried to bear it. I was willing to work, and ready to work hard too ; but to be tormented for nothing but their fancies angered me. What right had they to make me suffer like that? Besides the soreness in my mouth and the pain in my neck, the bearing-rein always made my windpipe feel bad ; and if I had stopped there long, I know it would have spoiled my breathing.

" I grew more and more restless and irritable ; I could not help it. Then I began to snap and kick when anyone came to harness me, and for this the groom beat me. One day, as they had just buckled us into the carriage and were straining my head up with that rein, I began to plunge and kick with all my might. I soon broke a lot of harness, and kicked myself clear ; so my stay there was ended.

" Soon I was sent to Tattersalls to be sold. Of course I could not be warranted free from vice ; so nothing was said about that. My handsome appearance and good pace soon brought a gentleman to bid for me, and I was bought by another dealer. He tried me in all kinds of ways and with different bits, and soon found out what I could bear. At last he drove me quite without a bearing-rein, and then sold me as a perfectly quiet horse to a gentleman in the country.

" He was a good master, and I was getting on very well, but his old groom left him and a new one came. This man was as hard-tempered and hard-handed as Samson ; he always spoke in a rough, impatient voice, and if I did not move in the stall the moment he wanted me, he would hit me above the hocks with a stable broom or the fork, which- ever he might have in his hand. Everything he did was rough, and I began to hate him ; he wanted to make me afraid of him, but I was too high-mettled for that.

" One day when he had aggravated me more than usual, I bit him ; this of course put him in a great rage ; and he began to hit me about the head with a riding whip. After that, he never dared to come into my stall again, either my heels or my teeth were ready for him, and he knew it. I was quite quiet with my master, but of course he listened to what the man said, and so I was sold again.

" The same dealer heard of me, and said he thought he knew of a place where I should do well. ' 'Twas a pity,' he said, ' that such a fine horse should go to the bad, for want of a real good chance ' ; and the end of it was that I came here not long before you did. I had now made up my mind that men were my natural enemies, and that I must defend myself. Of course it is very different here ; but who knows how long it will last ? I wish I could think about things as you do ; but I can't after all I have gone through."

" Well," I said, " I think it would be a real shame if you
were to bite or kick John or James."

" I don't mean to," she said, " while they are good to
me. I did once bite James pretty sharp, but John said, ' Try
her with kindness,' and instead of punishing me as I expected, James came to me with his arm bound up, and
brought me a bran mash and stroked me ; and I have never
snapped at him since ; and I won't again."

I was sorry for Ginger, but of course I knew very little
then, and I thought most likely she made the worst of it.
However, I found that as the weeks went on, she grew much
more gentle and cheerful, and lost the watchful, defiant
look that she used to turn on any strange person who came
near her. And one day James said, " I do believe that mare
is getting fond of me, she quite whinnied after me this morning when I had been rubbing her forehead."

" Aye, aye, Jim, 'tis the Birtwick balls," said John :
" she'll be as good as Black Beauty by and by ; kindness is
all the physic she wants, poor thing ! " Master noticed the
change too, and one day when he got out of the carriage
and came to speak to us as he often did, he stroked her
beautiful neck. " Well, my pretty one, well, how do things
go with you now ? You are a good bit happier than when
you came to us, I think."

She put her nose up to him in a friendly, trustful way,
while he rubbed it gently.

" We shall make a cure of her, John," he said.

" Yes, sir, she's wonderfully improved ; she's not the same
creature that she was. It's the Birtwick balls, sir," said John,
laughing.

This was a little joke of John's ; he used to say that a
regular course of the Birtwick horse-balls would cure almost
any vicious horse. These balls, he said, were made up of
patience and gentleness, firmness and petting : one pound
of each to be mixed with half a pint of common sense, and
given to the horse every day.

CHAPTER IX

Merrylegs

MR. BLOMEFIELD, the Vicar, had a large family of boys and girls, who sometimes came to play with Miss Jessie and Flora. One of the girls was as old as Miss Jessie ; two of the boys were older, and there were several little ones. When they came, there was plenty of work for Merrylegs, for nothing pleased them so much as getting on him in turn, and riding him all about the orchard and the home paddock by the hour together.

One afternoon he had been out with them a long time, and when James brought him in and put on his halter, he said :

" There, you rogue, mind how you behave yourself, or we shall get into trouble."

" What have you been doing, Merrylegs ? " I asked.

" Oh ! " said he, tossing his little head, " I have only been giving these young people a lesson. They did not know when they had had enough, nor when I had had enough ; so I just pitched them off backwards : that was the only thing they could understand."

" What ? " said I, " you threw the children off ? I thought you knew better than that ! Did you throw Miss Jessie or Miss Flora ? "

He looked very much offended, and said :

" Of course not ; I would not do such a thing for the best oats that ever came into the stable. Why, I am as careful of our young ladies as the master could be ; and as for the little ones, it is I who teach them to ride. When they seem frightened or a little unsteady on my back, I go as smoothly and as quietly as old pussy when she is after a bird ; and when they are all right, I go on again faster, just to use them to it. So don't you trouble yourself preaching to me ; I am the best friend and riding master those children have.

" It is not they ; it is the boys. Boys," said he, shaking his mane, " are quite different ; they must be broken in, as we were broken in when we were colts, and must just be taught what's what."

" The other children had ridden me about for nearly two hours, and then the boys thought it was their turn ; and so it was, and I was quite agreeable. They rode me in turn, and I galloped them about, up and down the fields and all about the orchard for a good hour.

" They had each cut a great hazel stick for a riding whip, and laid it on a little too hard ; but I took it in good part, till at last I thought we had had enough ; so I stopped two or three times by way of a hint. Boys, you see, think a horse or pony is like a steam-engine or threshing-machine, that can go on as long and as fast as they please. They never think that a pony can get tired, or have any feelings ; so as the one whipping me could not understand, I just rose on my hind legs and let him slip off behind—that was all. He mounted me again, and I did the same. Then the other boy got up ; and as soon as he began to use his stick, I laid him on the grass ; and so on, till they were able to under-stand : that was all.

" They are not bad boys ; they don't wish to be cruel. I like them very well ; but you see I had to give them a lesson. When they brought me to James and told him, I think he was very angry to see such big sticks. He said they were only fit for drovers or gipsies, and not for young gentlemen."

" If I had been you," said Ginger, " I would have given those boys a good kick, and that would have given them a lesson."

" No doubt you would," said Merrylegs ; " but then I am not quite such a fool (begging your pardon) as to anger our master or make James ashamed of me. Besides, those children are under my charge when they are riding ; I tell you they are entrusted to me. Why, only the other day I heard our master say to Mrs. Blomefield, ' My dear madam, you need not be anxious about the children ; my old Merry-legs will take as much care of them as you or I could : I assure you I would not sell that pony for any money, he is so perfectly good-tempered and trustworthy.' Do you think I am such an ungrateful brute as to forget all the kind treatment I have had here for five years, and all the trust they place in me, and turn vicious because a couple of ignorant boys used me badly ?

" No ! no ! you never had a good place where they were kind to you, and so you don't know. I'm sorry for you, but I can tell you good places make good horses. I wouldn't vex our people for anything ; I love them, I do," said Merrylegs ; and he gave a low " Ho, ho, ho," through his nose, as he used to do in the morning when he heard James's footstep at the door.

" Besides," he went on, " if I took to kicking, where should I be ? Why, sold off in a jiffy with no character ; and I might find myself slaved about under a butcher's boy ; or worked to death at some seaside place where no one cared for me, except to find out how fast I could go ; or flogged along in some cart with three or four great men in it going out for a Sunday spree, as I have often seen in the place I lived in before I came here. No," said he, shaking his head, " I hope I shall never come to that."

CHAPTER X

A Talk in the Orchard

GINGER and I were not of the regular tall, carriage-horse breed ; we had more of the racing blood in us. We stood about fifteen and a half hands high, and were therefore just as good for riding as for driving. Our master used to say that he disliked either horse or man that could do but one thing ; and as he did not want to show off in London parks, he preferred a more active and useful kind of horse.

As for us, our greatest pleasure was when we were saddled for a riding party—the master on Ginger, the mistress on me, and the young ladies on Sir Oliver and Merrylegs. It was so cheerful to be trotting and cantering all together that it always put us in high spirits. I had the best of it, for I always carried the mistress. Her weight was little, her voice sweet, and her hand so light on the rein that I was guided almost without feeling it.

Oh ! if people knew what a comfort to horses a light hand is, and how it keeps a good mouth and a good temper, they surely would not chuck, and drag, and pull at the rein as they often do. Our mouths are so tender, that where they have not been spoiled or hardened with bad or ignorant treatment, they feel the slightest movement of the driver's hand, and we know in an instant what is required of us. My mouth had never been spoiled, and I believe that was why the mistress preferred me to Ginger, although her paces were certainly quite as good. She used often to envy me, and said it was all the fault of breaking in, and the gag-bit in London, that her mouth was not so perfect as mine ; and then old Sir Oliver would say, " There, there ! don't vex yourself ; you have the greatest honour ; a mare that can carry a tall man of our master's weight, with all your spring and sprightly action, does not need to hold her head down because she does not carry the lady ; we horses must take things as they come, and always be contented and willing so long as we are kindly used."

I had often wondered how it was that Sir Oliver had such a very short tail ; it really was only six or seven inches long, with a tassel of hair hanging from it ; and on one of our holidays in the orchard, I ventured to ask him by what accident he had lost his tail.

" Accident ! " he snorted, with a fierce look, " it was no accident ! It was a cruel, shameful, cold-blooded act ! When I was young I was taken to a place where these cruel things were done. I was tied up, and made fast so that I could not stir ; and then they came and cut my long, beautiful tail through the flesh and through the bone, and took it away."

" How dreadful," I exclaimed.

" Dreadful ! Ah, it was dreadful ! but it was not only the pain, though that was terrible and lasted a long time ; it was not only the indignity of having my best ornament taken from me, though that was bad ; but it was this—how could I ever again brush the flies off my sides and off my hind legs ? You who have tails just whisk the flies off without thinking about it ; and you can't tell what a torment it is to have them settle upon you, and sting and sting, and yet have nothing in the world with which to lash them off. I tell you it is a lifelong wrong, and a lifelong loss. But, thank Heaven ! men don't do it now."

" What did they do it for then ? " said Ginger.

" For fashion ! " said the old horse, with a stamp of his foot. " For fashion ! if you know what that means. There was not a well-bred young horse in my time that had not his tail docked in that shameful way, just as if the good God that made us did not know what we wanted and what looked best."

" I suppose it is fashion that makes them strap our heads up with those horrid bits that I was tortured with in London," said Ginger.

" Of course it is," said he. " To my mind, fashion is one of the most wicked things in the world. Now look, for instance, at the way they serve dogs, cutting off their tails to make them look plucky, and shearing up their pretty little ears to a point, to make them look sharp, forsooth.

" I had a dear friend once, a brown terrier—' Skye,' they called her. She was so fond of me that she would never sleep out of my stall. She made her bed under the manger, and there she had a litter of five as pretty little puppies as need be. None were drowned, for they were a valuable kind ; and how pleased she was with them ! And when they got their eyes open and crawled about, it was a real pretty sight.

" But one day the man came and took them all away. I thought he might be afraid I should tread upon them ; but it was not so. In the evening poor Skye brought them back again, one by one, in her mouth ; not the happy little things that they were, but bleeding and crying pitifully. They had all had a piece of their tails cut off, and the soft

flap of their pretty little ears was cut quite off. How their
mother licked them, and how troubled she was, poor thing !
I never forgot it. The wounds healed in time, and they forgot the pain ; but the nice, soft flap, that of course was intended to protect the delicate part of their ears from dust
and injury, was gone for ever.

"Why don't they cut their own children's ears into points
to make them look sharp ? Why don't they cut the end off
their noses to make them look plucky ? One would be just
as sensible as the other. What right have they to torment
and disfigure God's creatures ? "

Sir Oliver, though he was so gentle, was a fiery old fellow ;
and what he said was all so new to me and so dreadful, that
I found a bitter feeling toward men that I had never had
before rise up in my mind. Of course, Ginger was much
excited. With flashing eyes and distended nostrils, she flung
up her head, declaring that men were both brutes and
blockheads.

"Who talks about blockheads ? " said Merrylegs, who
just came up from the old apple-tree, where he had been
rubbing himself against the low branch. "Who talks about
blockheads ? I believe that is a bad word."

"Bad words were made for bad things," said Ginger ;
and she told him what Sir Oliver had said. " It is all true,"
said Merrylegs sadly, " and I've seen that about the dogs
over and over again where I lived first ; but we won't talk
about it here. You know that master, John, and James are
always good to us ; and talking against men in such a place
as this doesn't seem fair or grateful. You know there are
good masters and good grooms besides ours, though of
course ours are the best."

This wise speech of good little Merrylegs, which we knew
was quite true, cooled us all down, specially Sir Oliver, who
was dearly fond of his master ; and to turn the subject I
said, " Can anyone tell me the use of blinkers ? "

"No ! " said Sir Oliver, shortly, " because they are no
use."

" They are supposed," said Justice in his calm way, " to prevent horses from shying and starting, and getting so frightened as to cause accidents."

" Then what is the reason they do not put them on riding horses, especially on ladies' horses ? " said I.

" There is no reason at all," said he quietly, " except the fashion. They say that a horse would be so frightened to see the wheels of his own cart or carriage coming behind him that he would be sure to run away, although of course when he is ridden he sees them all about him if the streets are crowded. I admit they do sometimes come too close to be pleasant, but we don't run away ; we are used to it, and understand it. If we never had blinkers put on, we should never want them ; we should see what was there, and know what was what, and be much less frightened than by only seeing bits of things that we can't understand."

Of course there may be some nervous horses which have been hurt or frightened when they were young ; these may be the better for them : but as I never was nervous, I can't judge.

" I consider," said Sir Oliver, " that blinkers are dangerous things in the night. We horses can see much better in the dark than men can, and many an accident would never have happened if horses might have had the full use of their eyes.

" Some years ago, I remember, there was a hearse with two horses returning one dark night, and just by Farmer Sparrow's house where the pond is close to the road, the wheels went too near the edge, and the hearse was overturned into the water. Both the horses were drowned, and the driver hardly escaped. Of course after this accident a stout white rail was put up that might easily be seen ; but if those horses had not been partly blinded, they would of themselves have kept farther from the edge, and no accident would have happened.

" When our master's carriage was overturned, before you came here, it was said that if the lamp on the left side had not gone out, John would have seen the great hole that the roadmakers had left ; and so he might. But if old Colin had not had blinkers on, he would have seen it, lamp or no lamp, for he was far too knowing an old horse to run into danger. As it was, he was very much hurt, the carriage was broken, and how John escaped nobody knew."

" I should say," said Ginger, curling her nostril, " that these men who are so wise had better give orders that in future all foals should be born with their eyes set just in the middle of their foreheads, instead of on the side. Men always think they can improve upon Nature and mend what God has made."

Things were getting rather sore again, when Merrylegs held up his knowing little face and said :

" I'll tell you a secret—I believe John does not approve of blinkers ; I heard him talking to master about it one day. The master said that if horses had been used to them, it might be dangerous in some cases to leave them off ; and John said he thought it would be a good thing if all colts were broken in without blinkers, as was done in some foreign countries ; so let us cheer up and have a run to the other end of the orchard. I believe the wind has blown down some apples, and we may just as well eat them as for the slugs to have them."

Merrylegs' suggestions could not be resisted ; so we broke off our long conversation and got up our spirits by munching some very sweet apples which lay scattered on the grass.

CHAPTER XI

Plain Speaking

THE LONGER I lived at Birtwick, the more proud and happy I felt at having such a place. Our master and mistress were respected and beloved by all who knew them ; they were good and kind to everybody and everything : not only to men and women, but to horses and donkeys, to dogs and cats, and to cattle and birds. There was no oppressed or ill-used creature that had not a friend in them, and their servants took the same tone. If any of the village children were known to treat any creature cruelly, they soon heard about it from the Hall.

The Squire and Farmer Grey had worked together, as they said, for more than twenty years to get bearing-reins on the cart horses done away with, and in our parts you seldom saw them : but sometimes if mistress met a heavily-laden horse, with his head strained up, she would stop the carriage and get out, and reason with the driver in her sweet, serious voice, and try to show him how foolish and cruel it was.

I don't think any man could withstand our mistress. I wish all ladies were like her.

Our master sometimes used to speak his mind very freely. I remember he was riding me towards home one morning, when he saw a powerful man driving towards us in a light pony chaise, with a beautiful little bay pony with slender legs and a high-bred, sensitive head and face. Just as he came to the park gates the little thing turned towards them.

The man, without word or warning, wrenched the creature's head round with such force and suddenness that he nearly threw it on its haunches. Recovering itself, it was going on when he began to lash it furiously. The pony plunged forward, but the strong, heavy hand held the pretty creature back with force almost enough to break its jaw, whilst the whip still cut into him. It was a dreadful sight to me, for I knew what fearful pain it gave that delicate little mouth ; but master gave me the word, and we were up with him in a second.

" Sawyer," he cried in a stern voice, " is that pony made of flesh and blood ? "

" Flesh and blood and temper," he said. " He's too fond of his own will, and that won't suit me."

The man spoke as if he was in a strong passion. He was a builder who had often been to the park on business.

" And do you think," said master sternly, " that treat-ment like this will make him fond of your will ? "

" He had no business to make that turn ; his road was straight on ! " said the man roughly.

" You have often driven that pony up to my place," said master ; " it only shows the creature's memory and intelligence. How did he know that you were not going there again ? But that has little to do with it. I must say, Mr. Sawyer, that more unmanly, brutal treatment of a little pony it was never my painful lot to witness ; and by giving way to such passion, you injure your own character as much, nay more than you injure your horse. And remember we shall all have to be judged according to our works, whether they be towards man or towards beast."

Master rode me home slowly, and I could tell by his voice how the thing had grieved him.

He was just as free in speaking to gentlemen of his own rank as to those below him ; for another day, when we were out, we met a Captain Langley, a friend of our master. He was driving a splendid pair of greys in a kind of brake. After a little conversation the Captain said, " What do you think of my new team, Mr. Gordon ? You know you are the judge of horses in these parts, and I should like your opinion."

The master backed me a little so as to get a good view of them. " They are an uncommonly handsome pair," he said, " and if they are as good as they look, I am sure you need not wish for anything better ; but I see you yet hold to that pet scheme of yours for worrying your horses and lessening their power."

" What do you mean," said the other—" the bearing-reins ? Oh, ah ! I know that's a hobby of yours. Well, the fact is, I like to see my horses hold their heads up."

" So do I," said master, " as well as any man, but I don't like to see them *held up* ; that takes all the shine out of it. Now you are a military man, Langley, and no doubt like to see your regiment look well on parade, ' Heads up,' and all that kind of thing. But you would not take much credit for your drill if all your men had their heads tied to a backboard !

" It might not do much harm on parade, except to worry and fatigue them, but how would it be in a bayonet charge against the enemy, when they want the free use of every muscle, and all their strength thrown forward ? I would not give much for their chance of victory ; and it is just the same with horses ; you fret and worry their temper and decrease their power ; you will not let them throw their weight against their work, and so they have to do too much with their joints and muscles, and of course it wears them up faster. You may depend upon it horses were intended to have their heads free, as free as men's are, and if we could act a little more according to common sense, and a good deal less according to fashion, we should find many things work easier ; besides, you know as well as I that if a horse makes a false step he has much less chance of recovering himself if his head and neck are fastened back.

" And now," said the master laughing, " I have given my hobby a good trot out, can't you make up your mind to mount him too, Captain ? Your example would go a long way."

" I believe you are right in theory," said the other, " and that's rather a hard hit about the soldiers ; but—well, I'll think about it," and so they parted.

CHAPTER XII

A Stormy Day

ONE DAY, late in the autumn, my master had a long journey to go on business. I was put into the dog-cart, and John went with his master. I always liked to go in the dog-cart, it was so light, and the high wheels ran along so pleasantly. There had been a great deal of rain, and now the wind was very high and blew the dry leaves across the road in a shower. We went merrily along till we came to the toll-bar and the low wooden bridge. The river banks were rather high, and the bridge, instead of rising, went across just level, so that in the middle, if the river was full, the water would be nearly up to the woodwork and planks ; but as there were good substantial rails on each side, people did not mind it.

The man at the gate said the river was rising fast, and he feared it would be a bad night. Many of the meadows were under water, and in one low part of the road the water was half-way up to my knees ; the bottom was good, and master drove gently, so it was no matter.

When we got to the town, of course I had a good bait ; but as the master's business engaged him a long time, we did not start for home till rather late in the afternoon. The wind was then much higher, and I heard the master say to John he had never been out in such a storm ; and so I thought, as we went along the skirts of a wood, where the great branches were swaying about like twigs, and the rushing sound of the wind through the trees was terrible.

" I wish we were well out of this wood," said my master.

" Yes, sir," said John, " it would be rather awkward if one of these branches came down upon us."

The words were scarcely out of his mouth, when there was a groan, a crack, and a splitting sound, and tearing, crashing down amongst the other trees, came an oak, torn up by the roots, which fell right across the road just before us. I will never say I was not frightened, for I was. I stopped still, and I believe I trembled. Of course I did not turn round or run away ; I was not brought up to do that. John jumped out and in a moment was at my head.

" That was a very near touch," said my master. " What's to be done now ? "

" Well, sir, we can't drive over that tree nor yet get round it ; there will be nothing for it but to go back to the four cross-ways, and that will be a good six miles before we get round to the wooden bridge again. It will make us late, but the horse is fresh."

So back we went, and round by the cross-roads ; but by the time we got to the bridge, it was very nearly dark, and we could just see that the water was over the middle of it ; but as that happened sometimes when the floods were out, master did not stop.

We were going along at a good pace, but the moment my feet touched the first part of the bridge, I felt sure there was something wrong. I dare not go forward, and so I made a dead stop. " Go on, Beauty," said my master, giving me a touch with the whip ; but I dare not stir. He gave me a sharp cut ; I jumped, but I dared not go forward.

" There's something wrong, sir," said John ; and he sprang out of the dog-cart and came to my head and looked all about. He tried to lead me forward. " Come on, Beauty, what's the matter ? " Of course I could not tell him, but I knew very well that the bridge was not safe.

Just then the man at the toll-gate on the other side ran out of the house, tossing a torch about like one mad.

" Hoy, hoy, hoy, hallo, stop ! " he cried.

" What's the matter ? " shouted my master.

" The bridge is broken in the middle, and part of it is carried away ; if you come on you'll be into the river."

" Thank God ! " said my master. " You Beauty ! " said John ; and taking the bridle, he gently turned me round to the right-hand road by the river-side. The sun had set some time, the wind seemed to have lulled off after that furious blast which tore up the tree. It grew darker and darker, and more and more still. I trotted quietly along, the wheels hardly making a sound on the soft road.

For a good while neither master nor John spoke ; and then the master began to speak in a serious voice. I could not understand much of what they said, but I found they thought that if I had gone on as the master wanted me, most likely the bridge would have given way under us, and horse, chaise, master, and man would have fallen into the river ; and as the current was flowing very strongly, and there was no light and no help at hand, it was more than likely we should all have been drowned. Master said, God had given men reason by which they could find out things for themselves ; but He had given animals knowledge which did not depend on reason, much more prompt and perfect in its way, by which they had often saved the lives of men.

John had many stories to tell of dogs and horses, and the wonderful things they had done. He thought people did not value their animals half enough, nor make friends of them as they ought to do. I am sure he makes friends of them if ever a man does.

At last we came to the park gates, and found the gardener looking out for us. He said that mistress had been in a dreadful way ever since dark, fearing some accident had happened ; and that she had sent James off on Justice, the roan cob, towards the wooden bridge to make inquiry after us.

We saw a light at the hall door and at the upper windows, and as we came up mistress ran out saying, " Are you really safe, my dear ? Oh ! I have been so anxious, fancying all sorts of things. Have you had an accident ? "

" No, my dear ; but if your Black Beauty had not been wiser than we were, we should all have been carried down the river at the wooden bridge."

I heard no more, as they went into the house and John took me to the stable. Oh ! what a good supper he gave me that night—a good bran mash and some crushed beans with my oats, and such a thick bed of straw. I was glad of it, for I was tired.

CHAPTER XIII

The Devil's Trade-Mark

ON E D A Y, when John and I had been out on some business for our master, and were returning gently on a long straight road, at some distance we saw a boy trying to leap a pony over a gate. The pony would not take the leap, and the boy cut him with the whip, but he only turned off on one side ; he whipped him again, but the pony turned off on the other side. Then the boy got off and gave him a hard thrashing, knocking him about the head ; then he got up again and tried to make him leap the gate, kicking him all the time shamefully ; but still the pony refused.

When we were nearly at the spot, the pony put down his head, threw up his heels, and sent the boy neatly over into a broad quickset hedge ; and with the rein dangling from his head, he set off home at a full gallop. John laughed out quite loudly. " Serve him right ! " he said.

" Oh ! oh ! oh ! " cried the boy, as he struggled about amongst the thorns ; " I say come and help me out."

" Thank ye," said John, " I think you are quite in the right place ; and maybe a little scratching will teach you not to leap a pony over a gate that is too high for him " ; and so with that John rode off.

" It may be," said he to himself, " that young fellow is a liar as well as cruel ; we'll just go home by Farmer Bushby's, Beauty, and then if anybody wants to know, you and I can tell 'em, ye see." So we turned off to the right, and soon came up to the stack-yard within sight of the house. The farmer was hurrying out into the road, and his wife was standing at the gate looking very frightened.

" Have you seen my boy ? " said Mr. Bushby, as we came up ; " he went out an hour ago on my black pony, and the creature is just come back without a rider."

" I should think, sir," said John, " he had better be without a rider, unless he can be ridden properly."

" What do you mean ? " said the farmer.

" Well, sir, I saw your son whipping, kicking, and knocking that good little pony about shamefully, because he would not leap a gate that was too high for him. The pony behaved well, sir, and showed no vice ; but at last he just threw up his heels and tipped the young gentleman into the thorn hedge. He wanted me to help him out ; but—I hope you will excuse me, sir—I did not feel inclined to do so. There are no bones broken, sir ; he'll only get a few scratches. I love horses, and it roiles me to see them badly used. It is a bad plan to aggravate an animal till he uses his heels ; the first time is not always the last."

During this time the mother began to cry, " Oh ! my poor Bill, I must go and meet him ; he must be hurt."

" You had better go into the house, wife," said the farmer ; " Bill wants a lesson about this, and I must see that he gets it. This is not the first time nor the second that he has ill-used that pony, and I shall stop it. I am much obliged to you, Manly. Good evening."

So we went on, John chuckling all the way home. He told James about it, who laughed and said, " Serve him right. I knew that boy at school ; he took great airs on himself because he was a farmer's son ; he used to swagger about and bully the little boys. Of course we elder ones would not have any of that nonsense, and let him know that in the school and playground farmers' sons and labourers' sons were all alike.

" I well remember one day, just before afternoon school, I found him at the large window catching flies and pulling off their wings. He did not see me, and I gave him a box on the ears that laid him sprawling on the floor. Well, angry as I was, I was almost frightened ; he roared and bellowed in such a style. The boys rushed in from the play-ground, and the master ran in from the road to see who was being murdered.

" Of course I said fair and square at once what I had done, and why ; then I showed the master the poor flies, some crushed and some crawling about helpless, and I showed him the wings on the window-sill. I never saw him so angry before ; but as Bill was still howling and whining, like the coward that he was, he did not give him any more punishment of that kind, but set him up on a stool for the rest of the afternoon, and said that he should not go out to play for that week.

" Then he talked to all the boys very seriously about cruelty, and said how hard-hearted and cowardly it was to hurt the weak and the helpless. But what stuck in my mind was this—he said that cruelty was the devil's own trademark, and if we saw any one who took pleasure in cruelty, we might know to whom he belonged, for the devil was a murderer from the beginning and a tormentor to the end. On the other hand, where we saw people who loved their neighbours and were kind to man and beast, we might know that was God's mark ; for ' God is Love.' "

" Your master never taught you a truer thing," said John ; " there is no religion without love. People may talk as much as they like about their religion, but if it does not teach them to be good and kind to man and beast, it is all a sham—all a sham, James ; and it won't stand when things come to be turned inside out and put down for what they are."

<h3 style="text-align:center">CHAPTER XIV</h3>

<h3 style="text-align:center">James Howard</h3>

ONE MORNING, early in December, John had just led me into my box after my daily exercise, and was strapping my cloth on. James was coming in from the corn-chamber with some oats, when the master came into the stable. He looked rather serious, and held an open letter in his hand. John fastened the door of my box, touched his cap, and waited for orders.

" Good morning, John," said the master ; " I want to know if you have any complaint to make of James ? "

" Complaint, sir ? No, sir."

" Is he industrious at his work and respectful to you ? "

" Yes, sir, always."

" You never find he slights his work when your back is turned ? "

" Never, sir."

" That's well ; but I must put another question ; have

you any reason to suspect that when he goes out with the horses to exercise them, or take a message, he stops about talking to his acquaintances, or goes into houses where he has no business, leaving the horses outside ? "

" No, sir, certainly not, and if anybody has been saying that about James, I don't believe it ; and I don't mean to believe it unless I have it fairly proved before witnesses. It's not for me to say who has been trying to take away James's character ; but I will say this, sir, that a steadier, smarter, more pleasant, honest young fellow I never had in this stable. I can trust his word and I can trust his work.

" He is gentle and clever with the horses, and I would rather have them in his charge than in that of half the young fellows I know in laced hats and liveries ; and whoever wants a character of James Howard," said John, with a decided jerk of his head, " let them come to John Manly."

The master stood all this time grave and attentive ; but as John finished his speech, a broad smile spread over his face, and looking kindly across at James, who all this time had stood still at the door, he said : " James, my lad, set down the oats and come here. I am very glad to find that John's opinion of your character agrees so exactly with my own. John is a cautious man," he said, with a droll smile, " and it is not always easy to get his opinion about people ; so I thought if I beat the bush on this side, the bird would fly out, and I should learn what I wanted to know quickly ; so now we will come to business.

" I have a letter from my brother-in-law, Sir Clifford Williams, of Clifford Hall. He wants me to find him a trustworthy young groom, about twenty or twenty-one, who knows his business. His old coachman, who has lived with him twenty years, is getting feeble, and he wants a man to work with him and get into his ways, so that he would be able, when the old man was pensioned off, to step into his place. He would have eighteen shillings a week at first, a stable suit, a driving suit, a bedroom over the coach-house, and a boy under him. Sir Clifford is a good master, and if you could get the place, it would be a good start for you. I don't want to part with you, and if you left us I know John would lose his right hand."

" That I should, sir," said John, " but I would not stand in his light for the world."

" How old are you, James ? " said master.

" Nineteen next May, sir."

" That's young. What do you think, John ? "

" Well, sir, it is young ; but he is as steady as a man, strong, and well grown ; and though he has not had much experience in driving, he has a light, firm hand, a quick eye, and is very careful. I am quite sure no horse of his will be ruined for want of having his feet and shoes looked after."

" Your word will go the farthest, John," said the master, " for Sir Clifford adds in a postscript, ' If I could find a man trained by your John, I should like him better than any other.' So James, lad, think it over ; talk to your mother at dinner-time, and then let me know what you wish."

In a few days after this conversation, it was fully settled that James should go to Clifford Hall in a month or six weeks as it best suited his master, and in the meantime he was to get all the practice in driving that could be given him.

I never knew the carriage go out so often before. When the mistress did not go out, the master usually drove himself in the two-wheeled chaise ; but now, whether it was master or the young ladies who wanted to go out, or whether it was only an errand had to be done, Ginger and I were put into the carriage and James drove us. At first, John rode with him on the box, telling him this and that, and afterwards James drove alone.

Then it was wonderful what a number of places the master would go to in the city on Saturday, and what queer streets we were driven through. He was sure to go to the railway-station just as the train was coming in, when cabs and carriages, carts and omnibuses were all trying to get over the bridge together. That bridge wanted good horses and good drivers when the railway bell was ringing, for it was narrow, and there was a very sharp turn up to the station where it would not have been at all difficult for people to run into each other if they did not look sharp and keep their wits about them.

CHAPTER XV

The Old Ostler

AFTER this, my master and mistress decided to pay a visit to some friends who lived about forty-six miles from our home, and James was to drive them. The first day we travelled thirty-two miles ; there were some long, heavy hills, but James drove so carefully and thoughtfully that we were not at all harassed. He never forgot to put on the drag as we went downhill, nor to take it off at the right place. He kept our feet on the smoothest part of the road ; and if the uphill was very long, he set the wheels a little across the road so that the carriage should not run back, and gave us breathing time. All these little things help a horse very much, particularly if he gets kind words into the bargain.

We stopped once or twice on the road ; and just as the sun was going down, we reached the town where we were to spend the night. We stopped at the principal hotel, a very large one in the Market Place. We drove under an archway into a long yard, at the further end of which were the stables and coach-houses. Two ostlers came to take us out. The head ostler was a pleasant, active little man, with a crooked leg and a yellow striped waistcoat. I never saw a man un-buckle harness so quickly as he did ; and then with a pat and a good word he led me to a long stable with six or eight stalls in it and two or three horses. The other man brought Ginger—James stood by whilst we were rubbed down and cleaned.

I never was cleaned so lightly and quickly as by that little old man. When he had done, James stepped up and felt me over, as if he thought I could not be thoroughly done ; but he found my coat as clean and smooth as silk.

" Well," he said, " I thought I was pretty quick, and our John quicker still, but you do beat all I ever saw for being quick and thorough at the same time."

" Practice makes perfect," said the crooked little ostler, " and 'twould be a pity if it didn't. Forty years' practice, and not perfect ! Ha ! ha ! that would be a pity. As to being quick, why, bless you ! that is only a matter of habit. If you get into the habit of being quick, it is just as easy as being slow—easier, I should say. In fact, it does not agree with my health to be hulking about over a job twice as long as it needs take. Bless you ! I couldn't whistle if I crawled over my work as some folks do.

" You see, I have been about horses ever since I was twelve years old, in hunting stables and racing stables. Being small, you see, I was a jockey for several years ; but at the Goodwood the turf was very slippery and my poor Larkspur got a fall, and I broke my knee ; and so of course I was of no more use there.

" But I could not live without horses, of course I couldn't, so I took to the hotels ; and I can tell you it is a downright pleasure to handle an animal like this : well-bred, well-mannered, well-cared-for. Bless you ! I can tell how a horse is treated. Give me the handling of a horse for twenty minutes, and I'll tell you what sort of a groom he has had.

" Look at this one, pleasant, quiet, turns about just as you want him to do, holds up his feet to be cleaned out, or anything else you please to wish. Then you'll find another fidgety, fretful, won't move the right way, or starts across the stall, tosses up his head as soon as you come near him, lays back his ears, and seems afraid of you, or else squares about at you with his heels.

" Poor things ! I know what sort of treatment they have had. If they are timid, the treatment makes them start or shy ; if they are high-mettled, it makes them vicious or dangerous ; their tempers are mostly made when they are young. Bless you ! they are like children ; train 'em up in the way they should go, as the good Book says, and when they are old they will not depart from it—if they have a chance, that is."

" I like to hear you talk," said James ; " that's the way we lay it down at home, at our master's."

" Who is your master, young man, if it be a proper question ? I should judge he is a good one, from what I see."

" He is Squire Gordon, of Birtwick Park, on the other side of the Beacon Hills," said James.

" Ah ! so, so, I have heard tell of him ; fine judge of horses, ain't he ? The best rider in the country ? "

" I believe he is," said James, " but he rides very little now, since the poor young master was killed."

" Ah ! poor gentleman ; I read all about it in the paper at the time ; a fine horse killed too, wasn't there ? "

" Yes," said James, " he was a splendid creature, brother to this one, and just like him."

" Pity ! pity ! " said the old man. " 'Twas a bad place to leap, if I remember—a thin fence at top, a steep bank down to the stream, wasn't it ? No chance for a horse to see where he is going. Now, I am for bold riding as much as any man, but still there are some leaps that only a very knowing huntsman has any right to take. A man's life and a horse's life are worth more than a fox's tail ; at least, I should say they ought to be."

During this time the other man had finished Ginger, and brought our corn ; so James and the old man left the stable together.

CHAPTER XVI

The Fire

LATER on in the evening, a traveller's horse was brought in by the second ostler, and whilst he was cleaning him, a young man with a pipe in his mouth lounged into the stable to gossip.

" I say, Towler," said the ostler, " just run up the ladder

into the loft and bring down some hay into this horse's rack, will you ? Only first lay down your pipe."

"All right," said the other, and went up through the trap door ; and I heard him step across the floor overhead and put down the hay. James came in to look at us the last thing, and then the door was locked.

I cannot say how long I had slept, nor what time in the night it was, but I woke up feeling very uncomfortable, though I hardly knew why. I got up : the air seemed all thick and choking. I heard Ginger coughing, and one of the other horses moved about restlessly. It was quite dark, and I could see nothing ; but the stable was full of smoke, and I hardly knew how to breathe.

The trap door had been left open, and I thought that was the place from which the smoke came. I listened and heard a soft, rushing sort of noise, and a low crackling and snapping. I did not know what it was, but there was something in the sound so strange that it made me tremble all over. The other horses were now all awake ; some were pulling at their halters, others were stamping.

At last I heard steps outside, and the ostler who had put up the traveller's horse burst into the stable with a lantern, and began to untie the horses, and try to lead them out ; but he seemed in such a hurry, and was so frightened himself, that he frightened me still more. The first horse would not go with him ; he tried the second and third, but they too would not stir. He came to me next and tried to drag me out of the stall by force ; of course that was no use. He tried us all by turns and then left the stable.

No doubt we were very foolish, but danger seemed to be all round ; there was nobody whom we knew to trust in, and all was strange and uncertain. The fresh air that had come in through the open door made it easier to breathe, but the rushing sound overhead grew louder, and as I looked upward, through the bars of my empty rack, I saw a red light flickering on the wall. Then I heard a cry of " Fire ! " outside, and the old ostler came quietly and quickly in. He got one horse out, and went to another ; but the flames were playing round the trap door, and the roaring overhead was dreadful.

The next thing I heard was James's voice, quiet and cheery, as it always was.

" Come, my beauties, it is time for us to be off, so wake up and come along." I stood nearest the door, so he came to me first, patting me as he came in.

" Come, Beauty, on with your bridle, my boy, we'll soon be out of this smother." It was on in no time ; then he took the scarf off his neck, and tied it lightly over my eyes, and, patting and coaxing, he led me out of the stable. Safe in the yard, he slipped the scarf off my eyes, and shouted, " Here, somebody ! take this horse while I go back for the other."

A tall, broad man stepped forward and took me, and James darted back into the stable. I set up a shrill whinny as I saw him go. Ginger told me afterwards that whinny was the best thing I could have done for her, for had she not heard me outside, she would never had had courage to come out.

There was much confusion in the yard ; the horses were being got out of other stables, and the carriages and gigs were being pulled out of houses and sheds, lest the flames should spread farther. On the other side of the yard windows were thrown up, and people were shouting all sorts of things ; but I kept my eye fixed on the stable door, where the smoked poured out thicker than ever, and I could see flashes of red light.

Presently I heard above all the stir and din a loud, clear voice, which I knew was master's :

" James Howard ! James Howard ! are you there ? " There was no answer, but I heard a crash of something falling in the stable, and the next moment I gave a loud, joyful neigh, for I saw James coming through the smoke, leading Ginger with him ; she was coughing violently, and he was not able to speak.

" My brave lad ! " said master, laying his hand on his shoulder, " are you hurt ? "

James shook his head, for he could not yet speak.

" Ay," said the big man who held me, " he is a brave lad, and no mistake."

" And now," said master, " when you have got your breath, James, we'll get out of this place as quickly as we can."

We were moving towards the entry when from the Market Place there came a sound of galloping feet and loud rumbling wheels.

" 'Tis the fire engine ! the fire engine ! " shouted two or three voices. " Stand back, make way ! " and clattering and thundering over the stones two horses dashed into the yard with the heavy engine behind them. The firemen leaped to the ground ; there was no need to ask where the fire was—it was torching up in a great blaze from the roof.

We got out as fast as we could into the broad, quiet Market Place. The stars were shining, and except for the noise behind us, all was still. Master led the way to a large hotel on the other side, and as soon as the ostler came, he said, " James, I must now hasten to your mistress ; I trust the horses entirely to you ; order whatever you think is needed " ; and with that he was gone. The master did not run, but I never saw mortal man walk so fast as he did that night.

There was a dreadful sound before we got into our stalls— the shrieks of those poor horses that were left burning to death in the stable were very terrible ! They made both Ginger and me feel very ill. We, however, were taken in and well done by.

The next morning the master came to see how we were and to speak to James. I did not hear much, for the ostler was rubbing me down ; but I could see that James looked very happy, and I thought the master was proud of him.

Our mistress had been so much alarmed in the night, that the journey was put off till the afternoon ; so James had the morning on hand, and went first to see about our harness and the carriage, and then to hear more about the fire. When he came back, we heard him tell the ostler about it.

At first no one could guess how the fire had been caused ; but at last a man said he saw Dick Towler go into the stable with a pipe in his mouth, and when he came out he had not one, and went to the tap for another. Then the under ostler said he had asked Dick to go up the ladder to get down some hay, but told him to lay his pipe down first. Dick denied taking his pipe with him, but no one believed him.

I remember our John Manly's rule, never to allow a pipe in the stable, and thought it ought to be the rule everywhere.

James said the roof and floor had all fallen in, and that only the black walls were standing. The two poor horses that could not be got out were buried under the burnt rafters and tiles.

CHAPTER XVII

John Manly's Talk

THE REST of our journey was very easy, and a little after sunset we reached the house of my master's friend. We were taken into a clean, snug stable, where a kind coachman made us very comfortable. He seemed to think a great deal of James when he heard about the fire.

" There is one thing quite clear, young man," he said. " Your horses know whom they can trust. It is one of the hardest things in the world to get horses out of a stable when there is either fire or flood. I don't know why they won't come out, but they won't—not one in twenty."

We stopped two or three days at this place and then returned home. All went well on the journey : we were glad to be in our own stable again, and John was equally glad to see us.

Before James and he had left us for the night, James said, " I wonder who is coming in my place."

" Little Joe Green at the Lodge," said John.

" Little Joe Green ! Why, he's a child ! "

" He is fourteen and a half," said John.

" But he is such a little chap ! "

" Yes, he is small, but he is quick, willing, and kind-hearted too, and wishes very much to come, and his father would like it ; and I know the master would like to give him the chance. He said, if I thought he would not do, he would look out for a bigger boy ; but I said I was quite agreeable to try him for six weeks."

" Six weeks ! " said James, " why, it will be six months before he can be of much use ! It will make you a deal of work, John."

" Well," said John with a laugh, " work and I are very good friends ; I never was afraid of work yet."

" You are a very good man," said James ; " I wish I may ever be like you."

" I don't often speak of myself," said John, " but as you are going away from us out into the world to shift for yourself, I'll just tell you how I look on these things. I was just as old as Joseph when my father and mother died of the fever, within ten days of each other, and left me and my crippled sister, Nelly, alone in the world, without a relation to whom we could look for help.

" I was a farmer's boy, not earning enough to keep my-self, much less both of us, and she must have gone to the workhouse but for our mistress (Nelly calls her her angel, and she has good right to do so). The mistress went and hired a room for her with old Widow Mallet, and she gave her knitting and needlework, when she was able to do it ; and when she was ill, she sent her dinners and many nice comfortable things, and was like a mother to her. Then the master took me into the stable under old Norman, the coachman that then was. I had my food at the house and my bed in the loft, and a suit of clothes and three shillings a week, so that I could help Nelly.

" Norman might have turned round and said that at his age he could not be troubled with a raw boy from

the plough-tail ; but he was like a father to me, and took
no end of pains with me. When the old man died some years
after, I stepped into his place ; and now, of course, I have
top wages, and can lay by for a rainy day or a sunny day,
as it may happen ; and Nelly is as happy as a bird.

"So you see, James, I am not the man that should
turn up his nose at a little boy, and vex a good, kind
master. No ! no ! I shall miss you very much, James, but
we shall pull through. There's nothing like doing a kindness
when 'tis put in your way, and I am glad I can do it."

"Then," said James, "you don't hold with that saying,
'Everybody look after himself, and take care of number
one'?"

"No, indeed," said John. "Where would Nelly and I
have been if master and mistress and old Norman had only
taken care of number one ? Why, she in the workhouse and
I hoeing turnips ! Where would Black Beauty and Ginger
have been if you had only thought of number one ? Why,
roasted to death ! No, Jim, no ! that is a selfish, heathenish
saying, whoever may use it, and any man who thinks he
has nothing to do but take care of number one, why, it's
a pity but what he had been drowned like a puppy or a
kitten before he got his eyes open ; that's what I think,"
said John, with a very decided jerk of his head.

James laughed at this ; but there was a thickness in
his voice when he said, "You have been my best friend
except my mother ; I hope you won't forget me."

"No, lad, no !" said John, "and if ever I can do you
a good turn, I hope you won't forget me."

The next day Joe came to the stables to learn all he could
before James left. He learned to sweep the stable, to bring
in the straw and hay, and began to clean the harness, and
help to wash the carriage. As he was quite too short to do
anything in the way of grooming Ginger and me, James
taught him upon Merrylegs, for, under John, he was to
have full charge of the pony. He was a nice little bright
fellow, and always came whistling to his work.

Merrylegs was a good deal put out at being " mauled about," as he said, " by a boy who knew nothing " ; but towards the end of the second week he told me confidentially that he thought the boy would turn out well.

At last the day came when James had to leave us ; cheerful as he always was, he looked quite down-hearted that morning.

" You see," he said to John, " I am leaving a great deal behind—my mother and Betsy, you, a good master and mistress, and the horses and my old Merrylegs. At the new place there will not be a soul I shall know. If it were not that I shall get a higher place, and be able to help my mother better, I don't think I should have made up my mind to it ; it is a real pinch, John."

" Ay, James, lad, so it is, but I should not think much of you if you could leave your home for the first time and not feel it. Cheer up ! you'll make friends there, and if you get on well—as I am sure you will—it will be a fine thing for your mother, and she will be proud enough that you have got into such a good place as that."

So John cheered him up, but every one was sorry to lose James. As for Merrylegs, he pined after him for several days, and went quite off his appetite. So when he exercised me, John took him out several mornings with a leading rein, and trotting and galloping by my side he got up the little fellow's spirits again, and Merrylegs was soon all right.

Joe's father would often come in and give a little help, as he understood the work, and Joe took a great deal of pains to learn, and John was quite encouraged about him.

CHAPTER XVIII

Going for the Doctor

ONE NIGHT, a few days after James had left, I had eaten my hay and was lying down in my straw fast asleep, when I was suddenly awakened by the stable bell ringing very loudly.

I heard the door of John's house opened and his feet running up to the Hall. He was back again in no time. He unlocked the stable door and came in, calling out, " Wake up, Beauty, you must go well now, if ever you did ! " and almost before I could think, he had placed the saddle on my back and the bridle on my head. He just ran round for his coat, and then took me at a quick trot up to the Hall door. The Squire stood there with the lamp in his hand.

" Now, John," he said, " ride for your life—that is for your mistress's life ; there is not a moment to lose. Give this note to Doctor White. Give your horse a rest at the inn, and be back as soon as you can."

John said, " Yes, sir," and was on my back in a minute. The gardener who lived at the lodge had heard the bell ring, and was ready with the gate open. Away we went through the park, through the village, and down the hill till we came to the toll-gate. John called very loudly and thumped upon the door : the man was soon out and flung open the gate.

" Now," said John, " do you keep the gate open for the doctor ; here's the money," and off we went again.

There was before us a long piece of level road by the river-side. John said to me, " Now, Beauty, do your best," and so I did ; I wanted neither whip nor spur, and for two miles I galloped as fast as I could lay my feet to the ground. I don't believe that my old grandfather, who won the race at Newmarket, could have gone faster. When we came to the bridge John pulled me up a little and patted my neck. " Well done, Beauty ! good old fellow," he said. He would have let me go more slowly, but my spirit was up, and I was off again as fast as before.

The air was frosty, the moon bright, and it was very pleasant. We went through a village, through a dark wood, then uphill, then downhill, till after an eight miles' run we came to the town. On through the streets we went and into the Market Place. All was quite still except for the clatter of my feet on the stones—everybody was asleep. The church clock struck three as we drew up at Doctor White's door.

John rang the bell twice, and then knocked at the door like thunder. A window was thrown up, and Doctor White, in his nightcap, put his head out and said, " What do you want ? "

" Mrs. Gordon is very ill, sir ; master wants you to come at once ; he thinks she will die if you cannot get there— here is a note."

" Wait," he said, " I will come."

He shut the window and was soon at the door.

" The worst of it is," he said, " that my horse has been out all day and is quite done up ; my son has just been sent for and he has taken the other. What is to be done ? Can I have your horse ? "

" He has come at a gallop nearly all the way, sir, and I was to give him a rest here, but I think my master would not be against it if you think fit, sir."

" All right," he said, " I will soon be ready."

John stood by me and stroked my neck. I was very hot. The Doctor came out with his riding-whip.

" You need not take that, sir," said John. " Black Beauty will go till he drops. Take care of him, sir, if you can ; I should not like any harm to come to him."

" No ! no ! John," said the Doctor, " I hope not," and in a minute we had left John far behind.

I will not describe our way back ; the Doctor was a heavier man than John, and not so good a rider ; however, I did my very best. The man at the toll-gate had it open. When we came to the hill, the Doctor drew me up. " Now my good fellow," he said, " take some breath." I was glad he did, for I was nearly spent ; but that breathing helped me on, and soon we were in the park. Joe was at the lodge gate, and my master was at the hall door, for he had heard us coming. He spoke not a word ; the Doctor went into the house with him, and Joe led me to the stable.

I was glad to get home ; my legs shook under me, and I could only stand and pant. I had not a dry hair on my body, the water ran down my legs, and I steamed all over—Joe used to say, like a pot on the fire. Poor Joe ! he was young and small, and as yet he knew very little, and his father, who would have helped him, had been sent to the next village ; but I am sure he did the very best he knew.

He rubbed my legs and my chest, but he did not put my warm cloth on me ; he thought I was so hot I should not like it. Then he gave me a pailful of water to drink. It was cold, and very good, and I drank it all ; then he gave me some hay and some corn, and thinking he had done right, he went away.

Soon I began to shake and tremble, and turned deadly cold ; my legs, loins, and chest ached, and I felt sore all over. Oh ! how I wished for my warm, thick cloth as I stood and trembled. I wished for John, but he had eight miles to walk, so I lay down in my straw and tried to go to sleep.

After a long while I heard John at the door ; I gave a low moan, for I was in great pain. He was at my side in a moment, stooping down by me. I could not tell him how ill I felt ; but he seemed to know it all. He covered me up with two or three warm cloths, and then ran to the house for some hot water ; then he made me some warm gruel, which I drank ; then, I think, I went to sleep.

John seemed to be very much put out. I heard him say to himself, over and over again, " Stupid boy ! stupid boy ! No cloth put on, and I daresay the water was cold too ; boys are no good " ; but Joe was a good boy after all.

I was now very ill ; a strong inflammation had attacked my lungs, and I could not draw my breath without pain. John nursed me night and day. He would get up two or three times in the night to come to me ; my master, too, often came to see. " My poor Beauty," he said one day ; " my good horse, you saved your mistress's life, Beauty ! Yes, you saved her life."

I was very glad to hear that, for it seems the Doctor had said if we had been a little longer it would have been too late. John told my master he never saw a horse go so fast in his life ; it seemed as if the horse knew what was the matter. Of course I did, though John thought I did not ; at least, I knew as much as this, that John and I must go at the top of our speed, and that it was for the sake of the mistress.

CHAPTER XIX

Only Ignorance

I DO NOT know how long I was ill. Mr. Bond, the horse doctor, came every day. One day he bled me, and John held a pail for the blood. I felt very faint after it, and thought I should die. I believe they all thought so too.

Ginger and Merrylegs had been moved into the other stable, so that I might be quiet, for the fever made me very quick of hearing ; any little noise seemed quite loud, and I could tell every one's footstep going to and from the house. I knew all that was going on. One night John had to give me a draught ; Thomas Green came in to help him.

After I had taken it and John had made me as comfortable as he could, he said he should stay half an hour to see how the medicine settled. Thomas said he would stay with him, so they went and sat down on a bench that had been brought into Merrylegs' stall, and put down the lantern at their feet that I might not be disturbed with the light.

For a while both men sat silent, and then Tom Green said in a low voice :

" I wish, John, you'd say a bit of a kind word to Joe ; the boy is quite broken-hearted ; he can't eat his meals, and he can't smile. He says he knows it was all his fault, though he is sure he did the best he knew ; and he says, if Beauty dies, no one will ever speak to him again. It goes to my heart to hear him ; I think you might give him just a word, he is not a bad boy."

After a short pause, John said slowly : " You must not be too hard upon me, Tom. I know he meant no harm ; I never said he did. I know he is not a bad boy, but you see

I am sore myself. That horse is the pride of my heart, to
say nothing of his being such a favourite with the master
and mistress ; and to think that his life may be flung away
in this manner is more than I can bear. But if you think I
am hard on the boy, I will try to give him a good word to-
morrow—that is, I mean, if Beauty is better.''

" Well, John ! thank you, I knew you did not wish to be
too hard, and I am glad you see it was only ignorance."

John's voice almost startled me as he answered, " *Only*
ignorance ! only *ignorance* ! how can you talk about *only*
ignorance ? Don't you know that ignorance is the worst
thing in the world, next to wickedness ?—and which does
the most mischief Heaven only knows. If people can say,
' Oh ! I did not know, I did not mean any harm,' they think
it is all right. I suppose Martha Mulwash did not mean to
kill that baby when she dosed it with Dalby and soothing
syrups ; but she did kill it, and was tried for manslaughter.''

" And serve her right too," said Tom. " A woman
should not undertake to nurse a tender little child without
knowing what is good or what is bad for it.''

" Bill Starkey," continued Tom, " did not mean to
frighten his brother into fits when he dressed up like a
ghost, and ran after him in the moonlight ; but he did ;
and that bright, handsome little fellow, that might have
been the pride of any mother's heart, is just no better than an
idiot, and never will be, if he lives to be eighty years old.''

" You were a good deal cut up yourself, Tom, two weeks
ago, when those young ladies left your hothouse door open,
with a frosty east wind blowing right in ; you said it killed
a good many of your plants.''

" A good many ! " said Tom. " There was not one of the
tender cuttings that was not nipped off. I shall have to
strike all over again, and the worst of it is, that I don't know
where to go to get fresh ones. I was nearly mad when I came
in and saw what was done.''

" And yet," said John, " I am sure the young ladies did
not mean it ; it was only ignorance ! "

I heard no more of this conversation, for the medicine took effect and sent me to sleep, and in the morning I felt much better ; but I often thought of John's words when I came to know more of the world.

CHAPTER XX
Joe Green

JOE GREEN went on very well ; he learned quickly, and was so attentive and careful that John began to trust him in many things ; but as I have said, he was small for his age, and it was seldom that he was allowed to exercise either Ginger or me. But it so happened one morning that John was out with Justice in the luggage-cart, and the master wanted a note to be taken immediately to a gentleman's house about three miles distant, and sent his orders for Joe to saddle me and take it, adding the caution that he was to ride carefully.

The note was delivered, and we were quietly returning till we came to the brickfield. Here we saw a cart heavily laden with bricks. The wheels had stuck fast in the stiff mud of some deep ruts ; and the carter was shouting and flogging the two horses unmercifully. Joe pulled up. It was a sad sight. There were the two horses straining and struggling with all their might to drag the cart out, but they could not move it ; the sweat streamed from their legs and flanks, their sides heaved, and every muscle was strained, whilst the man, fiercely pulling at the head of the fore horse, swore and lashed most brutally.

" Hold hard," said Joe, " don't go on flogging the horses like that ; the wheels are so stuck that they cannot move the cart." The man took no heed, but went on lashing.

" Stop ! pray~stop," said Joe ; " I'll help you to lighten the cart, they can't move it now."

" Mind your own business, you impudent young rascal, and I'll mind mine." The man was in a towering passion, and the worse for drink ; and so he laid on the whip again. Joe turned my head, and the next moment we were going at a round gallop towards the house of the master brick-maker. I cannot say if John would have approved of our pace, but Joe and I were both of one mind, and so angry that we could not go slower.

The house stood close by the roadside. Joe knocked at the door and shouted, " Hulloa ! is Mr. Clay at home ? " The door was opened, and Mr. Clay himself came out.

" Hulloa, young man ! you seem in a hurry ; any orders from the Squire this morning ? "

" No, Mr. Clay ; but there's a fellow in your brickyard flogging two horses to death. I told him to stop and he wouldn't. I said I'd help him to lighten the cart, and he wouldn't ; so I have come to tell you. Pray, sir, go." Joe's voice shook with excitement.

" Thank ye, my lad," said the man, running in for his hat. Then, pausing for a moment—" Will you give evidence of what you saw if I should bring the fellow up before a magistrate ? " he asked.

" That I will," said Joe, " and glad too." The man was gone, and we were on our way home at a smart trot.

" Why, what's the matter with you, Joe ? You look angry all over," said John, as the boy flung himself from the saddle.

" I am angry all over, I can tell you," said the boy, and then in hurried, excited words he told all that had happened. Joe was usually such a quiet, gentle little fellow that it was wonderful to see him so roused.

" Right, Joe ! you did right, my boy, whether the fellow gets a summons or not. Many folks would have ridden by and said 'twas not their business to interfere. Now, I say, that with cruelty and oppression it is everybody's business to interfere when they see it ; you did right, my boy."

Joe was quite calm by this time, and proud that John approved of him. He cleaned out my feet, and rubbed me down with a firmer hand than usual.

They were just going home to dinner when the footman came down to the stable to say that Joe was wanted directly in master's private room ; there was a man brought up for ill-using horses, and Joe's evidence was wanted. The boy flushed up to his forehead, and his eyes sparkled. " They shall have it," said he.

" Put yourself a bit straight," said John. Joe gave a pull at his necktie and a twitch at his jacket and was off in a moment. Our master being one of the county magistrates, cases were often brought to him to settle, or say what should be done.

In the stable we heard no more for some time, as it was the men's dinner-hour. But when Joe came next into the stable I saw he was in high spirits ; he gave me a good-natured slap and said, " We won't see such things done, will we, old fellow ? " We heard afterwards that he had given his evidence so clearly, and the horses were in such an exhausted state, bearing marks of such brutal usage, that the carter was committed to take his trial, and might possibly be sentenced to two or three months in prison.

It was wonderful what a change had come over Joe. John laughed, and said he had grown an inch taller in that week ; and I believe he had. He was just as kind and gentle as before, but there was more purpose and determination in all that he did—as if he had jumped at once from a boy into a man.

CHAPTER XXI

The Parting

I HAD NOW lived in this happy place three years, but sad changes were about to come over us. We heard from time to time that our mistress was ill. The Doctor was often at the house, and the master looked grave and anxious. Then we heard that she must leave her home at once and go to a warm country for two or three years. The news fell upon the household like the tolling of a death-bell.

Everybody was sorry ; but the master began directly to make arrangements for breaking up his establishment and leaving England. We used to hear it talked about in our stable ; indeed nothing else was talked about.

John went about his work silent and sad, and Joe scarcely whistled. There was a great deal of coming and going ; Ginger and I had full work.

The first to go were Miss Jessie and Miss Flora with their governess. They came to bid us good-bye. They hugged poor Merrylegs like an old friend, and so indeed he was. Then we heard what had been arranged for us. Master had sold Ginger and me to his old friend the Earl of W——, for he thought we should have a good place there. Merrylegs he had given to the Vicar, who was wanting a pony for Mrs. Blomefield ; but it was on condition that he should never be sold, and that when he was past work he should be shot and buried.

Joe was engaged to take care of him and to help in the house ; so I thought that Merrylegs was well off. John had the offer of several good places, but he said he should wait a little and look round.

The evening before they left, the master came into the stable to give some directions and to give his horses the last pat. He seemed very low-spirited ; I knew that by his voice. I believe we horses can tell more by the voice than many men can.

" Have you decided what to do, John ? " he said. " I find you have not accepted any of those offers."

" No, sir, I have made up my mind that if I could get a situation with some first-rate colt-breaker and horse-trainer, it would be the right thing for me. Many young animals are frightened and spoiled by wrong treatment, which need not be if the right man took them in hand. I always get on well with horses, and if I could help some of them to a fair start, I should feel as if I was doing some good. What do you think of it, sir ? "

" I don't know a man anywhere," said master, " that

I should think so suitable for it as yourself. You understand horses, and somehow they understand you, and in time you might set up for yourself ; I think you could not do better. If in any way I can help you, write to me ; I shall speak to my agent in London, and leave your character with him."

He asked John about his future, and then thanked him for his long and faithful service ; but that was too much for John. " Pray don't, sir, I can't bear it. You and my dear mistress have done so much for me that I could never repay it ; but we shall never forget you, sir, and please God we may some day see mistress back again like herself ; we must keep up hope, sir." Master gave John his hand, but he did not speak ; and they both left the stable.

The last sad day had come ; the footman and the heavy luggage had gone off the day before, and there was only master and mistress and her maid left. Ginger and I brought the carriage up to the hall door for the last time. The servants brought out cushions and rugs and many other things ; and when all were arranged, master came down the steps carrying the mistress in his arms (I was on the side next the house and could see all that went on). He placed her carefully in the carriage, while the house servants stood round crying.

" Good-bye again," he said as he got in ; " we shall not forget any of you—drive on, John."

Joe jumped up, and we trotted slowly through the park and through the village, where the people were standing at their doors to have a last look and to say, " God bless them."

When we reached the railway station, I think mistress walked from the carriage to the waiting-room. I heard her say in her own sweet voice, " Good-bye, John, God bless you." I felt the rein twitch, but John made no answer, perhaps he could not speak. As soon as Joe had taken the things out of the carriage, John called him to stand by the horses while he went on the platform. Poor Joe ! he stood close up to our heads to hide his tears.

Very soon the train came puffing up into the station. Two or three minutes after the doors were slammed to, the guard whistled, and the train glided away leaving behind it only clouds of white steam and some very heavy hearts.

When it was quite out of sight, John came back.

"We shall never see her again," he said—"never." He took the reins, mounted the box, and drove slowly home with Joe ; but it was not our home now.

CHAPTER XXII

Earlshall

THE NEXT morning after breakfast, Joe put Merrylegs into the mistress's low chaise to take him to the vicarage. He came first and said good-bye to us, and Merrylegs neighed to us from the yard. Then John put the saddle on Ginger and the leading rein on me, and rode us across the country about fifteen miles to Earlshall Park, where the Earl of W—— lived. Here was a very fine house and a great deal of stabling.

We went into the yard through a stone gateway, and John asked for Mr. York. It was some time before he came. He was a fine-looking, middle-aged man, and his voice said at once that he expected to be obeyed. He was very friendly and polite to John ; and after giving us a slight look, he called a groom to take us to our boxes, and invited John to take some refreshment.

We were taken to a light, airy stable and placed in boxes adjoining each other, where we were rubbed down and fed. In about half an hour John and Mr. York, who was to be our new coachman, came in to see us.

"Now, Mr. Manly," he said, after carefully looking at us both, " I can see no fault in these horses ; but we all know that horses as well as men have their peculiarities, and that sometimes they need different treatment. I should like to know if there is anything particular in either of these that you would like to mention."

"Well," said John, " I don't believe there is a better

pair of horses in the country, and right grieved I am to part with them, but they are not alike. The black one is the most perfect temper I ever knew ; I suppose he has never known a hard word or a blow since he was foaled, and all his pleasure seems to be what you wish to do.

" But the chestnut I fancy must have had bad treatment ; we heard as much from the dealer. She came to us snappish and suspicious, but when she found what sort of a place ours was, it went off by degrees. For three years I have never seen the smallest sign of temper, and if she is well treated there is not a better or more willing animal than she is ; but she is naturally of a more irritable constitution than the black horse—flies tease her more ; anything wrong in the harness frets her more ; and if she were ill-used or unfairly treated, she would not be unlikely to give tit for tat. You know that many high-mettled horses will do so."

" Of course," said York, " I quite understand ; but you know it is not easy in stables like these to have all the grooms just what they should be ; I do my best, and there I must leave it. I'll remember what you have said about the mare."

They were going out of the stable, when John stopped and said : " I had better mention that we have never used the bearing-rein with either of them ; the black horse never had one on, and the dealer said it was the gag-bit that spoiled the other's temper."

" Well," said York, " if they come here, they must wear the bearing-rein. I prefer a loose rein myself, and his lordship is always very reasonable about horses ; but my lady—that's another matter. She will have style ; and if her carriage horses were not reined up tight she wouldn't look at them. I always stand out against the gag-bit, and shall do so, but the rein must be tight up when my lady rides ! "

" I am sorry for it, very sorry," said John ; " but I must go now, or I shall lose the train."

He came round to each of us to pat and speak to us for the last time ; his voice sounded very sad.

I held my face close to him, as that was all I could do

to say good-bye; and then he was gone, and I have never seen him since.

The next day Lord W—— came to look at us; he seemed pleased with our appearance.

"I have great confidence in these horses," he said, "from the character my friend Mr. Gordon has given me of them. Of course they are not a match in colour, but my idea is that they will do very well for the carriage whilst we are in the country. Before we go to London I must try to match Baron; the black horse, I believe, is perfect for riding."

York then told him what John had said about us.

"Well," said he, "you must keep an eye to the mare, and put the bearing-rein easy; I daresay they will do very well with a little humouring at first. I'll mention it to her ladyship."

In the afternoon we were harnessed and put in the carriage, and as the stable clock struck three we were led round to the front of the house. It was all very grand, and the house three or four times as large as the old one at Birtwick, but not half so pleasant, if a horse may have an opinion. Two footmen, dressed in drab livery, with scarlet breeches and white stockings, were standing ready.

Presently we heard the rustling sound of silk as my lady came down the flight of stone steps. She stepped round to look at us. She was a tall, proud-looking woman, and did not seem pleased about something; but she said nothing, and got into the carriage. This was my first time of wearing a bearing-rein, and I must say, though it certainly was a nuisance not to be able to get my head down now and then it did not pull my head higher than I was accustomed to carry it. I felt anxious about Ginger, but she seemed to be quiet and content.

The next day at three o'clock we were again at the door, and the footmen were there as before. We heard the silk dress rustle as the lady came down the steps, and in an imperious voice she said; "York, you must put those horses' heads higher; they are not fit to be seen."

York got down and said very respectfully : " I beg your pardon, my lady, but these horses have not been reined up for three years, and my lord said it would be safer to bring them to it by degrees ; but if your ladyship pleases, I can take them up a little more."

" Do so," she said.

York came round to our heads and shortened the rein one hole, I think ; every little makes a difference, be it for better or worse, and that day we had a steep hill to go up. Then I began to understand what I had heard. Of course I wanted to put my head forward and take the carriage up with a will, as we had been used to do ; but no, I had now to pull with my head up, and that took all the spirit out of me, and brought the strain on my back and legs.

When we came in, Ginger said : " Now you see what it is like ; but this is not bad, and if it does not get much worse than this, I shall say nothing about it, for we are very well treated here. But if they strain me up tight, why, let 'em look out ! I can't bear it and I won't."

Day by day, hole by hole, our bearing-reins were shortened, and instead of looking forward with pleasure to having my harness put on as I used to do, I began to dread it. Ginger, too, seemed restless, though she said very little. At last I thought the worst was over ; for several days there had been no more shortening, and I determined to make the best of it and to do my duty, though now going out was a constant harass instead of a pleasure ; but the worst was not come.

CHAPTER XXIII

A Strike for Liberty

ONE DAY my lady came down later than usual, and the silk rustled more than ever.

" Drive to the Duchess of B——'s," she said. Then, after a pause, she added : " Are you never going to get those horses' heads up, York? Raise them at once, and let us have no more of this humouring nonsense."

York came to me first, whilst the groom stood at Ginger's head. He drew my head back and fixed the rein so tight that it was almost intolerable ; then he went to Ginger, who was impatiently jerking her head up and down against the bit, as was her way now. She had a good idea of what was coming, and the moment York took the rein off the terret in order to shorten it, she took her opportunity and reared up so suddenly that York had his nose roughly hit and his hat knocked off, and the groom was nearly thrown off his legs.

At once they both flew to her head, but she was a match for them, and went on plunging, rearing, and kicking in a most desperate manner. At last she kicked right over the carriage pole and fell down, after giving me a severe blow on my near quarter.

There is no knowing what further mischief she may have done had not York promptly sat himself down flat on her head to prevent her struggling, at the same time calling out, "Unbuckle the black horse ! Run for the winch and unscrew the carriage pole ; and somebody cut the trace if you can't unhitch it."

One of the footmen ran for the winch, and another brought a knife from the house. The groom set me free from Ginger and the carriage, and led me to my box. He just turned me in as I was, and ran back to York.

I was much excited by what had happened, and if I had ever been used to kick or rear, I am sure I should have done it then ; but I never had, so there I stood, angry, sore in my leg, my head still strained up to the terret on the saddle, and with no power to get it down. I was very miserable, and felt much inclined to kick the first person who came near me.

Before long, however, Ginger was led in by two grooms, a good deal knocked about and bruised. York came with her and gave his orders, and then came to look at me. In a moment he let down my head.

" Confound these bearing-reins ! " he said to himself.
" I thought we should have some mischief soon—master
will be sorely vexed ; but there—if a woman's husband
can't rule her, of course a servant can't ; so I wash my hands
of it, and if she can't get to the Duchess's garden party,
I can't help it."

York did not say this before the men ; he always spoke
respectfully when they were by. Now he felt me all over
and soon found the place above my hock where I had been
kicked. It was swollen and painful ; so he ordered it to
be sponged with hot water and then some lotion to be
rubbed in.

Lord W—— was much put out when he learned what
had happened. He blamed York for giving way to his mistress, to which York replied that in future he would much
prefer to receive his orders only from his lordship. But I
think nothing came of it, for things went on the same as
before. I thought York might have stood up better for his
horses ; but perhaps I am no judge.

Ginger was never put into the carriage again, but when
her bruises were healed, one of Lord W——'s younger
sons said he should like to have her ; he was sure she would
make a good hunter. As for me, I was obliged still to go in
the carriage, and had a fresh partner, called Max, who had
always been used to the tight rein. I asked him how it was
he bore it.

" Well," he said, " I bear it because I must, but it is
shortening my life, and it will shorten yours too if you
have to stick to it."

" Do you think," I said, " that our masters know how
bad it is for us ? "

" I can't say," he replied, " but the dealers and the
horse doctors know it very well. I was at a dealer's once,
who was training me and another horse to go as a pair ;
he was getting our heads up, as he said, a little higher and
a little higher every day. A gentleman who was there asked
him why he did so ; ' Because,' said he, ' people won't

buy them unless we do. The London people always want their horses to carry their heads high, and to step high ; of course it is very bad for the horses, but then it is good for trade. The horses soon wear up, or get diseased and they come for another pair.' That," said Max, " is what he said in my hearing, and you can judge for yourself."

What I suffered for four long months with that rein it would be hard to describe ; but I am quite sure that, had it lasted much longer, either my health or my temper would have given way. Before that, I never knew what it was to foam at the mouth ; but now the action of the sharp bit on my tongue and jaw and the constrained position of my head and throat, always caused me to froth more or less at the mouth.

Some people think it very fine to see this, and say, " What fine, spirited creatures ! " But it is just as unnatural for horses as for men to foam at the mouth : it is a sure sign of some discomfort, and should be attended to. Besides this, there was a pressure on my windpipe, which often made my breathing very uncomfortable. When I returned from my work, my neck and chest were strained and painful, my mouth and tongue tender, and I felt worn and depressed.

In my old home I always knew that John and my master were my friends ; but here, although in many ways I was well treated, I had no friend. York might have known, and very likely did know, how that rein harassed me ; but I suppose he took it as a matter of course that could not be helped ; at any rate, nothing was done to relieve me.

CHAPTER XXIV
Lady Anne, or a Runaway Horse

EARLY in the spring Lord W—— and part of his family went up to London and took York with them. Ginger and I and some other horses were left at home for use, and the head groom was left in charge.

The Lady Harriet, who remained at the Hall, was a great invalid, and never went out in the carriage, and the Lady Anne preferred riding on horseback with her brother or cousins. She was a perfect horsewoman, and as gay and gentle as she was beautiful. She chose me for her horse, and named me Black Auster. I enjoyed very much these rides in the clear, cold air, sometimes with Ginger,. sometimes with Lizzie. This Lizzie was a bright bay mare almost thoroughbred, and a great favourite with the gentlemen on account of her fine action and lively spirit ; but Ginger, who knew more of her than I did, told me she was rather nervous.

There was a gentleman of the name of Blantyre staying at the Hall ; he always rode Lizzie, and praised her so much that one day Lady Anne ordered the side-saddle to be put on Lizzie and the other saddle on me. When we came to the door, the gentleman seemed very uneasy.

" How is this ? " he said ; " are you tired of your good Black Auster ? "

" Oh, no, not at all," she replied, " but I am amiable enough to let you ride him for once, and I will try your charming Lizzie. You must confess that in size and appearance she is far more like a lady's horse than my own favourite."

" Do let me advise you not to mount her," he said ; " she is a charming creature, but she is too nervous for a lady. I assure you she is not perfectly safe ; let me beg you to have the saddles changed."

" My dear cousin," said Lady Anne, laughing, " pray do not trouble your good, careful head about me. I have been a horsewoman ever since I was a baby, and I have followed the hounds a great many times, though I know you do not approve of ladies hunting ; but still, that is the fact and I intend to try this Lizzie that you gentlemen are all so fond of ; so please help me to mount like the good friend you are."

There was no more to be said. He placed her carefully

on the saddle, looked to the bit and curb, gave the reins gently into her hand, and then mounted me. Just as we were moving off, a footman came out with a slip of paper and message from the Lady Harriet—" Would Mr. Blantyre ask this question for her at Dr. Ashley's, and bring the answer ? "

The village was about a mile off, and the Doctor's house was the last in it. We went along gaily enough till we came to his gate. There was a short drive up to the house between tall evergreens. Blantyre alighted at the gate and was going to open it for Lady Anne, but she said, " I will wait for you here ; you can hang Auster's rein on the gate."

He looked at her doubtfully—" I will not be five minutes," he said.

" Oh, do not hurry yourself ; Lizzie and I shall not run away from you."

He hung my rein on one of the iron spikes, and was soon hidden amongst the trees. By the side of the road, a few paces off, Lizzie was standing quietly with her back to me. My young mistress was sitting easily with a loose rein, humming a little song. I listened to my rider's footsteps until they reached the house, and heard him knock at the door.

There was a meadow on the opposite side of the road, the gate of which stood open. Just then some cart horses and several young colts came trotting out in a very disorderly manner, whilst a boy behind was cracking a great whip. The colts were wild and frolicsome, and one of them bolted across the road and blundered up against Lizzie's hind legs. Whether it was the stupid colt, or the loud cracking of the whip, or both together I cannot say ; but she gave a violent kick and dashed off into a headlong gallop. It was so sudden, that Lady Anne was nearly unseated, but she soon recovered herself.

I gave a loud, shrill neigh for help. Again and again I neighed, pawing the ground impatiently, and tossing my head to get the rein loose. I had not long to wait. Blantyre came running to the gate. He looked anxiously about, and just caught sight of the flying figure, now far away on the road. In an instant he sprang into the saddle. I needed no whip or spur, for I was as eager as my rider. He saw it, and giving me a free rein, and leaning a little forward, we dashed after them.

For about a mile and a half the road ran straight, then bent to the right, after which it divided into two roads. Long before we came to the bend Lady Anne was out of sight. Which way had she turned? A woman was standing at her garden gate, shading her eyes with her hand and looking eagerly up the road. Scarcely drawing the rein, Blantyre shouted, " Which way? " " To the right," cried the woman, pointing with her hand, and away we went up the right-hand road ; then for a moment we caught sight of her ; another bend and she was hidden again. Several times we caught glimpses, and then lost them. We scarcely seemed to gain ground upon them at all.

An old road-mender was standing near a heap of stones, with shovel dropped and hands raised. As we came near he made a sign to speak. Blantyre drew the rein a little. " To the common, to the common, sir ; she has turned off there." I knew this common very well. It was for the most part very uneven ground, covered with heather and dark green furze bushes, with here and there a scrubby old thorn-tree. There were also open spaces of fine, short grass, with ant-hills and mole-turns everywhere,—the worst place I ever knew for a headlong gallop.

We had hardly turned on the common, when we caught sight again of the green habit flying on before us. My lady's hat was gone, and her long brown hair was streaming behind her. Her head and body were thrown back, as if she were pulling with all her remaining strength, and as if that strength were nearly exhausted. It was clear that the roughness of the ground had very much lessened Lizzie's speed, and there seemed a chance that we might overtake her.

Whilst we were on the high-road, Blantyre had given me my head ; but now with a light hand and a practised eye, he guided me over the ground in such a masterly manner, that my pace was scarcely slackened, and we were decidedly gaining on them.

About half-way across the heath there had been a wide dyke recently cut, and the earth from the cutting was cast up roughly on the other side. Surely this would stop them ! But no ; with scarcely a pause Lizzie took the leap, stumbled among the rough clods, and fell. Blantyre groaned, " Now, Auster, do your best ! " He gave me a steady rein, I gathered myself well together, and with one determined leap cleared both dyke and bank.

Motionless among the heather, with her face to the earth, lay my poor young mistress. Blantyre kneeled down and called her name—there was no sound.

Gently he turned her face upward, it was ghastly white, and the eyes were closed. " Annie, dear Annie, do speak ! " but there was no answer. He unbuttoned her habit, loosened her collar, felt her hands and wrists, then started up and looked wildly round for help.

At no great distance were two men cutting turf, who, seeing Lizzie running wild without a rider, had left their work to catch her.

Blantyre's " Hallo ! " soon brought them to the spot. The foremost man seemed much troubled at the sight and asked what he could do.

" Can you ride ? "

" Well, sir, I bean't much of a horseman, but I'd risk my neck for the Lady Anne ; she was uncommon good to my wife in the winter."

" Then mount this horse, my friend ; your neck will be quite safe. Ride to the Doctor's and ask him to come instantly ; then go on to the Hall ; tell them all that you know, and bid them send me the carriage with Lady Anne's maid and other assistance. I shall stay here."

" All right, sir, I'll do my best, and I pray God the dear

young lady may open her eyes soon." Then, seeing the other man, he called out : " Here, Joe, run for some water, and tell my missis to come as quickly as she can to the Lady Anne."

He then somehow scrambled into the saddle, and with a " Gee up ! " and a clap on my sides with both his legs, he started on his journey, making a little circuit to avoid the dyke. He had no whip, which seemed to trouble him, but my pace soon cured that difficulty, and he found the best thing he could do was to stick to the saddle, and hold me in, which he did manfully. I shook him as little as I could help, but once or twice on the rough ground he called out, " Steady ! Woah ! Steady." On the high-road we were all right ; and at the Doctor's and at the Hall he did his errand like a good man and true. They asked him in to take a drop of something. " No ! no," he said ; " I'll be back to 'em again by a short cut through the fields, and be there before the carriage."

There was a great deal of hurry and excitement after the news became known. I was just turned into my box, the saddle and bridle were taken off, and a cloth thrown over me.

Ginger was saddled and sent off in great haste for Lord George, and I soon heard the carriage roll out of the yard.

It seemed a long time before Ginger came back and before we were left alone ; and then she told me all that she had seen.

" I can't tell much," she said ; " we went galloping nearly all the way, and got there just as the Doctor rode up. There was a woman sitting on the ground with the lady's head in her lap. The Doctor poured something into her mouth, but all that I heard was " She is not dead." Then I was led off by a man to a little distance. After a while the lady was taken to the carriage, and we came home together. I heard my master say to a gentleman who stopped him to inquire, that he hoped no bones were broken, but that she had not spoken yet."

When Lord George took Ginger for hunting, York shook his head ; he said it ought to be a steady hand to train a horse for the first season, and not a random rider like Lord George.

Ginger used to like it very much, but sometimes when she came back I could see that she had been very much strained, and now and then she gave a short cough. She had too much spirit to complain, but I could not help feeling anxious about her.

Two days after the accident Blantyre paid me a visit. He patted me and praised me very much, and told Lord George that he was sure the horse knew of Annie's danger as well as he did. " I could not have held him in if I would," said he ; " she ought never to ride any other horse."

I found by their conversation that my young mistress was now out of danger and would soon be able to ride again. This was good news to me, and I looked forward to a happy life.

CHAPTER XXV

Reuben Smith

I MUST now say a little about Reuben Smith, who was left in charge of the stables when York went to London. No one more thoroughly understood his business than he did, and when he was all right, there could not be a more faithful or valuable man. He was gentle and very clever in his management of horses, and could doctor them almost as well as a farrier, for he had lived two years with a veterinary surgeon. He was a first-rate driver, and could take a four-in-hand, or a tandem, as easily as a pair.

He was a handsome man, a good scholar, and had very pleasant manners. I believe everybody liked him ; certainly the horses did. The only wonder was that he should be in an under situation, and not in the place of a head coachman like York : but he had one great fault—the love of drink.

He was not like some men, always at it ; he used to keep steady for weeks or months together ; but then he would break out and have a " bout " of it, as York called it, and be a disgrace to himself, a terror to his wife, and a nuisance to all that had to do with him. He was, however, so useful that two or three times York had hushed the matter up and kept it from the Earl's knowledge.

But one night, when Reuben had to drive a party home from a ball, he was so drunk that he could not hold the reins, and a gentleman of the party had to mount the box and drive the ladies home. Of course this could not be hidden. Reuben was at once dismissed, and his poor wife and little children had to turn out of the pretty cottage by the park gate and go where they could.

Old Max told me all this, for it happened a good while ago ; but shortly before Ginger and I came Smith had been taken back again. York had interceded for him with the Earl, who is very kind-hearted, and the man had promised faithfully that he would never taste another drop as long as he lived there. Smith had kept his promise so well that York thought he might be safely trusted to fill his place whilst he was away ; and he was so clever and honest that no one else seemed so well fitted for it.

It was now early in April, and the family was expected home some time in May. The light brougham was to be fresh done up, and as Colonel Blantyre was obliged to return to his regiment, it was arranged that Smith should drive him to the town in it, and then ride back ; for this purpose he took the saddle with him, and I was chosen for the journey.

At the station the Colonel put some money into Smith's hand and bade him good-bye, saying : " Take care of your young mistress, Reuben, and don't let Black Auster be hacked about by any random young prig that wants to ride him—keep him for the lady."

We left the carriage at the maker's, and Smith drove me to the " White Lion," and ordered the ostler to feed me well and have me ready for him at four o'clock. A nail in one of my front shoes had started as I came along, but the ostler did not notice it till just about four o'clock. Smith did not come into the yard till six, as he had met with some old friends. The man then told him of the nail, and asked if he should have the shoe looked to.

" No," said Smith, " that will be all right till we get home."

He spoke in a very loud, off-hand way, and I thought it was very unlike him not to see about the shoe, as he was generally wonderfully particular about loose nails in our shoes. He came neither at six, seven, nor eight, and it was nearly nine o'clock before he called me ; and then it was with a loud, rough voice. He seemed in a very bad temper and abused the ostler, though I could not tell what for.

The landlord stood at the door, and said, " Have a care, Mr. Smith ! " but he answered angrily with an oath ; and almost before he was out of the town he began to gallop, frequently giving me a sharp cut with his whip, though I was going at full speed. The moon had not yet risen, and it was very dark. Having been recently mended, the roads were stony, and going over them at this pace made my shoe looser, so that when we were near the turnpike gate it came off.

If Smith had been in his right senses, he would have been sensible of something wrong in my pace ; but he was too madly drunk to notice anything.

Beyond the turnpike was a long piece of road, upon which some fresh stones had just been laid—large, sharp stones, over which no horse could be driven quickly without risk of danger. Over this road, with one shoe gone, I was forced to gallop at my utmost speed, my rider meanwhile cutting into me with his whip, and with wild curses urging me to go still faster. Of course my shoeless foot suffered dreadfully ; the hoof was broken and split down to the quick, and the inside was terribly cut by the sharpness of the stones.

This could not go on ; no horse could keep his footing under such circumstances as the pain was too great. I stumbled, and fell with violence on both my knees. Smith was flung off by my fall, and, owing to the speed at which I was going, he must have fallen with great force. I soon recovered my feet and limped to the side of the road, where it was free from stones.

The moon had just risen above the hedge, and by its light I could see Smith lying a few yards beyond me. After making one slight effort to rise, there was a heavy groan. He did not move. I could have groaned too, for I was suffering intense pain both from my foot and knees ; but horses are used to bear their pain in silence. I uttered no sound, but stood there and listened.

One more heavy groan from Smith ; but though he now lay in the full moonlight, I could see no motion. I could do nothing for him nor for myself. But, oh ! how I listened for the sound of horse, or wheels, or footsteps. The road was not much frequented, and at this time of the night we might stay for hours before help came to us.

I stood watching and listening. It was a calm, sweet April night ; there were no sounds except a few low notes of a nightingale ; and nothing moved but the white clouds near the moon, and a brown owl that flitted over the hedge. It made me think of the summer nights long ago, when I used to lie beside my mother in the green, pleasant meadow at Farmer Grey's.

CHAPTER XXVI

How it Ended

IT MUST have been nearly midnight when I heard at a great distance the sound of a horse's feet. Sometimes the sound died away, then it grew clearer again and nearer. The road to Earlshall led through plantations that belonged to the Earl ; the sound came in that direction, and I hoped it might be some one coming in search of us. As the sound came nearer and nearer, I was almost sure I could distinguish Ginger's step ; a little nearer still, and I could tell she was in the dog-cart. I neighed loudly, and was overjoyed to hear an answering neigh from Ginger and men's voices. They came slowly over the stones, and stopped at the dark figure that lay upon the ground.

One of the men jumped out, and stooped down over it. " It is Reuben ! " he said, " and he does not stir."

The other man followed and bent over him. " He's dead," he said ; " feel how cold his hands are."

They raised him up, but there was no life, and his hair was soaked with blood. Laying him down again, they came and looked at me and saw my cut knees.

" Why, the horse has been down and has thrown him ! Who would have thought the black horse would have done that ? Nobody thought he could fall. Reuben must have been lying here for hours ! Odd, too, that the horse has not moved from the place."

Robert then attempted to lead me forward. I made a step, but almost fell again.

" Hallo ! he's bad in his foot as well as his knees. Look here—his hoof is cut all to pieces ; he might well come down, poor fellow ! I tell you what, Ned, I'm afraid it hasn't been all right with Reuben ! Just think of him riding a horse over these stones without a shoe ! Why, if he had been in his right senses, he would just as soon have tried to ride him over the moon. I'm afraid it has been the old thing over again.

" Poor Susan ! she looked awfully pale when she came to my house to ask if he had come home. She made believe she was not a bit anxious, and talked of a lot of things that might have kept him. But for all that, she begged me to go and meet him. But what must we do ? There's the horse to get home as well as the body—and that will be no easy matter."

Then followed a conversation between them, till it was agreed that Robert, the groom, should lead me, and that

Ned should take the body ; it was a hard job to get it into the dog-cart, for there was no one to hold Ginger ; but she knew as well as I did what was going on, and stood as still as a stone. I noticed that, because, if she had a fault, it was that she was impatient in standing.

Ned started off very slowly with his sad load, and Robert came and looked at my foot again ; then he took his hand-kerchief and bound it closely round, and so led me home. I shall never forget that night walk ; it was more than three miles. Robert led me on very slowly, and I limped and hob-bled on as well as I could, suffering great pain. I am sure he was sorry for me, for he often patted and encouraged me, talking to me in a pleasant voice.

At last I reached my own box and had some corn ; and after Robert had wrapped up my knees in wet cloths, he tied up my foot in a bran poultice to draw out the heat, and to cleanse it before the horse doctor saw it in the morn-ing. Then I managed to get myself down on the straw and slept in spite of the pain.

The next day, after the farrier had examined my wounds, he said he hoped the joint was not injured, and if so, I should not be spoiled for work, but I should never lose the blemish. I believe they did the best to make a good cure, but it was a long and painful one. Proud flesh, as they called it, came up in my knees and was burnt out with caustic ; and when at last my knees were healed, they put a blistering fluid over the front of both to bring off all the hair ; they had some reason for this, and I suppose it was all right.

As Smith's death had been so sudden, and no one was there to see it, there was an inquest held. The landlord and ostler at the " White Lion," with several other people gave evidence that he was intoxicated when he started from the inn ; the keeper of the toll-gate said he rode at a hard gallop through the gate ; and my shoe was picked up amongst the stones ; so the case was quite plain to them, and I was cleared of all blame.

Everybody pitied Susan ; she was nearly out of her mind, and kept saying over and over again, " Oh ! he was so good —so good ! It was all that cursed drink ; why will they sell that cursed drink ? Oh, Reuben, Reuben ! " So she went on 'till after he was buried ; and then, as she had no home or relations, she, with her six little children, were obliged once more to leave the pleasant home by the tall oak-trees, and go into that great gloomy Union House.

CHAPTER XXVII

Ruined, and going Downhill

AS SOON as my knees were sufficiently healed, I was turned into a small meadow for a month or two. No other creature was there, and though I enjoyed the liberty and the sweet grass, yet I had been so long used to society that I felt very lonely. Ginger and I had become fast friends, and now I missed her company extremely.

I often neighed when I heard horses' feet passing in the road, but I seldom got an answer, till one morning the gate was opened, and who should come in but poor old Ginger ! The man slipped off her halter and left her there. With a joyful whinny I trotted up to her ; we were both glad to meet, but I soon found that it was not for our pleasure that she was brought to be with me. Her story would be too long to tell, but the end of it was that she had been ruined by hard riding, and was now turned off to see what rest would do.

Lord George was young and would take no warning. He was a hard rider, and would hunt whenever he could get a chance, quite careless of his horse. Soon after I left the stable there was a steeplechase, and he determined to ride. Though the groom told him the mare was a little strained, and was not fit for the race, he did not believe it, and on the day of the race he urged Ginger to keep up with the foremost riders. With her high spirit, she strained herself to the utmost and came in with the first three horses ; but her wind was touched, beside which, he was too heavy for her, and her back was strained.

" And so," she said, " here we are, ruined in the prime of our youth and strength—you by a drunkard, and I by a fool ; it is very hard."

We both felt in ourselves that we were not what we had been. However, that did not spoil the pleasure we had in each other's company. We did not gallop about as we once did, but we used to feed and lie down together, and stand for hours under one of the shady lime-trees with our heads close to each other ; and so we passed our time till the family returned from town.

One day we saw the Earl come into the meadow, and York was with him. Seeing who it was, we stood still under our lime-tree, and let them come up to us. They examined us carefully. The Earl seemed much annoyed.

" There is three hundred pounds flung away for no earthly use," said he ; " but what I care most for is, that these horses of my old friend, who thought they would find a good home with me, are ruined. The mare shall have a twelve-month's run, and we shall see what that will do for her ; but the black one must be sold ; 'tis a great pity, but I could not have knees like these in my stables."

" No, my lord, of course not," said York, " but he might get a place where appearance is not much of consequence, and still be well treated. I know a man in Bath, the master of some livery stables, who often wants a good horse at a low figure ; I know he looks well after his horses. The inquest cleared the horse's character, and your lordship's recommendation or mine would be sufficient warrant for him."

" You had better write to him, York. I should be more particular about the place than the money he would fetch."

After this they left us.

" They'll soon take you away," said Ginger, " and I shall lose the only friend I have, and most likely we shall never see each other again. 'Tis a hard world ! "

About a week after this, Robert came into the field with a halter, which he slipped over my head and led me away. There was no leave-taking of Ginger ; we neighed to each other as I was led off, and she trotted anxiously along by the hedge, calling to me as long as she could hear the sound of my feet.

Through the recommendation of York, I was bought by the master of the livery stables. I had to go by train, a new experience to me, requiring a good deal of courage the first time ; but as I found the puffing, rushing, whistling, and more than all, the trembling of the horse-box in which I stood did me no real harm, I soon took it quietly.

When I reached the end of my journey, I found myself in a tolerably comfortable stable and well attended to. These stables were not so airy and pleasant as those I had been used to. The stalls were laid on a slope instead of being level, and as my head was kept tied to the manger, I was obliged always to stand on the slope, which was very fatiguing. Men do not seem to know yet that horses can do more work if they can stand comfortably and can turn about.

However, I was well fed and well cleaned, and, on the whole, I think our master took as much care of us as he could. He kept a good many horses and carriages of different kinds, for hire. Sometimes his own men drove them ; at others the horse and chaise were let to gentlemen or ladies who drove themselves.

CHAPTER XXVIII

A Job Horse and His Drivers

HITHERTO I had always been driven by people who at least knew how to drive ; but in this place I was to get my experience of all the different kinds of bad and ignorant driving to which we horses are subjected ; for I was a "job horse," and was let out to all sorts of people who wished to hire me ; and as I was good-tempered and gentle, I think I was more often let out to the ignorant drivers than some of the other horses, because I could be depended upon. It would take a long time to tell of all the different styles in which I was driven, but I will mention a few of them.

First, there were the tight-rein drivers—men who seemed to think that all depended on holding the reins as hard as they could, never relaxing the pull on the horse's mouth or giving him the least liberty of movement. These are always talking about " keeping the horse well in hand," and " holding a horse up," just as if a horse was not made to hold himself up.

Some poor broken-down horses, whose mouths have been made hard and insensible by just such drivers as these, may, perhaps, find some support in it ; but for a horse who can depend upon its own legs, has a tender mouth, and is easily guided, it is not only tormenting, but stupid.

Then there are the loose-rein drivers, who let the reins lie easily on our backs and their own hands rest lazily on their knees. Of course, such gentlemen have no control over a horse, if anything happens suddenly. If a horse shies, starts, or stumbles, they are nowhere, and cannot help the horse or themselves till the mischief is done.

Of course, for myself, I had no objection to it, as I was not in the habit either of starting or stumbling, and had only been used to depend on my driver for guidance and encouragement ; still, one likes to feel the rein a little in going downhill, and likes to know that one's driver is not gone to sleep.

Besides, a slovenly way of driving gets a horse into bad, and often lazy, habits ; and when he changes hands he has to be whipped out of them with more or less pain and trouble. Squire Gordon always kept us to our best paces and our best manners. He said that spoiling a horse and letting him get into bad habits was just as cruel as spoiling a child, and both had to suffer for it afterwards.

Moreover, these drivers are often altogether careless, and will attend to anything else rather than to their horses. I went out in the phaeton one day with one of them ; he had a lady and two children behind. He flopped the reins about as we started, and, of course, gave me several unmeaning cuts with the whip, though I was fairly off. There had been a good deal of road-mending going on, and even where the stones were not freshly laid down there were a great many loose ones about. My driver was laughing and joking with the lady and the children, and talking about the country to the right and to the left ; but he never thought it worth while to keep an eye on his horse, or to drive on the smoothest parts of the road ; and so it easily happened that I got a stone in one of my fore feet.

Now, if Mr. Gordon or John, or, in fact, any good driver had been there, he would have seen that something was wrong before I had gone three paces. Or, even if it had been dark, a practised hand would have felt by the rein that there was something wrong in the step, and would have got down and picked out the stone. But this man went on laughing and talking, whilst at every step the stone became more firmly wedged between my shoe and the frog of my foot. The stone was sharp on the inside and round on the outside, which as every one knows, is the most dangerous kind that a horse can pick up, as it cuts his foot and at the same time makes him most liable to stumble and fall.

Whether the man was partly blind or only very careless I can't say ; but he drove me with that stone in my foot for a good half-mile before he saw anything was wrong. By that time I was going so lame with the pain that at last he saw it, and called out, " Well, here's a go ! Why, they have sent us out with a lame horse ! What a shame ! "

He then jerked the reins and flipped about with the whip, saying, " Now, then, it's no use playing the old soldier with me ; there's the journey to go, and it's no use turning lame and lazy."

Just at this time a farmer came riding up on a brown cob ; he lifted his hat and pulled up.

" I beg your pardon, sir," he said, " but I think there is something the matter with your horse ; he goes very much as if he had a stone in his shoe. If you will allow me, I will look at his feet ; these loose, scattered stones are very dangerous things for the horses."

" He's a hired horse," said the driver. " I don't know what's the matter with him, but it's a great shame to send out a lame beast like this."

The farmer dismounted, and, slipping his rein over his arm, at once took up my near foot.

" Bless me, there's a stone. Lame ! I should think so ! "

At first he tried to dislodge it with his hand, but as it was now very tightly wedged, he drew a stone-pick out of his pocket, and very carefully, and with some trouble, got it out. Then, holding it up, he said, " There, that's the stone your horse has picked up ; it is a wonder he did not fall down and break his knees into the bargain ! "

" Well, to be sure ! " said my driver. " That is a queer thing ! I never knew before that horses picked up stones."

" Didn't you ? " said the farmer rather contemptuously ; " but they do, though, and the best of them will do it, and can't help it sometimes on such roads as these. And if you don't want to lame your horse, you must look sharp and get them out quickly. This foot is very much bruised," he said, setting it gently down and patting me. " If I may advise, sir, you had better drive him gently for a while ; the foot is a good deal hurt, and the lameness will not go off directly."

Then, mounting his cob, and raising his hat to the lady, he drove off.

When he was gone, my driver began to flop the reins about and whip the harness, by which I understood that I was to go on, which of course I did, glad that the stone was gone, but still in a good deal of pain.

This was the sort of experience we job horses often had.

CHAPTER XXIX
Cockneys

THEN THERE is the steam-engine style of driving ; these
drivers were mostly people from towns, who never had a
horse of their own, and generally travelled by rail.

They always seemed to think that a horse was something
like a steam-engine, only smaller. At any rate, they think
that if only they pay for it, a horse is bound to go just as
far, and just as fast, and with just as heavy a load, as they
please. And be the roads heavy and muddy, or dry and
good, be they stony or smooth, uphill or downhill, it is all
the same—on, on, on, one must go at the same pace, with
no relief and no consideration.

These people never think of getting out to walk up a
steep hill. Oh, no, they have paid to ride, and ride they
will ! The horse ? Oh, he's used to it ! What were horses
made for, if not to drag people uphill ? Walk ! A good
joke, indeed ! And so the whip is plied and the rein is
jerked, and often a rough, scolding voice cries out, " Go
along, you lazy beast ! " And then comes another slash
of the whip, when all the time we are doing our very best
to get along, uncomplaining and obedient, though often
sorely harassed and downhearted.

This steam-engine style of driving wears us up faster than
any other kind. I would far rather go twenty miles with a
good, considerate driver than ten with some of these ; it
would take less out of me.

Another thing—they scarcely ever put on the drag, however steep the hill may be, and thus bad accidents sometimes
happen ; or if they do put it on, they often forget to take
it off at the bottom of the hill ; and more than once I
have had to pull half-way up the next hill with one of the
wheels lodged fast in the drag-shoe before my driver chose
to think about it ; and that is a terrible strain on a horse.

Then these Cockneys, instead of starting at an easy pace
as a gentleman would do, generally set off at full speed

from the very stable-yard ; and when they want to stop,
they first whip us and then pull up so suddenly that we are
nearly thrown on our haunches, and our mouths are jagged
with the bit ; they call that pulling up with a dash ! And
when they turn a corner they do it as sharply as if there was
no right side or wrong side of the road.

I well remember one spring evening. Rory and I had
been out for the day (Rory was the horse that mostly went
with me when a pair was ordered, and a good honest
fellow he was). We had our own driver, and, as he was
always considerate and gentle with us, we had a very
pleasant day. About twilight we were coming home at a
good smart pace. Our road turned sharp to the left ; but
as we were close to the hedge on our own side, and there
was plenty of room to pass, our driver did not pull us in.
As we neared the corner I heard a horse and two wheels
coming rapidly down the hill towards us. The hedge was
high, and I could see nothing ; but the next moment we
were upon each other. Happily for me, I was on the side
next the hedge. Rory was on the right side of the pole, and
had not even a shaft to protect him.

The man who was driving was making straight for the
corner, and when he came in sight of us he had no time to
pull over to his own side. The whole shock came upon
Rory. The gig shaft ran right into his chest, making him
stagger back with a cry that I shall never forget. The other
horse was thrown upon its haunches, and one shaft broken.
It turned out that it was a horse from our own stables, with
the high-wheeled gig that the young men were so fond of.

The driver was one of those random, ignorant fellows
who don't even know which is their own side of the road,
or, if they know, don't care. And there was poor Rory,
with his flesh torn open and bleeding and the blood
streaming down. They said if it had been a little more to
one side, it would have killed him ; and a good thing for
him, poor fellow, if it had.

As it was, it was a long time before the wound healed,

and then he was sold for coal carting ; and what that is, up and down those steep hills, only horses know. Some of the sights I saw there, where a horse had to come downhill with a heavily loaded two-wheel cart behind him, on which no drag could be placed, make me sad even now to think of.

After Rory was disabled I often went in the carriage with a mare named Peggy, who stood in the stall next to mine. She was a strong, well-made animal, of a bright dun colour, beautifully dappled, and with a dark-brown mane and tail. There was no high breeding about her, but she was very pretty, and remarkably sweet-tempered and will-ing. Still, there was an anxious look about her eye, by which I knew that she had some trouble. The first time we went out together I thought she had a very odd pace ; she seemed to go partly in a trot, partly in a canter—three or four paces, and then to make a little jump forward.

It was very unpleasant for any horse who pulled with her, and made me quite fidgety. When we got home, I asked her what made her go in that odd, awkward way.

" Ah," she said in a troubled manner, " I know my paces are very bad, but what can I do ? It really is not my fault, it is just because my legs are so short. I stand nearly as high as you, but your legs are a good three inches longer above your knees than mine, and of course you can take a much longer step, and go much faster. You see, I did not make myself ; I wish I could have done so, I would have had long legs then ; all my troubles come from my short legs," said Peggy, in a desponding tone.

" But how is it," I said, " when you are so strong and good-tempered and willing ? "

" Why, you see," said she, " men will go so fast, and if one can't keep up to other horses, it is nothing but whip, whip, whip, all the time. And so I have had to keep up as I could, and have got into this ugly, shuffling pace. It was not always so ; when I lived with my first master I always went a good regular trot, but then he was not in such a hurry. He was a young clergyman in the country, and a good kind master he was. He had two churches a good way apart, and a great deal of work, but he never scolded or whipped me for not going faster. He was very fond of me. I only wish I was with him now ; but he had to leave and go to a larger town, and then I was sold to a farmer.

" Some farmers, you know, are capital masters ; but I think this one was a low sort of man. He cared nothing about good horses or good driving ; he only cared for going fast. I went as fast as I could, but that would not do, and he always was whipping ; so I got into this way of making a spring forward to keep up. On market nights he used to stay very late at the inn, and then drive home at a gallop.

" One dark night he was galloping home as usual, when all on a sudden the wheel came against some great, heavy thing in the road, and turned the gig over in a minute. He was thrown out and his arm broken, and some of his ribs, I think. At any rate, it was the end of my living with him, and I was not sorry. But you see it will be the same everywhere for me, if men *must* go so fast. I wish my legs were longer ! "

Poor Peggy ! I was very sorry for her, and I could not comfort her, for I knew how hard it was upon slow-paced horses to be put with fast ones ; all the whipping comes to their share, and they can't help it.

She was often used in the phaeton, and was very much liked by some of the ladies, because she was so gentle ; and some time after this she was sold to two ladies who drove themselves, and wanted a safe, good horse.

I met her several times out in the country, going a good, steady pace, and looking as gay and contented as a horse could be. I was very glad to see her, for she deserved a good place.

After she left us, another horse came in her stead. He was young, and had a bad name for shying and starting, by which he had lost a good place. I asked him what made him shy.

" Well, I hardly know," he said. " I was timid when I

was young, and several times was a good deal frightened. If I saw anything strange, I used to turn and look at it— you see, with our blinkers one can't see or understand what a thing is unless one looks round—and then my master always gave me a whipping, which, of course, made me start on and did not make me less afraid. I think if he would have let me just look at things quietly to see that there was nothing to hurt me, it would have been all right and I should have got used to them.

" One day an old gentleman was riding with him, and a large piece of white paper or rag blew across just on one side of me. I shied and started forward—my master as usual whipped me smartly, but the old man cried out, ' You're wrong ! you're wrong ! You should never whip a horse for shying : he shies because he is frightened, and you only frighten him more, and make the habit worse.' So I suppose all men don't do so.

" I am sure I don't want to shy for the sake of it, but how should one know what is dangerous and what is not if one is never allowed to get used to anything ? I am never afraid of what I know. Now I was brought up in a park where there were deer. Of course, I knew them as well as I did a sheep or a cow ; but they are not common, and I know many sensible horses who are frightened at them and kick up quite a shindy before they will pass a paddock where there are deer."

I knew what my companion said was true, and I wished that every young horse had as good masters as Farmer Grey and Squire Gordon.

Of course we sometimes came in for good driving here. I remember one morning I was put into the light gig, and taken to a house in Pulteney Street. Two gentlemen came out ; the taller of them came round to my head. He looked at the bit and bridle, and just shifted the collar with his hand, to see if it fitted comfortably.

" Do you consider this horse wants a curb ? " he said to the ostler.

" Well," said the man, " I should say he would go just as well without, for he has an uncommonly good mouth, and though he has a fine spirit, he has no vice ; but we generally find people like the curb."

" I don't like it," said the gentleman ; " be so good as to take it off, and put the rein in at the cheek. An easy mouth is a great thing on a long journey, is it not, old fellow ? " he said, patting my neck.

Then he took the reins, and they both got up. I can remember now how quietly he turned me round, and then with a light feel of the rein, and a gentle drawing of the whip across my back, we were off.

I arched my neck and set off at my best pace. I found I had someone behind me who knew how a good horse ought to be driven. It seemed like old times again, and made me feel quite gay.

This gentleman took a great liking to me, and after trying me several times with the saddle, he prevailed upon my master to sell me to a friend of his who wanted a safe, pleasant horse for riding. And so it came to pass that in the summer I was sold to Mr. Barry.

CHAPTER XXX

A Thief

MY NEW master was an unmarried man. He lived at Bath, and was much engaged in business. His doctor advised him to take horse exercise, and for this purpose he bought me. He hired a stable a short distance from his lodgings, and engaged a man named Filcher as groom. My master knew very little about horses, but he treated me well, and I should have had a good and easy place but for circumstances of which he was ignorant. He ordered the best hay, with plenty of oats, crushed beans, and bran, with vetches or rye grass, as the man might think needful. I heard the master give the order, so I knew there was plenty of good food, and I thought I was well off.

For a few days all went on well ; I found that my groom understood his business. He kept the stable clean and airy, groomed me thoroughly, and was never otherwise than gentle. He had been an ostler in one of the great hotels in Bath. This he had given up, and now cultivated fruit and vegetables for the market ; and his wife reared and fattened poultry and rabbits for sale.

After a while it seemed to me that my oats became very short. I had the beans, but bran was mixed with them with a few oats ; certainly there were not more than a quarter of the oats there should have been. In two or three weeks this began to tell upon my strength and spirits. The grass food, though very good, was not the thing without corn to keep up my condition. However, I could not complain nor make known my wants. So it went on for about two months ; and I wondered my master did not see that something was the matter.

However, one afternoon he rode out into the country to see a friend of his—a gentleman farmer who lived on the road to Wells. This gentleman had a very quick eye for horses ; and after he had welcomed his friend, casting his eye over me, he said :

" It seems to me, Barry, that your horse does not look so well as he did when you first had him ; has he been well ? "

" Yes, I believe so," said my master, " but he is not nearly so lively as he was. My groom tells me that horses are always dull and weak in the autumn, and that I must expect it."

" Autumn ! fiddlestick ! " said the farmer ; " why, this is only August ; and with your light work and good food, he ought not to go down like this, even if it were autumn. How do you feed him ? "

My master told him. The other shook his head slowly, and began to feel me over.

" I can't say who eats your corn, my dear fellow, but I

am much mistaken if your horse gets it. Have you ridden
very fast ? "

" No, very gently."

" Then just put your hand here," said he, passing his
hand over my neck and shoulders ; " he is as warm and
damp as a horse just come up from grass. I advise you to
look into your stable a little more. I hate to be suspicious,
and, thank Heaven, I have no cause to be, for I can trust
my men, present or absent ; but there are mean scoundrels
wicked enough to rob a dumb beast of his food. You must
look into it." And turning to his man who had come to
take me, " Give this horse a good feed of bruised oats, and
don't stint him."

" Dumb beasts ! " yes, we are ; but if I could have spoken
I could have told my master where his oats went to. My
groom used to come every morning about six o'clock with a
little boy, who always had a covered basket with him. The
boy used to go with his father into the harness-room where
the corn was kept, and I could see them, when the door
stood ajar, fill a little bag with oats out of the bin, and then
the boy used to be off.

Five or six mornings after this, just as the boy had left
the stable, the door was pushed open and a policeman
walked in, holding the child tight by the arm. Another
policeman followed, and locked the door on the inside,
saying, " Show me the place were your father keeps his
rabbits' food."

The boy looked very frightened and began to cry ; but
there was no escape, and he led the way to the corn-bin.
Here the policeman found another empty bag like that
which was found full of oats in the boy's basket.

Filcher was cleaning my feet at the time, but they soon
saw him, and though he blustered a good deal, they walked
him off to the " lock-up," and his boy with him. I heard
afterwards that the boy was not held to be guilty, but the
man was sentenced to prison for two months.

CHAPTER XXXI

A Humbug

MY MASTER was not immediately suited, but in a few days my new groom came. He was a tall, good-looking fellow enough ; but if ever there was a humbug in the shape of a groom, Alfred Smirk was the man. He was very civil to me, and never used me ill ; in fact, he did a great deal of stroking and patting, when his master was there to see it. To make me look smart he always brushed my mane and tail with water, and my hoofs with oil, before he brought me to the door, but as to cleaning my feet, looking to my shoes, or grooming me thoroughly, he thought no more of these than if I had been a cow. He left my bit rusty, my saddle damp, and my crupper stiff.

Alfred Smirk considered himself very handsome ; he spent a great deal of time before a little looking-glass in the harness-room, attending to his hair, whiskers, and necktie. When his master was speaking to him, it was always, " Yes, sir ; yes, sir," touching his hat at every word ; and every one thought he was a very nice young man, and that Mr. Barry was very fortunate to meet with him. I should say he was the laziest, most conceited fellow I ever came near.

Of course it was a great thing not to be ill-used, but then a horse wants more than that. I had a loose box, and might have been very comfortable if he had not been too indolent to clean it out. He never took all the straw away, and the smell from what lay underneath was very bad, while the strong vapours that rose up from it made my eyes smart and inflame, and I had not the same appetite for my food.

One day my master came in and said, " Alfred, the stable smells rather strong ; should you not give that stall a good scrub, and throw down plenty of water ? "

" Well, sir," he said, touching his cap, " I'll do so if you please, sir, but it is rather dangerous, sir, throwing down

water in a horse's box ; horses are very apt to take cold, sir.
I should not like to do him an injury, but I'll do it if you
please, sir."

"Well," said his master, "I should not like him to take
cold, but I don't like the smell of this stable ; do you think
the drains are all right."

"Well, sir, now you mention it, I think the drain does
sometimes send back a smell ; there may be something
wrong, sir."

"Then send for the bricklayer and have it seen to," said
the master.

"Yes, sir, I will."

The bricklayer came and pulled up a great many bricks,
and found nothing amiss ; so he put down some lime and
charged the master five shillings ; but the smell in my box
was as bad as ever. This was not all. Standing as I did on a
quantity of moist straw, my feet grew unhealthy and tender,
and the master used to say :

"I don't know what is the matter with this horse, he
goes very fumble-footed. I am sometimes afraid he will
stumble."

"Yes, sir," said Alfred, "I have noticed the same myself,
when I have exercised him."

Now the fact was that he hardly ever did exercise me,
and when the master was busy, I often stood for days
together without stretching my legs at all, and yet was
fed just as high as if I were hard at work. This often dis-
ordered my health, and made me sometimes heavy and
dull, but more often restless and feverish.

He never even gave me a meal of green meat or a bran
mash, which would have cooled me, for he was altogether
as ignorant as he was conceited ; and then, instead of exercise or change of food, I had to take horse balls and draughts,
which, beside the nuisance of having them poured down my
throat, used to make me feel ill and uncomfortable.

One day my feet were so tender that, trotting over
some fresh stones with my master on my back, I made two

such serious stumbles that as we came down Lansdown into the city, master stopped at the farrier's and asked him to see what was the matter with me. The man took up my feet one by one and examined them ; then standing up and dusting his hands one against the other, he said—

" Your horse has got the ' thrush,' and badly too ; his feet are very tender ; it is fortunate that he has not been down. I wonder your groom has not seen to it before. This is the sort of thing we find in foul stables where the litter is never properly cleared out. If you will send him here to-morrow I will attend to the hoof, and I will direct your man how to apply some liniment which I will give him."

The next day I had my feet thoroughly cleansed and stuffed with tow soaked in some strong lotion, and a very unpleasant business it was.

The farrier ordered all the litter to be taken out of my box day by day, and the floor to be kept very clean. Then I was to have bran mashes, a little green meat, and not so much corn, till my feet were well again. With this treatment I soon regained my spirits, but Mr. Barry was so much disgusted at being twice deceived by his grooms that he determined to give up keeping a horse and to hire when he wanted one. I was therefore kept till my feet were quite sound, and was then sold again.

CHAPTER XXXII

A Horse Fair

No DOUBT a horse fair is a very amusing place to those who have nothing to lose ; at any rate, there is plenty to see—long strings of young horses out of the country, fresh from the marshes ; droves of shaggy little Welsh ponies, no higher than Merrylegs ; hundreds of cart horses of all sorts, some of them with their long tails braided up and tied with scarlet cord ; and a good many, like myself, handsome and high-bred, but fallen into the middle class through some accident or blemish, unsoundness of wind, or some other complaint.

There were some splendid animals quite in their prime and fit for anything, who were throwing out their legs and showing off their paces in high style as they were trotted out with a leading rein, the groom running by the side. But round in the background were a number of poor things, sadly broken down with hard work, their knees knuckling over, and their hind legs swinging out at every step ; some were very dejected-looking old horses, with the upper lip hanging down and the ears laying back heavily, as if there was no pleasure in life and no more hope ; again, some were so thin you could see all their ribs ; and some had old sores on their backs and hips. These were sad sights for a horse who knows not but that he may come to the same sad state.

There was a great deal of bargaining, running up, and beating down ; and if a horse may speak his mind so far as he understands, I should say there were more lies told and more trickery carried on at that horse fair than a clever man could give an account of. I was put with two or three other strong, useful-looking horses, and a good many people came to look at us. The gentlemen always turned from me when they saw my broken knees, though the man who had me swore it was only a slip in the stall.

To examine me, buyers began to pull my mouth open, then to look at my eyes, next to feel all the way down my legs, and to give me a hard feel of the skin and flesh, and, lastly, to try my paces. What a difference there was in the way these things were done ! Some did it in a rough, off-hand way, as if one was only a piece of wood ; while others would take their hands gently over one's body, with a pat now and then, as much as to say, " By your leave." Of course, I judged the buyers a good deal by their manners to myself.

There was one man of whom I thought that if he would

buy me I should be happy. He was not a gentleman, nor yet one of the loud, flashy sort that called themselves so. He was a rather small man, but well made, and quick in all his motions. I knew in a moment by the way he handled me that he was used to horses ; he spoke gently, and his grey eye had a kindly, cheery look in it. It may seem strange—but it is true all the same—that the clean, fresh smell there was about him made me take to him. There was no smell of old beer and tobacco, which I hated, but a fresh smell as if he had come out of a hay-loft. He offered twenty-three pounds for me ; but that was refused, and he walked away. I looked after him, but he was gone.

A very hard-looking, loud-voiced man came next. I was dreadfully afraid he would have me ; but he walked off. One or two more came who did not mean business. Then the hard-faced man came back again and offered twenty-three pounds. A very close bargain was being driven, for my salesman began to think he should not get all he asked, and must come down ; but just then the grey-eyed man came back again. I could not help reaching out my head towards him. He stroked my face kindly.

" Well, old chap," he said, " I think we should suit each other. I'll give twenty-four for him."

" Say twenty-five and you shall have him."

" Twenty-four ten," said my friend, in a very decided tone, " and not another sixpence—yes or no ? "

" Done," said the salesman, " and you may depend upon it there's a monstrous deal of quality in that horse, and if you want him for cab work, he's a bargain."

The money was paid on the spot, and my new master took my halter and led me out of the fair to an inn, where he had a saddle and bridle ready. He gave me a good feed of oats, and stood by whilst I ate it, talking to himself and talking to me. Half an hour after we were on our way to London, through pleasant lanes and country roads, until we came into the great London thoroughfare, on which we travelled steadily till in the twilight we reached the great City. The gas lamps were already lighted ; there were streets to the right, streets to the left, and streets crossing each other for mile upon mile. I thought we should never come to the end of them. At last, in passing through one, we came to a long cab-stand, when my rider called out in a cheery voice, " Good-night, Governor ! "

" Hallo ! " cried a voice, " have you got a good one ? "

" I think so," replied my owner.

" I wish you luck with him."

" Thank ye, Governor " ; and he rode on. We soon turned up one of the side streets, and about half-way up turned again into a very narrow one, with rather poor-looking houses on one side and what seemed to be coach-houses and stables on the other.

My owner pulled up at one of the houses and whistled. The door flew open, and a young woman, followed by a little girl and boy, ran out. There was a very lively greeting as my rider dismounted.

" Now then, Harry, my boy, open the gates, and mother will bring us the lantern."

The next minute they were all standing round me in a small stable yard.

" Is he gentle, father ? "

" Yes, Dolly, as gentle as your own kitten ; come and pat him."

At once the little hand was patting about fearlessly all over my shoulder. How good it felt !

" Let me get him a bran mash while you rub him down," said the mother.

" Do, Polly, it's just what he wants, and I know you've got a beautiful mash ready for me."

" Sausage dumpling and apple turnover," shouted the boy : this set them all laughing. I was led into a comfort-able, clean-smelling stall with plenty of dry straw, and, after a capital supper, I lay down, thinking I was going to be happy.

CHAPTER XXXIII

A London Cab Horse

MY NEW master's name was Jeremiah Barker, but as every one called him Jerry, I shall do the same. Polly, his wife, was just as good a match as a man could have. She was a plump, trim, tidy little woman with smooth, dark hair, dark eyes, and a merry little mouth. The boy was nearly twelve years old—a tall, frank, good-tempered lad ; and little Dorothy (Dolly they called her) was her mother over again at eight years old. They were all wonderfully fond of each other ; I never, before or since, knew such a happy merry family.

Jerry had a cab of his own and two horses, which he drove and attended to himself. His other horse was a tall, white, rather large-boned animal, called Captain. He was old now, but when he was young he must have been splendid ; there was still the proud way of holding his head and arching his neck, in fact, he was a high-bred, fine mannered, noble old horse, every inch of him.

He told me that in his early youth he went to the Crimean War, for he belonged to an officer in the cavalry, and used to lead the regiment : I will tell more of that hereafter.

The next morning, when I was well groomed, Polly and Dolly came into the yard to see me and to make friends. Harry had been helping his father since the early morning, and had stated his opinion that I should turn out " a regular brick." Polly brought me a slice of apple, and Dolly a piece of bread, and they made as much of me as if I had been the " Black Beauty " of olden time. To be petted again and talked to in a gentle voice was a great treat ; and I let them see as well as I could that I wished to be friendly. Polly thought I was very handsome and a great deal too good for a cab, if it was not for the broken knees.

" Of course, there's no one to tell us whose fault that was," said Jerry, " and as long as I don't know, I shall give him

the benefit of the doubt ; for a firmer, neater stepper I
never rode. We'll call him ' Jack,' after the old one—shall
we, Polly ? "

" Do," she said, " for I like to keep a good name going."

Captain went out in the cab all the morning. Harry
came in after school to feed me and give me water. In the
afternoon I was put into the cab. Jerry took as much pains
to see if the collar and bridle fitted comfortably as if he had
been John Manly over again. When the crupper was let
out a hole or two it all fitted well. There was no bearing-
rein or curb, nothing but a plain ring snaffle. What a blessing that was !

After driving through the side street we came to the
large cab-stand where Jerry had said " Good-night." On
one side of this wide street were high houses with wonderful
shop fronts, and on the other was an old church and churchyard surrounded by iron palisades. Alongside these iron
rails a number of cabs were drawn up, waiting for passen-
gers. Bits of hay were lying about on the ground. Some of
the men were standing together talking ; others were sitting
on their boxes reading the newspaper ; and one or two were
feeding their horses with bits of hay and a drink of water.
We pulled up in the rank at the back of the last cab. Two
or three men came round and began to look at me and to
pass their remarks.

" Very good for a funeral," said one.

" Too smart-looking," said another, shaking his head
in a very wise way ; " you'll find out something wrong one
of these fine mornings, or my name isn't Jones."

" Well," said Jerry pleasantly, " I suppose I need not
find it out till it finds me out, eh ? and, if so, I'll keep up
my spirits a little longer."

Then came up a broad-faced man dressed in a great
grey coat with great grey capes and great white buttons, a
grey hat, and a blue comforter loosely tied round his neck.
His hair was grey too, but he was a jolly-looking fellow,
and the other men made way for him. He looked me all

over, as if he had been going to buy me ; and then, straight-ening himself up, he said with a grunt, " He's the right sort for you, Jerry ; I don't care what you gave for him, he'll be worth it." Thus my character was established on the stand. This man's name was Grant, but he was called, " Grey Grant," or " Governor Grant." He had been the longest of any of the men on that stand, and he took it upon himself to settle matters and stop disputes. He was generally a good-humoured, sensible man ; but if his tem-per was a little out, as it was sometimes when he had drunk too much, nobody liked to come too near his fist for he could deal a very hard blow.

The first week of my life as a cab horse was very trying ; I had never been used to London, and the noise, the hurry, the crowds of horses, carts, and carriages through which I had to make my way, made me feel anxious and harassed ; but I soon found that I could perfectly trust my driver, and then I made myself easy and got used to it.

Jerry was as good a driver as I had ever known ; and, what was better, he took as much thought for his horses as he did for himself. He soon found out that I was willing to work and to do my best ; and he never laid the whip on me, unless it was to draw the end of it gently over my back when I was to go on. Generally I knew this quite well by the way in which he took up the reins ; and I believe his whip was more frequently stuck up by his side than in his hand.

In a short time my master and I understood each other as well as horse and man could do. In the stable, too, he did all that he could for our comfort. The stalls were of the old-fashioned style—too much on the slope ; but he had two movable bars fixed across the back of our stalls, so that at night and when we were resting, he just took off our halters and put up the bars, and thus we could turn about and stand whichever way we pleased : this is a great comfort.

Jerry kept us very clean, and gave us as much change of

food as he could, and always plenty of it ; and not only that, but he always gave us plenty of clean fresh water, which he allowed to stand by us both night and day, except of course when we came in warm.

Some people say that a horse ought not to drink as much as he wishes ; but I know if we are allowed to drink it when we want it, we drink only a little at a time, and it does us a great deal more good than swallowing it down half a bucketful at a time, as we do if we have been left without water till we are thirsty and miserable.

Some grooms will go home to their beer and leave us for hours with our dry hay and oats, with nothing to moisten them ; then, of course, we gulp down too much water at once, which helps to spoil our breathing and sometimes chills our stomachs.

But the best thing that we had here was our Sundays for rest. We worked so hard during the week that I do not think we could have kept up to it but for that day's rest ; besides, we then had time to enjoy each other's company. It was on these days that I learned my companion's history.

CHAPTER XXXIV

An Old War Horse

CAPTAIN had been broken in and trained for an army horse, his first owner being an officer of cavalry going out to the Crimean War. He said he quite enjoyed the training with all the other horses—trotting together, turning together to the right hand or the left, halting at the word of command, or dashing forward at full speed at the sound of the trumpet or signal of the officer. When young, he was a dark, dappled iron grey, and was considered very handsome. His master, a young, high-spirited gentleman, was very fond of him, and from the first treated him with the greatest care and kindness. He told me he thought the life of an army horse was very pleasant ; but when it came to being sent abroad in a great ship over the sea, he almost changed his mind.

"That part of it," he said, "was dreadful ! Of course we could not walk off the land into the ship ; so they were obliged to put strong straps under our bodies and then we were lifted off our legs in spite of our struggles, and were swung through the air, over water, on the deck of the great vessel. There we were placed in small close stalls, and never for a long time saw the sky, or were able to stretch our legs. The ship sometimes rolled about in high winds, and we were knocked about, and felt very ill. However, at last it came to an end, and we were hauled up and swung over again to the land. We were very glad, and snorted and neighed for joy when we once more felt firm ground under our feet.

"We soon found that the country to which we had come was very different from our own, and that we had many hardships to endure besides the fighting ; but many of the men were so fond of us that they did everything they could to make us confortable, in spite of snow, wet, and the fact that all things were out of order."

"But what about that fighting ? " said I. " Was not that worse than anything else ? "

"Well," said he, "I hardly know. We always liked to hear the trumpet sound, and to be called out, and were impatient to start off, though sometimes we had to stand for hours, waiting for the word of command. But when the word was given, we used to spring forward as gaily and eagerly as if there were no cannon-balls, bayonets, or bullets. I believe so long as we felt our rider firm in the saddle, and his hand steady on the bridle, not one of us gave way to fear, not even when the terrible bombshells whirled through the air and burst into a thousand pieces.

"With my noble master, I went into many actions without a wound ; and though I saw horses shot down with bullets, others pierced through with lances or gashed with fearful sabre-cuts, though I left them dead on the field, or dying in the agony of their wounds, I don't think I feared for myself. My master's cheery voice as he encouraged his men made me feel as if he and I could not be killed. I had such perfect trust in him that whilst he was guiding me, I was ready to charge up to the very cannon's mouth.

" I saw many brave men cut down, and many fall from their saddles mortally wounded. I have heard the cries and groans of the dying, cantered over ground slippery with blood, and frequently had to turn aside to avoid trampling on wounded man or horse ; but, until one dreadful day, I had never felt terror : that day I shall never forget."

Here old Captain paused for a while and drew a long breath ; I waited, and he went on.

" It was one autumn morning, and, as usual, an hour before daybreak our cavalry had turned out, ready caparisoned for the day's work, whether fighting or waiting. The men stood waiting by their horses, ready for orders. As the light increased, there seemed to be some excitement among the officers ; and before the day was well begun, we heard the firing of the enemy's guns.

" Then one of the officers rode up and gave the word for the men to mount, and in a second every man was in his saddle, and every horse stood expecting the touch of the rein, or the pressure of his rider's heels—all animated, all eager. But still we had been trained so well, that, except by the champing of our bits, and by the restive tossing of our heads from time to time, it could not be said that we stirred.

" My dear master and I were at the head of the line and as all sat motionless and watchful, he took a little stray lock of my mane which had turned over the wrong side, laid it over on the right and smoothed it down with his hand ; then, patting my neck, he said, ' We shall have a day of it to-day, Bayard, my beauty ; but we'll do our duty as we always have done.'

" That morning he stroked my neck more, I think, than he had ever done before ; quietly on and on, as if he were thinking of something else. I loved to feel his hand on my neck, and arched my crest proudly and happily ; but I stood very still, for I knew all his moods, and when he liked me to be quiet and when gay.

" I cannot tell all that happened that day, but I will tell of the last charge that we made together : it was across a valley right in front of the enemy's cannon. By this time we were well used to the roar of heavy guns, the rattle of musket fire, and the flying of shot near us ; but never had I been under such a fire as we rode through that day. From right, left, and front, shot and shell poured in upon us. Many a brave man went down, many a horse fell, flinging his rider to the earth ; many a horse without a rider ran wildly out of the ranks ; then, terrified at being alone with no hand to guide him, came pressing in amongst his old companions, to gallop with them to the charge.

" Fearful as it was, no one stopped, no one turned back. Every moment the ranks were thinned, but as our comrades fell we closed in to keep the others together ; and instead of being shaken or staggered in our pace, our gallop became faster and faster as we neared the cannon, all clouded in white smoke, while the red fire flashed through it.

" My master, my dear master, was cheering on his comrades, with his right arm raised on high, when one of the balls, whizzing close to my head, struck him. I felt him stagger with the shock, though he uttered no cry. I tried to check my speed, but the sword dropped from his right hand, the rein fell loose from the left, and sinking backward from the saddle, he fell to the earth ; the other riders swept past us, and by the force of their charge I was driven from the spot where he fell.

" I wanted to keep my place at his side, and not to leave him under that rush of horses' feet, but it was in vain. And now, without a master or a friend, I was alone on that great slaughter-ground. Then fear took hold of me, and I trembled as I had never trembled before. Then I, too, as I had seen other horses do, tried to join in the ranks and to gallop with them ; but I was beaten off by the swords of the soldiers.

" Just then, a soldier whose horse had been killed under him caught at my bridle and mounted me, and with this new master I was again going forward. But our gallant company was cruelly overpowered, and those who remained alive after the fierce fight for the guns came galloping back over the same ground.

" Some of the horses had been so badly wounded that they could scarcely move from loss of blood ; other noble creatures were trying on three legs to drag themselves along ; and others were struggling to rise on their fore feet when their hind legs had been shattered by shot. Their groans were piteous to hear, and the beseeching look in their eyes as those who escaped passed by and left them to their fate I shall never forget. After the battle, the wounded men were brought in, and the dead were buried."

" And what about the wounded horses ? " I said ; " were they left to die ? "

" No, the army farriers went over the field with their pistols, and shot all that were ruined. Some that had only slight wounds were brought back and attended to, but the greater part of the noble, willing creatures that went out that morning never came back ! In our stables there was only about one in four that returned.

" I never saw my dear master again. I believe he fell dead from the saddle. Never did I love any other master so well. I went into many other engagements, but was only once wounded, and then not seriously ; and when the war was over, I came back again to England, as sound and strong as when I went out."

I said, " I have heard people talk about war as if it was a very fine thing."

" Ah ! " said he, " I should think they have never seen it. No doubt it is very fine when there is no enemy, only just exercise, parade, and sham-fight. Yes, it is very fine then ; but when thousands of good, brave men and horses are killed or crippled for life, then it has a very different look."

" Do you know what they fought about ? " said I.

" No," he said, " that is more than a horse can understand ; but the enemy must have been awfully wicked
people if it was right to go all that way over the sea on purpose to kill them."

CHAPTER XXXV

Jerry Barker

I N E V E R knew a better man than my new master—kind
and good, as strong for the right as John Manly, and
so good-tempered and merry that very few people could
pick a quarrel with him. He was very fond of making little
songs, which he would sing to himself. His favourite was this :

> *Come, father and mother,*
> *And sister and brother,*
> *Come, all of you, turn to*
> *And help one another.*

And so they did ; Harry was as clever at stable-work as
a much older boy, and always wanted to do what he could.
Then Polly and Dolly used to come in the morning to help
with the cab—to brush and beat the cushions and rub the
glass, while Jerry was giving us a cleaning in the yard and
Harry was cleaning the harness. There used to be a great
deal of laughing and fun between them, and it put Captain
and me in much better spirits than if we had heard scolding
and hard words. They were always early in the morning,
for Jerry would say :

> *If you in the morning*
> *Throw minutes away,*
> *You can't pick them up*
> *In the course of the day.*
>
> *You may hurry and scurry,*
> *And flurry and worry,*
> *You've lost them for ever,*
> *For ever and ay.*

He could not bear any careless loitering and waste of time ; and nothing was so near making him angry as to find people who were always late wanting a cab horse to be driven hard to make up for their idleness.

One day two wild-looking young men came out of a tavern close by the stand, and called Jerry.

" Here, cabby ! look sharp, we are rather late ; put on the steam, will you, and take us to Victoria in time for the one o'clock train. You shall have a shilling extra."

" I will take you at the regular pace, gentlemen ; shillings don't pay for putting on the steam like that."

Larry's cab was standing next to ours. He flung open the door and said, " I'm your man, gentlemen ! Take my cab, my horse will get you there all right," and as he shut them in, with a wink towards Jerry, he said, " It's against his conscience to go beyond a jog-trot." Then, slashing his jaded horse, he set off as hard as he could. Jerry patted me on the neck—" No, Jack, a shilling would not pay for that sort of thing, would it, old boy ? "

Although Jerry was steadfastly set against hard driving to please careless people, he always went at a good fair pace, and was not against putting on the steam, as he said, if only he knew *why*.

I well remember one morning, as we were on the stand waiting for a fare, that a young man carrying a heavy portmanteau trod on a piece of orange-peel which lay on the pavement and fell down with great force.

Jerry was the first to run and lift him up. He seemed much stunned, and as they led him into a shop, he walked as if he were in great pain. Jerry, of course, came back to the stand, but in about ten minutes one of the shopmen called him so he drew up to the pavement.

" Can you take me to the South-Eastern Railway ? " said the young man. " This unlucky fall has made me late, I fear ; but it is of great importance that I should not lose the twelve o'clock train. I should be most thankful if you could get me there in time, and will gladly pay you an extra fare."

" I'll do my very best," said Jerry heartily, " if you think you are well enough, sir," for he looked dreadfully white and ill.

" *I must* go," he said earnestly. " Please open the door, and let us lose no time."

The next minute Jerry was on the box. He gave a cheery chirrup to me, and a twitch to the rein that I well understood.

" Now then, Jack, my boy," said he, " spin along ; we'll show them how we can get over the ground if we only know why."

It is always difficult to drive fast in the city in the middle of the day, when the streets are full of traffic, but we did what could be done ; and when a good driver and a good horse, who understand each other, are of one mind, it is wonderful what they can do. I had a very good mouth— that is, I could be guided by the slightest touch of the rein, and that is a great thing in London, amongst carriages, omnibuses, carts, vans, trucks, cabs, and great wagons creeping along at a walking pace ; some going one way, some another, some going slowly, others wanting to pass them, omnibuses stopping short every few minutes to take up a passenger, obliging the horse that is coming behind to pull up too, or to pass and get before them : perhaps you try to pass, but just then something else comes dashing in through the narrow opening, and you have to keep in behind the omnibus again ; presently you think you see a chance, and manage to get to the front, going so near the wheels on each side that half an inch nearer and they would scrape. Well, you get along for a bit, but soon find yourself in a long train of carts and carriages all obliged to go at a walk ; perhaps you come to a regular block-up and have to stand still for minutes together, till something clears out into a side street, or the policeman interferes ; you have to be ready for any chance—to dash forward if there be an opening, and be quick as a rat dog to see if there be room, and if there be time, lest you get your own wheels locked, or smashed, or the shaft of some other vehicle run into your chest or shoulder. All this is what you have to be ready for. If you want to get through London fast in the middle of the day, it wants a deal of practice.

Jerry and I were used to the thickest traffic, and no one could beat us at getting through when we were set on it. I was quick and bold, and could always trust my driver ; Jerry was quick and patient at the same time, and could trust his horse, which was a great thing too. He very seldom used the whip ; I knew by his voice and his click, click, when he wanted to get on fast, and the rein told me where I was to go, so there was no need for whipping.

The streets were very full that day, but we got on pretty well as far as the bottom of Cheapside, where there was a block for three or four minutes. The young man put his head out and said anxiously : " I think I had better get out and walk ; I shall never get there if this goes on."

" I'll do all that can be done, sir," said Jerry. " I think we shall be in time ; this block-up cannot last much longer, and your luggage is very heavy for you to carry, sir."

Just then the cart in front of us began to move on, and then we had a good turn. In and out, in and out we went, as fast as horse-flesh could do it, and for a wonder, we had a good clear time on London Bridge, for there was a whole train of cabs and carriages all going our way at a quick trot—perhaps wanting to catch that very train. At any rate, with many others, we whirled into the station just as the great clock pointed to eight minutes to twelve.

" Thank God ! we are in time," said the young man ; " and thank you, too, my friend, and your good horse. You have saved me more than money can ever pay for ; take this extra half-crown."

" No, sir, no, thank you all the same. So glad we hit the time, sir ; but don't stay now, sir, the bell is ringing. Here, porter ! take this gentleman's luggage—Dover line—twelve o'clock train—that's it " ; and without waiting for another word, Jerry wheeled me round to make room for other cabs that were dashing up at the last minute, and draw up on one side till the crush was past.

" So glad ! " he said, " so glad ! poor young fellow, I wonder what it was that made him so anxious."

Jerry often talked to himself, quite loud·enough for me to hear when we were not moving.

On Jerry's return to the rank there was a good deal of laughing and chaffing at him for driving hard to the train for an extra fare, as they said, all against his principles ; and they wanted to know how much he had pocketed.

" A good deal more than I generally get," said he, nodding slyly ; " what he gave me will keep me in little comforts for several days."

" Gammon ! " said one.

" He's a humbug," said another, " preaching to us and then doing the same himself."

" Look here, mates," said Jerry. " The gentleman offered me half a crown extra, but I didn't take it ; 'twas quite pay enough for me to see how glad he was to catch that train ; and if Jack and I choose to have a quick run now and then to please ourselves, that's our business and not yours."

" Well," said Larry, " *you'll* never be a rich man."

" Most likely not," said Jerry, " but I don't know that I shall be the less happy for that. I have heard the commandments read a great many times, and I never noticed that any of them said, ' Thou shalt be rich ' ; and there are a good many curious things said in the New Testament about rich men that, I think, would make me feel rather queer if I was one of them."

" If you ever do get rich," said Governor Grant, looking over his shoulder across the top of his cab, " you'll deserve it, Jerry, and you won't find a curse come with your wealth. As for you, Larry, you'll die poor, you spend too much in whipcord."

"Well," said Larry, "what is a fellow to do if his horse won't go without it?"

"You never take the trouble to see if he will go without it; your whip is always going as if you had the St. Vitus's dance in your arm; and if it does not wear you out, it wears your horses out. You know you are always changing your horses, and why? Because you never give them any peace or encouragement."

"Well, I have not had good luck," said Larry, "that's where it is."

"And you never will," said the Governor. "Good Luck is rather particular with whom she rides, and mostly prefers those who have common sense and a good heart; at least, that is my experience."

Governor Grant turned round again to his newspaper, and the other men went to their cabs.

CHAPTER XXXVI

The Sunday Cab

ONE MORNING, as Jerry had just put me into the shafts and was fastening the traces, a gentleman walked into the yard. "Your servant, sir," said Jerry.

"Good-morning, Mr. Barker," said the gentleman. "I should be glad to make some arrangement with you for taking Mrs. Briggs regularly to church on Sunday mornings. We go to the New Church now, and that is rather farther than she can walk."

"Thank you, sir," said Jerry, "but I have only taken out a six days' licence,[1] and therefore I could not take a fare on a Sunday, it would not be legal."

"Oh!" said the other, "I did not know yours was a six days' cab; but of course it would be very easy to alter your licence. I would see that you did not lose by it; the

---

[1] Some years since the annual charge for a cab licence was very much reduced, and the difference between the six and seven days' cabs was abolished.

fact is, Mrs. Briggs very much prefers you to drive her."

"I should be glad to oblige the lady, sir, but I had a seven days' licence once, and the work was too hard for me and too hard for my horses. Year in and year out, not a day's rest, never a Sunday with my wife and children, and never able to go to a place of worship, which I had always been used to do before I took to the driving box ; so for the last five years I have taken only a six days' licence, and I find it better all the way round."

"Well, of course," replied Mr. Briggs, "it is very proper that every person should have rest and be able to go to church on Sundays, but I should have thought you would not have minded such a short distance for the horse, and only once a day ; you would have all the afternoon and evening for yourself, and we are very good customers, you know."

"Yes, sir, that is true, and I'm grateful for all favours, I am sure, and anything that I could do to oblige you or the lady, I should be proud and happy to do ; but I can't give up my Sundays, sir, indeed I can't. I read that God made man, and He made horses and all the other beasts ; and as soon as He had made them, He made a day of rest, and bade that all should rest one day in seven. I think, sir, He must have known what was good for them, and I am sure it is good for me. I am stronger and healthier altogether now that I have a day of rest ; the horses are fresh too, and do not wear up nearly so fast. The six-day drivers all tell me the same, and I have laid more money in the Savings Bank than ever I did before ; and as for my wife and children, sir—why, heart alive ! they would not go back to the seven days' work for all they could get by it."

"Oh, very well," said the gentleman. "Don't trouble yourself, Mr. Barker, any further ; I will inquire somewhere else " ; and he walked away.

"Well," says Jerry to me, "we can't help it, Jack, old boy, we must have our Sundays.

"Polly ! " he shouted. "Polly ! come here."

She was there in a minute.

" What is it all about, Jerry ? "

" Why, my dear, Mr. Briggs wants me to take Mrs. Briggs to church every Sunday morning. I said I had only a six days' licence. He said, ' Get a seven days' licence, and I'll make it worth your while ' ; and you know, Polly, they are very good customers to us. Mrs. Briggs often goes out shopping for hours, or makes calls, and then she pays down fair and honourable like a lady ; there's no beating down, or making three hours into two hours and a half, as some folks do. Besides, it is easy work for the horses ; not like tearing along to catch trains for people that are always a quarter of an hour too late. If I don't oblige her in this matter, it is very likely we shall lose them altogether. What do you say, little woman ? "

" I say, Jerry," says she, speaking very slowly, " I say, if Mrs. Briggs would give you a sovereign every Sunday morning, I would not have you a seven days' cabman again. We have known what it was to have no Sundays, and now we know what it is to call them our own. Thank God ! you earn enough to keep us, though it is sometimes close work to pay for all the oats and hay, in addition to the licence and the rent.

" But Harry will soon be earning something, and I would rather struggle on harder than we do than go back to those horrid times when you hardly had a minute to look at your own children, and we never could go to a place of worship together, or have a happy, quiet day. God forbid that we should ever turn back to those times ! that's what I say, Jerry."

" And that is just what I told Mr. Briggs, my dear," said Jerry, " and that is what I mean to stick to ; so don't go and fret yourself, Polly " (for she had begun to cry) ; " I would not go back to the old times if I earned twice as much ; so that is settled, little woman. Now cheer up, and I'll be off to the stand."

Three weeks had passed away after this conversation,

and no order had come from Mrs. Briggs ; so there was
nothing but taking jobs from the stand. Jerry took it to
heart a good deal, for of course the work was harder for
horse and man. But Polly would always cheer him up and
say, " Never mind, father, never mind—

> *Do your best,*
> *And leave the rest,*
> *'Twill all come right*
> *Some day or night.*"

It soon became known that Jerry had lost his best cus-
tomer, and for what reason ; most of the men said he was a
fool, but two or three took his part.

" If working men don't stick to their Sunday," said
Truman, " they'll soon have none left ; it is every man's
right, and every beast's right. By God's law we have a day
of rest, and by the law of England we have a day of rest,
and I say we ought to hold to the rights these laws give us,
and keep them for our children."

" All very well for you religious chaps to talk so," said
Larry, " but I'll turn a shilling when I can. I don't believe
in religion, for I don't see that your religious people are
any better than the rest."

" If they are not better," put in Jerry, " it is because
they are not religious. You might as well say that our
country's laws are not good because some people break
them. If a man gives way to his temper, and speaks evil of
his neighbour, and does not pay his debts, he is *not* religious ;
I don't care how much he goes to church. If some men are
shams and humbugs, that does not make religion untrue.
Real religion is the best and the truest thing in the world,
and the only thing that can make a man really happy, or
make the world any better."

" If religion was good for anything," said Jones, " it
would prevent your religious people from making us work
on Sundays as you know many of them do, and that's why

I say religion is nothing but a sham—why, if it was not for the church- and chapel-goers it would be hardly worth while our coming out on a Sunday ; but they have their privileges, as they call them, and I go without. I shall expect them to answer for my soul, if I can't get a chance of saving it."

Several of the men applauded this, till Jerry said :

" That may sound well enough, but it won't do ; every man must look after his own soul ; you can't lay it down at another man's door like a foundling, and expect him to take care of it ; and don't you see, if you are always sitting on your box, waiting for a fare, they will say, ' If we don't take him, some one else will, and he does not look for any Sunday.' Of course they don't go to the bottom of it, or they would see if they never came for a cab, it would be no use your standing there ; but people don't always like to go to the bottom of things ; it may not be convenient to do it ; but if you Sunday drivers would all strike for a day of rest, the thing would be done."

" And what would all the good people do if they could not get to their favourite preachers ? " said Larry.

" 'Tis not for me to lay down plans for other people," said Jerry, " but if they can't walk so far, they can go to what is nearer ; and if it should rain they can put on their mackintoshes as they do on a week-day. If a thing is right, it *can* be done and if it is wrong, it *can be done without* ; and a good man will find a way ; and that is as true for us cabmen as it is for the church-goers."

CHAPTER XXXVII
The Golden Rule

TWO OR three weeks after this, as we came into the yard rather late in the evening, Polly came running across the road with the lantern (she always brought it to him if it was not very wet).

"It has all come right, Jerry ; Mrs. Briggs sent her servant this afternoon, to ask you to take her out to-morrow at eleven o'clock. I said, yes, I thought you could, but we supposed she employed some one else now.

"'Well,' says he, 'the real fact is, master was put out because Mr. Barker refused to come on Sundays, and he has been trying other cabs, but there's something wrong with them all ; some drive too fast, and some too slow ; and the mistress says there is not a cab so nice and clean as yours ; so nothing will suit her but Mr. Barker's cab again.'"

Polly was almost out of breath, and Jerry broke out into a merry laugh :

> "All will come right
> Some day or night.

You were right, my dear ; you generally are. Run in and get the supper, and I'll have Jack's harness off and make him snug and happy in no time."

After this Mrs. Briggs wanted Jerry's cab quite as often as before ; never, however, on a Sunday. But there came a day when we had Sunday work, and this was how it happened.

We had all come home on the Saturday night very tired, and very glad to think that the next day would be all rest ; but it was not to be so.

On Sunday morning Jerry was cleaning me in the yard, when Polly stepped up to him, looking very full of something.

"What is it ? " said Jerry.

"Well, my dear," she said, " poor Dinah Brown has just received a letter to say that her mother is dangerously ill, and that she must go directly if she wishes to see her alive. The place is more than ten miles away from here, right out in the country ; and she says if she took the train she should still have four miles to walk ; and so weak as she is, and the baby only four weeks old, of course that would be impossible. She wants to know if you would take her in your cab, and she promises to pay you faithfully as soon as she can get the money."

" Tut, tut, we'll see about that. It was not the money I was thinking about, but of losing our Sunday ; the horses are tired, and I am tired too—that's where it pinches."

" It pinches all round, for that matter," said Polly, " for it's only half Sunday without you. But you know we should do to other people as we would like them to do to us. I know very well what I should like if my mother was dying ; and, Jerry, dear, I am sure it won't break the Sabbath ; for if pulling a poor beast or donkey out of a pit would not spoil the Sabbath, I am quite sure taking poor Dinah would not."

" Why, Polly, you are as good as the minister ; so, as I've had my Sunday morning sermon early to-day, you may go and tell Dinah that I'll be ready for her as the clock strikes ten. But stop—just step round to Butcher Braydon's, with my compliments, and ask him if he would lend me his light trap ; I know he never uses it on the Sunday, and it would make a wonderful difference to the horse."

Away she went, and soon returned, saying that he could have the trap and welcome.

" All right," said he ; " now put me up a bit of bread and cheese, and I'll be back in the afternoon as soon as I can."

" And I'll have the meat pie ready for an early tea instead of for dinner," said Polly. And away she went, whilst he made his preparations to the tune of " Polly, the woman and no mistake," of which tune he was very fond.

I was selected for the journey, and at ten o'clock we started in a light, high-wheeled gig, which ran so easily that, after the four-wheeled cab, it seemed like nothing.

It was a fine May day, and as soon as we were out of the town the sweet air, the smell of the fresh grass, and the soft country roads were as pleasant as they used to be in the old times, and I soon began to feel quite fresh.

Dinah's family lived in a small farmhouse up a green lane, close by a meadow with some fine shady trees : there were two cows feeding in it. A young man asked Jerry to bring his trap into the meadow, and he would tie me up in the cowshed ; he wished he had a better stable to offer.

" If your cows would not be offended," said Jerry, " there is nothing my horse would like so well as to have an hour or two in your beautiful meadow. He's quiet, and it would be a rare treat for him."

" Put him there and welcome," said the young man. " The best we have is at your service for your kindness to my sister ; we shall be having some dinner in an hour, and I hope you'll come in, though with mother so ill we are all out of sorts in the house."

Jerry thanked him kindly, but said as he had some dinner with him, there was nothing he should like so well as walking about in the meadow.

When my harness was taken off, I did not know what I should do first—eat the grass, roll over on my back, lie down and rest, or have a gallop across the meadow out of sheer spirits at being free ; so I did all by turns. Jerry seemed to be quite as happy as I was. He sat down by a bank under a shady tree, and listened to the birds ; then he sang to himself, and read out of the little brown book he is so fond of ; next he wandered round the meadow and down by a little brook, where he picked the flowers and the haw-thorn, and tied them up with long sprays of ivy ; lastly he gave me a good feed of the oats which he had brought with him. But the time seemed all too short—I had not been in a field since I left poor Ginger at Earlshall.

We came home at a gentle pace, and Jerry's first words were as we came into the yard, " Well, Polly, I have not lost my Sunday after all, for the birds were singing hymns in every bush, and I joined in the service ; and as for Jack, he was like a young colt."

When he handed Dolly the flowers she jumped about for joy.

CHAPTER XXXVIII
Dolly and a Real Gentleman

THE WINTER came in early with a great deal of cold and wet. There was snow, sleet, or rain almost every day for weeks, changing only to keen, driving winds or sharp frosts. We all felt it very much. When it is a dry cold, a couple of good thick rugs will keep the warmth in us ; but when it is a soaking rain, they soon get wet through and are no good. Some of the drivers had a waterproof cover to throw over us ; this was a fine thing.

But some of the men were so poor that they could not protect either themselves or their horses, and many of them suffered very much that winter. When we horses had worked half the day we went to our dry stables, and could rest ; whilst the drivers had to sit on their boxes, sometimes staying out as late as one or two o'clock in the morning if they had to wait for a party.

When the streets were slippery with frost or snow, that was the worst of all for us horses ; one mile of such travelling, with a weight to draw and no firm footing, would take more out of us than four on a good road. Every nerve and muscle of our body is on the strain to keep our balance ; and added to this, the fear of falling is more exhausting than anything else. If the roads are very bad indeed, our shoes are roughed, but this makes us feel nervous at first.

When the weather was very bad, many of the men would go and sit in the tavern close by, and get some one to watch for them ; but they often lost a fare in this way, and could not, as Jerry said, be there without spending money.

He never went to the " Rising Sun." There was a coffee-shop near, where he now and then went ; or he bought of an old man who came to our rank with tins of hot coffee and pies. It was Jerry's opinion that spirits and beer made a man colder afterwards, and that dry clothes, good food, cheerfulness, and a comfortable wife at home were the best things to keep a cabman warm.

Polly always supplied him with something to eat when he could not get home, and sometimes he would see little Dolly peeping from the corner of the street, to make sure if "Father" was on the stand. If she saw him, she would run off at full speed and soon come back with something in a tin or basket—some hot soup or pudding that Polly had ready.

It was wonderful how such a little thing could get safely across the street, often thronged with horses and carriages ; but she was a brave little maid, and felt it quite an honour to bring " Father's first course," as he called it. She was a general favourite on the stand, and there was not a man who would not have seen her safely across the street if Jerry had not been able to do so.

One cold, windy day, Dolly had brought Jerry a basin of something hot, and was standing by him whilst he ate it. He had scarcely begun, when a gentleman walking towards us very quickly held up his umbrella. Jerry touched his hat in return, gave the basin to Dolly, and was taking off my cloth, when the gentleman, hastening up, cried out, "No, no, finish your soup, my friend ; I have not much time to spare, but I can wait till you have done, and have set your little girl safely on the pavement." So saying, he seated himself in the cab. Jerry thanked him kindly, and came back to Dolly.

" There, Dolly, that's a gentleman ; that's a real gentleman, Dolly ; he has both time and thought for the comfort of a poor cabman and a little girl."

Jerry finished his soup, saw the child safely across the road, and then took his orders to drive to Clapham Rise. Several times after this the same gentleman took our cab. I think he was very fond of dogs and horses, for whenever we took him to his own door, two or three dogs would come bounding out to meet him. Sometimes he came round and patted me, saying in his quiet, pleasant way, " This horse has a good master, and he deserves it."

It was a very rare thing for anyone to notice the horse that had been working for him. I have known ladies do it now and then, and this gentleman, and one or two others have given me a pat and a kind word ; but ninety-nine out of a hundred would as soon think of patting the steam-engine that drew the train.

This gentleman was not young, and there was a forward stoop in his shoulders as if he was always going at something. His lips were thin and close shut, though they had a very pleasant smile ; his eye was keen, and there was something in his jaw and the motion of his head that made one think he was very determined in anything he set about doing. His voice was pleasant and kind ; any horse would trust that voice, though it was just as decided as everything else about him.

One day, he and another gentleman took our cab. They stopped a shop in R—— Street, and whilst his friend went in he stood at the door. A little ahead of us, on the other side of the street, a cart with two very fine horses was standing before some wine-vaults ; the carter was not with them, and I cannot tell how long they had been standing, but they seemed to think they had waited long enough, and began to move off. Before they had gone many paces the carter came running out and caught them. He seemed furious at their having moved, and with whip and rein punished them brutally, even beating them about the head.

Our gentleman saw it all, and stepping quickly across the street, said in a decided voice, " If you don't stop that directly, I'll have you summoned for leaving your horses and for brutal conduct."

The man, who had clearly been drinking, poured forth some abusive language, but he left off knocking the horses about, and taking the reins, got into his cart. Meanwhile our friend had quietly taken a notebook from his pocket, and looking at the name and address painted on the cart, he wrote something down.

" What do you want with that ? " growled the carter, as he cracked his whip and was moving on. A nod and a grim smile was the only answer he got.

On returning to the cab, our friend was joined by his

companion, who said laughingly, " I should have thought, Wright, you had enough business of your own to look after without troubling yourself about other people's horses and servants."

Our friend stood still for a moment, and throwing his head a little back, said, " Do you know why this world is as bad as it is ? "

" No," said the other.

" Then I'll tell you. It is because people think only about their own business, and won't trouble themselves to stand up for the oppressed, nor bring the wrong-doer to light. I never see a wicked thing like this without doing what I can, and many a master has thanked me for letting him know how his horses have been used."

" I wish there were more gentlemen like you, sir," said Jerry, " for they are wanted badly enough in this city."

After this we continued our journey, and as they got out of the cab our friend was saying, " My doctrine is this, that if we see cruelty or wrong that we have the power to stop, and yet do nothing, we make ourselves sharers in the guilt."

CHAPTER XXXIX
Seedy Sam

I SHOULD say that for a cab horse I was very well off indeed ; my driver was my owner, and it was to his interest to treat me well and not to overwork me, even had he not been so good a man as he was : but there were a great many horses which belonged to the large cab-owners, who let them out to their drivers for so much money a day. As the horses did not belong to these men, the only thing they thought of was how to get their money out of the horses, first to pay the master, and then to provide their own living ; and a dreadful time some of these horses had of it. Of course I understood but little, but it was often talked over on the stand, and the Governor, who was a kind-hearted man and fond of horses, would sometimes speak his mind if a horse came in very much jaded or ill-used.

One day, a shabby, miserable-looking driver, who went by the name of " Seedy Sam," brought in his horse looking dreadfully beat, and the Governor said, " You and your horse look more fit for the police-station than for this rank."

The man flung his tattered rug over the horse, turned full round upon the Governor, and said, in a voice that sounded almost desperate :

" If the police have any business with the matter, it ought to be with the masters who charge us so much, or with the fares that are fixed so low. If a man has to pay eighteen shillings a day for the use of a cab and two horses, as many of us have to do in the season, and must make that up before he earns a penny for himself—I say, 'tis more than hard work. Nine shillings a day to get out of each horse before you begin to get your own living ! You know that's true, and if the horses don't work we must starve.

" My children and I have known what that is before now. I've six of 'em, and only one earns anything. I am on the stand fourteen or sixteen hours a day, and I haven't had a Sunday these ten or twelve weeks. You know, Skinner never gives a day if he can help it ; and if I don't work hard, tell me who does ! I want a warm coat and a mackintosh, but with so many to feed, how can a man get it ? I had to pledge my clock a week ago to pay Skinner, and I shall never see it again."

Some of the other drivers stood round nodding their heads, and saying he was right. The man went on, " You that have your own horses and cabs, or drive for good masters, have a chance of getting on, and a chance of doing right ; I haven't. Within the four-mile radius we can't charge more than sixpence a mile after the first mile.

" This very morning I had to go a clear six miles and took only three shillings. I could not get a return fare, and had to come half the way back ; there's twelve miles for the horse and three shillings for me.

" After that I had a three-mile fare, and there were bags and boxes enough to have brought in a good many two-pences if they had been put outside. But you know how people do—all that could be piled up inside on the front seat were put in, and three heavy boxes went on the top— that was sixpence, and the fare one and sixpence. Then I got a return for a shilling ; now that makes eighteen miles for the horse and six shillings for me. There's three shillings still for that horse to earn, and nine shillings for the after-noon horse before I touch a penny.

" Of course it is not always as bad as that, but you know it often is ; and I say it 'tis mockery to tell a man he must not overwork his horse, for when a beast is downright tired, there's nothing but the whip that will keep his legs going— you can't help yourself. You must put your wife and children before the horse ; the masters must look to that, we can't. I don't ill-use my horse for the sake of doing so ; none of you can say I do.

" There's wrong lying somewhere—never a day's rest, never a quiet hour with the wife and children. I often feel like an old man, though I'm only forty-five. You know how quick some of the gentry are to suspect us of cheating and over-charging. Why, they stand with their purses in their hands, counting the fare over to a penny, and looking at us as if we were pickpockets. I wish some of 'em had got to sit on my box sixteen hours a day, and had to get a living out of it and eighteen shillings besides, and to do it in all weathers : they would not then be so uncommonly par-ticular never to give us a sixpence over, nor would they then cram all the luggage inside. Of course, some of 'em tip us pretty handsomely now and then, or else we could not live : but we can't *depend* upon that."

The men who stood round much approved of this speech. One of them said, " It is desperate hard ; and if a man sometimes does what is wrong, it is no wonder ; and if he gets a dram too much, who's to blow him up ? "

Jerry had taken no part in this conversation, but I never

saw his face look so sad before. The Governor had stood
with both his hands in his pockets ; now he took his handkerchief out of his hat, and wiped his forehead.

" You've beaten me, Sam," he said, " for it's all true, and
I won't cast it up against you any more about the police. It
was the look in that horse's eye that came over me. It is
hard lines for both man and beast, and who's to mend it
I don't know ; but anyway you might tell the poor beast
that you were sorry to take it out of him in that way. Sometimes a kind word is all we can give 'em, poor brutes, and
'tis wonderful what they understand."

A few mornings after this talk a new man came on the
stand with Sam's cab.

" Hallo ! " said one, " what's up with Seedy Sam ? "

" He's ill in bed," said the man ; " he was taken ill last
night in the yard, and could scarcely crawl home. His wife
sent a boy this morning to say his father was in a high fever
and could not get out ; so I'm here instead."

The next morning the same man came again.

" How is Sam ? " inquired the Governor.

" He's gone," said the man.

" What ! gone ? You don't mean to say he's dead ? "

" Just snuffed out," said the other ; " he died at four
o'clock this morning. All yesterday he was raving—raving
about Skinner and about having no Sundays. ' I never had
a Sunday's rest,' these were his last words."

No one spoke for a while, and then the Governor said,
" I tell you what, mates, this is a warning to us all."

CHAPTER XL

Poor Ginger

ONE DAY, whilst our cab and many others were waiting
outside one of the parks where a band was playing, a
shabby old cab drove up beside ours. The horse was an old
worn-out chestnut with an ill-kept coat, and with bones

E*

that snowed plainly through it. The knees knuckled over, and the fore legs were very unsteady.

I had been eating some hay, and the wind rolling a little lock of it that way, the poor creature put out her long, thin neck and picked it up, and then turned round and looked about for more. There was a hopeless look in the dull eye that I could not help noticing ; and then, as I was thinking where I had seen that horse before, she looked full at me and said, " Black Beauty, is that you ? "

It was Ginger ! but how changed ! The beautifully arched and glossy neck was now straight, lank, and fallen in ; the clean, straight legs and delicate fetlocks were swollen ; the joints were grown out of shape with hard work ; the face that was once so full of spirit and life was now full of suffering ; and I could tell by the heaving of her sides and by her frequent cough how bad her breath was.

Our drivers were standing together a little way off, so I sidled up to her a step or two that we might have a little quiet talk. It was a sad tale that she had to tell.

After a twelve month's run off at Earlshall, she was considered to be fit for work again and was sold to a gentleman. For a little while she got on very well, but after a longer gallop than usual, the old strain returned, and, after being rested and doctored, she was again sold. In this way she changed hands several times, but always getting lower down.

" And so at last," said she, " I was bought by a man who keeps a number of cabs and horses, and lets them out. You look well off, and I am glad of it ; but I cannot tell you what my life has been. When they found out my weakness, they said I was not worth what they gave for me, and that I must go into one of the low cabs and just be used up ; that is what they are doing—whipping and working me, with never one thought of what I suffer. They paid for me, and must get the money out of me, they say. The man who hires me now pays a deal of money to the owner every day, and so he has to get it out of me first ; and so it goes on all the weeks round, with never a Sunday rest."

I said, " You used to stand up for yourself if you were ill-used."

" Ah ! " she said, " I did once, but it's no use ; men are stronger, and if they are cruel and have no feeling, there is nothing that we can do but just bear it—bear it on and on to the end. I wish the end was come ; I wish I was dead. I have seen dead horses, and I am sure they do not suffer pain ; I hope I may drop down dead at my work, and not be sent off to the knacker's."

I was very much troubled, and I put my nose up to hers, but I could say nothing to comfort her. I think she was pleased to see me, for she said, " You are the only friend I ever had."

Just then her driver came up, and with a tug at her mouth backed her out of the line and drove off, leaving me very sad indeed.

A short time after this a cart with a dead horse in it passed our cab-stand. The head hung out of the cart tail, the life-less tongue was slowly dropping blood ; and the sunken eyes !—but I can't speak of them, the sight was too dread-ful. It was a chestnut horse with a long, thin neck. I saw a white streak down the forehead. I believe it was Ginger ; I hoped it was, for then her troubles would be over. Oh ! if men were more merciful, they would shoot us before we come to such misery.

CHAPTER XLI

The Butcher

I s a w a great deal of trouble amongst the horses in London, much of which might have been prevented by a little com-mon sense. We horses do not mind hard work if we are treated reasonably ; and I am sure there are many driven by quite poor men who have a happier life than I had when, with my silver-mounted harness, I used to go in the Countess of W——'s carriage.

It often went to my heart to see how badly the little

ponies were used—straining along with heavy loads, or staggering under heavy blows from some low, cruel boy. Once I saw a little grey pony with a thick mane and a pretty head, and so much like Merrylegs that if I had not been in harness I should have neighed to him. He was doing his best to pull a heavy cart, while a strong, rough boy was cutting him under the belly with his whip, and chucking cruelly at his little mouth.

Could it be Merrylegs? It was just like him; but then Mr. Blomefield was never to sell him, and I do not think he would have done so. Yet this may have been quite as good a little fellow, and have had as happy a place when he was young.

I often noticed the great speed at which butchers' horses were made to go, though I did not know why they were driven so fast till one day when we had to wait some time in St. John's Wood. There was a butcher's shop next door, and as we were standing a butcher's cart came dashing up at a great pace. The horse was hot and much exhausted; he hung his head down, while his heaving sides and trembling legs showed how hard he had been driven. The lad jumped out of the cart and was getting the basket when the master came out of the shop much displeased. After looking at the horse, he turned angrily to the lad.

"How many times shall I tell you not to drive in this way? You ruined the last horse and broke his wind, and you are going to ruin this in the same way. If you were not my own son, I would dismiss you on the spot; it is a disgrace to have a horse brought to the shop in such a condition. You are liable to be taken up by the police for furious driving, and if you are, you need not look to me for bail, for I have spoken to you till I am tired; you must look out for yourself."

During this speech the boy had stood by, sullen and dogged; but when his father ceased, he broke out angrily, "It wasn't my fault, and I won't take the blame: I am only going by orders all the time.

" You always say, ' Now, be quick ; now look sharp ! '
And when I go to the houses, one person wants a leg of
mutton for an early dinner, and I must be back with it in
a quarter of an hour ; another has forgotten to order the
beef, and I must go and fetch it and be back in no time or
the mistress will scold ; the third says they have company
coming unexpectedly and must have some chops sent up
directly ; and the lady at No. 4 in the Crescent *never* orders
her dinner till the meat comes in for lunch—it's nothing
but hurry, hurry, all the time. If the gentry would think of
what they want, and order their meat the day before, there
need not be this blow up ! "

" I wish to goodness they would," said the butcher ;
" 'twould save me a wonderful deal of harass, and I could
suit my customers much better if I knew beforehand. But
there—what's the use of talking ? Whoever thinks of a
butcher's convenience, or a butcher's horse ? Now then,
take him in, and look to him well. Mind, he does not go
out again to-day, and if anything else is wanted, you must
carry it yourself in the basket." With that he went in, and
the horse was led away.

But all boys are not cruel. I have seen some as fond of
their pony or donkey as if it had been a favourite dog ; and
the little creatures have worked away as cheerfully and
willingly for their young drivers as I work for Jerry. It may
be hard work sometimes, but a friend's hand and voice
make it easy.

There was a young coster-boy who came up our street
with greens and potatoes. He had an old pony, not very
handsome, but the most cheerful and plucky little thing I
ever saw ; and to see how fond those two were of each other
was a treat. The pony followed his master like a dog ; and
when the boy got into his cart, the pony would trot off without a whip or a word, and rattle down the street as merrily
as if he had come out of the Queen's stables. Jerry liked the
boy and called him " Prince Charlie," for he said he would
make a king of drivers some day.

There was an old man, too, who used to come up our street with a little coal cart. He wore a coal-heaver's hat, and looked rough and black. He and his old horse used to plod together along the street like two good partners who understood each other. The horse would stop of his own accord at the doors where they took coal of him. He used to keep one ear bent towards his master. The old man's cry could be heard up the street long before he came near. I never knew what he said, but the children called him " Old Ba-a-ar Hoo," for it sounded like that. Polly bought her coal of him, and was very friendly ; and Jerry said it was a comfort to think how happy an old horse may be in a poor place.

CHAPTER XLII

The Election

As we came into the yard one afternoon, Polly came out. " Jerry ! I've had Mr. B—— here asking about your vote, and he wants to hire your cab for the election ; he will call for an answer."

" Well, Polly, you may say that my cab will be otherwise engaged ; I should not like to have it pasted over with their great bills, and as to make Jack and Captain race about to the public-houses to bring up half-drunken voters, why, I think 'twould be an insult to the horses. No, I shan't do it."

" I suppose you'll vote for the gentleman ? He said he was of your politics."

" So he is in some things, but I shall not vote for him, Polly ; you know what his trade is ? "

" Yes."

" Well, a man who gets rich by that trade may be all very well in some ways, but he is blind as to what working men want ; I could not in my conscience send him up to make the laws. I daresay they'll be angry, but every man must do what he thinks to be the best for his country."

On the morning before the election Jerry was putting me into the shafts, when Dolly came into the yard sobbing and crying, with her little blue frock and white pinafore spattered all over with mud.

"Why, Dolly, what is the matter?"

"Those naughty boys," she sobbed, "have thrown the dirt all over me, and called me a little raga—raga——"

"They called her a little blue ragamuffin, father," said Harry, who ran in looking very angry; "but I have given it to them, they won't insult my sister again. I have given them a thrashing they will remember; a set of cowardly, rascally, orange blackguards!"

Jerry kissed the child and said, "Run in to mother, my pet, and tell her I think you had better stay at home to-day and help her."

Then, turning gravely to Harry:

"My boy, I hope you will always defend your sister, and give anybody who insults her a good thrashing—that is as it should be; but mind, I won't have any election blackguarding on my premises. There are as many blue blackguards as there are orange, and as many white as there are purple, or any other colour, and I won't have any of my family mixed up with it. Even women and children are ready to quarrel for the sake of a colour, and not one in ten of them know what it is about."

"Why, father, I thought blue was for Liberty."

"My boy, Liberty does not come from colours, they only show party, and all the liberty you can get out of them is, liberty to get drunk at other people's expense, liberty to ride to the poll in a dirty old cab, liberty to abuse anyone that does not wear your colour, and to shout yourself hoarse at what you only half understand—that's your liberty!"

"Oh, father, you are laughing."

"No, Harry, I am serious, and I am ashamed to see how men go on that ought to know better. An election is a very serious thing; at least, it ought to be, and every man ought to vote according to his conscience, and let his neighbour do the same."

CHAPTER XLIII

A Friend in Need

IT WAS the day of the election. Jerry would not let his cab to either party, but there was no lack of work for us.

First came a stout, puffy gentleman with a carpet-bag, who wanted to go to the Bishopsgate Station ; then we were called by a party who wished to be taken to the Regent's Park ; and next we were wanted in a side street, where a timid, anxious old lady was waiting to be taken to the Bank. There we had to stop to take her back again ; and just as we had set her down, a red-faced gentleman with a handful of papers came running up, out of breath ; and before Jerry could get down, he had opened the door, popped himself in, and called out, " Bow Street Police Station, quick ! " So off we went with him ; and when after another turn or two we came back, there was no other cab on the stand. Jerry put on my nose-bag, for, as he said, " We must eat when we can on such days as these ; so munch away, Jack, and make the best of your time, old boy."

I found I had a good feed of crushed oats, wetted with a little bran ; this would be a treat any day, but was specially refreshing now. Jerry was so thoughtful and kind—what horse would not do his best for such a master ? Then he took out one of Polly's meat pies, and standing near me, he began to eat it.

The streets were very full, and the cabs with the candidates' colours on them were dashing about through the crowd as if life and limb were of no consequence. We saw two people knocked down that day, and one was a woman. The horses were having a bad time of it, poor things ! but the voters inside thought nothing of that, for many of them were half drunk, hurrahing out of the cab windows if their own party came by. It was the first election I had seen, and I don't want to be in another, though I have heard things are better now.

Jerry and I had not eaten many mouthfuls before a poor young woman, carrying a heavy child, came along the street. She was looking this way and that way, and seemed quite bewildered. Presently she made her way up to Jerry and asked if he could tell her the way to St. Thomas's Hospital, and how far it was to get there. She had come from the country that morning in a market cart, and did not know it was the election. She was quite a stranger in London, but had got an order for the hospital for her little boy, who was crying with a feeble, pining cry.

" Poor little fellow ! " she said, " he suffers a deal of pain. He is four years old, and can't walk any more than a baby ; but the doctor said if I could get him into the hospital, he might get well. Pray, sir, how far is it ? and which way must I go ? "

" Why, missis," said Jerry, " you can't get there walking through crowds like this ! Why, it is three miles away, and that child is heavy."

" Yes, bless him, he is, but I am strong, thank God ; and if I knew the way, I think I could get on somehow : please tell me the way."

" You can't do it," said Jerry ; " you might be knocked down and the child be run over. Now look here, just get into this cab, and I'll drive you safely to the hospital : don't you see the rain is coming on ? "

" No, sir, no, I can't do that, thank you ; I have only just money enough to get back with. Please tell me the way."

" Look you here, missis," said Jerry, " I've got a wife and dear children at home, and I know a father's feelings. Now get into that cab and I'll take you there for nothing ; I'd be ashamed of myself to let a woman and a sick child run a risk like that."

" Heaven bless you ! " said the woman, and she burst into tears.

" There, there, cheer up, my dear, I'll soon take you there. Come, let me put you inside."

As Jerry went to open the door, two men with colours

in their hats and button-holes ran up, calling out " Cab ! "

" Engaged ! " cried Jerry. But one of the men, pushing past the woman, sprang into the cab, followed by the other. Jerry looked as stern as a policeman : " This cab is already engaged, gentlemen, by that lady."

" Lady ! " said one of them ; " oh ! she can wait, our business is very important : besides, we were in first. It is our right, and we shall stay in."

A droll smile came over Jerry's face as he shut the door upon them. " All right, gentlemen ; pray stay in as long as it suits you. I can wait while you rest yourselves " ; and turning his back upon them, he walked up to the young woman, who was standing near me. "They'll soon be gone," he said, laughing ; " don't trouble yourself, my dear."

And they soon were gone ; for when they understood Jerry's dodge, they got out, calling him all sorts of bad names, and blustering about his number and getting a summons. After this little stoppage we were soon on our way to the hospital, going as much as possible through by-streets. Jerry rang the great bell, and helped the young woman out.

" Thank you a thousand times," she said ; " I could never have got here alone."

" You're kindly welcome, and I hope the dear child will soon be better."

He watched her go in at the door, and he said to himself quietly, " ' Inasmuch as ye have done it to one of the least of these.' " Then he patted my neck ; this was always his way when anything pleased him.

The rain was now coming down fast, and just as we were leaving the hospital the door opened again, and the porter called out, " Cab ! " We stopped, and a lady came down the steps. Jerry seemed to know her at once. She put back her veil, and said, " Barker ! Jeremiah Barker ! is it you ? I am very glad to find you here ; you are just the friend I want, for it is very difficult to get a cab in this part of London to-day."

" I shall be proud to serve you, ma'am ; I am right glad

I happened to be here. Where may I take you to, ma'am?"

"To the Paddington Station, and then if we are in good time, as I think we shall be, you shall tell me all about Mary and the children."

We got to the station in good time, and being under shelter, the lady stood a good while talking to Jerry. I found she had been Polly's mistress, and after many inquiries about her, she said, "How do you find the cab-work suit you in winter? I know Mary was rather anxious about you last year."

"Yes, ma'am, she was; I had a bad cough that followed me up quite into the warm weather, and when I am kept out late she does worry herself a good deal. You see, ma'am, my work is at all hours and in all weathers, and that does try a man's constitution; but I am getting on pretty well, and I should feel quite lost if I had not horses to look after. I was brought up to it, and I am afraid I should not do as well at anything else."

"Well, Barker," she said, "it would be a great pity that you should seriously risk your health in this work, not only for your own but for Mary's and the children's sake. There are many places where good drivers or good grooms are wanted; and if ever you think you ought to give up this cab-work, let me know." Then sending some kind messages to Mary, she put something into his hand, saying, "There are five shillings each for the two children; Mary will know how to spend it."

Jerry thanked her and seemed much pleased; then, turning out of the station, we at last reached home: I, at least, was tired.

CHAPTER XLIV

Old Captain and His Successor

CAPTAIN and I were great friends. He was a noble old fellow, and a very good companion. I never thought that he would have to leave his home and go down the hill, but his turn

came ; and this is how it happened. I was not there, but I
heard all about it.

Jerry and he had taken a party to the great railway station over London Bridge, and were coming back, somewhere between the bridge and the Monument, when Jerry
saw a brewer's empty dray coming along, drawn by two
powerful horses. The drayman was lashing his horses with
his heavy whip. The dray was light, and they were going
at a furious rate. The man had no control over them.

The street was full of traffic ; one young girl was knocked
down and run over, and the next moment the dray dashed
up against our cab ; both the wheels were torn off, and the
cab was thrown over. Captain was dragged down, the
shafts splintered, and one of them ran into his side. Jerry,
too, was thrown, but was only bruised. Nobody could tell
how he escaped ; he always said 'twas a miracle.

When poor Captain was got up, he was found to be very
much cut and knocked about. Jerry led him home gently,
and a sad sight it was to see the blood soaking into his white
coat and dropping from his side and shoulder. The drayman being proved to be drunk, was fined, and the brewer
had to pay damages to our master ; but there was no one
to pay damages to poor Captain.

The farrier and Jerry did the best they could to ease his
pain and make him comfortable. The fly had to be mended,
and for several days I did not go out ; so Jerry earned
nothing. The first time we went to the stand after the accident the Governor came up to hear how Captain was.

" He'll never get over it," said Jerry—" at least, not for
my work, so the farrier said this morning. He says he may
do for carting and that sort of work. It has put me out very
much. Carting indeed ! I've seen what horses come to at
that work round London. I only wish all the drunkards
could be put in a lunatic asylum, instead of being allowed
to run foul of sober people.

" If they would break their *own* bones, and smash their
own carts, and lame their *own* horses, that would be their

own affair, and we might let them alone ; but it seems to me that the innocent always suffer ; and then they talk about compensation ! You can't make compensation—there's all the trouble and vexation and loss of time, besides losing a good horse that's like an old friend—it's nonsense talking of compensation ! If there's one devil more than another that I should like to see in the bottomless pit, it's the drink devil."

" I say, Jerry," said the Governor, " you are treading pretty hard on my toes, you know ; I'm not as good as you are, more shame for me—I wish I were."

" Well," said Jerry, " why don't you cut the drink, Governor ? You are too good a man to be the slave of such a thing."

" I'm a great fool, Jerry, but I tried once for two days, and I thought I should have died : how did you do ? "

" I had hard work at it for several weeks. You see, I never did get drunk, but I found that I was not my own master, and that when the craving came on, it was hard work to say ' no.' I saw that one of us must knock under—the drink devil or Jerry Barker ; and I said that it should not be Jerry Barker, God helping me.

" But it was a struggle, and I wanted all the help I could get ; for till I tried to break the habit, I did not know how strong it was. Polly took pains that I should have good food, and when the craving came on, I used to get a cup of coffee, or some peppermint, or I used to read a bit in my book, and that was a help to me.

" Sometimes I had to say over and over to myself, ' Give up the drink or lose your soul. Give up the drink or break Polly's heart.' But thanks be to God and my dear wife, my chains were broken, and now for ten years I have not tasted a drop, and never wish for it."

" I've a great mind to try it," said Grant, " for 'tis a poor thing not to be one's own master."

" Do, Governor, do ; you'll never repent it ; and what a help it would be to some of the poor fellows in our rank if they saw you do without it ! I know there are two or three would like to keep out of that tavern if they could."

At first Captain seemed to do well, but he was a very old horse, and it was only his wonderful constitution and Jerry's care that had kept him up at the cab-work so long ; now he broke down very much. The farrier said he might mend up enough to sell for a few pounds, but Jerry said, No ! a few pounds got by selling a good old servant into hard work and misery would canker all the rest of his money. He thought the kindest thing he could do for the fine old fellow would be to put a sure bullet through his heart, and then he would never suffer more ; for he did not know where to find him a kind master for the rest of his days.

The day after this was decided Harry took me to the forge for some new shoes. When I returned Captain was gone. The family and I all felt it very much.

Jerry had now to look out for another horse, and he soon heard of one through an acquaintance who was under-groom in a nobleman's stables. He was a valuable young horse, but he had run away, smashed into another carriage, flung his lordship out, and so cut and blemished himself that he was no longer fit for a gentleman's stables, and the coachman had orders to look round and sell him as well as he could.

" I can do with high spirits," said Jerry, " if a horse is not vicious or hard-mouthed."

" There is not a bit of vice in him," said the man ; " his mouth is very tender, and I think myself that was the cause of the accident. You see, he had just been clipped, and the weather was bad, and he had not had exercise enough, and when he did go out, he was as full of spring as a balloon. Our governor (the coachman, I mean) had him harnessed in as tight and strong as he could, with the martingale, and the bearing-rein, a very sharp curb, and the reins put in at the bottom bar ; it is my belief that it made the horse mad, being tender in the mouth and so full of spirit."

" Likely enough ; I'll come and see him," said Jerry.

The next day Hotspur—that was his name—came home ; he was a fine brown horse, without a white hair in him, as tall as Captain, with a very handsome head, and only five years old. I gave him a friendly greeting by way of good-fellowship, but did not ask him any questions. The first night he was very restless ; instead of lying down, he kept jerking his halter rope up and down through the ring, and knocking the block about against the manger so that I could not sleep. However, the next day, after five or six hours in the cab, he came in quiet and sensible. Jerry patted and talked to him a good deal, and very soon they understood each other, and Jerry said that with an easy bit and plenty of work he would be as gentle as a lamb, and that it was an ill wind that blew nobody good, for if his lordship had lost a hundred-guinea favourite, the cabman had gained a good horse with all his strength in him.

Hotspur thought it a great come-down to be a cab horse, and was disgusted at standing in the rank, but he confessed to me at the end of the week that an easy mouth and a free head made up for a great deal, and, after all, the work was not so degrading as having one's head and tail fastened to each other at the saddle. In fact, he settled in well, and Jerry liked him very much.

CHAPTER XLV

Jerry's New Year

CHRISTMAS and the New Year are very merry times for some people ; but for cabmen and cabmen's horses these times are no holiday, though they may be a harvest. There are so many parties, balls, and places of amusement open that the work is hard and often late. Sometimes driver and horse, shivering with cold, have to wait for hours in the rain or frost, whilst the merry people within are dancing to the music. I wonder if the beautiful ladies ever think of the weary cabman waiting on his box, and of his patient beast standing till his legs get stiff with cold !

I had now most of the evening work as I was well accustomed to standing, and Jerry was also more afraid of Hotspur, the new horse, taking cold. We had a great deal of late work in the Christmas week, and Jerry's cough was bad, but, however late we were, Polly sat up for him, and, looking anxious and troubled, she came out with the lantern to meet him.

On the evening of the New Year we had to take two gentlemen to a house in one of the West End squares. We set them down at nine o'clock, and were told to come again at eleven. " But," said one of them, " as it is a card party, you may have to wait a few minutes, but don't be late."

As the clock struck eleven we were at the door, for Jerry was always punctual. The clock chimed the quarters—one, two, three, and then struck twelve ; but the door did not open.

The wind had been very changeable, with squalls of rain during the day, but now it came on sharp, driving sleet, which seemed to come all the way round one ; it was very cold, and there was no shelter. Jerry got off his box and came and pulled one of my cloths a little more over my neck ; then, stamping his feet, he took a turn or two up and down ; then he began to beat his arms, but that set him on coughing ; so he opened the cab door and sat at the bottom with his feet on the pavement, and was thus a little sheltered. Still the clock chimed the quarters, but no one came. At half-past twelve he rang the bell, and asked the servant if he would be wanted that night.

" Oh ! yes, you'll be wanted safe enough," said the man ; " you must not go, it will soon be over." And again Jerry sat down, but his voice was so hoarse I could hardly hear him.

At a quarter past one the door opened, and the two gentlemen came out ; they got into the cab without a word, and told Jerry where to drive ; it was nearly two miles away. My legs were numb with cold, and I thought I should have stumbled. When the men got out, they never said they were sorry to have kept us waiting so long, but were angry at the charge. However, as Jerry never charged more than was his due, he never took less, and so they had to pay for the two hours and a quarter of waiting ; but it was hard-earned money to Jerry.

At last we got home. He could hardly speak, and his cough was dreadful. Polly asked no questions but opened the door and held the lantern for him.

" Can't I do something ? " she said.

" Yes ; get Jack something warm, and then boil me some gruel."

This was said in a hoarse whisper. He could hardly get his breath, but he gave me a rub down as usual, and even went up into the hayloft for an extra bundle of straw for my bed. Polly brought me a warm mash that made me comfortable ; and then they locked the door.

It was late the next morning before anyone came, and then it was only Harry. He cleaned and fed us, and swept out the stalls ; then he put the straw back again as if it was Sunday. He was very still, and neither whistled nor sang. At noon he came again and gave us our food and water : this time Dolly came with him. She was crying, and I could gather from what they said that Jerry was dangerously ill, and the doctor said it was a bad case. So two days passed, and there was great trouble indoors. We saw only Harry and sometimes Dolly. I think she came for company, for Polly was always with Jerry, who had to be kept very quiet.

On the third day, whilst Harry was in the stable, a tap came at the door, and Governor Grant came in.

" I wouldn't go to the house, my boy," he said, " but I want to know how your father is."

" He is very bad," said Harry, " he can't be much worse. They call it bronchitis, and the doctor thinks it will turn one way or another to-night."

" That's bad, very bad," said Grant, shaking his head. " I know two men who died of that last week. It takes 'em off in no time ; but whilst there's life there's hope, so you must keep up your spirits."

" Yes," said Harry quickly, " and the doctor said that father had a better chance than most men, because he didn't drink. He said yesterday the fever was so high that if father had been a drinking man, it would have burnt him up like a piece of paper ; but I believe he thinks he will get over it ; don't you think he will, Mr. Grant ? "

The Governor looked puzzled.

" If there's any rule that good men should get over these things, I am sure he will, my boy. He's the best man I know. I'll look in early to-morrow."

Early next morning he was there.

" Well ? " said he.

" Father is better," said Harry. " Mother hopes he will get over it."

" Thank God ! " said the Governor ; " and now you must keep him warm, and keep his mind easy. And that brings me to the horses. You see, Jack will be all the better for the rest of a week or two in a warm stable, and you can easily take him a turn up and down the street to stretch his legs ; but this young one, if he does not get work, will soon be all up on end as you may say, and will be rather too much for you ; and when he does go out, there'll be an accident."

" He is like that now," said Harry ; " I have kept him short of corn, but he's so full of spirit I don't know what to do with him."

" Just so," said Grant. " Now look here. Will you tell your mother that, if she is agreeable, I will come for him every day till something is arranged, and take him for a good spell of work ; and whatever he earns, I'll bring your mother half of it, and that will help with the horses' feed. Your father is in a good club, I know, but that won't keep the horses, and they'll be eating their heads off all this time : I'll come at noon to hear what she says " ; and without waiting for Harry's thanks, he was gone.

At noon I think he went and saw Polly, for Harry and he came to the stable together, harnessed Hotspur, and took him out.

For a week or more he came for Hotspur, and when Harry thanked him or said anything about his kindness, he laughed it off, saying, it was all good luck for him, for his horses were wanting a little rest which they could not otherwise have had.

Jerry steadily grew better, but the doctor said that he must never go back to the cab-work again if he wished to be an old man. The children had many consultations together about what father and mother would do, and how they could help to earn money.

One afternoon Hotspur was brought in very wet and dirty.

" The streets are nothing but slush," said the Governor ; " it will give you a good warming, my boy, to get him clean and dry."

" All right, Governor," said Harry, " I shall not leave him till he is ; you know I have been trained by my father."

" I wish all the boys had been trained like you," said the Governor.

While Harry was sponging off the mud from Hotspur's body and legs, Dolly came in, looking very full of something.

" Who lives at Fairstowe, Harry ? Mother has got a letter from Fairstowe ; she seemed so glad, and ran upstairs to father with it."

" Don't you know ? Why, it is the name of Mrs. Fowler's place—mother's old mistress, you know—the lady that father met last summer, who sent you and me five shillings each."

" Oh ! Mrs. Fowler ; of course I know all about her. I wonder what she is writing to mother about."

" Mother wrote to her last week," said Harry. " You know she told father if ever he gave up the cab-work, she would like to know. I wonder what she says ; run in and see, Dolly."

Harry scrubbed away at Hotspur with a " huish ! huish ! " like any old ostler.

In a few minutes Dolly came dancing into the stable.

" Oh, Harry ! was there ever anything so beautiful ? Mrs. Fowler says we are all to go and live near her. There is a cottage now empty that will just suit us, with a garden, a hen-house, apple-trees, and everything ! Her coachman is going away in the spring, and then she will want father in his place. And there are good families round, where you can get a place in the garden or stable, or as a page-boy ; and there's a good school for me. Mother is laughing and crying by turns, and father does look *so* happy ! "

" That's uncommon jolly," said Harry, " and just the right thing, I should say. It will suit father and mother both ; but I don't intend to be a page-boy with tight clothes and rows of buttons. I'll be a groom or a gardener."

It was quickly settled that, as soon as Jerry was well enough, they should remove to the country, and that the cab and horses should be sold as soon as possible.

This was heavy news for me, for I was not young now, and could not look for any improvement in my condition. Since I left Birtwick I had never been so happy as with my dear master, Jerry ; but three years of cab-work, even under the best conditions, will tell on one's strength, and I felt that I was not the horse that I had been.

Grant said at once that he would take Hotspur. There were men on the stand who would have bought me ; but Jerry said I should not go to cab-work again with just anybody, and the Governor promised to find a place for me where I should be comfortable.

The day came for going away. Jerry had not been allowed to go out yet, and I never saw him after that New Year's Eve. Polly and the children came to bid me good-bye. " Poor old Jack ! dear old Jack ! I wish we could take you with us," she said ; and then, laying her hand on my mane, she put her face close to my neck and kissed me. Dolly was crying, and she kissed me too. Harry stroked me a great deal, but said nothing, only he seemed very sad ; and so I was led away to my new place.

CHAPTER XLVI
Jakes and the Lady

I WAS sold to a corn dealer and baker whom Jerry knew, and with him he thought I should have good food and fair work. In the first he was quite right, and if my master had always been on the premises, I do not think I should have been overloaded ; but there was a foreman who was always hurrying and driving every one, and frequently when I had quite a full load, he would order something else to be taken on. My carter, whose name was Jakes, often said it was more than I ought to take, but the other always overruled him, saying, " 'Tis no use going twice when once will do, and I choose to get business forward."

Jakes, like the other carters, always had the bearing-rein up, which prevented me from drawing easily ; and by the time I had been there three or four months, I found the work telling very much on my strength.

One day, I was loaded more than usual, and part of the road was up a steep hill : I used all my strength, but I could not get on, and was obliged continually to stop. This did not please my driver, and he laid his whip on badly. " Get on, you lazy fellow," he said, " or I'll make you."

Again I started the heavy load, and struggled on a few yards ; again the whip came down, and again I struggled forward. The pain of that great cart whip was sharp, but my mind was hurt quite as much as my poor sides. To be punished and abused when I was doing my very best was so hard that it took the heart out of me. A third time he was flogging me cruelly, when a lady stepped quickly up to him, and said in a sweet, earnest voice :

" Oh ! pray do not whip your good horse any more ; I am sure he is doing all he can. The road is very steep, and I am sure he is doing his best."

" If doing his best won't get this load up, he must do something more than his best ; that's all I know, ma'am." said Jakes.

" But is it not a very heavy load ? " she said.

" Yes, yes, too heavy," he said, " but that's not my fault ; the foreman came just as we were starting, and would have three hundredweight more put on to save him trouble. I must get on with it as well as I can."

He was raising the whip again, when the lady said :

" Pray, stop, I think I can help you if you will let me." The man laughed.

" You see," she said, " you do not give him a fair chance. He cannot use all his power with his head held back as it is with that bearing-rein ; if you would take it off, I am sure he would do better—*do* try it," she said persuasively ; " I should be very glad if you would."

" Well, well," said Jakes, with a short laugh, " anything to please a lady, of course. How far would you wish it down, ma'am ? "

" Quite down ; give him his head altogether."

The rein was taken off, and in a moment I put my head down to my very knees. What a comfort it was ! Then I tossed it up and down several times to get the aching stiffness out of my neck.

" Poor fellow ! that is what you wanted," said she, patting and stroking me with her gentle hand ; " and now if you will speak kindly to him and lead him on, I believe he will be able to do better."

Jakes took the rein—" Come on, Blackie." I put down my head, and threw my whole weight against the collar. I spared no strength ; the load moved on, and I pulled it steadily up the hill, and then stopped to take breath.

The lady had walked along the footpath, and now came across into the road. She stroked and patted my neck, as I had not been patted for many a long day.

" You see, he was quite willing when you gave him the chance ; I am sure he is a fine-tempered creature, and I daresay has known better days. You won't put that rein on again, will you ? " for he was just going to hitch it up on the old plan.

" Well, ma'am, I can't deny that having his head has helped him up the hill, and I'll remember it another time, and thank you, ma'am ; but if he went without a bearing-rein, I should be the laughing-stock of all the carters ; it is the fashion, you see."

" Is it not better," she said, " to lead a good fashion than to follow a bad one ? A great many gentlemen do not use bearing-reins now ; our carriage horses have not worn them for fifteen years, and work with much less fatigue than those which have them ; besides," she added in a very serious voice, " we have no right to distress any of God's creatures without a very good reason ; we call them dumb animals, and so they are, for they cannot tell us how they feel, but they do not suffer less because they have no words. But I must not detain you now ; I thank you for trying my plan with your good horse, and I am sure you will find it far better than the whip. Good day." And with another soft pat on my neck, she stepped lightly across the path, and I saw her no more.

" That was a real lady, I'll be bound for it," said Jakes to himself ; " she spoke just as politely as if I was a gentleman. I'll try her plan, uphill, at any rate."

I must do him the justice to say that he let my rein out several holes, and after that, going uphill, he always gave me my head ; but the heavy loads went on.

Good food and fair rest will keep up one's strength under full work, but no horse can stand against overloading ; and I was getting so thoroughly pulled down from this cause that a younger horse was bought in my place. I may as well mention here what I suffered at this time from another cause. I had heard horses speak of it, but had never myself had experience of the evil of a badly-lighted stable. There was only one very small window at the end, and the consequence was that the stalls were almost dark.

Besides the depressing effect this had on my spirits, it very much weakened my sight, and when I was suddenly brought out of the darkness into the glare of daylight, it was very painful to my eyes. Several times I stumbled over the threshold, and could scarcely see where I was going.

I believe, had I stayed there very long, I should have become purblind, and that would have been a great misfortune ; for I have heard men say that a stone-blind horse is safer to drive than one which has imperfect sight, as purblindness generally makes them very timid. However, I escaped without any permanent injury to my sight, and was sold to a large cab-owner.

CHAPTER XLVII
Hard Times

I SHALL never forget my new master. He had black eyes and a hooked nose ; his mouth was as full of teeth as a bulldog's, and his voice was as harsh as the grinding of cart wheels over gravel-stones. His name was Nicholas Skinner, and I believe he was the same man for whom poor Seedy Sam had driven.

I have heard men say that seeing is believing ; but I should say that *feeling* is believing ; for much as I had seen before, I never knew till now the utter misery of a cab horse's life.

Skinner had a low set of cabs and a low set of drivers ; he was hard on the men, and the men were hard on the horses. In this place we had no Sunday rest, and it was in the heat of summer.

Sometimes on a Sunday morning a party of fast men would hire a cab for the day—four of them inside and another with the driver, and I had to take them ten or fifteen miles out into the country, and back again : never would any of them get down to walk up a hill, let it be ever so steep or the day ever so hot—unless indeed, when the driver was afraid I should not manage it, and sometimes I was so fevered and worn that I could hardly touch my food. How I used to long for the nice bran mash with nitre in it that Jerry used to give us on Saturday nights in hot weather, that used to cool us down and make us so comfortable. Then we had two nights and a whole day for unbroken rest, and on Monday morning we were as fresh as young horses again ; but here, there was no rest, and my driver was just as hard as his master.

He had a cruel whip with something so sharp at the end that it sometimes drew blood, and he would even whip me under the belly, and flip out the lash at my head. Indignities like these took the heart out of me terribly, but still I did my best and never hung back ; for, as poor Ginger said, it was no use ; men are the stronger.

My life was now so utterly wretched that I wished I might, like Ginger, drop down dead at my work, and so be out of my misery ; and one day my wish very nearly came to pass.

I went on the stand at eight in the morning, and had done a good share of work when we had to take a fare to the railway. A long train was just expected in, so my driver pulled up at the back of some of the outside cabs to take the chance of a return fare. It was a very heavy train, and as all the cabs were soon engaged, ours was called for.

There was a party of four : a noisy, blustering man with a lady, a little boy, a young girl, and a great deal of luggage. The lady and the boy got into the cab, and while the man ordered about the luggage, the young girl came and looked at me.

" Papa," she said, " I am sure this poor horse cannot take us and all our luggage so far ; he is so very weak and worn out ; do look at him."

" Oh ! he's all right, miss," said my driver, " he's strong enough."

The porter, who was pulling about some heavy boxes, suggested to the gentleman that, as there was so much luggage, he should take a second cab.

" Can your horse do it, or can't he ? " said the blustering man.

" Oh ! he can do it all right, sir. Send up the boxes, porter ; he can take more than that." Saying this, he helped to haul up a box so heavy that I could feel the springs go down.

" Papa, papa, do take a second cab," said the young girl in a beseeching tone ; " I am sure we are wrong ; I am sure it is very cruel."

" Nonsense, Grace, get in at once, and don't make all this fuss ; a pretty thing it would be if a man of business had to examine every cab horse before he hired it—the man knows his own business of course : there, get in and hold your tongue ! "

My gentle friend had to obey ; and box after box was dragged up and lodged on the top of the cab, or settled by the side of the driver. At last all was ready, and with his usual jerk of the rein and slash of the whip, he drove out of the station.

The load was very heavy, and I had had neither food nor rest since the morning ; but I did my best, as I always had done in spite of cruelty and injustice.

I got along fairly till we came to Ludgate Hill ; but there, the heavy load and my own exhaustion were too much. I was struggling to keep on, goaded by constant chucks of the rein and use of the whip, when, in a single moment—I cannot tell how—my feet slipped from under me, and I fell heavily to the ground on my side. The suddenness and the force with which I fell seemed to beat all the breath out of my body.

I lay perfectly still ; indeed, I had no power to move, and I thought now I was going to die. I heard a sort of confusion round me—loud, angry voices, and the getting down of the luggage ; but it was all like a dream. I thought I heard that sweet, pitiful voice saying, " Oh ! that poor horse ! it is all our fault."

Some one came and loosened the throat strap of my bridle, and undid the traces which kept the collar so tight upon me. Some one said, " He's dead, he'll never get up again." Then I could hear a policeman giving orders, but I did not even open my eyes ; I could only draw a gasping breath now and then. Some cold water was thrown over my head, some cordial was poured into my mouth, and something was covered over me.

I cannot tell how long I lay there, but I found my life coming back, and a kind-voiced man was patting me and encouraging me to rise. After some more cordial had been given me, and after one or two attempts, I staggered to my feet, and was gently led to some stables which were close by. Here I was put into a well-littered stall, and some warm gruel was brought to me : this I drank thankfully.

In the evening I was sufficiently recovered to be led back to Skinner's stables, where I think they did the best for me they could. In the morning Skinner came with a farrier to look at me. He examined me very closely, and said :

" This is a case of overwork more than disease, and if you could give him a run off for six months, he would be able to work again ; but now there is not an ounce of strength in him."

" Then he must just go to the dogs," said Skinner. " I have no meadows to nurse sick horses in—he may get well or he may not ; that sort of thing does not suit my business. My plan is to work 'em as long as they'll go, and then sell 'em for what they'll fetch at the knacker's or elsewhere."

" If he was broken-winded," said the farrier, " you had better have had him killed out of hand, but he is not ; there is a sale of horses coming off in about ten days, if you rest him and feed him up, he may pick up, and you may at any rate get more than his skin is worth."

Upon this advice Skinner, rather unwillingly, I think, gave orders that I should be well fed and cared for ; and the stableman, happily for me, carried out the orders with a much better will than his master had shown in giving them.

Ten days of perfect rest, plenty of good oats, hay, and bran mashes with boiled linseed mixed in them, did more to get up my condition than anything else could have done. Those linseed mashes were delicious, and I began to think that after all it might be better to live than go to the dogs. When the twelfth day after the accident came, I was taken to the sale, a few miles out of London. I felt that any change from my present place must be an improvement ; so I held up my head, and hoped for the best.

CHAPTER XLVIII

Farmer Thoroughgood and His Grandson Willie

AT THIS sale of course I found myself in company with the old broken-down horses—some lame, some broken-winded, some old, and some that I am sure it would have been merciful to shoot.

The buyers and sellers, too, many of them looked not much better off than the poor beasts for which they were bargaining. There were poor old men trying to get a horse or pony for a few pounds to drag about some little wood or coal cart. There were poor men trying to sell a worn-out beast for two or three pounds, rather than have the greater loss of killing him.

Some of them looked as if poverty and hard times had hardened them all over ; but there were others for whom I would willingly have used the last of my strength—poor and shabby, but kind and human, with voices that I could trust. There was one tottering old man that took a great fancy to me, and I to him, but I was not strong enough—it was an anxious time !

Coming from the better part of the fair, I noticed a man who looked like a gentleman farmer, with a young boy by his side. He had a broad back and round shoulders, a kind, ruddy face, and he wore a broad-brimmed hat. When he came up to me and my companions, he stood still and gave a pitiful look round upon us. I saw his eye rest on me ; I had still a good mane and tail, which did something for my appearance. I pricked my ears and looked at him.

"There's a horse, Willie, that has known better days."

"Poor old fellow!" said the boy. "Do you think, grandpapa, he was ever a carriage horse?"

"Oh, yes, my boy," said the farmer, coming closer, "he might have been anything when he was young. Look at his nostrils and his ears, and the shape of his neck and shoulders; there'a deal of breeding about that horse." He put out his hand and gave me a kind pat on the neck. I put out my nose in answer to his kindness, and the boy stroked my face.

"Poor old fellow! See, grandpapa, how well he understands kindness. Could you not buy him and make him young again, as you did Ladybird?"

"My dear boy, I can't make all old horses young. Besides, Ladybird was not so old as she was run down and badly used."

"Well, grandpapa, I don't believe that this one is old; look at his mane and tail. I wish you would look into his mouth, and then you could tell. Though he is so very thin, his eyes are not sunken like some old horses."

The old gentleman laughed. "Bless the boy! he is as horsey as his old grandfather."

"But do look at his mouth, grandpapa, and ask the price; I am sure he would grow young in our meadows."

The man who had brought me for sale now put in his word.

"The young gentleman's a real knowing one, sir. Now, the fact is, this 'ere hoss is just pulled down with overwork in the cabs. He's not an old one, and I heard as how the vet. should say that a six months' run off would set him right up, being as how his wind was not broken. I've had the tending of him these ten days past, and a more grateful and pleasant animal I never met. 'Twould be worth a gentleman's while to give a five-pound note for him and let him have a chance. I'll be bound he'd be worth twenty pounds next spring."

The old gentleman laughed, and the little boy looked up eagerly.

"Oh ! grandpapa, did you not say the colt sold for five pounds more than you expected ? You would not be poorer if you did buy this one."

The farmer slowly felt my legs, which were much swollen and strained ; then he looked at my mouth—" Thirteen or fourteen, I should say. Just trot him out, will you ? "

I arched my poor thin back, raised my tail a little, and threw out my legs as well as I could, for they were very stiff.

"What is the lowest you will take for him ? " said the farmer as I came back.

"Five pounds, sir ; that was the lowest price my master set."

" 'Tis a speculation," said the old gentleman, shaking his head, but at the same time slowly drawing out his purse— " quite a speculation ! Have you any more business here ? " he said, counting the sovereigns into the man's hand.

"No, sir, I can take him for you to the inn if you please."

"Do so ; I am now going there."

They walked forward, and I was led behind. The boy could hardly control his delight, and the old gentleman seemed to enjoy his pleasure. I had a good feed at the inn, and was then gently ridden home by a servant of my new master and turned into a large meadow with a shed in one corner of it.

Mr. Thoroughgood, for that was the name of my benefactor, gave orders that I should have hay and oats every night and morning, and the run of the meadow during the day. "You, Willie," said he, "must take the oversight of him ; I give him into your charge."

The boy was proud of his charge, and undertook it in all seriousness. There was not a day when he did not pay me a visit, picking me out from among the other horses to give me a bit of carrot or some other good thing, or sometimes to stand by me whilst I ate my oats. He always came with kind words and caresses, and of course I grew very fond of him. He called me Old Crony, as I used to come to him in the field and follow him about. Sometimes he brought his grandfather, who always looked closely at my legs.

" That is our point, Willie," he would say ; " but he is improving so steadily that I think we shall see a change for the better in the spring."

The perfect rest, the good food, the soft turf, and gentle exercise soon began to tell on my condition and my spirits. I had a good constitution from my mother, and I was never strained when I was young, so that I had a better chance than many horses who have been worked before they came to their full strength.

During the winter my legs improved so much that I began to feel quite young again. The spring came round, and one day in March Mr. Thoroughgood determined that he would try me in the phaeton. I was well pleased, and he and Willie drove me a few miles. My legs were not stiff now and I did the work with perfect ease.

" He's growing young, Willie ; we must give him a little gentle work now, and by midsummer he will be as good as Ladybird ; he has a beautiful mouth and good paces ; these could not be better."

" Oh, grandpapa, how glad I am you bought him ! "

" So am I, my boy, but he has to thank you more than me. We must now be looking out for a quiet, genteel place for him where he will be valued."

CHAPTER XLIX

My Last Home

O NE D A Y during this summer the groom cleaned and dressed me with such extraordinary care that I thought some new change must be at hand. He trimmed my fetlocks and legs, passed the tar-brush over my hoofs, and even parted my forelock. I think the harness also had an extra polish. Willie seemed half anxious, half merry, and he got into the chaise with his grandfather.

" If the ladies take to him," said the old gentleman, " they'll be suited, and he'll be suited : we can but try."

At the distance of a mile or two from the village we came to a pretty, low house with a lawn and shrubbery at the front and a drive up to the door. Willie rang the bell, and asked if Miss Blomefield or Miss Ellen was at home. Yes, they both were. So whilst Willie stayed with me, Mr. Thoroughgood went into the house.

In about ten minutes he returned, followed by three ladies. One tall, pale lady, wrapped in a white shawl, leaned on a younger lady with dark eyes and a merry face ; the third, a very stately-looking person, was Miss Blomefield. They all came to look at me and ask questions. The younger lady—this was Miss Ellen—took to me very much ; she said she was sure she should like me, for I had such a good face. The tall, pale lady said that she should always be nervous in riding behind a horse that had once been down, as I might come down again ; and if I did, she should never get over the fright.

" You see, ladies," said Mr. Thoroughgood, " many first-rate horses have had their knees broken through the carelessness of their drivers, without any fault of their own ; and from what I see of this horse, I should say that is his case : but of course I do not wish to influence you. If you wish, you can have him on trial, and then your coachman will see what he thinks of him."

" You have always been such a good adviser to us about our horses," said the stately lady, " that your recommendation would go a long way with me, and if my sister Lavinia sees no objection, we will accept with thanks, your offer of a trial."

It was then arranged that I should be sent for the next day.

In the morning a smart-looking young man came for me. At first he looked pleased, but when he saw my knees, he said in a disappointed voice : " I didn't think, sir, you would have recommended my ladies a blemished horse like this."

" Handsome is that handsome does," said my master. " You are only taking him on trial, and I am sure you will do fairly by him, young man ; and if he is not as safe as any horse you ever drove, send him back."

I was led home, placed in a comfortable stable, fed, and left to myself. The next day, when my groom was cleaning my face, he said : " That is just like the star that Black Beauty had, and he is much the same height, too ; I wonder where he is now."

A little farther on he came to the place in my neck where I was bled, and where a little knot was left in the skin. He almost started, and began to look me over carefully, talking to himself.

" White star in the forehead, one white foot on the off-side, this little knot just in that place " ; then, looking at the middle of my back—" and as I am alive, there is that little patch of white hair that John used to call ' Beauty's threepenny-bit.' It *must* be Black Beauty ! Why, Beauty ! Beauty ! do you know me, little Joe Green that almost killed you ? " And he began patting and patting me as if he was quite overjoyed.

I could not say that I remembered him, for now he was a fine, grown young fellow with black whiskers and a man's voice, but I was sure he knew me, and that he was Joe Green ; so I was very glad. I put my nose up to him, and tried to say that we were friends. I never saw a man so pleased.

" Give him a fair trial ! I should think so indeed ! I wonder who the rascal was that broke your knees, my old Beauty ! You must have been badly served out somewhere. Well, well, it won't be my fault if you haven't good times of it now. I wish John Manly were here to see you."

In the afternoon I was put into a low park chair and brought to the door. Miss Ellen was going to try me, and Green went with her. I soon found that she was a good driver, and she seemed pleased with my paces. I heard

Joe telling her about me, and that he was sure I was Squire Gordon's old Black Beauty.

When we returned, the other sisters came out to hear how I had behaved myself. She told them what she had just heard, and said, " I shall certainly write to Mrs. Gordon to tell her that her favourite horse has come to us. How pleased she will be ! "

After this I was driven every day for a week or so, and as I appeared to be quite safe, Miss Lavinia at last ventured out in the small close carriage. After this, it was quite decided to keep me and to call me by my old name of " Black Beauty."

I have now lived in this happy place a whole year. Joe is the best and kindest of grooms. My work is easy and pleasant, and I feel my strength and spirits all coming back again. Mr. Thoroughgood said to Joe the other day, " In your place he will last till he is twenty years old—perhaps more."

Willie always speaks to me when he can, and treats me as his special friend. My ladies have promised that I shall never be sold, and so I have nothing to fear ; and here my story ends. My troubles are all over and I am at home ; and often before I am quite awake, I fancy I am still in the orchard at Birtwick, standing with my old friends under the apple-trees.

HORATIUS

A Lay made about the Year of the City CCCLX

by LORD MACAULAY

Lars Porsena of Clusium
  By the Nine Gods he swore
That the great house of Tarquin
  Should suffer wrong no more.
By the Nine Gods he swore it,
  And named a trysting day,
And bade his messengers ride forth,
East and west and south and north,
  To summon his array.

East and west and south and north
  The messengers ride fast,
And tower and town and cottage
  Have heard the trumpet's blast.
Shame on the false Etruscan
  Who lingers in his home,
When Porsena of Clusium
  Is on the march for Rome.

The horsemen and the footmen
  Are pouring in amain
From many a stately market-place ;
  From many a fruitful plain ;
From many a lonely hamlet,
  Which, hid by beech and pine,
Like an eagle's nest, hangs on the crest
  Of purple Apennine ;

From lordly Volaterræ,
    Where scowls the far-famed hold
Piled by the hands of giants
    For godlike kings of old ;
From seagirt Populonia,
    Whose sentinels descry
Sardinia's snowy mountain-tops
    Fringing the southern sky ;

From the proud mart of Pisæ,
    Queen of the western waves,
Where ride Massilia's triremes
    Heavy with fair-haired slaves ;
From where sweet Clanis wanders
    Through corn and vines and flowers ;
From where Cortona lifts to heaven
    Her diadem of towers.

Tall are the oaks whose acorns
    Drop in dark Auser's rill ;
Fat are the stags that champ the boughs
    Of the Ciminian hill ;
Beyond all streams Clitumnus
    Is to the herdsman dear ;
Best of all pools the fowler loves
    The great Volsinian mere.

But now no stroke of woodman
    Is heard by Auser's rill ;
No hunter tracks the stag's green path
    Up the Ciminian hill ;
Unwatched along Clitumnus
    Grazes the milk-white steer ;
Unharmed the water fowl may dip
    In the Volsinian mere.

The harvests of Arretium,
  This year, old men shall reap,
This year, young boys in Umbro
  Shall plunge the struggling sheep ;
And in the vats of Luna,
  This year, the must shall foam
Round the white feet of laughing girls
  Whose sires have marched to Rome.

There be thirty chosen prophets,
  The wisest of the land,
Who alway by Lars Porsena
  Both morn and evening stand :
Evening and morn the Thirty
  Have turned the verses o'er,
Traced from the right on linen white
  By mighty seers of yore.

And with one voice the Thirty
  Have their glad answer given :
" Go forth, go forth, Lars Porsena ;
  Go forth, beloved of Heaven ;
Go, and return in glory
  To Clusium's royal dome ;
And hang round Nurscia's altars
  The golden shields of Rome."

And now hath every city
  Sent up her tale of men ;
The foot are fourscore thousand,
  The horse are thousands ten ;
Before the gates of Sutrium
  Is met the great array.
A proud man was Lars Porsena
  Upon the trysting day.

For all the Etruscan armies
    Were ranged beneath his eye,
And many a banished Roman,
    And many a stout ally ;
And with a mighty following
    To join the muster came
The Tusculan Mamilius,
    Prince of the Latian name.

But by the yellow Tiber
    Was tumult and affright :
From all the spacious champaign
    To Rome men took their flight.
A mile around the city,
    The throng stopped up the ways ;
A fearful sight it was to see
    Through two long nights and days.

For aged folks on crutches,
    And women great with child,
And mothers sobbing over babes
    That clung to them and smiled,
And sick men borne in litters
    High on the necks of slaves,
And troops of sun-burned husbandmen
    With reaping-hooks and staves,

And droves of mules and asses
    Laden with skins of wine,
And endless flocks of goats and sheep,
    And endless herds of kine,
And endless trains of waggons
    That creaked beneath the weight
Of corn-sacks and of household goods,
    Choked every roaring gate.

Now, from the rock Tarpeian,
  Could the wan burghers spy
The line of blazing villages
  Red in the midnight sky.
The Fathers of the City,
  They sat all night and day,
For every hour some horseman came
  With tidings of dismay.

To eastward and to westward
  Have spread the Tuscan bands ;
Nor house, nor fence, nor dovecote
  In Crustumerium stands.
Verbenna down to Ostia
  Hath wasted all the plain ;
Astur hath stormed Janiculum,
  And the stout guards are slain.

I wis, in all the Senate,
  There was no heart so bold,
But sore it ached, and fast it beat,
  When that ill news was told.
Forthwith up rose the Consul,
  Up rose the Fathers all ;
In haste they girded up their gowns,
  And hied them to the wall.

They held a council standing
  Before the River-Gate ;
Short time was there, ye well may guess,
  For musing or debate.
Out spake the Consul roundly :
  " The bridge must straight go down ;
For, since Janiculum is lost,
  Nought else can save the town."

Just then a scout came flying,
　　All wild with haste and fear :
" To arms ! to arms ! Sir Consul :
　　Lars Porsena is here."
On the low hills to westward
　　The Consul fixed his eye,
And saw the swarthy storm of dust
　　Rise fast along the sky.

And nearer fast and nearer
　　Doth the red whirlwind come ;
And louder still and still more loud,
From underneath that rolling cloud,
Is heard the trumpet's war-note proud,
　　The trampling, and the hum.
And plainly and more plainly
　　Now through the gloom appears,
Far to left and far to right,
In broken gleams of dark-blue light,
The long array of helmets bright,
　　The long array of spears.

And plainly and more plainly,
　　Above that glimmering line,
Now might ye see the banners
　　Of twelve fair cities shine ;
But the banner of proud Clusium
　　Was highest of them all,
The terror of the Umbrian,
　　The terror of the Gaul.

And plainly and more plainly
　　Now might the burghers know,
By port and vest, by horse and crest,
　　Each warlike Lucumo.
There Cilnius of Arretium
　　On his fleet roan was seen ;

And Astur of the fourfold shield,
Girt with the brand none else may wield,
Tolumnius with the belt of gold,
And dark Verbenna from the hold
  By reedy Thrasymene.

Fast by the royal standard,
  O'erlooking all the war,
Lars Porsena of Clusium
  Sat in his ivory car.
By the right wheel rode Mamilius,
  Prince of the Latian name ;
And by the left false Sextus,
  That wrought the deed of shame.

But when the face of Sextus
  Was seen among the foes,
A yell that rent the firmament
  From all the town arose.
On the house-tops was no woman
  But spat towards him and hissed,
No child but screamed out curses,
  And shook its little fist.

But the Consul's brow was sad,
  And the Consul's speech was low,
And darkly looked he at the wall,
  And darkly at the foe.
" Their van will be upon us
  Before the bridge goes down ;
And if they once may win the bridge,
  What hope to save the town ? "

Then out spake brave Horatius,
  The Captain of the Gate :
" To every man upon this earth
  Death cometh soon or late.

And how can man die better
  Than facing fearful odds,
For the ashes of his fathers,
  And the temples of his Gods,

" And for the tender mother
  Who dandled him to rest,
And for the wife who nurses
  His baby at her breast,
And for the holy maidens
  Who feed the eternal flame,
To save them from false Sextus
  That wrought the deed of shame ?

" Hew down the bridge, Sir Consul,
  With all the speed ye may ;
I, with two more to help me,
  Will hold the foe in play.
In yon strait path a thousand
  May well be stopped by three.
Now who will stand on either hand,
  And keep the bridge with me ? "

Then out spake Spurius Lartius ;
  A Ramnian proud was he :
" Lo, I will stand at thy right hand,
  And keep the bridge with thee."
And out spake strong Herminius ;
  Of Titian blood was he :
" I will abide on thy left side,
  And keep the bridge with thee."

" Horatius," quoth the Consul,
  " As thou sayest, so let it be."
And straight against that great array
  Forth went the dauntless Three.

For Romans in Rome's quarrel
  Spared neither land nor gold,
Nor son nor wife, nor limb nor life,
  In the brave days of old.

Then none was for a party ;
  Then all were for the state ;
Then the great man helped the poor,
  And the poor man loved the great :
Then lands were fairly portioned ;
  Then spoils were fairly sold :
The Romans were like brothers
  In the brave days of old.

Now Roman is to Roman
  More hateful than a foe,
And the Tribunes beard the high,
  And the Fathers grind the low.
As we wax hot in faction,
  In battle we wax cold :
Wherefore men fight not as thy fought
  In the brave days of old.

Now while the Three were tightening
  Their harness on their backs,
The Consul was the foremost man
  To take in hand an axe :
And Fathers mixed with Commons
  Seized hatchet, bar, and crow,
And smote upon the planks above,
  And loosed the props below.

Meanwhile the Tuscan army,
  Right glorious to behold,
Came flashing back the noonday light,
Rank behind rank, like surges bright
  Of a broad sea of gold.

Four hundred trumpets sounded
  A peal of warlike glee,
As that great host, with measured tread,
And spears advanced, and ensigns spread,
Rolled slowly toward the bridge's head,
  Where stood the dauntless Three.

The Three stood calm and silent,
  And looked upon the foes,
And a great shout of laughter
  From all the vanguard rose :
And forth three chiefs came spurring
  Before that deep array ;
To earth they sprang, their swords they drew,
And lifted high their shields, and flew
  To win the narrow way ;

Aunus from green Tifernum,
  Lord of the Hill of Vines ;
And Seius, whose eight hundred slaves
  Sicken in Ilva's mines ;
And Picus, long to Clusium
  Vassal in peace and war,
Who led to fight his Umbrian powers
From that grey crag where, girt with towers,
The fortress of Nequinum lowers
  O'er the pale waves of Nar.

Stout Lartius hurled down Aunus
  Into the stream beneath :
Herminius struck at Seius,
  And clove him to the teeth :
At Picus brave Horatius
  Darted one fiery thrust ;
And the proud Umbrian's gilded arms
  Clashed in the bloody dust.

Then Ocnus of Falerii
  Rushed on the Roman Three :
And Lausulus of Urgo,
  The rover of the sea ;
And Aruns of Volsinium,
  Who slew the great wild boar,
The great wild boar that had his den
Amidst the reeds of Cosa's fen,
And wasted fields, and slaughtered men,
  Along Albinia's shore.

Herminius smote down Aruns :
  Lartius laid Ocnus low :
Right to the heart of Lausulus
  Horatius sent a blow.
" Lie there," he cried, " fell pirate !
  No more, aghast and pale,
From Ostia's walls the crowd shall mark
The track of thy destroying bark.
No more Campania's hinds shall fly
To woods and caverns when they spy
  Thy thrice accursed sail."

But now no sound of laughter
  Was heard among the foes.
A wild and wrathful clamour
  From all the vanguard rose.
Six spears' lengths from the entrance
  Halted that deep array,
And for a space no man came forth
  To win the narrow way.

But hark ! the cry is Astur :
  And lo ! the ranks divide ;
And the great Lord of Luna
  Comes with his stately stride.

Upon his ample shoulders
   Clangs loud the fourfold shield,
And in his hand he shakes the brand
   Which none but he can wield.

He smiled on those bold **Romans**
   A smile serene and high ;
He eyed the flinching Tuscans,
   And scorn was in his eye.
Quoth he, " The she-wolf's litter
   Stand savagely at bay :
But will ye dare to follow,
   If Astur clears the way ? "

Then, whirling up his broadsword
   With both hands to the height,
He rushed against Horatius,
   And smote with all his might.
With shield and blade Horatius
   Right deftly turned the blow.
The blow, though turned, came yet too nigh ;
It missed his helm, but gashed his thigh :
The Tuscans raised a joyful cry
   To see the red blood flow.

He reeled, and on Herminius
   He leaned one breathing-space ;
Then, like a wild cat mad with wounds,
   Sprang right at Astur's face.
Through teeth, and skull, and helmet
   So fierce a thrust he sped,
The good sword stood a hand-breadth out
   Behind the Tuscan's head.

And the great Lord of Luna
   Fell at that deadly stroke,
As falls on Mount Alvernus
   A thunder-smitten oak.

Far o'er the crashing forest
  The giant arms lie spread ;
And the pale augurs, muttering low,
  Gaze on the blasted head.

On Astur's throat Horatius
  Right firmly pressed his heel,
And thrice and four times tugged amain,
  Ere he wrenched out the steel.
" And see," he cried, " the welcome,
  Fair guests, that waits you here !
What noble Lucumo comes next
  To taste our Roman cheer ? "

But at his haughty challenge
  A sullen murmur ran,
Mingled of wrath, and shame, and dread,
  Along that glittering van.
There lacked not men of prowess,
  Nor men of lordly race ;
For all Etruria's noblest
  Were round the fatal place.

But all Etruria's noblest
  Felt their hearts sink to see
On the earth the bloody corpses,
  In the path the dauntless Three :
And, from the ghastly entrance
  Where those bold Romans stood,
All shrank, like boys who unaware,
Ranging the woods to start a hare,
Come to the mouth of the dark lair
Where, growling low, a fierce old bear
  Lies amidst bones and blood.

Was none who would be foremost
   To lead such dire attack :
But those behind cried " Forward ! "
   And those before cried " Back ! "
And backward now and forward
   Wavers the deep array ;
And on the tossing sea of steel,
To and fro the standards reel ;
And the victorious trumpet-peal
   Dies fitfully away.

Yet one man for one moment
   Stood out before the crowd ;
Well known was he to all the Three,
   And they gave him greeting loud ;
" Now welcome, welcome, Sextus !
   Now welcome to thy home !
Why dost thou stay, and turn away ?
   Here lies the road to Rome."

Thrice looked he at the city ;
   Thrice looked he at the dead ;
And thrice came on in fury
   And thrice turned back in dread :
And, white with fear and hatred,
   Scowled at the narrow way
Where, wallowing in a pool of blood,
   The bravest Tuscans lay.

But meanwhile axe and lever
   Have manfully been plied ;
And now the bridge hangs tottering
   Above the boiling tide.
" Come back, come back, Horatius ! "
   Loud cried the Fathers all.
" Back, Lartius ! back, Herminius !
   Back, ere the ruin fall ! "

Back darted Spurius Lartius ;
   Herminius darted back :
And, as they passed, beneath their feet
   They felt the timbers crack.
But when they turned their faces,
   And on the farther shore
Saw brave Horatius stand alone,
   They would have crossed once more.

But with a crash like thunder
   Fell every loosened beam,
And, like a dam, the mighty wreck
   Lay right athwart the stream :
And a long shout of triumph
   Rose from the walls of Rome,
As to the highest turret-tops
   Was splashed the yellow foam.

And, like a horse unbroken
   When first he feels the rein,
The furious river struggled hard,
   And tossed his tawny mane,
And burst the curb, and bounded,
   Rejoicing to be free,
And whirling down, in fierce career,
Battlement, and plank, and pier,
   Rushed headlong to the sea.

Alone stood brave Horatius,
   But constant still in mind ;
Thrice thirty thousand foes before,
   And the broad flood behind.
" Down with him ! " cried false Sextus,
   With a smile on his pale face.
   Now yield thee," cried Lars Porsena,
   " Now yield thee to our grace."

Round turned he, as not deigning
   Those craven ranks to see ;
Nought spake he to Lars Porsena,
   To Sextus nought spake he ;
But he saw on Palatinus
   The white porch of his home ;
And he spake to the noble river
   That rolls by the towers of Rome.

" Oh, Tiber ! father Tiber !
   To whom the Romans pray,
A Roman's life, a Roman's arms,
   Take thou in charge this day ! "
So he spake, and speaking sheathed
   The good sword by his side,
And with his harness on his back
   Plunged headlong in the tide.

No sound of joy or sorrow
   Was heard from either bank ;
But friends and foes in dumb surprise,
With parted lips and straining eyes,
   Stood gazing where he sank ;
And when above the surges
   They saw his crest appear,
All Rome sent forth a rapturous cry,
And even the ranks of Tuscany
   Could scarce forbear to cheer.

But fiercely ran the current,
   Swollen high by months of rain :
And fast his blood was flowing ;
   And he was sore in pain,
And heavy with his armour,
   And spent with changing blows :
And oft they thought him sinking,
   But still again he rose.

Never, I ween, did swimmer,
   In such an evil case,
Struggle through such a raging flood
   Safe to the landing-place :
But his limbs were borne up bravely
   By the brave heart within,
And our good father Tiber
   Bare bravely up his chin.

" Curse on him ! " quoth false Sextus ;
   " Will not the villain drown ?
But for this stay, ere close of day
   We should have sacked the town ! "
" Heaven help him ! " quoth Lars Porsena,
   " And bring him safe to shore ;
For such a gallant feat of arms
   Was never seen before."

And now he feels the bottom ;
   Now on dry earth he stands ;
Now round him throng the Fathers
   To press his gory hands ;
And now, with shouts and clapping,
   And noise of weeping loud,
He enters through the River-Gate,
   Borne by the joyous crowd.

They gave him of the corn-land,
   That was of public right,
As much as two strong oxen
   Could plough from morn till night ;
And they made a molten image,
   And set it up on high,
And there it stands unto this day
   To witness if I lie.

It stands in the Comitium,
　Plain for all folk to see ;
Horatius in his harness,
　Halting upon one knee :
And underneath is written,
　In letters all of gold,
How valiantly he kept the bridge
　In the brave days of old.

And still his name sounds stirring
　Unto the men of Rome,
As the trumpet-blast that cries to them
　To charge the Volscian home ;
And wives still pray to Juno
　For boys with hearts as bold
As his who kept the bridge so well
　In the brave days of old.

And in the nights of winter,
　When the cold north winds blow,
And the long howling of the wolves
　Is heard amidst the snow ;
When round the lonely cottage
　Roars loud the tempest's din,
And the good logs of Algidus
　Roar louder yet within ;

When the oldest cask is opened,
　And the largest lamp is lit ;
When the chestnuts glow in the embers,
　And the kid turns on the spit ;
When young and old in circle
　Around the firebrands close ;
When the girls are weaving baskets,
　And the lads are shaping bows ;

When the goodman mends his armour,
  And trims his helmet's plume ;
When the goodwife's shuttle merrily
  Goes flashing through the loom ;
With weeping and with laughter
  Still is the story told,
How well Horatius kept the bridge
  In the brave days of old.

THE HISTORY OF THE SEVEN FAMILIES OF THE LAKE PIPPLE-POPPLE

by EDWARD LEAR

CHAPTER I

Introductory

IN FORMER days—that is to say, once upon a time, there lived in the Land of Gramble-Blamble, Seven Families. They lived by the side of the great Lake Pipple-Popple (one of the Seven Families, indeed, lived *in* the Lake), and on the outskirts of the City of Tosh, which, excepting when it was quite dark, they could see plainly. The names of all these places you have probably heard of, and you have only not to look in your Geography books to find out all about them.

Now the Seven Families who lived on the borders of the great Lake Pipple-Popple, were as follows in the next Chapter.

CHAPTER II

The Seven Families

THERE WAS a family of Two old Parrots and Seven young Parrots.

There was a family of Two old Storks and Seven young Storks.

There was a Family of Two old Geese and Seven young Geese.

There was a Family of Two old Owls and Seven young Owls.

There was a Family of Two old Guinea Pigs and Seven young Guinea Pigs.

There was a Family of Two old Cats and Seven young Cats.

And there was a Family of Two old Fishes and Seven young Fishes.

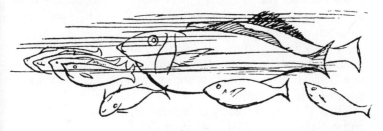

CHAPTER III
The Habits of the Seven Families

THE PARROTS lived upon the Soffsky-Poffsky trees,— which were beautiful to behold, and covered with blue leaves,—and they fed upon fruit, artichokes, and striped beetles.

The Storks walked in and out of the Lake Pipple-Popple, and ate frogs for breakfast and buttered toast for tea ; but on account of the extreme length of their legs, they could not sit down, and so they walked about continually.

The Geese, having webs to their feet, caught quantities of flies, which they ate for dinner.

The Owls anxiously looked after mice, which they caught and made into sago puddings.

The Guinea Pigs toddled about the gardens, and ate lettuces and Cheshire cheese.

The Cats sate still in the sunshine, and fed upon sponge biscuits.

The Fishes lived in the Lake, and fed chiefly on boiled periwinkles.

And all these Seven Families lived together in the utmost fun and felicity.

CHAPTER IV

The Children of the Seven Families are Sent Away

ONE DAY all the Seven Fathers and the Seven Mothers of the Seven Families agreed that they would send their children out to see the world.

So they called them all together, and gave them each eight shillings and some good advice, some chocolate drops, and a small green morocco pocket-book to set down their expenses in.

They then particularly entreated them not to quarrel, and all the parents sent off their children with a parting injunction.

" If," said the old Parrots, " you find a Cherry, do not fight about who shall have it."

" And," said the old Storks, " if you find a Frog, divide it carefully into seven bits, but on no account quarrel about it."

And the old Geese said to the Seven young Geese, " Whatever you do, be sure you do not touch a Plum-pudding Flea."

And the old Owls said, " If you find a Mouse, tear him up into seven slices, and eat him cheerfully, but without quarrelling."

And the old Guinea Pigs said, " Have a care that you eat your Lettuces, should you find any, not greedily but calmly."

And the old Cats said, " Be particularly careful not to meddle with a Clangle-Wangle, if you should see one."

And the old Fishes said, " Above all things avoid eating a blue Boss-Woss, for they do not agree with Fishes, and give them a pain in their toes."

So all the Children of each Family thanked their parents, and making in all forty-nine polite bows, they went into the wide world.

CHAPTER V

The History of the Seven Young Parrots

THE SEVEN young Parrots had not gone far, when they saw a tree with a single Cherry on it, which the oldest Parrot picked instantly, but the other six being extremely hungry, tried to get it also. On which all the Seven began to fight, and they scuffled,
> and huffled,
> > and ruffled,
> > > and shuffled,
> > > > and puffled,
> > > > > and muffled,
> > > > > > and buffled,
> > > > > > > and duffled,
> > > > > > > > and fluffled,
> > > > > > > > > and guffled,
> > > > > > > > > > and bruffled, and
screamed, and shrieked, and squealed, and squeaked, and clawed, and snapped, and bit, and bumped, and thumped, and dumped, and flumped each other till they were all torn into little bits, and at last there was nothing left to record this painful incident, except the Cherry and seven small green feathers.

And that was the vicious and voluble end of the Seven young Parrots.

CHAPTER VI

The History of the Seven Young Storks

WHEN THE Seven young Storks set out, they walked or flew for fourteen weeks in a straight line, and for six weeks more in a crooked one ; and after that they ran as hard as they could for one hundred and eight miles ; and after that they stood still and made a himmeltanious chatter-clatter-blattery noise with their bills.

About the same time they perceived a large Frog, spotted with green, and with a sky-blue stripe under each ear.

So being hungry, they immediately flew at him and were going to divide him into seven pieces, when they began to quarrel as to which of his legs should be taken off first. One said this, and another said that, and while they were all quarrelling the Frog hopped away. And when they saw that he was gone, they began to chatter-clatter,
> blatter-platter,
> > patter-blatter,
> > > matter-clatter,
> > > > flatter-quatter, more violently than

ever. And after they had fought for a week they pecked each other to little pieces, so that at last nothing was left of any of them except their bills.

And that was the end of the Seven young Storks.

CHAPTER VII

The History of the Seven Young Geese

WHEN THE Seven young Geese began to travel, they went over a large plain, on which there was but one tree, and that was a very bad one.

So four of them went up to the top of it, and looked about them, while the other three waddled up and down, and repeated poetry, and their last six lessons in Arithmetic, Geography, and Cookery.

Presently they perceived, a long way off, an object of the most interesting and obese appearance, having a perfectly round body, exactly resembling a boiled plum-pudding, with two little wings, and a beak, and three feathers growing out of his head, and only one leg.

So after a time all the Seven young Geese said to each

other, " Beyond all doubt this beast must be a Plum-pudding Flea ! "

On which they incautiously began to sing aloud,

> "Plum-pudding Flea,
> "Plum-pudding Flea,
> "Wherever you be,
> "O come to our tree,
> "And listen, O listen, O listen to me ! "

And no sooner had they sung this verse than the Plum-pudding Flea began to hop and skip on his one leg with the most dreadful velocity, and came straight to the tree, where he stopped and looked about him in a vacant and volum-inous manner.

On which the Seven young Geese were greatly alarmed, and all of a tremble-bemble : so one of them put out his long neck and just touched him with the tip of his bill,—but no sooner had he done this than the Plum-pudding Flea skipped and hopped about more and more and higher and higher, after which he opened his mouth, and to the great surprise and indignation of the Seven Geese, began to bark so loudly and furiously and terribly that they were totally unable to bear the noise, and by degrees every one of them suddenly tumbled down quite dead.

So that was the end of the Seven young Geese.

CHAPTER VIII

The History of the Seven Young Owls

WHEN THE Seven young Owls set out, they sat every now and then on the branches of old trees, and never went far at one time.

And one night when it was quite dark, they thought they heard a mouse, but as the gas lamps were not lighted, they could not see him.

So they called out, " Is that a mouse ? "

On which a Mouse answered, " Squeaky-peeky-weeky, yes it is."

And immediately all the young Owls threw themselves off the tree, meaning to alight on the ground ; but they did not perceive that there was a large well below them into which they all fell superficially, and were every one of them drowned in less than half a minute.

So that was the end of the Seven young Owls.

CHAPTER IX

The History of the Seven Young Guinea Pigs

THE SEVEN young Guinea Pigs went into a garden full of Gooseberry-bushes and Tiggory-trees, under one of which they fell asleep. When they awoke they saw a large Lettuce which had grown out of the ground while they had been sleeping, and which had an immense number of green leaves. At which they all exclaimed,

> " Lettuce ! O Lettuce !
> " Let us, O let us,
> " O Lettuce leaves,
> " O let us leave this tree and eat
> " Lettuce, O let us, Lettuce leaves ! "

And instantly the Seven young Guinea Pigs rushed with such extreme force against the Lettuce-plant, and hit their heads so vividly against its stalk, that the concussion brought on directly an incipient transitional inflammation of their noses, which grew worse and worse and worse and worse till it incidentally killed them all Seven.

And that was the end of the Seven young Guinea Pigs.

CHAPTER X

The History of the Seven Young Cats

THE SEVEN young Cats set off on their travels with great delight and rapacity. But, on coming to the top of a high hill, they perceived at a long distance of a Clangle-Wangle (or, as it is more properly written, Clangel-Wangel), and in spite of the warning they had had, they ran straight up to it.

(Now the Clangle-Wangle is a most dangerous and delusive beast, and by no means commonly to be met with. They live in the water as well as on land, using their long tail as a sail when in the former element. Their speed is extreme, but their habits of life are domestic and superfluous, and their general demeanour pensive and pellucid. On summer evenings they may sometimes be observed near the Lake Pipple-Popple, standing on their heads and humming their national melodies : they subsist entirely on vegetables, excepting when they eat veal, or mutton, or pork, or beef, or fish, or saltpetre.)

The moment the Clangle-Wangle saw the Seven young Cats approach, he ran away ; and as he ran straight on for four months, and the Cats, though they continued to run, could never overtake him,—they all gradually *died* of fatigue and exhaustion, and never afterwards recovered.

And this was the end of the Seven young Cats.

CHAPTER XI

The History of the Seven Fishes

THE SEVEN young Fishes swam across the Lake Pipple-Popple, and into the river, and into the ocean, where most unhappily for them they saw, on the fifteenth day of their travels, a bright-blue Boss-Woss, and instantly swam after him. But the Blue Boss-Woss plunged into a perpendicular,
　　　spicular,
　　　　　orbicular,
　　　　　　quadrangular,
　　　　　　　circular depth of soft mud,
where in fact his house was.

And the Seven young Fishes, swimming with great and uncomfortable velocity, plunged also into the mud, quite against their will, and not being accustomed to it, were all suffocated in a very short period.

And that was the end of the Seven young Fishes.

CHAPTER XII

Of What Occurred Subsequently

AFTER IT was known that the Seven young Parrots, and the Seven young Storks, and the Seven young Geese, and the Seven young Owls, and the Seven young Guinea Pigs, and the Seven young Cats, and the Seven young Fishes, were all dead, then the Frog, and the Plum-pudding Flea, and the Mouse, and the Clangel-Wangel, and the Blue Boss-Woss, all met together to rejoice over their good fortune. And they collected the Seven Feathers of the Seven young Parrots, and the Seven Bills of the Seven young Storks, and the Lettuce, and the Cherry, and having placed the latter on the Lettuce, and the other objects in a circular arrangement at their base, they danced a hornpipe round all these memorials until they were quite tired ; after which they gave a tea-party, and a garden-party, and a ball, and a concert, and then returned to their respective homes full of joy and respect, sympathy, satisfaction, and disgust.

CHAPTER XIII

Of What Became of the Parents of the Forty-nine Children

BUT WHEN the two old Parrots, and the two old Storks, and the two old Geese, and the two old Owls, and the two old Guinea Pigs, and the two old Cats, and the two old Fishes, became aware, by reading in the newspapers, of the calamitous extinction of the whole of their families, they refused all further sustenance ; and sending out to various shops, they purchased great quantities of Cayenne Pepper, and Brandy, and Vinegar, and blue Sealing-wax, besides Seven immense glass Bottles with air-tight stoppers. And having done this, they ate a light supper of brown bread and Jerusalem Artichokes, and took an affecting and formal leave of the whole of their acquaintance, which was very numerous and distinguished, and select, and responsible, and ridiculous.

CHAPTER XIV

Conclusion

AND AFTER this, they filled the bottles with the ingredients for pickling, and each couple jumped into a separate bottle, by which effort of course they all died immediately, and became thoroughly pickled in a few minutes ; having previously made their wills (by the assistance of the most eminent Lawyers of the District), in which they left strict orders that the Stoppers of the Seven Bottles should be carefully sealed up with the blue Sealing-wax they had purchased ; and that they themselves in the Bottles should be presented to the principal museum of the city of Tosh, to be labelled with Parchment or any other anti-congenial succedaneum, and to be placed on a marble table with silver-gilt legs, for the daily inspection and contemplation, and for the perpetual benefit of the pusillanimous public.

And if ever you happen to go to Gramble-Blamble, and visit that museum in the city of Tosh, look for them on the Ninety-eighth table in the Four hundred and twenty-seventh room of the right-hand corridor of the left wing of the Central Quadrangle of that magnificent building ; for if you do not, you certainly will not see them.

THREE NONSENSE SONGS

by EDWARD LEAR

I

THE JUMBLIES

I

THEY WENT to sea in a Sieve, they did,
   In a Sieve they went to sea :
In spite of all their friends could say,
On a winter's morn, on a stormy day,
   In a Sieve they went to sea !
And when the Sieve turned round and round,
And every one cried, " You'll all be drowned ! "

They called aloud, " Our Sieve ain't big,
But we don't care a button ! we don't care a fig !
  In a Sieve we'll go to sea ! "
    Far and few, far and few,
      Are the lands where the Jumblies live ;
    Their heads are green, and their hands are blue,
      And they went to sea in a Sieve.

II

They sailed away in a Sieve, they did,
  In a Sieve they sailed so fast,
With only a beautiful pea-green veil
Tied with a riband by way of a sail,
  To a small tobacco-pipe mast ;
And every one said, who saw them go,
" O won't they be soon upset, you know !
For the sky is dark, and the voyage is long,
And happen what may, it's extremely wrong
  In a Sieve to sail so fast ! "
    Far and few, far and few,
      Are the lands where the Jumblies live ;
    Their heads are green, and their hands are blue,
      And they went to sea in a Sieve.

III

The water it soon came in, it did,
  The water it soon came in ;
So to keep them dry, they wrapped their feet
In a pinky paper all folded neat,
  And they fastened it down with a pin.
And they passed the night in a crockery-jar,
And each of them said, " How wise we are !

Though the sky be dark, and the voyage be long,
Yet we never can think we were rash or wrong,
  While round in our Sieve we spin ! "
    Far and few, far and few,
      Are the lands where the Jumblies live ;
      Their heads are green, and their hands are blue,
        And they went to sea in a Sieve.

IV

And all night long they sailed away ;
  And when the sun went down,
They whistled and warbled a moony song
To the echoing sound of a coppery gong,
  In the shade of the mountains brown.
" O Timballo ! How happy we are,
When we live in a sieve and a crockery-jar,
And all night long in the moonlight pale,
We sail away with a pea-green sail,
  In the shade of the mountains brown ! "
    Far and few, far and few,
      Are the lands where the Jumblies live ;
      Their heads are green, and their hands are blue,
        And they went to sea in a Sieve.

V

They sailed to the Western Sea, they did,
  To a land all covered with trees,
And they bought an Owl, and a useful Cart,
And a pound of Rice, and a Cranberry Tart,
  And a hive of silvery Bees.
And they bought a Pig, and some green Jack-daws,
And a lovely Monkey with lollipop paws,

And forty bottles of Ring-Bo-Ree,
  And no end of Stilton Cheese.
    Far and few, far and few,
      Are the lands where the Jumblies live ;
    Their heads are green, and their hands are blue,
      And they went to sea in a Sieve.

VI

And in twenty years they all came back,
  In twenty years or more,
And every one said, " How tall they've grown !
For they've been to the Lakes, and the Terrible Zone,
  And the hills of the Chankly Bore " ;
And they drank their health, and gave them a feast
Of dumplings made of beautiful yeast ;
And every one said, " If we only live,
We too will go to sea in a Sieve,—
  To the hills of the Chankly Bore ! "
    Far and few, far and few,
      Are the lands where the Jumblies live ;
    Their heads are green, and their hands are blue,
      And they went to sea in a Sieve.

II

THE POBBLE WHO HAS NO TOES

I

THE POBBLE who has no toes
  Had once as many as we ;
When they said, " Some day you may lose them all " ;—
  He replied,—" Fish fiddle de-dee ! "
And his Aunt Jobiska made him drink,
Lavender water tinged with pink,
For she said, " The World in general knows
There's nothing so good for a Pobble's toes ! "

II

The Pobble who has no toes,
  Swam across the Bristol Channel ;
But before he set out he wrapped his nose,
  In a piece of scarlet flannel.
For his Aunt Jobiska said, " No harm
" Can come to his toes if his nose is warm ;
" And it's perfectly known that a Pobble's toes
" Are safe,—provided he minds his nose."

III

The Pobble swam fast and well,
  And when boats or ships came near him
He tinkledy-binkledy-winkled a bell,
  So that all the world could hear him.
And all the Sailors and Admirals cried,
When they saw him nearing the further side,—
" He has gone to fish, for his Aunt Jobiska's
" Runcible Cat with crimson whiskers ! "

IV

But before he touched the shore,
   The shore of the Bristol Channel,
A sea-green Porpoise carried away
   His wrapper of scarlet flannel.
And when he came to observe his feet,
Formerly garnished with toes so neat,
His face at once became forlorn
On perceiving that all his toes were gone !

V

And nobody ever knew
   From that dark day to the present,
Whoso had taken the Pobble's toes,
   In a manner so far from pleasant.
Whether the shrimps or crawfish gray,
Or crafty Mermaids stole them away—
Nobody knew ; and nobody knows
How the Pobble was robbed of his twice five toes !

VI

The Pobble who has no toes
   Was placed in a friendly Bark,
And they rowed him back, and carried him up,
   To his Aunt Jobiska's Park.
And she made him a feast at his earnest wish
Of eggs and buttercups fried with fish ;—
And she said,—" It's a fact the whole world knows,
" That Pobbles are happier without their toes."

III

THE TWO OLD BACHELORS

Two old Bachelors were living in one house ;
One caught a Muffin, the other caught a Mouse.
Said he who caught the Muffin to him who caught the
    Mouse,—
" This happens just in time ! For we've nothing in the house,
" Save a tiny slice of lemon and a teaspoonful of honey,
" And what to do for dinner—since we haven't any money ?
" And what can we expect if we haven't any dinner,
" But to lose our teeth and eyelashes and keep on growing
    thinner ? "

Said he who caught the Mouse to him who caught the
    Muffin,—
" We might cook this little Mouse, if we only had some
    Stuffin' !
" If we had but Sage and Onion we could do extremely well,
" But how to get that Stuffin' it is difficult to tell ! "—

Those two old Bachelors ran quickly to the town
And asked for Sage and Onion as they wandered up and
    down ;
They borrowed two large Onions, but no Sage was to be
    found
In the Shops, or in the Market, or in all the Gardens round.

But some one said,—" A hill there is, a little to the north,
" And to its purpledicular top a narrow way leads forth ;—
" And there among the rugged rocks abides an ancient
    Sage,—
" An earnest Man, who reads all day a most perplexing
    page.
" Climb up, and seize him by the toes !—all studious as he
    sits,—
" And pull him down,—and chop him into endless little
    bits !
" Then mix him with your Onion, (cut up likewise into
    Scraps,)—
" When your Stuffin' will be ready—and very good :
    perhaps."

Those two old Bachelors without loss of time
The nearly purpledicular crags at once began to climb ;
And at the top, among the rocks, all seated in a nook,
They saw that Sage, a-reading of a most enormous book.
" You earnest Sage ! " aloud they cried, " you're book
    you've read enough in !—
"We wish to chop you into bits to mix you into Stuffin' ! "—

But that old Sage looked calmly up, and with his awful
    book,
At those two Bachelors' bald heads a certain aim he took ;—
And over crag and precipice they rolled promiscuous
    down,—
At once they rolled, and never stopped in lane or field or
    town,—

And when they reached their house, they found (besides
    their want of Stuffin',)
The Mouse had fled ; —and, previously, had eaten up the
    Muffin.

They left their home in silence by the once convivial door.
And from that hour those Bachelors were never heard of
    more.

THE ROSE AND THE RING

OR, THE

HISTORY OF PRINCE GIGLIO
AND PRINCE BULBO

A Fireside Pantomime for Great and Small Children

By MR. M. A. TITMARSH
(William Makepeace Thackeray)

I

Shows how the Royal Family Sate Down to Breakfast

THIS IS Valoroso XXIV, King of Paflagonia, seated with his Queen and only child at their royal breakfast-table, and receiving the letter which announces to His Majesty a proposed visit from Prince Bulbo, heir of Padella, reigning King of Crim Tartary. Remark the delight upon the monarch's royal features. He is so absorbed in the perusal of the King of Crim Tartary's letter, that he allows his eggs to get cold, and leaves his august muffins untasted.

"What! that wicked, brave, delightful Prince Bulbo!" cries Princess Angelica; "so handsome, so accomplished, so witty—the conqueror of Rimbombamento, where he slew ten thousand giants!"

"Who told you of him, my dear?" asks His Majesty.

"A little bird," says Angelica.

"Poor Giglio!" says mamma, pouring out the tea.

"Bother Giglio!" cries Angelica, tossing up her head, which rustled with a thousand curl-papers.

"I wish," growls the King—"I wish Giglio was . . ."

"Was better? Yes, dear, he is better," says the Queen. "Angelica's little maid, Betsinda, told me so when she came to my room this morning with my early tea."

"You are always drinking tea," said the monarch, with a scowl.

"It is better than drinking port or brandy and water," replies Her Majesty.

"Well, well, my dear, I only said you were fond of drinking tea," said the King of Paflagonia, with an effort as if to command his temper. "Angelica! I hope you have plenty of new dresses; your milliners' bills are long enough. My dear Queen, you must see and have some parties. I prefer dinners, but of course you will be for balls. Your everlasting blue velvet quite tires me: and, my love, I should like you to have a new necklace. Order one. Not more than a hundred or a hundred and fifty thousand pounds."

"And Giglio, dear?" says the Queen.

"GIGLIO MAY GO TO THE——"

"Oh, sir," screams Her Majesty. "Your own nephew! our late King's only son."

"Giglio may go to the tailor's, and order the bills to be sent in to Glumboso to pay. Confound him! I mean bless his dear heart. He need want for nothing; give him a couple of guineas for pocket-money, my dear; and you may as well order yourself bracelets while you are about the necklace, Mrs. V."

Her Majesty, or *Mrs. V.*, as the monarch facetiously called her (for even royalty will have its sport, and this august family were very much attached), embraced her husband, and, twining her arm round her daughter's waist, they quitted the breakfast-room in order to make all things ready for the princely stranger.

When they were gone, the smile that had lighted up the eyes of the *husband* and *father* fled—the pride of the *King* fled —the MAN was alone. Had I the pen of a G. P. R. James, I would describe Valoroso's torments in the choicest language ; in which I would also depict his flashing eye, his distended nostril—his dressing-gown, pocket-handkerchief, and boots. But I need not say I have *not* the pen of that novelist ; suffice it to say, Valoroso was alone.

He rushed to the cupboard, seizing from the table one of the many egg-cups with which his princely board was served for the matin meal, drew out a bottle of right Nantz or Cognac, filled and emptied the cup several times, and laid it down with a hoarse " Ha, ha, ha ! now Valoroso is a man again ! "

" But oh ! " he went on (still sipping, I am sorry to say), " ere I was a king, I needed not this intoxicating draught ; once I detested the hot brandy wine, and quaffed no other fount but nature's rill. It dashes not more quickly o'er the rocks than I did, as, with blunderbuss in hand, I brushed away the early morning dew, and shot the partridge, snipe, or antlered deer ! Ah ! well may England's dramatist remark, ' Uneasy lies the head that wears a crown ! ' Why did I steal my nephew's, my young Giglio's—— ? Steal ! said I ? no, no, no, not steal, not steal. Let me withdraw that odious expression. I took, and on my manly head I set, the royal crown of Paflagonia ; I took, and with my royal arm I wield, the sceptral rod of Paflagonia ; I took, and in my outstretched hand I hold, the royal orb of Paflagonia ! Could a poor boy, a snivelling, drivelling boy

—was in his nurse's arms but yesterday, and cried for sugar-plums and puled for pap—bear up the awful weight of crown, orb, sceptre ? gird on the sword my royal fathers wore, and meet in fight the tough Crimean foe ? "

And then the monarch went on to argue in his own mind (though we need not say that blank verse is not argument) that what he had got it was his duty to keep, and that, if at one time he had entertained ideas of a certain restitution, which shall be nameless, the prospect by a *certain marriage* of uniting two crowns and two nations which had been engaged in bloody and expensive wars, as the Paflagonians and the Crimeans had been, put the idea of Giglio's restoration to the throne out of the question : nay, were his own brother, King Savio, alive, he would certainly will away the crown from his own son in order to bring about such a desirable union.

Thus easily do we deceive ourselves ! Thus do we fancy what we wish is right ! The King took courage, read the papers, finished his muffins and eggs, and rang the bell for his Prime Minister. The Queen, after thinking whether she should go up and see Giglio, who had been sick, thought " Not now. Business first ; pleasure afterwards. I will go and see dear Giglio this afternoon ; and now I will drive to the jeweller's, to look for the necklace and bracelets." The Princess went up into her own room, and made Betsinda, her maid, bring out all her dresses ; and as for Giglio, they forgot him as much as I forget what I had for dinner last Tuesday twelvemonth.

II

How King Valoroso got the Crown, and Prince Giglio Went Without

PAFLAGONIA, ten or twenty thousand years ago, appears to have been one of those kingdoms where the laws of succession were not settled ; for when King Savio died, leaving his brother Regent of the kingdom, and guardian of Savio's

orphan infant, this unfaithful regent took no sort of regard
of the late monarch's will ; had himself proclaimed sovereign of Paflagonia under the title of King Valoroso XXIV.,
had a most splendid coronation, and ordered all the nobles
of the kingdom to pay him homage. So long as Valoroso
gave them plenty of balls at Court, plenty of money and
lucrative places, the Paflagonian nobility did not care who

was king ; and as for the people, in those early times, they
were equally indifferent. The Prince Giglio, by reason of
his tender age at his royal father's death, did not feel the
loss of his crown and empire. As long as he had plenty of toys
and sweetmeats, a holiday five times a week, and a horse
and gun to go out shooting when he grew a little older, and,
above all, the company of his darling cousin, the King's
only child, poor Giglio was perfectly contented ; nor did he
envy his uncle the royal robes and sceptre, the great hot

uncomfortable throne of state, and the enormous cumber-
some crown in which that monarch appeared from morning till night. King Valoroso's portrait has been left to us ;
and I think you will agree with me that he must have been
sometimes *rather tired* of his velvet, and his diamonds, and
his ermine, and his grandeur. I shouldn't like to sit in that
stifling robe with such a thing as that on my head.

No doubt, the Queen must have been lovely in her
youth ; for though she grew rather stout in after life, yet
her features, as shown in her portrait, are certainly *pleasing*.
If she was fond of flattery, scandal, cards, and fine clothes,
let us deal gently with her infirmities, which, after all, may
be no greater than our own. She was kind to her nephew ;
and if she had any scruples of conscience about her husband's taking the young Prince's crown, consoled herself

by thinking that the King, though a usurper, was a most respectable man, and that at his death Prince Giglio would be restored to his throne, and share it with his cousin, whom he loved so fondly.

The Prime Minister was Glumboso, an old statesman, who most cheerfully swore fidelity to King Valoroso, and in whose hands the monarch left all the affairs of his kingdom. All Valoroso wanted was plenty of money, plenty of hunting, plenty of flattery, and as little trouble as possible. As long as he had his sport, this monarch cared little how his people paid for it : he engaged in some wars, and of course the Paflagonian newspapers announced that he gained prodigious victories : he had statues erected to himself in every city of the empire ; and of course his pictures placed everywhere, and in all the print-shops : he was Valoroso the Magnanimous, Valoroso the Victorious, Valoroso the Great, and so forth ;—for even in these early early times courtiers and people knew how to flatter.

This royal pair had one only child, the Princess Angelica, who, you may be sure, was a paragon in the courtiers' eyes, in her parents', and in her own. It was said she had the longest hair, the largest eyes, the slimmest waist, the smallest foot, and the most lovely complexion of any young lady in the Paflagonian dominions. Her accomplishments were announced to be even superior to her beauty ; and governesses used to shame their idle pupils by telling them what Princess Angelica could do. She could play the most difficult pieces of music at sight. She could answer any one of *Mangnall's Questions*. She knew every date in the history of Paflagonia, and every other country. She knew French, English, Italian, German, Spanish, Hebrew, Greek, Latin, Cappadocian, Samothracian, Ægean, and Crim Tartar. In a word, she was a most accomplished young creature ; and her governess and lady-in-waiting was the severe Countess Gruffanuff.

Would you not fancy, from this picture, that Gruffanuff must have been a person of the highest birth ? She looks so

haughty that I should have thought her a Princess at the
very least, with a pedigree reaching as far back as the
Deluge. But this lady was no better born than many other
ladies who give themselves airs ; and all sensible people
laughed at her absurd pretensions. The fact is, she had been
maid-servant to the Queen when her Majesty was only
Princess, and her husband had been head footman ; but

after his death or *disappearance*, of which you shall hear
presently, this Mrs. Gruffanuff, by flattering, toadying,
and wheedling her royal mistress, became a favourite with
the Queen (who was rather a weak woman), and Her
Majesty gave her a title, and made her nursery governess
to the Princess.

And now I must tell you about the Princess's learning
and accomplishments, for which she had such a wonderful

character. Clever Angelica certainly was, but as *idle as possible*. Play at sight, indeed ! she could play one or two pieces, and pretend that she had never seen them before ; she could answer half a dozen *Mangnall's Questions* ; but then you must take care to ask the *right* ones. As for her languages, she had masters in plenty, but I doubt whether she knew more than a few phrases in each, for all her pretence ; and as for her embroidery and her drawing, she showed beautiful specimens, it is true, but *who did them* ?

This obliges me to tell the truth, and to do so I must go back ever so far, and tell you about the FAIRY BLACKSTICK.

III

Tells who the Fairy Blackstick was, and who were ever so many Grand Personages besides

BETWEEN the kingdoms of Paflagonia and Crim Tartary, there lived a mysterious personage, who was known in those countries as the Fairy Blackstick, from the ebony wand or crutch which she carried ; on which she rode to the moon sometimes, or upon other excursions of business or pleasure, and with which she performed her wonders.

When she was young, and had been first taught the art of conjuring by the necromancer, her father, she was always practising her skill, whizzing about from one kingdom to another upon her black stick, and conferring her fairy favours upon this Prince or that. She had scores of royal godchildren ; turned numberless wicked people into beasts, birds, millstones, clocks, pumps, bootjacks, umbrellas, or other absurd shapes ; and, in a word, was one of the most active and officious of the whole College of fairies.

But after two or three thousand years of this sport, I suppose Blackstick grew tired of it. Or perhaps she thought, " What good am I doing by sending this Princess to sleep for a hundred years ? by fixing a black pudding on to that booby's nose ? by causing diamonds and pearls to drop from one little girl's mouth, and vipers and toads from another's ? I begin to think I do as much harm as good by my performances. I might as well shut my incantations up, and allow things to take their natural course.

"There were my two young goddaughters, King Savio's wife, and Duke Padella's wife, I gave them each a present, which was to render them charming in the eyes of their husbands, and secure the affection of those gentlemen as long as they lived. What good did my Rose and my Ring do these two women ? None on earth. From having all their whims indulged by their husbands, they became capricious, lazy, ill-humoured, absurbly vain, and leered and languished, and fancied themselves irresistibly beautiful, when they were really quite old and hideous, the ridiculous creatures ! They used actually to patronise me when I went to pay them a visit—*me*, the Fairy Blackstick, who knows all the wisdom of the necromancers, and who could have turned them into baboons, and all their diamonds into strings of onions, by a single wave of my rod !" So she locked up her books in her cupboard, declined further magical performances, and scarcely used her wand at all except as a cane to walk about with.

So when Duke Padella's lady had a little son (the Duke was at that time only one of the principal noblemen in Crim Tartary), Blackstick, although invited to the christening, would not so much as attend ; but merely sent her compliments and a silver papboat for the baby, which was really not worth a couple of guineas. About the same time the Queen of Paflagonia presented His Majesty with a son and heir ; and guns were fired, the capital illuminated, and no end of feasts ordained to celebrate the young Prince's birth. It was thought the fairy, who was asked to be his godmother, would at least have presented him with an invisible jacket, a flying horse, a Fortunatus's purse, or some other valuable token of her favour ; but instead, Blackstick went up to the cradle of the child Giglio, when everybody was admiring him and complimenting his royal papa and mamma, and said, " My poor child, the best thing I can send you is a little *misfortune* " ; and this was all she would utter, to the disgust of Giglio's parents, who died very soon after, when Giglio's uncle took the throne, as we read in Chapter I.

In like manner, when CAVOLFIORE, King of Crim Tartary, had a christening of his only child, ROSALBA, the Fairy Blackstick, who had been invited, was not more gracious than in Prince Giglio's case. Whilst everybody was expatiating over the beauty of the darling child, and congratulating its parents, the Fairy Blackstick looked very sadly at the baby and its mother, and said, " My good woman (for the Fairy was very familiar, and no more minded a Queen than a washerwoman)—my good woman, these people who are following you will be the first to turn against you ; and as for this little lady, the best thing I can wish her is a *little misfortune*." So she touched Rosalba with her black wand, looked severely at the courtiers, motioned the Queen an adieu with her hand, and sailed slowly up into the air out of window.

When she was gone, the Court people, who had been awed and silent in her presence, began to speak. " What an odious Fairy she is (they said)—a pretty Fairy, indeed ! Why, she went to the King of Paflagonia's christening, and pretended to do all sorts of things for that family ; and what has happened—the Prince, her godson, has been turned off his throne by his uncle. Would we allow our sweet Princess to be deprived of her rights by any enemy ? Never, never, never, never ! "

And they all shouted in a chorus, " Never, never, never, never ! "

Now, I should like to know, and how did these fine courtiers show their fidelity ? One of King Cavolfiore's vassals, the Duke Padella just mentioned, rebelled against the King, who went out to chastise his rebellious subject.

" Any one rebel against our beloved and august Monarch ! " cried the courtiers ; " any one resist *him* ? Pooh !

He is invincible, irresistible. He will bring home Padella a prisoner, and tie him to a donkey's tail, and drive him round the town, saying, ' This is the way the Great Cavolfiore treats rebels.' "

The King went forth to vanquish Padella ; and the poor Queen, who was a very timid, anxious creature, grew so frightened and ill, that I am sorry to say she died ; leaving injunctions with her ladies to take care of the dear little Rosalba.—Of course they said they would. Of course they vowed they would die rather than any harm should happen

to the Princess. At first the *Crim Tartar Court Journal* stated that the King was obtaining great victories over the audacious rebel : then it was announced that the troops of the infamous Padella were in flight : then it was said that the royal army would soon come up with the enemy, and then —then the news came that King Cavolfiore was vanquished and slain by His Majesty, King Padella the First !

At this news, half the courtiers ran off to pay their duty to the conquering chief, and the other half ran away, laying hands on all the best articles in the palace ; and poor little Rosalba was left there quite alone—quite alone ; and she

toddled from one room to another, crying, " Countess !
Duchess ! " (only she said " Tountess, Duttess," not being
able to speak plain) " bring me my mutton sop ; my Royal
Highness hungy ! Tountess ! Duttess ! " And she went
from the private apartments into the throne-room and
nobody was there ;—and thence into the ball-room and
nobody was there ;—and thence into the pages' room
and nobody was there ;—and she toddled down the great
staircase into the hall and nobody was there ;—and the door
was open, and she went into the court, and into the garden,
and thence into the wilderness, and thence into the forest
where the wild beasts live, and was never heard of any
more !

A piece of her torn mantle and one of her shoes were
found in the wood in the mouths of two lionesses' cubs,
whom KING PADELLA and a royal hunting party shot—for
he was King now, and reigned over Crim Tartary. " So
the poor little Princess is done for," said he ; " well, what's
done can't be helped. Gentlemen, let us go to luncheon ! "
And one of the courtiers took up the shoe and put it in his
pocket. And there was an end of Rosalba !

IV

How Blackstick was not asked to the Princess Angelica's Christening

WHEN THE Princess Angelica was born, her parents not only
did not ask the Fairy Blackstick to the christening party,
but gave orders to their porter absolutely to refuse her if
she called. This porter's name was Gruffanuff, and he had
been selected for the post by their Royal Highnesses because he was a very tall fierce man, who could say " Not
at home " to a tradesman or an unwelcome visitor with a
rudeness which frightened most such persons away. He was
the husband of that Countess whose picture we have just

seen, and as long as they were together they quarrelled
from morning till night. Now this fellow tried his rudeness
once too often, as you shall hear. For the Fairy Blackstick
coming to call upon the Prince and Princess, who were
actually sitting at the open drawing-room window, Gruffanuff not only denied them, but made the most *odious
vulgar sign* as he was going to slam the door in the Fairy's
face ! " Git away, hold Blackstick " ! said he. " I tell you,
Master and Missis ain't at home to you " ; and he was, as
we have said, *going* to slam the door.

But the Fairy, with her wand, prevented the door being
shut ; and Gruffanuff came out again in a fury, swearing in
the most abominable way, and asking the Fairy " whether
she thought he was a going to stay at that there door hall
day ? "

" You *are* going to stay at that door all day and all night,
and for many a long year," the Fairy said, very majestically;
and Gruffanuff, coming out of the door, straddling before
it with his great calves, burst out laughing, and cried,
" Ha, ha, ha ! this *is* a good un ! Ha—ah—what's this ?
Let me down—O—o—H'm ! " and then he was dumb !

For, as the Fairy waved her wand over him, he felt himself rising off the ground, and fluttering up against the door, and then, as if a screw ran into his stomach, he felt a dreadful pain there, and was pinned to the door ; and then his arms flew up over his head ; and his legs, after writhing about wildly, twisted under his body ; and he felt cold, cold, growing over him, as if he was turning into metal ; and he said, " O—o—H'm ! " and could say no more, because he was dumb.

He *was* turned into metal ! He was, from being *brazen*, *brass* ! He was neither more nor less than a knocker ! And there he was, nailed to the door in the blazing summer day, till he burned almost red-hot ; and there he was, nailed

RING ALSO

to the door all the bitter winter nights, till his brass nose was dropping with icicles. And the postman came and rapped at him, and the vulgarest boy with a letter came and hit him up against the door. And the King and Queen (Princess and Prince they were then) coming home from a walk that evening, the King said, " Hullo, my dear ! you have had a new knocker put on the door. Why, it's rather like our porter in the face ! What has become of that boozy vagabond ? " And the housemaid came and scrubbed his nose with sand-paper ; and once, when the Princess Angelica's little sister was born, he was tied up in an old kid glove ; and, another night, some *larking* young men tried to wrench him off, and put him to the most excruciating agony with a turnscrew. And then the Queen had a fancy to have the colour of the door altered ; and the painters dabbed him over the mouth and eyes, and nearly choked him, as they painted him pea-green. I warrant he had leisure to repent of having been rude to the Fairy Blackstick !

As for his wife, she did not miss him ; and as he was always guzzling beer at the public-house, and notoriously quarrelling with his wife, and in debt to the tradesmen, it was supposed he had run away from all these evils, and emigrated to Australia or America. And when the Prince and Princess chose to become King and Queen, they left their old house, and nobody thought of the porter any more.

V

How Princess Angelica took a Little Maid

ONE DAY, when the Princess Angelica was quite a little girl, she was walking in the garden of the palace, with Mrs. Gruffanuff, the governess, holding a parasol over her head, to keep her sweet complexion from the freckles, and Angelica was carrying a bun, to feed the swans and ducks in the royal pond.

They had not reached the duck-pond, when there came toddling up to them such a funny little girl ! She had a great quantity of hair blowing about her chubby little cheeks, and looked as if she had not been washed or combed for ever so long. She wore a ragged bit of a cloak, and had only one shoe on.

" You little wretch, who let you in here ? " asked Gruffanuff.

" Div me dat bun," said the little girl, " me vely hungry."

" Hungry ! what is that ? " asked Princess Angelica, and gave the child the bun.

" Oh, Princess ! " says Gruffanuff, " how good, how kind, how truly angelical you are ! See, your Majesties," she said to the King and Queen, who now came up, along

with their nephew, Prince Giglio, " how kind the Princess
is ! She met this little dirty wretch in the garden—I can't
tell how she came in here, or why the guards did not shoot
her dead at the gate !—and the dear darling of a Princess
has given her the whole of her bun ! "

" I didn't want it," said Angelica.

" But you are a darling little angel all the same," says
the governess.

" Yes ; I know I am," said Angelica. " Dirty little girl

don't you think I am very pretty ? " Indeed, she had on
the finest of little dresses and hats ; and, as her hair was
carefully curled, she really looked very well.

" Oh, pooty, pooty ! " says the little girl, capering about,
laughing, and dancing, and munching her bun ; and as she
ate it she began to sing, " Oh, what fun to have a plum
bun ! how I wis it never was done ! " At which, and her
funny accent, Angelica, Giglio, and the King and Queen
began to laugh very merrily.

" I can dance as well as sing," says the little girl. " I can
dance, and I can sing, and I can do all sorts of ting." And

she ran to a flower-bed, and pulling a few polyanthuses, rhododendrons, and other flowers, made herself a little wreath, and danced before the King and Queen so drolly and prettily, that everybody was delighted.

" Who was your mother—who were your relations, little girl ? " said the Queen.

The little girl said, " Little lion was my brudder ; great big lioness my mudder ; neber heard of any udder." And

she capered away on her one shoe, and everybody was exceedingly diverted.

So Angelica said to the Queen, " Mamma, my parrot flew away yesterday out of its cage, and I don't care any more for any of my toys ; and I think this funny little dirty child will amuse me. I will take her home, and give her some of my old frocks."

" Oh, the generous darling ! " says Gruffanuff.

" Which I have worn ever so many times, and am quite

tired of," Angelica went on ; " and she shall be my little maid. Will you come home with me, little dirty girl ? "

The child clapped her hands, and said, " Go home with you—yes ! You pooty Princess !—Have a nice dinner, and wear a new dress ! "

And they all laughed again, and took home the child to the palace, where, when she was washed and combed, and had one of the Princess's frocks given to her, she looked as handsome as Angelica, almost. Not that Angelica ever thought so ; for this little lady never imagined that anybody in the world could be as pretty, as good, or as clever as herself. In order that the little girl should not become too proud and conceited, Mrs. Gruffanuff took her old ragged mantle and one shoe, and put them into a glass box, with a card laid upon them, upon which was written, " These were the old clothes in which little BETSINDA was found when the great goodness and admirable kindness of her Royal Highness the Princess Angelica received this little outcast." And the date was added, and the box locked up.

For a while little Betsinda was a great favourite with the Princess, and she danced, and sang, and made her little rhymes, to amuse her mistress. But then the Princess got a monkey, and afterwards a little dog, and afterwards a doll, and did not care for Betsinda any more, who became very melancholy and quiet, and sang no more funny songs, because nobody cared to hear her. And then, as she grew older, she was made a little lady's-maid to the Princess ; and though she had no wages, she worked and mended, and put Angelica's hair in papers, and was never cross when scolded, and was always eager to please her mistress, and was always up early and to bed late, and at hand when wanted, and in fact became a perfect little maid. So the two girls grew up, and, when the Princess came out, Betsinda was never tired of waiting on her ; and made her dresses better than the best milliner, and was useful in a hundred ways. Whilst the Princess was having her masters, Betsinda would sit and watch them ; and in this way she picked up a great deal of learning ; for she was always awake, though her mistress was not, and listened to the wise professors when Angelica was yawning or thinking of the next ball. And when the dancing-master came, Betsinda learned along with Angelica ; and when the music-master came, she watched him, and practised the Princess's pieces when Angelica was away at balls and parties ; and when the drawing-master came, she took note of all he said and did ; and the same with French, Italian, and all other languages —she learned them from the teacher who came to Angelica. When the Princess was going out of an evening she would say, " My good Betsinda, you may as well finish what I have begun." " Yes, miss," Betsinda would say, and sit down very cheerful, not to *finish* what Angelica began, but to *do* it.

For instance, the Princess would begin the head of a warrior, let us say, and when it was begun it was something like this—

But when it was done, the warrior was like this—

(only handsomer still if possible), and the Princess put her name to the drawing ; and the Court and King and Queen, and above all poor Giglio, admired the picture of all things, and said, " Was there ever a genius like Angelica ? " So, I am sorry to say, was it with the Princess's embroidery and other accomplishments ; and Angelica actually believed that she did these things herself, and received all the flattery of the Court as if every word of it was true. Thus she began to think that there was no young woman in all the world equal to herself, and that no young man was good enough for her. As for Betsinda, as she heard none of these praises, she was not puffed up by them, and being a most grateful, good-natured girl, she was only too anxious to do everything which might give her mistress pleasure. Now you begin to perceive that Angelica had faults of her own, and was by no means such a wonder of wonders as people represented Her Royal Highness to be.

VI

How Prince Giglio Behaved Himself

AND NOW let us speak about Prince Giglio, the nephew of the reigning monarch of Paflagonia. It has already been stated, in page 174, that as long as he had a smart coat to wear, a good horse to ride, and money in his pocket, or rather to take out of his pocket, for he was very good-natured, my young Prince did not care for the loss of his crown and sceptre, being a thoughtless youth, not much inclined to politics or any kind of learning. So his tutor had a sinecure. Giglio would not learn classics or mathematics, and the Lord Chancellor of Paflagonia, SQUARETOSO, pulled a very long face because the Prince could not be got to study the Paflagonian laws and constitution ; but, on the other hand, the King's gamekeepers and huntsmen found the Prince an apt pupil ; the dancing-master pronounced that he was a most elegant and assiduous scholar ; the First Lord of the Billiard Table gave the most flattering reports of the Prince's skill ; so did the Groom of the Tennis Court ; and

as for the Captain of the Guard and Fencing-Master, the *valiant* and *veteran* Count KUTASOFF HEDZOFF, he avowed that since he ran the General of Crim Tartary, the dreadful Grumbuskin, through the body, he never had encountered so expert a swordsman as Prince Giglio.

I hope you do not imagine that there was any impropriety in the Prince and Princess walking together in the palace garden, and because Giglio kissed Angelica's hand in a polite manner. In the first place they are cousins ; next

the Queen is walking in the garden too (you cannot see her, for she happens to be behind that tree), and Her Majesty always wished that Angelica and Giglio should marry : so did Giglio : so did Angelica sometimes, for she thought her cousin very handsome, brave, and good-natured : but then you know she was so clever and knew so many things, and poor Giglio knew nothing, and had no conversation. When they looked at the stars, what did Giglio know of the heavenly bodies ? Once, when on a sweet night in a balcony where they were standing, Angelica said, " There is

the Bear." " Where ? " says Giglio. " Don't be afraid, Angelica ! if a dozen bears come, I will kill them rather than they shall hurt you." " Oh, you silly creature ! " says she ; " you are very good, but you are not very wise." When they looked at the flowers, Giglio was utterly unacquainted with botany, and had never heard of Linnæus. When the butterflies passed, Giglio knew nothing about them, being as ignorant of entomology as I am of algebra. So you see, Angelica, though she liked Giglio pretty well, despised him on account of his ignorance. I think she probably valued *her own learning* rather too much ; but to think too well of one's self is the fault of people of all ages and both sexes. Finally, when nobody else was there, Angelica liked her cousin well enough.

King Valoroso was very delicate in health, and withal so fond of good dinners (which were prepared for him by his French cook Marmitonio), that it was supposed he could not live long. Now the idea of anything happening to the King struck the artful Prime Minister and the designing old lady-in-waiting with terror. For, thought Glumboso and the Countess, " when Prince Giglio marries his cousin and

comes to the throne, what a pretty position we shall be in, whom he dislikes, and who have always been unkind to him. We shall lose our places in a trice ; Gruffanuff will have to give up all the jewels, laces, snuff-boxes, rings, and watches which belonged to the Queen, Giglio's mother ; and Glumboso will be forced to refund two hundred and seventeen thousand millions nine hundred and eighty-seven thousand four hundred and thirty-nine pounds, thirteen shillings, and sixpence halfpenny, money left to Prince Giglio by his poor dear father." So the Lady of Honour and the Prime Minister hated Giglio because they had done him a wrong ; and these unprincipled people invented a

hundred cruel stories about poor Giglio, in order to influence the King, Queen, and Princess against him ; how
he was so ignorant that he could not spell the commonest
words, and actually wrote Valoroso Valloroso, and spelt
Angelica with two l's ; how he drank a great deal too much
wine at dinner, and was always idling in the stables with
the grooms ; how he owed ever so much money at the
pastrycook's and the haberdasher's ; how he used to go to
sleep at church ; how he was fond of playing cards with the
pages. So did the Queen like playing cards ; so did the King
go to sleep at church, and eat and drink too much ; and, if
Giglio owed a trifle for tarts, who owed him two hundred
and seventeen thousand millions nine hundred and eighty-
seven thousand four hundred and thirty-nine pounds, thirteen shillings, and sixpence halfpenny, I should like to
know ? Detractors and tale-bearers (in my humble opinion)
had much better look at *home*. All this backbiting and slan-
dering had effect upon Princess Angelica, who began to
look coldly on her cousin, then to laugh at him and scorn
him for being so stupid, then to sneer at him for having
vulgar associates ; and at Court balls, dinners, and so forth
to treat him so unkindly that poor Giglio became quite ill,
took to his bed, and sent for the doctor.

His Majesty King Valoroso, as we have seen, had his own
reasons for disliking his nephew ; and as for those innocent
readers who ask why ?—I beg (with the permission of their
dear parents) to refer them to Shakespeare's pages, where
they will read why King John disliked Prince Arthur. With
the Queen, his royal but weak-minded aunt, when Giglio
was out of sight he was out of mind. While she had her
whist and her evening parties, she cared for little else.

I dare say *two villains*, who shall be nameless, wished
Doctor Pildrafto, the Court Physician, had killed Giglio
right out, but he only bled and physicked him so severely
that the Prince was kept to his room for several months,
and grew as thin as a post.

Whilst he was lying sick in this way, there came to the

Court of Paflagonia a famous painter, whose name was Tomaso Lorenzo, and who was Painter in Ordinary to the King of Crim Tartary, Paflagonia's neighbour. Tomaso Lorenzo painted all the Court, who were delighted with his works ; for even Countess Gruffanuff looked young and Glumboso good-humoured in his pictures. " He flatters very much," some people said. " Nay ! " says Princess Angelica, " I am above flattery, and I think he did not make my picture handsome enough. I can't bear to hear a man of genius unjustly cried down, and I hope my dear

papa will make Lorenzo a knight of his Order of the Cucumber."

The Princess Angelica, although the courtiers vowed Her Royal Highness could draw so *beautifully* that the idea of her taking lessons was absurd, yet chose to have Lorenzo for a teacher, and it was wonderful, *as long as she painted in his studio*, what beautiful pictures she made ! Some of the performances were engraved for the Book of Beauty : others were sold for enormous sums at Charity Bazaars. She wrote the *signatures* under the drawings, no doubt, but I think I know who did the pictures—this artful painter, who had come with other designs on Angelica than merely to teach her to draw.

One day, Lorenzo showed the Princess a portrait of a young man in armour, with fair hair and the loveliest blue eyes, and an expression at once melancholy and interesting.

" Dear Signor Lorenzo, who is this ? " asked the Princess.

" I never saw anyone so handsome," says Countess Gruffanuff (the old humbug).

" That," said the painter, " that, madam, is the portrait of my august young master, His Royal Highness Bulbo, Crown Prince of Crim Tartary, Duke of Acroceraunia, Marquis of Poluphloisboio, and Knight Grand Cross of the Order of the Pumpkin. That is the Order of the Pumpkin glittering on his manly breast, and received by His Royal Highness from his august father, His Majesty King PADELLA I., for his gallantry at the battle of Rimbombamento, when he slew with his own princely hand the King of Ograria and two hundred and eleven giants of the two hundred and eighteen who formed the King's bodyguard. The remainder were destroyed by the brave Crim Tartar army after an obstinate combat, in which the Crim Tartars suffered severely."

What a Prince ! thought Angelica : so brave—so calm-looking—so young—what a hero !

" He is as accomplished as he is brave," continued the Court Painter. " He knows all languages perfectly : sings deliciously : plays every instrument : composes operas which have been acted a thousand nights running at the Imperial Theatre of Crim Tartary, and danced in a ballet there before the King and Queen ; in which he looked so beautiful, that his cousin, the lovely daughter of the King of Circassia, died for love of him."

"Why did he not marry the poor Princess?" asked Angelica, with a sigh.

"Because they were *first cousins*, madam, and the clergy forbid these unions," said the Painter. "And, besides, the young Prince had given his royal heart *elsewhere*."

"And to whom?" asked Her Royal Highness.

"I am not at liberty to mention the Princess's name," answered the Painter.

"But you may tell me the first letter of it," gasped out the Princess.

"That your Royal Highness is at liberty to guess," said Lorenzo.

"Does it begin with a Z?" asked Angelica.

The Painter said it wasn't a Z; then she tried a Y; then an X; then a W, and went so backwards through almost the whole alphabet.

When she came to D, and it wasn't D, she grew very much excited; when she came to C, and it wasn't C, she was still more nervous; when she came to B, *and it wasn't B*, "O dearest Gruffanuff," she said, "lend me your smelling-bottle!" and, hiding her head in the Countess's shoulder, she faintly whispered, "Ah, Signor, can it be A?"

"It was A; and though I may not, by my Royal Master's orders, tell your Royal Highness the Princess's name, whom he fondly, madly, devotedly, rapturously loves, I may show you her portrait," says this slyboots: and leading the Princess up to a gilt frame, he drew a curtain which was before it.

O goodness! the frame contained A LOOKING-GLASS! and Angelica saw her own face!

VII

How Giglio and Angelica had a Quarrel

THE COURT PAINTER of His Majesty the King of Crim Tartary returned to that monarch's dominions, carrying away a number of sketches which he had made in the Paflagonian capital (you know, of course, my dears, that the name of that capital is Blombodinga) ; but the most charming of all his pieces was a portrait of the Princess Angelica, which all the Crim Tartar nobles came to see. With this work the King was so delighted, that he decorated the Painter with his Order of the Pumpkin (sixth class), and the artist became Sir Tomaso Lorenzo, K.P., thenceforth.

King Valoroso also sent Sir Tomaso his Order of the Cucumber, besides a handsome order for money, for he painted the King, Queen, and principal nobility while at Blombodinga, and became all the fashion, to the perfect rage of all the artists in Paflagonia, where the King used to point to the portrait of Prince Bulbo, which Sir Tomaso had left behind him, and say, " Which among you can paint a picture like that ? "

It hung in the royal parlour over the royal sideboard, and Princess Angelica could always look at it as she sat making the tea. Each day it seemed to grow handsomer and handsomer, and the Princess grew so fond of looking at it, that she would often spill the tea over the cloth, at which her father and mother would wink and wag their heads, and say to each other, " Aha ! we see how things are going."

In the meanwhile poor Giglio lay upstairs very sick in his chamber, though he took all the doctor's horrible medicines like a good young lad ; as I hope *you* do, my dears, when you are ill and mamma sends for the medical man. And the only person who visited Giglio (besides his friend the captain of the guard, who was almost always busy or on parade), was little Betsinda the housemaid, who used to do his bedroom and sitting-room out, bring him his gruel, and warm his bed.

When the little housemaid came to him in the morning and evening, Prince Giglio used to say, " Betsinda, Betsinda, how is the Princess Angelica ? "

And Betsinda used to answer, " The Princess is very well, thank you, my Lord." And Giglio would heave a sigh, and think, if Angelica were sick, I am sure *I* should not be very well.

Then Giglio would say, " Betsinda, has the Princess Angelica asked for me to-day ? " And Betsinda would answer, " No, my Lord, not to-day " ; or, " she was very busy practising the piano when I saw her " ; or, " she was writing invitations for an evening party, and did not speak to me " ; or make some excuse or other, not strictly consonant with truth : for Betsinda was such a good-natured creature, that she strove to do everything to prevent annoyance to Prince Giglio, and even brought him up roast chicken and jellies from the kitchen (when the Doctor allowed them, and Giglio was getting better), saying, " that the Princess had made the jelly, or the bread-sauce, with her own hands, on purpose for Giglio."

When Giglio heard this he took heart and began to mend immediately ; and gobbled up all the jelly, and picked the last bone of the chicken—drumsticks, merry-thought, sides'-bones, back, pope's nose, and all—thanking his dear Angelica ; and he felt so much better the next day, that he dressed and went downstairs, where, whom should he meet but Angelica going into the drawing-room ? All the covers were off the chairs, the chandeliers taken out of the bags, the damask curtains uncovered, the work and things carried away, and the handsomest albums on the tables. Angelica had her hair in papers : in a word, it was evident there was going to be a party.

" Heavens, Giglio ! " cries Angelica ; " *you* here in such a dress ! What a figure you are ! "

" Yes, dear Angelica, I am come downstairs, and feel so well to-day, thanks to the *fowl* and the *jelly*."

" What do I know about fowls and jellies, that you allude to them in that rude way ? " says Angelica.

" Why, didn't—didn't you send them, Angelica dear ? " says Giglio.

" I send them indeed ! Angelica dear ! No, Giglio dear," says she, mocking him, " *I* was engaged in getting the rooms ready for His Royal Highness the Prince of Crim Tartary, who is coming to pay my papa's Court a visit."

" The — Prince — of — Crim — Tartary ! " Giglio said, aghast.

" Yes, the Prince of Crim Tartary," says Angelica, mocking him. " I dare say you never heard of such a country. What *did* you ever hear of ? You don't know whether Crim Tartary is on the Red Sea or on the Black Sea, I dare say."

" Yes, I do, it's on the Red Sea," says Giglio, at which the Princess burst out laughing at him, and said, " Oh, you ninny ! You are so ignorant, you are really not fit for society ! You know nothing but about horses and dogs, and are only fit to dine in a mess-room with my Royal father's heaviest dragoons. Don't look so surprised at me, sir : go and put your best clothes on to receive the Prince, and let me get the drawing-room ready."

Giglio said, " Oh, Angelica, Angelica, I didn't think this of you. *This* wasn't your language to me when you gave me this ring, and I gave you mine in the garden, and you gave me that k——"

But what k was we never shall know, for Angelica, in a rage, cried, " Get out, you saucy, rude creature ! How dare you to remind me of your rudeness ? As for your little trumpery twopenny ring, there, sir, there ! " And she flung it out of the window.

" It was my mother's marriage-ring," cried Giglio.

" *I* don't care whose marriage-ring it was," cries Angelica. " Marry the person who picks it up if she's a woman ; you shan't marry *me*. And give me back *my* ring. I've no patience with people who boast about the things they give away ! *I* know who'll give me much finer things than you ever gave me. A beggarly ring indeed, not worth five shillings ! "

Now Angelica little knew that the ring which Giglio had given her was a fairy ring : if a man wore it, it made all the women in love with him ; if a woman, all the gentlemen. The Queen, Giglio's mother, quite an ordinary-looking person, was admired immensely whilst she wore this ring, and her husband was frantic when she was ill. But when she called her little Giglio to her, and put the ring on his finger, King Savio did not seem to care for his wife so much any more, but transferred all his love to little Giglio. So did everybody love him as long as he had the ring ; but when, as quite a child, he gave it to Angelica, people began to love and admire *her* ; and Giglio, as the saying is, played only second fiddle.

" Yes," says Angelica, going on in her foolish ungrateful way. " *I* know who'll give me much finer things than your beggarly little pearl nonsense."

" Very good, miss ! You may take back your ring too ! " says Giglio, his eyes flashing fire at her, and then, as if his eyes had been suddenly opened, he cried out, " Ha ! what does this mean ? Is *this* the woman I have been in love with all my life ? Have I been such a ninny as to throw away my regard upon *you* ? Why—actually—yes—you are a little crooked ! "

" Oh, you wretch ! " cries Angelica.

" And, upon my conscience, you—you squint a little."

" Eh ! " cries Angelica.

" And your hair is red—and you are marked with the smallpox—and what ? you have three false teeth—and one leg shorter than the other ! "

" You brute, you brute, you ! " Angelica screamed out : and as she seized the ring with one hand, she dealt Giglio one, two, three smacks on the face, and would have pulled the hair off his head had he not started laughing, and crying—

" Oh dear me, Angelica, don't pull out *my* hair, it hurts ! You might remove a great deal of *your own*, as I perceive, without scissors or pulling at all. Oh, ho, ho ! ha, ha, ha ! he, he, he ! "

And he nearly choked himself with laughing, and she with rage ; when, with a low bow, and dressed in his Court habit, Count Gambabella, the first lord-in-waiting, entered,

and said, " Royal Highnesses ! Their Majesties expect you
in the Pink Throne-room, where they await the arrival of
the Prince of CRIM TARTARY."

VIII

How Gruffanuff Picked the Fairy Ring Up, and Prince Bulbo Came to Court

PRINCE BULBO'S arrival had set all the Court in a flutter :
everybody was ordered to put his or her best clothes on :
the footmen had their gala liveries ; the Lord Chancellor
his new wig ; the Guards their last new tunics ; and Countess Gruffanuff, you may be sure, was glad of an opportunity of decorating *her* old person with her finest things.
She was walking through the court of the Palace on her
way to wait upon their Majesties, when she spied something glittering on the pavement, and bade the boy in
buttons who was holding up her train to go and pick up
the article shining yonder. He was an ugly little wretch, in
some of the late groom-porter's old clothes cut down, and
much too tight for him ; and yet, when he had taken up
the ring (as it turned out to be), and was carrying it to his
mistress, she thought he looked like a little Cupid. He gave
the ring to her ; it was a trumpery little thing enough, but

too small for any of her old knuckles, so she put it into her pocket.

"Oh, mum!" says the boy, looking at her, "how—how beyoutiful you do look, mum, to-day, mum!"

"And you, too, Jacky," she was going to say; but, looking down at him—no, he was no longer good-looking at all

—but only the carroty-haired little Jacky of the morning. However, praise is welcome from the ugliest of men or boys, and Gruffanuff, bidding the boy hold up her train, walked on in high good-humour. The guards saluted her with peculiar respect. Captain Hedzoff, in the ante-room, said, "My dear madam, you look like an angel to-day." And so, bowing and smirking, Gruffanuff went in and took her place behind her Royal Master and Mistress, who were in the throne-room, awaiting the Prince of Crim Tartary.

Princess Angelica sat at their feet, and behind the King's chair stood Prince Giglio, looking very savage.

The Prince of Crim Tartary made his appearance, attended by Baron Sleibootz, his chamberlain, and followed by a black page carrying the most beautiful crown you ever saw ! He was dressed in his travelling costume, and his hair, as you see, was a little in disorder. " I have ridden

HIS R.H. THE PRINCE OF CRIM TARTARY

three hundred miles since breakfast," said he, " so eager was I to behold the Prin—the Court and august family of Paflagonia, and I could not wait one minute before appearing in your Majesties' presences."

Giglio, from behind the throne, burst out into a roar of contemptuous laughter ; but all the Royal party, in fact, were so flurried, that they did not hear this little outbreak. " Your R.H. is welcome in any dress," says the King. " Glumboso, a chair for His Royal Highness."

" Any dress his Royal Highness wears *is* a Court dress,"
says Princess Angelica, smiling graciously.

" Ah ! but you should see my other clothes," said the
Prince. " I should have had them on, but that stupid
carrier has not brought them. Who's that laughing ? "

It was Giglio laughing. " I was laughing," he said,
" because you said just now that you were in such a hurry
to see the Princess, that you could not wait to change your
dress ; and now you say you come in those clothes because
you have no others."

" And who are you ? " says Prince Bulbo, very fiercely.

" My father was King of this country, and I am his only
son, Prince ! " replies Giglio, with equal haughtiness.

" Ha ! " said the King and Glumboso, looking very
flurried ; but the former, collecting himself, said, " Dear
Prince Bulbo, I forgot to introduce to your Royal Highness
my dear nephew, His Royal Highness Prince Giglio !
Know each other ! Embrace each other ! Giglio, give His
Royal Highness your hand ! " and Giglio, giving his hand,
squeezed poor Bulbo's until the tears ran out of his eyes.
Glumboso now brought a chair for the royal visitor, and
placed it on the platform on which the King, Queen, and
Prince were seated ; but the chair was on the edge of the
platform, and as Bulbo sat down, it toppled over, and he
with it, rolling over and over, and bellowing like a bull.
Giglio roared still louder at this disaster, but it was with
laughter ; so did all the Court when Prince Bulbo got up :
for though when he entered the room he appeared not very
ridiculous, as he stood up from his fall for a moment he
looked so exceedingly plain and foolish, that nobody could
help laughing at him. When he had entered the room, he
was observed to carry a rose in his hand, which fell out of
it as he tumbled.

" My rose ! my rose ! " cried Bulbo ; and his chamberlain dashed forwards and picked it up, and gave it to the
Prince, who put it in his waistcoat. Then people wondered
why they had laughed ; there was nothing particularly

ridiculous in him. He was rather short, rather stout, **rather** red-haired, but, in fine, for a Prince, not so bad.

So they sat and talked, the royal personages together, **the** Crim Tartar officers with those of Paflagonia—Giglio **very** comfortable with Gruffanuff behind the throne. He looked at her with such tender eyes, that her heart was all in **a** flutter. " Oh, dear Prince," she said, " how could you speak so haughtily in presence of their Majesties ? I pro-test I thought I should have fainted."

" I should have caught you in my arms," said Giglio, looking raptures.

" Why were you so cruel to Prince Bulbo, dear Prince ? " says Gruff.

" Because I hate him," says Gil.

" You are jealous of him, and still love poor Angelica," cries Gruffanuff, putting her handkerchief to her eyes.

" I did, but I love her no more ! " Giglio cried. " I despise her ! Were she heiress to twenty thousand thrones, I would despise her and scorn her. But why speak of thrones ? I have lost mine. I am too weak to recover it—I am alone, and have no friend."

" Oh, say not so, dear Prince ! " says Gruffanuff.

" Besides," says he, " I am so happy here *behind the throne*
that I would not change my place, no, not for the throne
of the world ! "

" What are you two people chattering about there ? "
says the Queen, who was rather good-natured, though not
over-burthened with wisdom. " It is time to dress for dinner.
Giglio, show Prince Bulbo to his room. Prince, if your
clothes have not come, we shall be very happy to see you
as you are." But when Prince Bulbo got to his bedroom, his
luggage was there and unpacked ; and the hairdresser
coming in, cut and curled him entirely to his own satisfaction ; and when the dinner-bell rang, the royal company
had not to wait above five-and-twenty minutes until Bulbo
appeared, during which time the King, who could not bear
to wait, grew as sulky as possible. As for Giglio, he never
left Madam Gruffanuff all this time, but stood with her in
the embrasure of a window, paying her compliments. At
length the Groom of the Chambers announced His Royal
Highness the Prince of Crim Tartary ! and the noble company went into the royal dining-room. It was quite a small
party ; only the King and Queen, the Princess, whom Bulbo
took out, the two Princes, Countess Gruffanuff, Glumboso
the Prime Minister, and Prince Bulbo's chamberlain. You
may be sure they had a very good dinner—let every boy
or girl think of what he or she likes best, and fancy it on
the table.[1]

The Princess talked incessantly all dinner-time to the
Prince of Crimea, who ate an immense deal too much, and
never took his eyes off his plate, except when Giglio, who
was carving a goose, sent a quantity of stuffing and onion
sauce into one of them. Giglio only burst out a-laughing as
the Crimean Prince wiped his shirt-front and face with his
scented pocket-handkerchief. He did not make Prince Bulbo
any apology. When the Prince looked at him, Giglio would

[1] Here a very pretty game may be played by all the children saying
what they like best for dinner.

not look that way. When Prince Bulbo said, " Prince
Giglio, may I have the honour of taking a glass of wine
with you ? " Giglio *wouldn't* answer. All his talk and his
eyes were for Countess Gruffanuff, who you may be sure
was pleased with Giglio's attentions—the vain old creature ! When he was not complimenting her, he was making
fun of Prince Bulbo, so loud that Gruffanuff was always

tapping him with her fan, and saying—" Oh, you satirical
Prince ! Oh, fie, the Prince will hear ! " " Well, I don't
mind," says Giglio, louder still. The King and Queen
luckily did not hear ; for Her Majesty was a little deaf,
and the King thought so much about his own dinner, and,
besides, made such a dreadful noise, hobgobbling in eating
it, that he heard nothing else. After dinner, His Majesty
and the Queen went to sleep in their arm-chairs.

This was the time when Giglio began his tricks with Prince Bulbo, plying that young gentleman with port, sherry, madeira, champagne, marsala, cherry-brandy, and pale ale, of all of which Master Bulbo drank without stint. But in plying his guest, Giglio was obliged to drink himself, and, I am sorry to say, took more than was good for him, so that the young men were very noisy, rude, and foolish when they joined the ladies after dinner ; and dearly did they pay for that imprudence, as now, my darlings, you shall hear !

Bulbo went and sat by the piano, where Angelica was playing and singing, and he sang out of tune, and he upset

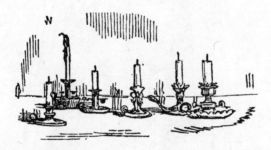

the coffee when the footman brought it, and he laughed out of place, and talked absurdly, and fell asleep and snored horribly. Booh, the nasty pig ! But as he lay there stretched on the pink satin sofa, Angelica still persisted in thinking him the most beautiful of human beings. No doubt the magic rose which Bulbo wore caused this infatuation on Angelica's part ; but is she the first young woman who has thought a silly fellow charming ?

Giglio must go and sit by Gruffanuff, whose old face he too every moment began to find more lovely. He paid the most outrageous compliments to her :—There never was such a darling—Older than he was ?—Fiddle-de-dee ! He would marry her—he would have nothing but her !

To marry the heir to the throne ! Here was a chance ! The artful hussy actually got a sheet of paper, and wrote upon it, " This is to give notice that I, Giglio, only son of Savio, King of Paflagonia, hereby promise to marry the charming and virtuous Barbara Griselda, Countess Gruff-anuff, and widow of the late Jenkins Gruffanuff, Esq."

" What is it you are writing, you charming Gruffy ? " says Giglio, who was lolling on the sofa, by the writing-table.

" Only an order for you to sign, dear Prince, for giving coals and blankets to the poor, this cold weather. Look ! the King and Queen are both asleep, and your Royal Highness's order will do."

So Giglio, who was very good-natured, as Gruffy well knew, signed the order immediately ; and, when she had it in her pocket, you may fancy what airs she gave herself. She was ready to flounce out of the room before the Queen herself, as now she was the wife of the *rightful* King of Paflagonia ! She would not speak to Glumboso, whom she thought a brute, for depriving her *dear husband* of the crown ! And when candles came, and she had helped to undress the Queen and Princess, she went into her own room, and actually practised on a sheet of paper, " Griselda Paflagonia," " Barbara Regina," " Griselda Barbara, Paf. Reg.," and I don't know what signatures besides, against the day when she should be Queen, forsooth !

IX

How Betsinda got the Warming-Pan

L I T T L E Betsinda came in to put Gruffanuff's hair in papers ; and the Countess was so pleased, that, for a wonder, she complimented Betsinda. " Betsinda ! " she said, " you dressed my hair very nicely to-day ; I promised you a little present. Here are five sh—— no, here is a pretty little ring, that I picked—that I have had some time." And she gave Betsinda the ring she had picked up in the court. It fitted Betsinda exactly.

"It's like the ring the Princess used to wear," says the maid.

"No such thing," says Gruffanuff, "I have had it this ever so long. There, tuck me up quite comfortable ; and now, as it's a very cold night (the snow was beating in at the window), you may go and warm dear Prince Giglio's bed, like a good girl, and then you may unrip my green silk, and then you can just do me up a little cap for the morning, and then you can mend that hole in my silk stocking, and then you can go to bed, Betsinda. Mind I shall want my cup of tea at five o'clock in the morning."

"I suppose I had best warm both the young gentlemen's beds, ma'am," says Betsinda.

Gruffanuff, for reply, said, "Hau-au-ho !—Grau-haw-hoo !—Hong-hrho !" In fact, she was snoring sound asleep.

Her room, you know, is next to the King and Queen, and the Princess is next to them. So pretty Betsinda went away for the coals to the kitchen, and filled the royal warming-pan.

Now, she was a very kind, merry, civil, pretty girl ; but there must have been something very captivating about her this evening, for all the women in the servant's hall began to scold and abuse her. The housekeeper said she was a pert, stuck-up thing ; the upper-housemaid asked, how dare she wear such ringlets and ribbons, it was quite improper ! The cook (for there was a woman-cook as well as a man-cook) said to the kitchen-maid that *she* never could see anything in that creetur : but as for the men, every one of them, Coachman, John, Buttons the page, and Monsieur, the Prince of Crim Tartary's valet, started up, and said—

"My eyes !"
"O mussey !"   "What a pretty girl Betsinda is !"
"O jemmany !"
"O ciel !"

"Hands off ; none of your impertinence, you vulgar, low

people ! " says Betsinda, walking off with her pan of coals.
She heard the young gentlemen playing at billiards as she
went upstairs : first to Prince Giglio's bed, which she
warmed, and then to Prince Bulbo's room.

He came in just as she had done ; and as soon as he saw
her, " O ! O ! O ! O ! O ! O ! what a beyou—oo—ootiful
creature you are ! You angel—you peri—you rosebud, let
me be thy bulbul—thy Bulbo, too ! Fly to the desert, fly
with me ! I never saw a young gazelle to glad me with its
dark blue eye that had eyes like thine. Thou nymph of

beauty, take, take this young heart. A truer never did itself
sustain within a soldier's waistcoat. Be mine ! Be mine ! Be
Princess of Crim Tartary ! My Royal father will approve
our union ; and, as for that little carroty-haired Angelica,
I do not care a fig for her any more."

" Go away, your Royal Highness, and go to bed, please,"
said Betsinda, with the warming-pan.

But Bulbo said, " No, never, till thou swearest to be mine,
thou lovely, blushing, chambermaid divine ! Here, at thy
feet, the Royal Bulbo lies, the trembling captive of Betsinda's eyes."

10

And he went on, making himself so *absurd and ridiculous*, that Betsinda, who was full of fun, gave him a touch with the warming-pan, which I promise you, made him cry ' O-o-o-o ! '' in a very different manner.

Prince Bulbo made such a noise that Prince Giglio, who heard him from the next room, came in to see what was

THE RIVALS

the matter. As soon as he saw what was taking place, Giglio, in a fury, rushed on Bulbo, kicked him in the rudest manner up to the ceiling, and went on kicking him till his hair was quite out of curl.

Poor Betsinda did not know whether to laugh or to cry ; the kicking certainly must hurt the Prince, but then he looked so droll ! When Giglio had done knocking him up and down to the ground, and whilst he went into a corner rubbing himself, what do you think Giglio does? He goes down on his own knees to Betsinda, takes her hand, begs her to accept his heart, and offers to marry her that moment. Fancy Betsinda's condition, who had been in love with the Prince ever since she first saw him in the palace garden, when she was quite a little child.

"Oh, divine Betsinda!" says the Prince, "how have I lived fifteen years in thy company without seeing thy perfections? What woman in all Europe, Asia, Africa, and America, nay, in Australia, only it is not yet discovered, can presume to be thy equal? Angelica? Pish! Gruffanuff? Phoo! The Queen? Ha, ha! Thou art my Queen. Thou art the real Angelica, because thou art really angelic."

"Oh, Prince! I am but a poor chambermaid," says Betsinda, looking, however, very much pleased.

"Didst thou not tend me in my sickness, when all forsook me?" continues Giglio. "Did not thy gentle hand smooth my pillow, and bring me jelly and roast chicken?"

"Yes, dear Prince, I did," says Betsinda, "and I sewed your Royal Highness's shirt-buttons on too, if you please, your Royal Highness," cries this artless maiden.

When poor Prince Bulbo, who was now madly in love with Betsinda, heard this declaration, when he saw the unmistakable glances which she flung upon Giglio, Bulbo began to cry bitterly, and tore quantities of hair out of his head, till it all covered the room like so much tow.

Betsinda had left the warming-pan on the floor while the Princes were going on with their conversation, and as they began now to quarrel and be very fierce with one another, she thought proper to run away.

"You great big blubbering booby, tearing your hair in the corner there; of course you will give me satisfaction for insulting Betsinda. *You* dare to kneel down at Princess Giglio's knees and kiss her hand!"

"She's not Princess Giglio!" roars out Bulbo. "She

shall be Princess Bulbo, no other shall be Princess Bulbo."

" You are engaged to my cousin ! " bellows out Giglio.

" I hate your cousin," says Bulbo.

" You shall give me satisfaction for insulting her ! " cries Giglio in a fury.

" I'll have your life."

" I'll run you through."

" I'll cut your throat."

" I'll blow your brains out."

" I'll knock your head off."

" I'll send a friend to you in the morning."

" I'll send a bullet into you in the afternoon."

" We'll meet again," says Giglio, shaking his fist in Bulbo's face ; and seizing up the warming-pan, he kissed it, because, forsooth, Betsinda had carried it, and rushed downstairs. What should he see on the landing but His Majesty talking to Betsinda, whom he called by all sorts of fond names. His Majesty had heard a row in the building, so he stated, and smelling something burning, had come out to see what the matter was.

" It's the young gentlemen smoking, perhaps, sir," says Betsinda.

" Charming chambermaid," says the King (like all the

rest of them), " never mind the young men ! Turn thy eyes on a middle-aged autocrat, who has been considered not ill-looking in his time."

" Oh, sir ! what will Her Majesty say ? " cries Betsinda.

" Her Majesty ! " laughs the monarch. " Her Majesty be hanged. Am I not Autocrat of Paflagonia ? Have I not blocks, ropes, axes, hangmen—ha ? Runs not a river by my palace wall ? Have I not sacks to sew up wives withal ? Say but the word, that thou wilt be mine own, your mistress straightway in a sack is sewn, and thou the sharer of my heart and throne."

When Giglio heard these atrocious sentiments, he forgot the respect usually paid to Royalty, lifted up the warming-pan, and knocked down the King as flat as a pancake ; after which, Master Giglio took to his heels and ran away, and Betsinda went off screaming, and the Queen, Gruff-anuff, and the Princess, all came out of their rooms. Fancy their feelings on beholding their husband, father, sovereign, in this posture !

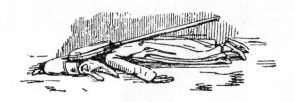

X

How King Valoroso was in a Dreadful Passion

As soon as the coals began to burn him, the King came to himself and stood up. " Ho ! my captain of the guards ! " His Majesty exclaimed, stamping his royal feet with rage. O piteous spectacle ! the King's nose was bent quite crooked by the blow of Prince Giglio ! His Majesty ground his teeth with rage. " Hedzoff," he said, taking a death-warrant out

of his dressing-gown pocket, " Hedzoff, good Hedzoff, seize upon the Prince. Thou'lt find him in his chamber two pair up. But now he dared, with sacrilegious hand, to strike the sacred night-cap of a king—Hedzoff, and floor me with a warming-pan ! Away, no more demur, the villain dies ! See it be done, or else,—h'm !—ha !—h'm mind thine own eyes ! " and followed by the ladies, and lifting up the tails of his dressing-gown, the King entered his own apartment.

Captain Hedzoff was very much affected, having a sincere love for Giglio. "Poor, poor Giglio!" he said, the tears rolling over his manly face, and dripping down his moustachios; "my noble young Prince, is it my hand must lead thee to death?"

"Lead him to fiddlestick, Hedzoff," said a female voice. It was Gruffanuff, who had come out in her dressing-gown, when she heard the noise. "The King said you were to hang the Prince. Well, hang the Prince."

"I don't understand you," says Hedzoff, who was not a very clever man.

"You Gaby! he didn't say *which* Prince," says Gruffanuff.

"No; he didn't say which, certainly," said Hedzoff.

"Well then, take Bulbo, and hang *him*!"

When Captain Hedzoff heard this, he began to dance about for joy. "Obedience is a soldier's honour," says he. "Prince Bulbo's head will do capitally," and he went to arrest the Prince the very first thing next morning.

He knocked at the door. "Who's there?" says Bulbo. "Captain Hedzoff? Step in, pray, my good Captain; I'm delighted to see you; I have been expecting you."

"Have you?" says Hedzoff.

"Sleibootz, my Chamberlain, will act for me," says the Prince.

"I beg your Royal Highness's pardon, but you will have to act for yourself, and it's a pity to wake Baron Sleibootz."

The Prince Bulbo still seemed to take the matter very coolly. "Of course, Captain," says he, "you are come about that affair with Prince Giglio?"

"Precisely," says Hedzoff, "that affair of Prince Giglio."

"Is it to be pistols, or swords, Captain?" asks Bulbo. "I'm a pretty good hand with both, and I'll do for Prince Giglio as sure as my name is my Royal Highness Prince Bulbo."

" There's some mistake, my Lord," says the Captain.
" The business is done with *axes* among us."

" Axes ? That's sharp work," says Bulbo. " Call my
Chamberlain, he'll be my second, and in ten minutes, I
flatter myself, you'll see Master Giglio's head off his impertinent shoulders. I'm hungry for his blood. Hoo-oo,
aw ! " and he looked as savage as an ogre.

" I beg your pardon, sir, but by this warrant I am to take
you prisoner, and hand you over to—to the executioner."

" Pooh, pooh, my good man !—Stop, I say,—ho !—

hulloa ! " was all that this luckless Prince was enabled to
say, for Hedzoff's guards seizing him, tied a handkerchief
over his mouth and face, and carried him to the place of
execution.

The King, who happened to be talking to Glumboso,
saw him pass, and took a pinch of snuff and said, " So
much for Giglio. Now let's go to breakfast."

The Captain of the Guard handed over his prisoner to
the Sheriff, with the fatal order,

" AT SIGHT CUT OFF THE BEARER'S HEAD.

" VALOROSO XXIV."

" It's a mistake," says Bulbo, who did not seem to understand the business in the least.

" Poo—poo—pooh," says the Sheriff. " Fetch Jack Ketch instantly. Jack Ketch ! "

And poor Bulbo was led to the scaffold, where an executioner with a block and a tremendous axe was always ready in case he should be wanted.

But we must now revert to Giglio and Betsinda.

XI

What Gruffanuff Did to Giglio and Betsinda

GRUFFANUFF, who had seen what had happened with the King, and knew that Giglio must come to grief, got up very early the next morning, and went to devise some plans for rescuing her darling husband, as the silly old thing insisted on calling him. She found him walking up and down the garden, thinking of a rhyme for Betsinda (*tinder* and *winda* were all he could find), and indeed having forgotten all about the past evening, except that Betsinda was the most lovely of beings.

" Well, dear Giglio," says Gruff.

" Well, dear Gruffy," says Giglio, only *he* was quite satirical.

" I have been thinking, darling, what you must do in this scrape. You must fly the country for a while."

" What scrape ?—fly the country ? Never without her I love, Countess," says Giglio.

" No, she will accompany you, dear Prince," she says, in her most coaxing accents. " First, we must get the jewels belonging to our royal parents, and those of her and his present Majesty. Here is the key, duck ; they are all yours, you know, by right, for you are the rightful King of Paflagonia, and your wife will be the rightful Queen."

" Will she ? " says Giglio.

" Yes ; and having got the jewels, go to Glumboso's

apartment, where, under his bed, you will find sacks containing money to the amount of £217,000,000,987,439, 13s. 6½d., all belonging to you, for he took it out of your royal father's room on the day of his death. With this we will fly."

" *We* will fly ? " says Giglio.

" Yes, you and your bride—your affianced love—your Gruffy! " says the Countess, with a languishing leer.

" *You* my bride ! " says Giglio. "You, you hideous old woman ! "

" Oh, you—you wretch ! didn't you give me this paper promising marriage ? " cries Gruff.

" Get away, you old goose ! I love Betsinda, and Betsinda only ! " And in a fit of terror he ran from her as quickly as he could.

" He ! he ! he ! " shrieks out Gruff; " a promise is a promise if there are laws in Paflagonia ! And as for that monster, that wretch, that fiend, that ugly little vixen— as for that upstart, that ingrate, that beast, Betsinda, Master Giglio will have no little difficulty in discovering her whereabouts. He may look very long before finding *her*, I warrant. He little knows that Miss Betsinda is——"

Is—what ? Now, you shall hear. Poor Betsinda got up at five in winter's morning to bring her cruel mistress her tea ;

and instead of finding her in a good humour, found Gruffy
as cross as two sticks. The Countess boxed Betsinda's ears
half a dozen times whilst she was dressing; but as poor
little Betsinda was used to this kind of treatment, she did
not feel any special alarm. " And now," says she, " when
Her Majesty rings her bell twice, I'll trouble you, miss, to
attend."

So when the Queen's bell rang twice, Betsinda came to
Her Majesty and made a pretty little curtsey. The Queen,
the Princess, and Gruffanuff were all three in the room. As
soon as they saw her they began,

" You wretch ! " says the Queen.

" You little vulgar thing ! " says the Princess.

" You beast ! " says Gruffanuff.

" Get out of my sight ! " says the Queen.

" Go away with you, do ! " says the Princess.

" Quit the premises ! " says Gruffanuff.

" Alas ! and woe is me ! " Very lamentable events had
occurred to Betsinda that morning, and all in consequence
of that fatal warming-pan business of the previous night.
The King had offered to marry her ; of course Her Majesty
the Queen was jealous : Bulbo had fallen in love with her ;
of course Angelica was furious : Giglio was in love with her,
and oh, what a fury Gruffy was in !

" Take off that $\left\{ \begin{array}{l} \text{cap} \\ \text{petticoat} \\ \text{gown} \end{array} \right\}$ $\begin{array}{l} \text{I gave you,"} \\ \text{they said, all} \\ \text{at once,} \end{array}$

and began tearing the clothes off poor Betsinda.

" How $\left\{ \begin{array}{l} \text{the King?"} \\ \text{Prince Bulbo?"} \\ \text{Prince Giglio?"} \end{array} \right.$ $\begin{array}{l} \text{cried the Queen,} \\ \text{the Princess, and} \\ \text{Countess.} \end{array}$

" Give her the rags she wore when she came into the
house, and turn her out of it ! " cries the Queen.

" Mind she does not go with *my* shoes on, which I lent
her so kindly," says the Princess ; and indeed the Princess's
shoes were a great deal too big for Betsinda.

" Come with me, you filthy hussy ! " and taking up the

Queen's poker, the cruel Gruffanuff drove Betsinda into her room.

The Countess went to the glass box in which she had kept Betsinda's old cloak and shoe this ever so long, and said, " Take those rags, you little beggar creature, and strip off everything belonging to honest people, and go about your business " ; and she actually tore off the poor little delicate thing's back almost all her things, and told her to be off out of the house.

Poor Betsinda huddled the cloak round her back, on which were embroidered the letters PRIN . . . . ROSAL . . . . and then came a great rent.

As for the shoe, what was she to do with one poor little tootsey sandal ? the string was still to it, so she hung it round her neck.

" Won't you give me a pair of shoes to go out in the snow, mum, if you please, mum ? " cried the poor child.

" No, you wicked beast ! " says Gruffanuff, driving her along with the poker—driving her down the cold stairs—

driving her through the cold hall—flinging her out into the cold street, so that the knocker itself shed tears to see her !

But a kind fairy made the soft snow warm for her little feet, and she wrapped herself up in the ermine of her mantle, and was gone !

" And now let us think about breakfast," says the greedy Queen.

" What dress shall I put on, mamma ? the pink or the pea-green ? " says Angelica. " Which do you think the dear Prince will like best ? "

" Mrs. V. ! " sings out the King from his dressing-room, " let us have sausages for breakfast ! Remember we have Prince Bulbo staying with us ! "

And they all went to get ready.

Nine o'clock came, and they were all in the breakfast room, and no Prince Bulbo as yet. The urn was hissing and humming : the muffins were smoking—such a heap of muffins ! the eggs were done, there was a pot of raspberry jam, and coffee, and a beautiful chicken and tongue on the side-table. Marmitonio the cook brought in the sausages. Oh, how nice they smelt !

" Where is Bulbo ? " said the King. " John, where is His Royal Highness ? "

John said he had a took hup His Roilighnessesses shaving-water, and his clothes and things, and he wasn't in his room, which he sposed His Royliness was just stepped hout.

" Stepped out before breakfast in the snow ! Impossible !" says the King, sticking his fork into a sausage. " My dear, take one. Angelica, won't you have a saveloy ? " The Princess took one, being very fond of them ; and at this moment Glumboso entered with Captain Hedzoff, both looking very much disturbed.

" I am afraid your Majesty——" cries Glumboso.

" No business before breakfast, Glum ! " says the King. " Breakfast first, business next. Mrs. V., some more sugar ! "

" Sire, I am afraid if we wait till after breakfast it will be too late," says Glumboso. " He—he—he'll be hanged at half-past nine."

" Don't talk about hanging and spoil my breakfast, you unkind vulgar man you," cries the Princess. " John, some mustard. Pray who is to be hanged ? "

" Sire, it is the Prince," whispers Glumboso to the King.

" Talk about business after breakfast, I tell you ! " says His Majesty, quite sulky.

" We shall have a war, Sire, depend on it," says the Minister. " His father, King Padella. . . . "

" His father, King *who* ? " says the King. " King Padella is not Giglio's father. My brother, King Savio, was Giglio's father."

" It's Prince Bulbo they are hanging, Sire, not Prince Giglio," says the Prime Minister.

" You told me to hang the Prince, and I took the ugly one," says Hedzoff. " I didn't, of course, think your Majesty intended to murder your own flesh and blood ! "

The King for all reply flung the plate of sausages at Hedzoff's head. The Princess cried out " Hee-karee-karee ! " and fell down in a fainting fit.

" Turn the cock of the urn upon Her Royal Highness," said the King, and the boiling water gradually revived her. His Majesty looked at his watch, compared it by the clock in the parlour, and by that of the church in the square opposite ; then he wound it up ; then he looked at it again. " The great question is," says he, " am I fast or am I slow ? If I'm slow, we may as well go on with breakfast. If I'm fast, why, there is just the possibility of saving Prince Bulbo. It's a doosid awkward mistake, and upon my word, Hedzoff, I have the greatest mind to have you hanged too."

" Sire, I did but my duty ; a soldier has but his orders. I didn't expect after forty-seven years of faithful service that my sovereign would think of putting me to a felon's death ! "

" A hundred thousand plagues upon you ! Can't you

see that while you are talking my Bulbo is being hung ? "
screamed the Princess.

" By Jove ! she's always right, that girl, and I'm so
absent," says the King, looking at his watch again. " Ha !
there go the drums ! What a doosid awkward thing
though ! "

" Oh, papa, you goose ! Write the reprieve, and let me
run with it," cries the Princess—and she got a sheet of
paper, and pen and ink, and laid them before the King.

" Confound it ! where are my spectacles ? " the Monarch
exclaimed. " Angelica ! go up into my bedroom, look under
my pillow, not your mamma's ; there you'll see my keys.
Bring them down to me, and—Well, well ! what impetuous
things these girls are ! " Angelica was gone, and had run
up panting to the bedroom, and found the keys, and was
back again before the King had finished a muffin. " Now,
love," says he, " you must go all the way back for my desk,
in which my spectacles are. If you *would* but have heard me
out. . . . Be hanged to her ! There she is off again. Angelica !
ANGELICA ! " When His Majesty called in his *loud* voice,
she knew she must obey, and came back.

" My dear, when you go out of a room, how often have I
told you, *shut the door*. That's a darling. That's all. At last
the keys and the desk and the spectacles were got, and the
King mended his pen, and signed his name to a reprieve,
and Angelica ran with it as swift as the wind. " You'd
better stay, my love, and finish the muffins. There's no use
going. Be sure it's too late. Hand me over that raspberry
jam, please," said the Monarch. " Bong ! Bawong ! There
goes the half-hour. I knew it was."

Angelica ran, and ran, and ran, and ran. She ran up
Fore Street, and down High Street, and through the Market
place, and down to the left, and over the bridge, and up the
blind alley, and back again, and round by the Castle, and
so along by the Haberdasher's on the right, opposite the
lamp-post, and round the square, and she came—she came
to the *Execution place*, where she saw Bulbo laying his head

on the block ! ! ! The executioner raised his axe, but at
that moment the Princess came panting up and cried
" Reprieve ! "   " Reprieve ! " screamed the Princess.
" Reprieve ! " shouted all the people. Up the scaffold stairs
she sprang, with the agility of a lighter of lamps ; and

ANGELICA ARRIVES JUST IN TIME

flinging herself in Bulbo's arms, regardless of all ceremony,
she cried out, " Oh, my Prince ! my lord ! my love ! my
Bulbo ! Thine Angelica has been in time to save thy precious
existence, sweet rosebud ; to prevent thy being nipped in
thy young bloom ! Had aught befallen thee, Angelica too

had died, and welcomed death that joined her to her Bulbo."

" H'm ! there's no accounting for tastes," said Bulbo, looking so very much puzzled and uncomfortable that the Princess, in tones of tenderest strain, asked the cause of his disquiet.

" I tell you what it is, Angelica," said he, " since I came here yesterday, there has been such a row, and disturbance, and quarrelling, and fighting, and chopping of heads off, and the deuce to pay, that I am inclined to go back to Crim Tartary."

" But with me as thy bride, my Bulbo ! Though wherever thou art is Crim Tartary to me, my bold, my beautiful, my Bulbo ! "

" Well, well, I suppose we must be married," says Bulbo. " Doctor, you came to read the Funeral Service— read the Marriage Service, will you ? What must be, must. That will satisfy Angelica, and then, in the name of peace and quietness, do let us go back to breakfast."

Bulbo had carried a rose in his mouth all the time of the dismal ceremony. It was a fairy rose, and he was told by his mother that he ought never to part with it. So he had kept it between his teeth, even when he laid his poor head upon the block, hoping vaguely that some chance would turn up in his favour. As he began to speak to Angelica, he forgot about the rose, and of course it dropped out of his mouth. The romantic Princess instantly stooped and seized it. " Sweet rose ! " she exclaimed, " that bloomed upon my Bulbo's lip, never, never will I part from thee ! " and she placed it in her bosom. And you know Bulbo *couldn't* ask her to give the rose back again. And they went to breakfast ; and as they walked, it appeared to Bulbo that Angelica became more exquisitely lovely every moment.

He was frantic until they were married ; and now, strange to say, it was Angelica who didn't care about him ! He knelt down, he kissed her hand, he prayed and begged ; he cried with admiration ; while she for her part said she really thought they might wait ; it seemed to her he was not handsome any more—no, not at all, quite the reverse ; and not clever, no, very stupid ; and not well bred, like Giglio ; no, on the contrary, dreadfully vul——

What, I cannot say, for King Valoroso roared out " *Pooh*, stuff ! " in a terrible voice. " We will have no more of this shilly-shallying ! Call the Archbishop, and let the Prince and Princess be married offhand ! "

So, married they were, and I am sure for my part I trust they will be happy.

XII

How Betsinda Fled, and What Became of Her

BETSINDA wandered on and on, till she passed through the town gates, and so on the great Crim Tartary road, the very way on which Giglio too was going. " Ah ! " thought she, as the diligence passed her, of which the conductor was blowing a delightful tune on his horn, " how I should like to be on that coach ! " But the coach and the jingling horses were very soon gone. She little knew who was in it, though very likely she was thinking of him all the time.

Then came an empty cart, returning from market ; and the driver being a kind man, and seeing such a very pretty girl trudging along the road with bare feet, most good-naturedly gave her a seat. He said he lived on the confines of the forest, where his old father was a woodman, and, if she liked, he would take her so far on her road. All roads were the same to little Betsinda, so she very thankfully took this one.

And the carter put a cloth round her bare feet, and gave her some bread and cold bacon, and was very kind to her. For all that she was very cold and melancholy. When after travelling on and on, evening came, and all the black pines were bending with snow, and there, at last, was the comfortable light beaming in the woodman's windows ; and so they arrived, and went into his cottage. He was an old man, and had a number of children, who were just at supper, with nice hot bread-and-milk, when their elder brother arrived with the cart. And they jumped and clapped their hands ; for they were good children ; and he had brought them toys from the town. And when they saw the pretty stranger, they ran to her, and brought her to the fire, and rubbed her poor little feet, and brought her bread-and-milk.

" Look, father ! " they said to the old woodman, " look at this poor girl, and see what pretty cold feet she has. They

are as white as our milk ! And look and see what an odd cloak she has, just like the bit of velvet that hangs up in our cupboard, and which you found that day the little cubs were killed by King Padella, in the forest ! And look, why, bless us all ! she has got round her neck just such another little shoe as that you brought home, and have shown us so often—a little blue velvet shoe ! "

" What," said the old woodman, " what is all this about a shoe and a cloak ? "

And Betsinda explained that she had been left, when quite a little child, at the town with this cloak and this shoe. And the persons who had taken care of her had—had been angry with her, for no fault, she hoped, of her own. And they had sent her away with her old clothes—and here, in fact, she was. She remembered having been in a forest—and perhaps it was a dream—it was so very odd and strange—having lived in a cave with lions there ; and, before that, having lived in a very, very fine house, as fine as the King's, in the town.

When the woodman heard this, he was so astonished, it was quite curious to see how astonished he was. He went to his cupboard, and took out of a stocking a five-shilling piece of King Cavolfiore, and vowed it was exactly like the young woman. And then he produced the shoe and piece of velvet

which he had kept so long, and compared them with the things which Betsinda wore. In Betsinda's little shoe was written, " Hopkins, maker to the Royal Family " ; so in the other shoe was written, " Hopkins, maker to the Royal Family." In the inside of Betsinda's piece of cloak was embroidered, " PRIN ROSAL " ; in the other piece of cloak was embroidered " CESS BA. No. 246." So that when put together you read, " PRINCESS ROSALBA. No. 246."

On seeing this, the dear old woodman fell down on his knee, saying, " O my Princess, O my gracious royal lady, O my rightful Queen of Crim Tartary,—I hail thee—I acknowledge thee—I do thee homage ! " And in token of his fealty, he rubbed his venerable nose three times on the ground, and put the Princess's foot on his head.

" Why," said she, " my good woodman, you must be a

nobleman of my royal father's Court ! " For in her lowly
retreat, and under the name of Betsinda, HER MAJESTY,
ROSALBA, Queen of Crim Tartary, had read of the customs
of all foreign courts and nations.

" Marry, indeed, am I, my gracious liege—the poor Lord
Spinachi once—the humble woodman these fifteen years
syne. Ever since the tyrant Padella (may ruin overtake the
treacherous knave !) dismissed me from my post of First
Lord."

" First Lord of the Toothpick and Joint Keeper of the
Snuffbox ? I mind me ! Thou heldest these posts under our
royal Sire. They are restored to thee, Lord Spinachi ! I
make thee knight of the second class of our Order of the
Pumpkin (the first class being reserved for crowned heads
alone). Rise, Marquis of Spinachi ! " And with indescribable majesty, the Queen, who had no sword handy, waved
the pewter spoon with which she had been taking her bread-
and-milk, over the bald head of the old nobleman, whose
tears absolutely made a puddle on the ground, and whose
dear children went to bed that night Lords and Ladies
Bartolomeo, Ubaldo, Catarina, and Ottavia degli Spinachi.

The acquaintance HER MAJESTY showed with the history,
and *noble families* of her empire, was wonderful. " The House
of Broccoli should remain faithful to us," she said ; " they
were ever welcome at our Court. Have the Articiocchi, as
was their wont, turned to the Rising Sun ? The family of
Sauerkraut must sure be with us—they were ever welcome
in the halls of King Cavolfiore." And so she went on enu-
merating quite a list of the nobility and gentry of Crim
Tartary, so admirably had Her Majesty profited by her
studies while in exile.

The old Marquis of Spinachi said he could answer for
them all ; that the whole country groaned under Padella's
tyranny, and longed to return to its rightful sovereign ; and
late as it was, he sent his children, who knew the forest well,
to summon this nobleman and that ; and when his eldest
son, who had been rubbing the horse down and giving him

his supper, came into the house for his own, the Marquis told him to put his boots on, and a saddle on the mare, and ride hither and thither to such and such people.

When the young man heard who his companion in the cart had been, he too knelt down and put her royal foot on his head ; he too bedewed the ground with his tears ; he was frantically in love with her, as everybody now was who saw her : so were the young Lords Bartolomeo and Ubaldo, who punched each other's little heads out of jealousy ; and

so, when they came from east and west at the summons of the Marquis degli Spinachi, were the Crim Tartar Lords who still remained faithful to the House of Cavolfiore. They were such very old gentlemen for the most part that Her Majesty never suspected their absurd passion, and went among them quite unaware of the havoc her beauty was causing, until an old blind Lord who had joined her party told her what the truth was ; after which, for fear of making the people too much in love with her, she always wore a veil. She went about privately, from one nobleman's castle to another ; and they visited among themselves again, and had meetings, and composed proclamations and counter-proclamations, and distributed all the best places of the kingdom amongst one another, and selected who of the opposition party should be executed when the Queen came to her own. And so in about a year they were ready to move.

The party of Fidelity was in truth composed of very feeble old fogies for the most part ; they went about the country waving their old swords and flags, and calling " God save the Queen ! " and King Padella happening to be absent upon an invasion, they had their own way for a little, and to be sure the people were very enthusiastic whenever they saw the Queen ; otherwise the vulgar took matters very quietly, for they said, as far as they could recollect, they were pretty well as much taxed in Cavolfiore's time, as now in Padella's.

XIII

How Queen Rosalba Came to the Castle of the Bold Count Hogginarmo

HER MAJESTY, having indeed nothing else to give, made all her followers Knights of the Pumpkin, and Marquises, Earls, and Baronets ; and they had a little court for her, and made her a little crown of gilt paper, and a robe of cotton velvet ; and they quarrelled about the places to be given away in her court, and about rank and precedence and dignities ;—you can't think how they quarrelled ! The poor Queen was very tired of her honours before she had had them a month, and I dare say sighed sometimes even to be a lady's-maid again. But we must all do our duty in our respective stations, so the Queen resigned herself to perform hers.

We have said how it happened that none of the Usurper's troops came out to oppose this Army of Fidelity : it pottered along as nimbly as the gout of the principal commanders allowed : it consisted of twice as many officers as soldiers :

and at length passed near the estates of one of the most powerful noblemen of the country, who had not declared for the Queen, but of whom her party had hopes, as he was always quarrelling with King Padella.

When they came close to his park gates, this nobleman sent to say he would wait upon Her Majesty : he was a most powerful warrior, and his name was Count Hogginarmo, whose helmet it took two strong negroes to carry. He knelt

down before her and said, " Madam and liege lady ! it becomes the great nobles of the Crimean realm to show every outward sign of respect to the wearer of the Crown, whoever that may be. We testify to our own nobility in acknowledging yours. The bold Hogginarmo bends the knee to the first of the aristocracy of his country."

Rosalba said, " The bold Count of Hogginarmo was uncommonly kind." But she felt afraid of him, even while he was kneeling, and his eyes scowled at her from between his whiskers, which grew up to them.

" The first Count of the Empire, madam," he went on, " salutes the Sovereign. The Prince addresses himself to the not more noble lady ! Madam, my hand is free, and I offer it, and my heart and my sword to your service ! My three wives lie buried in my ancestral vaults. The third perished but a year since ; and this heart pines for a consort ! Deign to be mine, and I swear to bring to your bridal table the head of King Padella, the eyes and nose of his son Prince Bulbo, the right hand and ears of the usurping Sovereign of Paflagonia, which country shall thenceforth be an appanage to your—to *our* Crown ! Say yes ; Hogginarmo is not accustomed to be denied. Indeed I cannot contemplate the possibility of a refusal : for frightful will be the result ; dreadful the murders ; furious the devastations ; horrible the tyranny ; tremendous the tortures, misery, taxation, which the people of this realm will endure, if Hogginarmo's wrath be aroused ! I see consent in your Majesty's lovely eyes— their glances fill my soul with rapture ! "

" Oh, sir ! " Rosalba said, withdrawing her hand in great fright. " Your Lordship is exceedingly kind ; but I am sorry to tell you that I have a prior attachment to a young gentleman by the name of—Prince—Giglio—and never—never can marry anyone but him."

Who can describe Hogginarmo's wrath at this remark ? Rising up from the ground, he ground his teeth so that fire flashed out of his mouth, from which at the same time issued remarks and language, so *loud, violent, and improper*, that this pen shall never repeat them ! " R-r-r-r-r-r—Rejected ! Fiends and perdition ! The bold Hogginarmo rejected ! All the world shall hear of my rage ; and you, madam, you above all shall rue it ! " And kicking the two negroes before him, he rushed away, his whiskers streaming in the wind.

Her Majesty's Privy Council was in a dreadful panic when they saw Hogginarmo issue from the royal presence in such a towering rage, making footballs of the poor negroes —a panic which the events justified. They marched off from

Hogginarmo's park very crestfallen ; and in another half-hour they were met by that rapacious chieftain with a few of his followers, who cut, slashed, charged, whacked, banged, and pommelled amongst them, took the Queen prisoner, and drove the Army of Fidelity to I don't know where.

Poor Queen ! Hogginarmo, her conqueror, would not condescend to see her. " Get a horse-van ! " he said to his grooms, " clap the hussy into it, and send her, with my compliments, to His Majesty King Padella."

Along with his lovely prisoner, Hogginarmo sent a letter full of servile compliments and loathsome flatteries to King Padella, for whose life, and that of his royal family, the *hypocritical humbug* pretended to offer the most fulsome prayers. And Hogginarmo promised speedily to pay his humble homage at his august master's throne, of which he begged leave to be counted the most loyal and constant defender. Such a *wary* old *bird* as King Padella was not to be caught by Master Hogginarmo's *chaff*, and we shall hear

presently how the tyrant treated his upstart vassal. No, no ;
depend on't, two such rogues do not trust one another.

So this poor Queen was laid in the straw like Margery
Daw, and driven along in the dark ever so many miles to
the Court, where King Padella had now arrived, having
vanquished all his enemies, murdered most of them, and
brought some of the richest into captivity with him for the

purpose of torturing them and finding out where they had
hidden their money.

Rosalba heard their shrieks and groans in the dungeon in
which she was thrust ; a most awful black hole, full of bats,
rats, mice, toads, frogs, mosquitoes, bugs, fleas, serpents,
and every kind of horror. No light was let into it, otherwise
the gaolers might have seen her and fallen in love with her,
as an owl that lived up in the roof of the tower did, and a
cat, you know, who can see in the dark, and having set its
green eyes on Rosalba, never would be got to go back to the

turnkey's wife to whom it belonged. And the toads in the dungeon came and kissed her feet, and the vipers wound round her neck and arms, and never hurt her, so charming was this poor Princess in the midst of her misfortunes.

At last, after she had been kept in this place *ever so long*, the door of the dungeon opened, and the terrible KING PADELLA came in.

But what he said and did must be reserved for another chapter, as we must now back to Prince Giglio.

XIV

What Became of Giglio

THE IDEA of marrying such an old creature as Gruffanuff frightened Prince Giglio so, that he ran up to his room, packed his trunks, fetched in a couple of porters, and was off to the diligence office in a twinkling.

It was well that he was so quick in his operations, did not dawdle over his luggage, and took the early coach, for as soon as the mistake about Prince Bulbo was found out, that cruel Glumboso sent up a couple of policemen to Prince Giglio's room, with orders that he should be carried to Newgate, and his head taken off before twelve o'clock. But the coach was out of the Paflagonian dominions before two o'clock ; and I dare say the express that was sent after Prince Giglio did not ride very quick, for many people in Paflagonia had a regard for Giglio, as the son of their old sovereign ; a Prince who, with all his weaknesses, was very much better than his brother, the usurping, lazy, careless, passionate, tyrannical, reigning monarch. That Prince busied himself with the balls, fêtes, masquerades, hunting-parties, and so forth, which he thought proper to give on occasion of his daughter's marriage to Prince Bulbo ; and let us trust was not sorry in his own heart that his brother's son had escaped the scaffold.

It was very cold weather, and the snow was on the

ground, and Giglio, who gave his name as simple Mr. Giles,
was very glad to get a comfortable place in the coupé of the
diligence, where he sat with the conductor and another
gentleman. At the first stage from Blombodinga, as they
stopped to change horses, there came up to the diligence a
very ordinary, vulgar-looking woman, with a bag under her
arm, who asked for a place. All the inside places were taken,
and the young woman was informed that if she wished to

travel, she must go upon the roof ; and the passenger inside
with Giglio (a rude person, I should think), put his head out
of the window, and said, " Nice weather for travelling outside ! I wish you a pleasant journey, my dear." The poor
woman coughed very much, and Giglio pitied her. " I will
give up my place to her," says he, " rather than she should
travel in the cold air with that horrid cough." On which the
vulgar traveller said, " *You'd* keep her warm, I am sure, if
it's a *muff* she wants." On which Giglio pulled his nose,

boxed his ears, hit him in the eye, and gave this vulgar person a warning never to call him *muff* again.

Then he sprang up gaily on to the roof of the diligence, and made himself very comfortable in the straw. The vulgar traveller got down only at the next station, and Giglio took his place again, and talked to the person next to him. She appeared to be a most agreeable, well-informed, and entertaining female. They travelled together till night, and she gave Giglio all sorts of things out of the bag which she carried, and which indeed seemed to contain the most wonderful collection of articles. He was thirsty—out there came a pint bottle of Bass's pale ale, and a silver mug! Hungry—she took out a cold fowl, some slices of ham, bread, salt, and

a most delicious piece of cold plum-pudding, and a little glass of brandy afterwards.

As they travelled, this plain-looking, queer woman talked to Giglio on a variety of subjects, in which the poor Prince showed his ignorance as much as she did her capacity. He owned, with many blushes, how ignorant he was ; on which the lady said, " My dear Gigl—my good Mr. Giles, you are a young man, and have plenty of time before you. You have nothing to do but to improve yourself. Who knows but that you may find use for your knowledge some day ? When—when you may be wanted at home, as some people may be."

" Good heavens, madam ! " says he, " do you know me ? "

" I know a number of funny things," says the lady. " I

have been at some people's christenings, and turned away
from other folks' doors. I have seen some people spoilt by
good fortune, and others, as I hope, improved by hardship.
I advise you to stay at the town where the coach stops for
the night. Stay there and study, and remember your old
friend to whom you were kind."

" And who is my old friend ? " asked Giglio.

" When you want anything," says the lady, " look in this
bag, which I leave to you as a present, and be grateful
to——"

" To whom, madam ? " says he.

" To the Fairy Blackstick," says the lady, flying out of
the window. And when Giglio asked the conductor if he
knew where the lady was ?

" What lady ? " says the man ; " there has been no lady
in this coach, except the old woman, who got out at the last
stage." And Giglio thought he had been dreaming. But
there was the bag which Blackstick had given him lying on
his lap ; and when he came to the town he took it in his
hand and went into the inn.

They gave him a very bad bedroom, and Giglio, when he
woke in the morning, fancying himself in the Royal Palace
at home, called, " John, Charles, Thomas ! My chocolate—
my dressing-gown—my slippers " ; but nobody came. There
was no bell, so he went out and bawled out for waiter on
the top of the stairs.

The landlady came up, looking—looking like this—

"What are you a hollaring and a bellaring for here, young man?" says she.

"There's no warm water—no servants; my boots are not even cleaned."

"He, he! Clean 'em yourself," says the landlady. "You young students give yourselves pretty airs. I never heard such impudence."

"I'll quit the house this instant," says Giglio.

"The sooner the better, young man. Pay your bill and be off. All my rooms is wanted for gentlefolks, and not for such as you."

"You may well keep the Bear Inn," said Giglio. "You should have yourself painted as the sign."

The landlady of the Bear went away *growling*. And Giglio returned to his room, where the first thing he saw was the fairy bag lying on the table, which seemed to give a little hop as he came in. "I hope it has some breakfast in it," says Giglio, "for I have only a very little money left." But on opening the bag, what do you think was there? A blacking-brush and a pot of Warren's jet, and on the pot was written—

> *Poor young men their boots must black :*
> *Use me and cork me and put me back.*

So Giglio laughed and blacked his boots, and put back the brush and the bottle into the bag.

When he had done dressing himself, the bag gave another little hop, and he went to it and took out—

1. A tablecloth and a napkin.
2. A sugar-basin full of the best loaf-sugar.

4, 6, 8, 10. Two forks, two teaspoons, two knives, and a pair of sugar-tongs, and a butter-knife, all marked G.

11, 12, 13. A teacup, saucer, and slop-basin.

14. A jug full of delicious cream.

15. A canister with black tea and green.

16. A large tea-urn and boiling water.
17. A saucepan, containing three eggs nicely done.
18. A quarter of a pound of best Epping butter.
19. A brown loaf.

And if he hadn't enough now for a good breakfast, I should like to know who ever had one ?

Giglio, having had his breakfast, popped all the things back into the bag, and went out looking for lodgings. I forgot to say that this celebrated university town was called Bosforo.

He took a modest lodging opposite the Schools, paid his bill at the inn, and went to his apartment with his trunk, carpet-bag, and not forgetting, we may be sure, his *other* bag.

When he opened his trunk, which the day before he had filled with his best clothes, he found it contained only books. And in the first of them which he opened there was written—

Clothes for the back, books for the head :
Read and remember them when they are read.

And in his bag, when Giglio looked in it, he found a student's cap and gown, a writing-book full of paper, an inkstand, pens, and a Johnson's dictionary, which was very useful to him, as his spelling had been sadly neglected.

So he sat down and worked away, very, very hard for a whole year, during which " Mr. Giles " was quite an example to all the students in the University of Bosforo. He never got into any riots or disturbances. The Professors all spoke well of him, and the students liked him too ; so that, when at examination, he took all the prizes, viz.—

The Spelling Prize	The French Prize
The Writing Prize	The Arithmetic Prize
The History Prize	The Latin Prize
The Catechism Prize	The Good Conduct Prize,

all his fellow-students said, " Hurray ! Hurray for Giles ! Giles is the boy—the student's joy ! Hurray for Giles ! " And he brought quite a quantity of medals, crowns, books, and tokens of distinction home to his lodgings.

One day after the Examinations, as he was diverting himself at a coffee-house with two friends—(Did I tell you that in his bag, every Saturday night, he found just enough to pay his bills, with a guinea over, for pocket-money ? Didn't I tell you ? Well, he did, as sure as twice twenty makes forty-five)—he chanced to look in the *Bosforo Chronicle*, and read off, quite easily (for he could spell, read, and write the longest words now), the following :—

" ROMANTIC CIRCUMSTANCE.—One of the most extraordinary adventures that we have ever heard has set the neighbouring country of Crim Tartary in a state of great excitement.

" It will be remembered that when the present revered sovereign of Crim Tartary, His Majesty King *Padella*, took possession of the throne, after having vanquished, in the terrific battle of Blunderbusco, the late King *Cavolfiore*, that

Prince's only child, the Princess Rosalba, was not found in the royal palace, of which King Padella took possession, and, it was said, had strayed into the forest (being abandoned by all her attendants) where she had been eaten up by those ferocious lions, the last pair of which were captured some time since, and brought to the Tower, after killing several hundred persons.

" His Majesty King Padella, who has the kindest heart in the world, was grieved at the accident which had occurred to the harmless little Princess, for whom His Majesty's known benevolence would certainly have provided a fitting establishment. But her death seemed to be certain. The mangled remains of a cloak, and a little shoe, were found in the forest, during a hunting-party, in which the intrepid sovereign of Crim Tartary slew two of the lions' cubs with his own spear. And these interesting relics of an innocent little creature were carried home and kept by their finder, the Baron Spinachi, formerly an officer in Cavolfiore's household. The Baron was disgraced in consequence of his known legitimist opinions, and has lived for some time in the humble capacity of a woodcutter, in a forest on the outskirts of the Kingdom of Crim Tartary.

" Last Tuesday week Baron Spinachi and a number of gentlemen, attached to the former dynasty, appeared in arms, crying, ' God save Rosalba, the first Queen of Crim Tartary ! ' and surrounding a lady whom report describes as ' *beautiful exceedingly*.' Her history *may* be authentic, *is* certainly most romantic.

" The personage calling herself Rosalba states that she was brought out of the forest, fifteen years since, by a lady in a car drawn by dragons (this account is certainly *improbable*), that she was left in the Palace Garden of Blombodinga, where Her Royal Highness the Princess Angelica, now married to His Royal Highness Bulbo, Crown Prince of Crim Tartary, found the child, and, with *that elegant benevolence* which has always distinguished the heiress of the throne of Paflagonia, gave the little outcast a *shelter and a home*! Her parentage not being known, and her garb very humble, the foundling was educated in the Palace in a menial capacity, under the name of *Betsinda*.

"She did not give satisfaction, and was dismissed, carrying with her, certainly, part of a mantle and a shoe, which she had on when first found. According to her statement she quitted Blombodinga about a year ago, since which time she has been with the Spinachi family. On the very same morning the Prince Giglio, nephew to the King of Paflagonia, a young Prince whose character for *talent* and *order* were, to say truth, *none of the highest*, also quitted Blombodinga, and has not been since heard of!"

"What an extraordinary story!" said Smith and Jones, two young students, Giglio's especial friends.

"Ha! what is this?" Giglio went on, reading—

"SECOND EDITION, EXPRESS.—We hear that the troop under Baron Spinachi has been surrounded, and utterly routed, by General Count Hogginarmo, and the *soi-disant* Princess is sent a prisoner to the capital.

"UNIVERSITY NEWS.—Yesterday, at the Schools, the distinguished young student, Mr. Giles, read a Latin oration, and was complimented by the Chancellor of Bosforo, Dr. Prugnaro, with the highest University honour —the wooden spoon."

"Never mind that stuff," says *Giles*, greatly disturbed. "Come home with me, my friends. Gallant Smith! intrepid Jones! friends of my studies—partakers of my academic toils—I have that to tell shall astonish your honest minds."

"Go it, old boy!" cries the impetuous Smith.

"Talk away, my buck!" says Jones, a lively fellow.

With an air of indescribable dignity, Giglio checked their natural, but no more seemly, familiarity. "Jones, Smith, my good friends," said the PRINCE, "disguise is henceforth

useless ; I am no more the humble student Giles, I am the
descendant of a royal line."

" *Atavis edite regibus*, I know, old co——," cried Jones. He
was going to say old cock, but a flash from THE ROYAL EYE
again awed him.

TO ARMS !

" Friends," continued the Prince, " I am that Giglio, I
am, in fact, Paflagonia. Rise, Smith, and kneel not in the
public street. Jones, thou true heart ! My faithless uncle,
when I was a baby, filched from me that brave crown my
father left me, bred me, all young and careless of my

rights, like unto hapless Hamlet Prince of Denmark ; and
had I any thoughts about my wrongs, soothed me with
promises of near redress. I should espouse his daughter,
young Angelica ; we two indeed should reign in Paflagonia.
His words were false—false as Angelica's heart !—false as
Angelica's hair, colour, front teeth ! She looked with her

PRINCE GIGLIO'S SPEECH TO THE ARMY

skew eyes upon young Bulbo, Crim Tartary's stupid heir,
and she preferred him. 'Twas then I turned my eyes upon
Betsinda—Rosalba, as she now is. And I saw in her the
blushing sum of all perfection ; the pink of maiden modesty ;
the nymph that my fond heart had ever woo'd in dreams,"
etc., etc.

(I don't give this speech, which was very fine, but very long ; and though Smith and Jones knew nothing about the circumstances, my dear reader does, so I go on.)

The Prince and his young friends hastened home to his apartment, highly excited by the intelligence, as no doubt by the *royal narrator's* admirable manner of recounting it and they ran up to his room where he had worked so hard at his books.

On his writing-table was his bag, grown so long that the Prince could not help remarking it. He went to it, opened it, and what do you think he found in it ?

A splendid long, gold-handled, red-velvet-scabbarded, cut-and-thrust sword, and on the sheath was embroidered " ROSALBA FOR EVER ! "

He drew out the sword, which flashed and illuminated the whole room, and called out " Rosalba for ever ! " Smith and Jones following him, but quite respectfully this time, and taking the time from His Royal Highness.

And now his trunk opened with a sudden pong, and out there came three ostrich feathers in a gold crown, surrounding a beautiful shining steel helmet, a cuirass, a pair of spurs, finally a complete suit of armour.

The books on Giglio's shelves were all gone. Where there had been some great dictionaries, Giglio's friends found two pairs of jack-boots labelled, " Lieutenant Smith," " —— Jones, Esq.," which fitted them to a nicety. Besides, there were helmets, back and breast plates, swords, etc., just like in Mr. G. P. R. James's novels ; and that evening three cavaliers might have been seen issuing from the gates of Bosforo, in whom the porters, proctors, etc., never thought of recognising the young Prince and his friends.

They got horses at a livery stablekeeper's, and never drew bridle until they reached the last town on the frontier before you come to Crim Tartary. Here, as their animals were tired, and the cavaliers hungry, they stopped and refreshed at an hostel. I could make a chapter of this if I were like some writers, but I like to cram my measure tight down, you see, and give you a great deal for your money, and, in a word, they had some bread and cheese and ale upstairs on the balcony of the inn. As they were drinking, drums and trumpets sounded nearer and nearer, the market-place was filled with soldiers, and His Royal Highness looking forth, recognised the Paflagonian banners, and the Paflagonian national air which the bands were playing.

The troops all made for the tavern at once, and as they came up Giglio exclaimed, on beholding their leader, " Whom do I see? Yes! No! It is, it is! Phoo! No, it can't be! Yes! It is my friend, my gallant faithful veteran, Captain Hedzoff! Ho! Hedzoff! Knowest thou not thy Prince, thy Giglio? Good Corporal, methinks we once were friends. Ha, Sergeant, an my memory serves me right, we have had many a bout at singlestick."

" I' faith, we have a many, good my Lord," says the Sergeant.

" Tell me, what means this mighty armament," continued His Royal Highness from the balcony, " and whither march my Paflagonians? "

Hedzoff's head fell. " My Lord," he said, " we march as the allies of great Padella, Crim Tartary's monarch."

" Crim Tartary's usurper, gallant Hedzoff! Crim Tartary's grim tyrant, honest Hedzoff! " said the Prince, on the balcony, quite sarcastically.

" A soldier, Prince, must needs obey his orders : mine are to help His Majesty Padella. And also (though alack that I should say it!) to seize wherever I should light upon him——"

" First catch your hare! ha, Hedzoff! " exclaimed His Royal Highness.

" —On the body of *Giglio*, whilome Prince of Paflagonia," Hedzoff went on, with indescribable emotion. " My Prince, give up your sword without ado. Look! we are thirty thousand men to one! "

" Give up my sword! Giglio give up his sword! " cried

the Prince ; and stepping well forward on to the balcony, the royal youth, *without preparation*, delivered a speech so magnificent, that no report can do justice to it. It was all in blank verse (in which, from this time, he invariably spoke, as more becoming his majestic station). It lasted for three days and three nights, during which not a single person who heard him was tired, or remarked the difference between daylight and dark. The soldiers only cheering tremendously, when occasionally, once in nine hours, the Prince paused to suck an orange, which Jones took out of the bag. He explained, in terms which we say we shall not attempt to convey, the whole history of the previous transaction, and his determination not only not to give up his sword, but to assume his rightful crown ; and at the end of this extraordinary, this truly *gigantic* effort, Captain Hedzoff flung up his helmet, and cried, " Hurray ! Hurray ! Long live King Giglio ! "

Such were the consequences of having employed his time well at College !

When the excitement had ceased, beer was ordered out for the army, and their Sovereign himself did not disdain a little ! And now it was with some alarm that Captain Hedzoff told him his division was only the advanced guard of the Paflagonian contingent, hastening to King Padella's aid ; the main force being a day's march in the rear under His Royal Highness Prince Bulbo.

" We will wait here, good friend, to beat the Prince," His Majesty said, " and *then* will make his royal father wince."

XV

We Return to Rosalba

KING PADELLA made very similar proposals to Rosalba to those which she had received from the various princes who, as we have seen, had fallen in love with her. His Majesty was a widower, and offered to marry his fair captive that instant, but she declined his invitation in her usual polite gentle manner, stating that Prince Giglio was her love, and that any other union was out of the question. Having tried tears and supplications in vain, this violent-tempered monarch menaced her with threats and tortures ; but she declared she would rather suffer all these than accept the hand of her father's murderer, who left her finally, uttering the most awful imprecations, and bidding her prepare for death on the following morning.

All night long the King spent in advising how he should get rid of this obdurate young creature. Cutting off her head was much too easy a death for her ; hanging was so common in His Majesty's dominions that it no longer afforded him any sport ; finally, he bethought himself of a pair of fierce lions which had lately been sent to him as presents, and he determined, with these ferocious brutes, to hunt poor Rosalba down. Adjoining his castle was an amphitheatre where the Prince indulged in bull-baiting, rat-hunting, and other ferocious sports. The two lions were kept in a cage under this place ; their roaring might be heard over the whole city, the inhabitants of which, I am sorry to say, thronged in numbers to see a poor young lady gobbled up by two wild beasts.

The King took his place in the royal box, having the officers of his Court around and the Count Hogginarmo by his side, upon whom His Majesty was observed to look very fiercely ; the fact is, royal spies had told the monarch of Hogginarmo's behaviour, his proposals to Rosalba, and his offer to fight for the crown. Black as thunder looked King Padella at this proud noble, as they sat in the front seats of the theatre waiting to see the tragedy whereof poor Rosalba was to be the heroine.

At length that Princess was brought out in her night-gown, with all her beautiful hair falling down her back, and looking so pretty that even the beef-eaters and keepers of the wild animals wept plentifully at seeing her. And she walked with her poor little feet (only luckily the arena was

covered with sawdust), and went and leaned up against a great stone in the centre of the amphitheatre, round which the Court and the people were seated in boxes, with bars

before them, for fear of the great, fierce, red-maned, black-throated, long-tailed, roaring, bellowing, rushing lions.

And now the gates were opened, and with a wurrawarrura-warar two great lean, hungry, roaring lions rushed out of their den, where they had been kept for three weeks on nothing but a little toast-and-water, and dashed straight up to the stone where poor Rosalba was waiting. Commend her to your patron saints, all you kind people, for she is in a dreadful state !

There was a hum and a buzz all through the circus, and the fierce King Padella even felt a little compassion. But Count Hogginarmo, seated by His Majesty, roared out " Hurray ! Now for it ! Soo-soo-soo ! " that nobleman being uncommonly angry still at Rosalba's refusal of him.

But O strange event ! O remarkable circumstance ! O extraordinary coincidence, which I am sure none of you could *by any possibility* have divined ! When the lions came to Rosalba, instead of devouring her with their great teeth, it was with kisses they gobbled her up ! They licked her pretty feet, they nuzzled their noses in her lap, they moo'd, they seemed to say, " Dear, dear sister, don't you recollect your brothers, in the forest ? " And she put her pretty white arms round their tawny necks, and kissed them.

King Padella was immensely astonished. The Count Hogginarmo was extremely disgusted. " Pooh ! " the Count cried. " Gammon ! " exclaimed his Lordship. " These lions are tame beasts come from Wombwell's or Astley's. It is a shame to put people off in this way. I believe they are little boys dressed up in door-mats. They are no lions at all."

" Ha ! " said the King, " you dare to say ' gammon ' to your Sovereign, do you ? These lions are no lions at all, aren't they ? Ho ! my beef-eaters ! Ho ! my bodyguard ! Take this Count Hogginarmo and fling him into the circus ! Give him a sword and buckler, let him keep his armour on, and his weather-eye out, and fight these lions."

The haughty Hogginarmo laid down his opera-glass, and looked scowling round at the King and his attendants.

" Touch me not, dogs ! " he said, " or by St. Nicholas the Elder, I will gore you ! Your Majesty thinks Hogginarmo is afraid ? No, not of a hundred thousand lions ! Follow me down into the circus, King Padella, and match thyself against one of yon brutes. Thou darest not. Let them both come on, then ! " And opening a grating of the box, he jumped lightly down into the circus.

Wurra wurra wurra wur-aw-aw-aw ! ! !
In about two minutes
The Count Hogginarmo was
GOBBLED UP
by
those lions,
bones, boots, and all,'
and
There was an
End of him.

At this, the King said, " Serve him right, the rebellious ruffian ! And now, as those lions won't eat that young woman———"

" Let her off !—let her off ! " cried the crowd.

" NO ! " roared the King. " Let the beef-eaters go down and chop her into small pieces. If the lions defend her, let the archers shoot them to death. That hussy shall die in tortures ! "

" A-a-ah ! " cried the crowd. " Shame ! shame ! "

" Who dares cry out shame ? " cried the furious potentate (so little can tyrants command their passions). " Fling any scoundrel who says a word down among the lions ! "

I warrant you there was a dead silence then, which was broken by a Pang arang pang pangkarangpang, and a Knight and a Herald rode in at the further end of the circus : the Knight, in full armour, with his vizor up, and bearing a letter on the point of his lance.

" Ha ! " exclaimed the King, " by my fay, 'tis Elephant and Castle, pursuivant of my brother of Paflagonia ; and the Knight, an my memory serves me, is the gallant Captain Hedzoff! What news from Paflagonia, gallant Hedzoff? Elephant and Castle, beshrew me, thy trumpeting must have made thee thirsty. What will my trusty herald like to drink?"

"Bespeaking first safe conduct from your Lordship," said Captain Hedzoff, "before we take a drink of anything, permit us to deliver our King's message."

"My Lordship, ha!" said Crim Tartary, frowning terrifically. "That title soundeth strange in the anointed ears of a crowned King. Straightway speak out your message, Knight and Herald!"

Reining up his charger in a most elegant manner close under the King's balcony, Hedzoff turned to the Herald, and bade him begin.

Elephant and Castle, dropping his trumpet over his shoulder, took a large sheet of paper out of his hat, and began to read:—

"O Yes! O Yes! O Yes! Know all men by these presents, that we, Giglio, King of Paflagonia, Grand Duke of Cappadocia, Sovereign Prince of Turkey and the Sausage Islands, having assumed our rightful throne and title, long time falsely borne by our usurping Uncle, styling himself King of Paflagonia——"

"Ha!" growled Padella.

"Hereby summon the false traitor, Padella, calling himself King of Crim Tartary——"

The King's curses were dreadful. "Go on, Elephant and Castle!" said the intrepid Hedzoff.

"—To release from cowardly imprisonment his liege lady and rightful Sovereign, ROSALBA, Queen of Crim Tartary, and restore her to her royal throne: in default of which, I, Giglio, proclaim the said Padella sneak, traitor, humbug, usurper, and coward. I challenge him to meet me, with fists or with pistols, with battle-axe or sword, with blunderbuss or singlestick, alone or at the head of his army, on foot or on horseback ; and will prove my words upon his wicked ugly body ! ''

" God save the King ! '' said Captain Hedzoff, executing a demivolte, two semilunes, and three caracols.

" Is that all ? '' said Padella, with the terrific calm of concentrated fury.

" That, sir, is all my royal master's message. Here is His Majesty's letter in autograph, and here is his glove, and if any gentleman of Crim Tartary chooses to find fault with His Majesty's expressions, I, Tuffskin Hedzoff, Captain of the Guard, am very much at his service," and he waved his lance, and looked at the assembly all round.

" And what says my good brother of Paflagonia, my dear son's father-in-law, to this rubbish ? " asked the King.

" The King's uncle hath been deprived of the crown he unjustly wore," said Hedzoff gravely. " He and his ex-minister, Glumboso, are now in prison waiting the sentence of my royal master. After the battle of Bombardaro——"

" Of what ? " asked the surprised Padella.

" Of Bombardaro, where my liege, his present Majesty, would have performed prodigies of valour, but that the whole of his uncle's army came over to our side, with the exception of Prince Bulbo."

" Ah ! my boy, my boy, my Bulbo was no traitor ! " cried Padella.

" Prince Bulbo, far from coming over to us, ran away, sir ; but I caught him. The Prince is a prisoner in our army, and the most terrific tortures await him if a hair of the Princess Rosalba's head is injured."

" Do they ? " exclaimed the furious Padella, who was now perfectly *livid* with rage. " Do they indeed ? So much the worse for Bulbo. I've twenty sons as lovely each as Bulbo. Not one but is as fit to reign as Bulbo. Whip, whack, flog, starve, rack, punish, torture Bulbo—break all his bones—roast him or flay him alive—pull all his pretty teeth out one by one ! But justly dear as Bulbo is to me,— joy of my eyes, fond treasure of my soul !—Ha, ha, ha, ha ! revenge is dearer still. Ho ! torturers, rack-men, executioners—light up the fires and make the pincers hot ! get lots of boiling lead !—Bring out ROSALBA ! "

XVI

How Hedzoff Rode Back again to King Giglio

CAPTAIN HEDZOFF rode away when King Padella uttered this cruel command, having done his duty in delivering the message with which his royal master had entrusted him. Of course he was very sorry for Rosalba, but what could he do ?

So he returned to King Giglio's camp, and found the young monarch in a disturbed state of mind, smoking cigars in the royal tent. His Majesty's agitation was not appeased by the news that was brought by his ambassador. " The brutal ruthless ruffian royal wretch ! " Giglio exclaimed. " As England's poesy has well remarked, ' The man that lays his hand upon a woman, save in the way of kindness, is a villain.' Ha, Hedzoff ! "

" That he is, your Majesty," said the attendant.

" And didst thou see her flung into the oil ? and didn't the soothing oil—the emollient oil refuse to boil, good Hedzoff—and to spoil the fairest lady ever eyes did look on ? "

" Faith, good my liege, I had no heart to look and see a beauteous lady boiling down ; I took your royal message to Padella, and bore his back to you. I told him you would hold Prince Bulbo answerable. He only said that he had twenty sons as good as Bulbo, and forthwith he bade the ruthless executioners proceed."

" O cruel father—O unhappy son ! " cried the King. " Go, some of you, and bring Prince Bulbo hither."

Bulbo was brought in chains, looking very uncomfortable. Though a prisoner, he had been tolerably happy, perhaps because his mind was at rest, and all the fighting was over, and he was playing at marbles with his guards when the King sent for him.

" Oh, my poor Bulbo," said His Majesty, with looks of infinite compassion, " hast thou heard the news ? " (for you see Giglio wanted to break the thing gently to the Prince), " thy brutal father has condemned Rosalba— p-p-p-ut her to death, P-p-p-prince Bulbo ! "

" What, killed Betsinda ! Boo-hoo-hoo," cried out Bulbo. " Betsinda ! pretty Betsinda ! dear Betsinda ! She was the dearest little girl in the world. I love her better twenty thousand times even than Angelica," and he went on expressing his grief in so hearty and unaffected a manner that the King was quite touched by it, and said, shaking Bulbo's hand, that he wished he had known Bulbo sooner.

Bulbo, quite unconsciously, and meaning for the best, offered to come and sit with His Majesty, and smoke a cigar with him, and console him. The *royal kindness* supplied Bulbo with a cigar ; he had not had one, he said, since he was taken prisoner.

And now think what must have been the feelings of the most *merciful of monarchs*, when he informed his prisoner that, in consequence of King Padella's *cruel and dastardly behaviour* to Rosalba, Prince Bulbo must instantly be executed ! The noble Giglio could not restrain his tears, nor could the Grenadiers, nor the officers, nor could Bulbo himself, when the matter was explained to him, and he was brought to understand that His Majesty's promise, of course, was *above every* thing, and Bulbo must submit. So poor Bulbo was led out, Hedzoff trying to console him, by pointing out that if he had won the battle of Bombardaro he might have hanged Prince Giglio. " Yes ! But that is no comfort to me now ! " said poor Bulbo ; nor indeed was it, poor fellow !

He was told the business would be done the next

morning at eight, and was taken back to his dungeon, where
every attention was paid to him. The gaoler's wife sent
him tea, and the turnkey's daughter begged him to write
his name in her album, where a many gentlemen had
wrote it on like occasions ! " Bother your album ! " says
Bulbo. The Undertaker came and measured him for the
handsomest coffin which money could buy—even this
didn't console Bulbo. The Cook brought him dishes which
he once used to like ; but he wouldn't touch them : he sat
down and began writing an adieu to Angelica, as the clock

kept always ticking, and the hands drawing nearer to next
morning. The Barber came in at night, and offered to shave
him for the next day. Prince Bulbo kicked him away, and
went on writing a few words to Princess Angelica, as the
clock kept always ticking, and the hands hopping nearer
and nearer to next morning. He got up on the top of a
hat-box, on the top of a chair, on the top of his bed, on the
top of his table, and looked out to see whether he might
escape as the clock kept always ticking and the hands
drawing nearer, and nearer, and nearer.

But looking out of the window was one thing, and jumping another : and the town clock struck seven. So he got into bed for a little sleep, but the gaoler came and woke him, and said, " Git up, your Royal Ighness, if you please, it's *ten minutes to eight* ! "

So poor Bulbo got up : he had gone to bed in his clothes (the lazy boy), and he shook himself, and said he didn't mind about dressing, or having any breakfast, thank you ; and he saw the soldiers who had come for him. " Lead on ! " he said ; and they led the way, deeply affected ; and

they came into the courtyard, and out into the square, and there was King Giglio come to take leave of him, and His Majesty most kindly shook hands with him, and the *gloomy procession* marched on :—when hark !

Haw—wurraw—wurraw—aworr !

A roar of wild beasts was heard. And who should come riding into the town, frightening away the boys, and even the beadle and policeman, but ROSALBA !

The fact is, that when Captain Hedzoff entered into the court of Snapdragon Castle, and was discoursing with

King Padella, the lions made a dash at the open gate, gobbled up the six beef-eaters in a jiffy, and away they went with Rosalba on the back of one of them, and they carried her, turn and turn about, till they came to the city where Prince Giglio's army was encamped.

When the KING heard of the QUEEN's arrival, you may think how he rushed out of his breakfast-room to hand Her Majesty off her lion ! The lions were grown as fat as pigs now, having had Hogginarmo and all those beef-eaters, and were so tame, anybody might pat them.

While Giglio knelt (most gracefully) and helped the Princess, Bulbo, for his part, rushed up and kissed the lion. He flung his arms round the forest monarch ; he hugged him, and laughed and cried for joy. " Oh, you darling old beast, oh, how glad I am to see you, and the dear, dear Bets—that is, Rosalba."

" What, is it you ? poor Bulbo ? " said the Queen. " Oh, how glad I am to see you," and she gave him her hand to kiss. King Giglio slapped him most kindly on the back, and said, " Bulbo, my boy, I am delighted, for your sake, that Her Majesty has arrived."

" So am I," said Bulbo ; " and *you know why*." Captain Hedzoff here came up. " Sire, it is half-past eight : shall we proceed with the execution ? "

" Execution ! what for ? " asked Bulbo.

" An officer only knows his orders," replied Captain Hedzoff, showing his warrant, on which His Majesty King Giglio smilingly said, " Prince Bulbo was reprieved this time," and most graciously invited him to breakfast.

XVII

How a Tremendous Battle took place, and Who Won It

As soon as King Padella heard, what we know already, that his victim, the lovely Rosalba, had escaped him, His Majesty's fury knew no bounds, and he pitched the Lord Chancellor, Lord Chamberlain, and every officer of the

Crown whom he could set eyes on, into the cauldron of boiling oil prepared for the Princess. Then he ordered out his whole army, horse, foot and artillery ; and set forth at the head of an innumerable host, and I should think twenty thousand drummers, trumpeters, and fifers.

King Giglio's advanced guard, you may be sure, kept that monarch acquainted with the enemy's dealings, and he was in no wise disconcerted. He was much too polite to alarm the Princess, his lovely guest, with any unnecessary rumours of battles impending ; on the contrary, he did everything to amuse and divert her ; gave her a most elegant breakfast, dinner, lunch, and got up a ball for her that evening, when he danced with her every single dance.

Poor Bulbo was taken into favour again, and allowed to go quite free now. He had new clothes given him, was called " My good cousin " by His Majesty, and was treated with the greatest distinction by everybody. But it was easy to see he was very melancholy. The fact is, the sight of Betsinda, who looked perfectly lovely in an elegant new dress, set poor Bulbo frantic in love with her again. And he never thought about Angelica, now Princess Bulbo, whom he had left at home, and who, as we know, did not care much about him.

The King, dancing the twenty-fifth polka with Rosalba, remarked with wonder the ring she wore ; and then Rosalba told him how she had got it from Gruffanuff, who no doubt had picked it up when Angelica flung it away.

" Yes," says the Fairy Blackstick, who had come to see the young people, and who had very likely certain plans regarding them. " That ring I gave the Queen, Giglio's mother, who was not, saving your presence, a very wise woman ; it is enchanted, and whoever wears it looks beautiful in the eyes of the world. I made poor Prince Bulbo, when he was christened, the present of a rose which made him look handsome while he had it ; but he gave it to Angelica, who instantly looked beautiful again, whilst Bulbo relapsed into his natural plainness."

" Rosalba needs no ring, I am sure," says Giglio, with a low bow. " She is beautiful enough, in my eyes, without any enchanted aid."

" Oh, sir ! " said Rosalba.

" Take off the ring and try," said the King, and resolutely drew the ring off her finger. In *his* eyes she looked just as handsome as before !

The King was thinking of throwing the ring away, as it was so dangerous and made all the people so mad about Rosalba ; but being a Prince of great humour, and good humour too, he cast eyes upon a poor youth who happened to be looking on very disconsolately, and said—

" Bulbo, my poor lad ! come and try on this ring. The Princess Rosalba makes it a present to you."

The magic properties of this ring were uncommonly strong, for no sooner had Bulbo put it on, but lo and behold, he appeared a personable, agreeable young Prince enough—with a fine complexion, fair hair, rather stout, and with bandy legs ; but these were encased in such a beautiful pair of yellow morocco boots that nobody remarked them. And Bulbo's spirits rose up almost immediately after he had looked in the glass, and he talked to their Majesties in the most lively, agreeable manner, and danced opposite the Queen with one of the prettiest maids of honour, and after looking at Her Majesty, could not help saying—

" How very odd ! she is very pretty, but not so *extraordinarily* handsome."

" Oh no, by no means ! " says the Maid of Honour.

" But what care I, dear sir," says the Queen, who overheard them, " if *you* think I am good-looking enough ? "

His Majesty's glance in reply to this affectionate speech was such that no painter could draw it. And the Fairy Blackstick said, " Bless you, my darling children ! Now you are united and happy ; and now you see what I said from the first, that a little misfortune has done you both good. *You*, Giglio, had you been bred in prosperity, would scarcely have learned to read or write—you would have been idle and extravagant, and could not have been a good King as now you will be. You, Rosalba, would have been so flattered, that your little head might have been turned like Angelica's, who thought herself too good for Giglio."

" As if anybody could be good enough for *him*," cried Rosalba.

" Oh, you, you darling ! " says Giglio. And so she was ; and he was just holding out his arms in order to give her a hug before the whole company, when a messenger came rushing in, and said, " My Lord, the enemy ! "

" To arms ! " cries Giglio.

" Oh, mercy ! " says Rosalba, and fainted of course.

He snatched one kiss from her lips, and rushed *forth to the field* of battle !

The Fairy had provided King Giglio with a suit of armour, which was not only embroidered all over with jewels, and blinding to your eyes to look at, but was waterproof, gun-proof, and sword-proof ; so that in the midst of the very hottest battles His Majesty rode about as calmly as if he had been a British Grenadier at Alma. Were I engaged in fighting for my country, *I* should like such a suit of armour as Prince Giglio wore ; but, you know, he was a Prince of a fairy tale, and they always have these wonderful things.

Besides the fairy armour, the Prince had a fairy horse, which would gallop at any pace you please ; and a fairy sword, which would lengthen and run through a whole regiment of enemies at once. With such a weapon at command, I wonder, for my part, he thought of ordering his army out ; but forth they all came, in magnificent new uniforms, Hedzoff and the Prince's two college friends each commanding a division, and His Majesty prancing in person at the head of them all.

Ah ! if I had the pen of a Sir Archibald Alison, my dear friends, would I not now entertain you with the account of a most tremendous shindy ? Should not fine blows be

struck ? dreadful wounds be delivered ? arrows darken the
air ? cannon balls crash through the battalions ? cavalry
charge infantry ? infantry pitch into cavalry ? bugles
blow ; drums beat ; horses neigh ; fifes sing ; soldiers roar,
swear, hurray ; officers shout out " Forward, my men ! "
" This way, lads ! " " Give it 'em, boys ! " " Fight for
King Giglio, and the cause of right ! " " King Padella for
ever ! " Would I not describe all this, I say, and in the very
finest language too ? But this humble pen does not possess
the skill necessary for the description of combats. In a word,
the overthrow of King Padella's army was so complete, that
if they had been Russians you could not have wished them
to be more utterly smashed and confounded.

As for that usurping monarch, having performed acts
of valour much more considerable than could be expected
of a royal ruffian and usurper, who had such a bad cause,
and who was so cruel to women,—as for King Padella, I
say, when his army ran away, the King ran away too,
kicking his first general, Prince Punchikoff, from his saddle,
and galloping away on the Prince's horse, having, indeed,
had twenty-five or twenty-six of his own shot under him.
Hedzoff coming up, and finding Punchikoff down, as you
may imagine, very speedily disposed of *him.* Meanwhile
King Padella was scampering off as hard as his horse could
lay legs to ground. Fast as he scampered, I promise you
somebody else galloped faster ; and that individual, as no
doubt you are aware, was the Royal Giglio, who kept
bawling out, " Stay, traitor ! Turn, miscreant, and defend
thyself ! Stand, tyrant, coward, ruffian, royal wretch, till I
cut thy ugly head from thy usurping shoulders ! " And, with
his fairy sword, which elongated itself at will, His Majesty
kept poking and prodding Padella in the back, until that
wicked monarch roared with anguish.

When he was fairly brought to bay, Padella turned and
dealt Prince Giglio a prodigious crack over the sconce with
his battle-axe, a most enormous weapon, which had cut
down I don't know how many regiments in the course of

the afternoon. But, Law bless you ! though the blow fell right down on His Majesty's helmet, it made no more impression than if Padella had struck him with a pat of butter : his battle-axe crumpled up in Padella's hand, and the Royal Giglio laughed for very scorn at the impotent efforts of that atrocious usurper.

At the ill success of his blow the Crim Tartar monarch was justly irritated. " If," says he to Giglio, " you ride a

THE TERRIFIC COMBAT BETWEEN KING GIGLIO
AND KING PADELLA

fairy horse, and wear fairy armour, what on earth is the use of my hitting you ? I may as well give myself up a prisoner at once. Your Majesty won't, I suppose, be so mean as to strike a poor fellow who can't strike again ? "

The justice of Padella's remark struck the magnanimous Giglio. " Do you yield yourself a prisoner, Padella ? " says he.

" Of course I do," says Padella.

" Do you acknowledge Rosalba as your rightful Queen, and give up the crown and all your treasures to your rightful mistress ? "

" If I must, I must," says Padella, who was naturally very sulky.

By this time King Giglio's aides-de-camp had come up, whom His Majesty ordered to bind the prisoner. And they tied his hands behind him, and bound his legs tight under his horse, having set him with his face to the tail ; and in this fashion he was led back to King Giglio's quarters, and thrust into the very dungeon where young Bulbo had been confined.

Padella (who was a very different person in the depth of his distress, to Padella, the proud wearer of the Crim Tartar crown), now most affectionately and earnestly asked to see his son—his dear eldest boy—his darling Bulbo ; and that good-natured young man never once reproached his haughty parent for his unkind conduct the day before, when he would have left Bulbo to be shot without any pity, but came to see his father, and spoke to him through the grating of the door, beyond which he was not allowed to go ; and brought him some sandwiches from the grand supper which His Majesty was giving above stairs, in honour of the brilliant victory which had just been achieved.

" I cannot stay with you long, sir," says Bulbo, who was in his best ball dress, as he handed his father in the prog, " I am engaged to dance the next quadrille with Her Majesty Queen Rosalba, and I hear the fiddles playing at this very moment."

So Bulbo went back to the ball-room, and the wretched Padella ate his solitary supper in silence and tears.

All was now joy in King Giglio's circle. Dancing, feasting, fun, illuminations, and jollifications of all sorts ensued. The people through whose villages they passed were ordered to illuminate their cottages at night, and scatter flowers on the roads during the day. They were requested, and I promise you they did not like to refuse, to serve the troops liberally with eatables and wine ; besides, the army was enriched by the immense quantity of plunder which was found in King Padella's camp, and taken from his soldiers ; who (after they had given up everything) were allowed to fraternise with the conquerors ; and the united forces marched back by easy stages towards King Giglio's capital, his royal banner and that of Queen Rosalba being carried in front of the troops. Hedzoff was made a Duke and a Field-Marshal. Smith and Jones were promoted to be Earls ; the Crim Tartar Order of the Pumpkin and the Paflagonian decoration of the Cucumber were freely distributed by their Majesties to the army. Queen Rosalba wore the Paflagonian Ribbon of the Cucumber across her riding-habit, whilst King Giglio never appeared without the grand Cordon of the Pumpkin. How the people cheered them as they rode along side by side ! They were pronounced to be the handsomest couple ever seen : that was a matter of course ; but they really *were* very handsome, and, had they been otherwise, would have looked so, they were so happy ! Their Majesties were never separated during the whole day, but breakfasted, dined, and supped together always, and rode side by side, interchanging elegant compliments, and indulging in the most delightful conversation. At night, Her Majesty's ladies of honour (who had all rallied round her the day after King Padella's defeat) came and conducted her to the apartments prepared for her ; whilst King Giglio, surrounded by his gentlemen, withdrew to his own Royal quarters. It was agreed they should be married as soon as they reached the capital, and orders were despatched to the Archbishop of Blombodinga, to hold himself in readiness to perform the interesting ceremony. Duke Hedzoff carried the message, and gave instructions to have the Royal Castle splendidly refurnished and painted afresh. The Duke seized Glumboso, the Ex-Prime Minister, and made him refund that considerable sum of money which the old scoundrel had secreted out of the late King's treasure. He also clapped Valoroso into prison (who, by the way, had been dethroned for some considerable period past), and when the Ex-Monarch weakly remonstrated, Hedzoff said, "A soldier, sir, knows but his duty ; my orders are to lock you up along with the Ex-King Padella, whom I have brought hither a

prisoner under guard." So these two Ex-Royal personages were sent for a year to the House of Correction, and thereafter were obliged to become monks of the severest Order of Flagellants, in which state, by fasting, by vigils, by flogging (which they administered to one another, humbly but resolutely), no doubt they exhibited a repentance for their past misdeeds, usurpations, and private and public crimes.

As for Glumboso, that rogue was sent to the galleys, and never had an opportunity to steal any more.

XVIII

How They All Journeyed Back to the Capital

THE FAIRY BLACKSTICK, by whose means this young King and Queen had certainly won their respective crowns back, would come not unfrequently, to pay them a little visit—as they were riding in their triumphal progress towards Giglio's capital—change her wand into a pony, and travel by their Majesties' side, giving them the very best advice. I am not sure that King Giglio did not think the Fairy and her advice rather a bore, fancying it was his own valour and merits which had put him on his throne, and conquered Padella : and, in fine, I fear he rather gave himself airs towards his best friend and patroness. She exhorted him to deal justly by his subjects, to draw mildly on the taxes, never to break his promise when he had once given it—and in all respects to be a good King.

" A good King, my dear Fairy ! " cries Rosalba. " Of course he will. Break his promise ! can you fancy my Giglio would ever do anything so improper, so unlike him ? No ! never ! " And she looked fondly towards Giglio, whom she thought a pattern of perfection.

" Why is Fairy Blackstick always advising me, and telling me how to manage my government, and warning me to keep my word ? Does she suppose that I am not a man of sense, and a man of honour ? " asks Giglio testily. " Methinks she rather presumes upon her position."

" Hush ! dear Giglio," says Rosalba. " You know Blackstick has been very kind to us, and we must not offend her." But the Fairy was not listening to Giglio's testy observations, she had fallen back, and was trotting on her pony now, by Master Bulbo's side, who rode a donkey, and made himself generally beloved in the army by his cheerfulness, kindness, and good-humour to everybody. He was eager to see his darling Angelica. He thought there never was such a charming being. Blackstick did not tell him it was the possession of the magic rose that made Angelica so lovely in his eyes. She brought him the very best accounts of his little wife, whose misfortunes and humiliations had indeed very greatly improved her ; and, you see, she could whisk off on her wand a hundred miles in a minute, and be back in no time, and so carry polite messages from Bulbo to Angelica, and from Angelica to Bulbo, and comfort that young man upon his journey.

When the Royal party arrived at the last stage before you reach Blombodinga, who should be in waiting, in her carriage there with her lady of honour by her side, but the Princess Angelica ! She rushed into her husband's arms, scarcely stopping to make a passing curtsey to the King and Queen. She had no eyes but for Bulbo, who appeared perfectly lovely to her on account of the fairy ring which he wore ; whilst she herself, wearing the magic rose in her bonnet, seemed entirely beautiful to the enraptured Bulbo.

A splendid luncheon was served to the Royal party, of which the Archbishop, the Chancellor, Duke Hedzoff, Countess Gruffanuff, and all our friends partook, the Fairy Blackstick being seated on the left of King Giglio, with Bulbo and Angelica beside her. You could hear the joy-bells ringing in the capital, and the guns which the citizens were firing off in honour of their Majesties.

" What can have induced that hideous old Gruffanuff to dress herself up in such an absurd way ? Did you ask her to be your bridesmaid, my dear ? " says Giglio to Rosalba. " What a figure of fun Gruffy is ! "

Gruffy was seated opposite their Majesties, between the Archbishop and the Lord Chancellor, and a figure of fun she certainly was, for she was dressed in a low white silk dress, with lace over, a wreath of white roses on her wig, a splendid lace veil, and her yellow old neck was covered with diamonds. She ogled the King in such a manner that His Majesty burst out laughing.

" Eleven o'clock ! " cries Giglio, as the great Cathedral

bell of Blombodinga tolled that hour. "Gentlemen and ladies, we must be starting. Archbishop, you must be at church, I think, before twelve?"

"We must be at church before twelve," sighs out Gruffanuff in a languishing voice, hiding her old face behind her fan.

"And then I shall be the happiest man in my dominions," cries Giglio, with an elegant bow to the blushing Rosalba.

"Oh, my Giglio! Oh, my dear Majesty!" exclaims Gruffanuff; "and can it be that this happy moment at length has arrived——"

"Of course it has arrived," says the King.

" —And that I am about to become the enraptured bride of my adored Giglio!" continues Gruffanuff. "Lend me a smelling-bottle, somebody. I certainly shall faint with joy."

"*You* my bride?" roars out Giglio.

"*You* marry my Prince?" cried poor little Rosalba.

"Pooh! Nonsense! The woman's mad!" exclaims the King. And all the courtiers exhibited by their countenances and expressions, marks of surprise, or ridicule, or incredulity, or wonder.

"I should like to know who else is going to be married, if I am not?" shrieks out Gruffanuff. "I should like to know if King Giglio is a gentleman, and if there is such a thing as justice in Paflagonia? Lord Chancellor! my Lord Archbishop! will your Lordships sit by and see a poor, fond, confiding, tender creature put upon? Has not Prince Giglio promised to marry his Barbara? Is not this Giglio's signature? Does not this paper declare that he is mine, and only mine?" And she handed to his Grace the Archbishop the document which the Prince signed that evening when she wore the magic ring, and Giglio drank so much champagne. And the old Archbishop, taking out his eyeglasses, read—" ' This is to give notice, that I, Giglio, only son of Savio, King of Paflagonia, hereby promise to marry the charming Barbara Griselda, Countess Gruffanuff, and widow of the late Jenkins Gruffanuff, Esq.'

" H'm," says the Archbishop, " the document is certainly a—a document."

" Phoo ! " says the Lord Chancellor, " the signature is not in His Majesty's handwriting." Indeed, since his studies at Bosforo, Giglio had made an immense improvement in caligraphy.

" Is it your handwriting, Giglio ? " cries the Fairy Blackstick, with an awful severity of countenance.

" Y—y—y—es," poor Giglio gasps out, " I had quite forgotten the confounded paper : she can't mean to hold me by it. You old wretch, what will you take to let me off ? Help the Queen, some one—Her Majesty has fainted."

" Chop her head off ! "
" Smother the old witch ! "
" Pitch her into the river ! "
exclaim the impetuous Hedzoff, the ardent Smith, and the faithful Jones.

But Gruffanuff flung her arms round the Archbishop's neck, and bellowed out, " Justice, justice, my Lord Chancellor ! " so loudly, that her piercing shrieks caused everybody to pause. As for Rosalba, she was borne away lifeless by her ladies ; and you may imagine the look of agony which Giglio cast towards that lovely being, as his hope, his joy, his darling, his all in all, was thus removed, and in her place the horrid old Gruffanuff rushed up to his side, and once more shrieked out, " Justice, justice ! "

" Won't you take that sum of money which Glumboso hid ? " says Giglio ; " two hundred and eighteen thousand millions, or thereabouts. It's a handsome sum."

" I will have that and you too ! " says Gruffanuff.

" Let us throw the crown jewels into the bargain," gasps out Giglio.

" I will wear them by my Giglio's side ! " says Gruffanuff.

" Will half, three-quarters, five-sixths, nineteen-twentieths, of my kingdom do, Countess ? " asks the trembling monarch.

"What were all Europe to me without *you*, my Giglio?" cries Gruff, kissing his hand.

"I won't, I can't, I shan't,—I'll resign the crown first," shouts Giglio, tearing away his hand; but Gruff clung to it.

"I have a competency, my love," she says, "and with thee and a cottage thy Barbara will be happy."

Giglio was half mad with rage by this time. "I will not marry her," says he. "Oh, Fairy, Fairy, give me counsel?" And as he spoke he looked wildly round at the severe face of the Fairy Blackstick.

"'Why is Fairy Blackstick always advising me, and warning me to keep my word? Does she suppose that I am not a man of honour?'" said the Fairy, quoting Giglio's own haughty words. He quailed under the brightness of her eyes; he felt that there was no escape for him from that awful inquisition.

"Well, Archbishop," said he in a dreadful voice, that made his Grace start, "since this Fairy has led me to the height of happiness but to dash me down into the depths of despair, since I am to lose Rosalba, let me at least keep my honour. Get up, Countess, and let us be married; I can keep my word, but I can die afterwards."

"Oh, dear Giglio," cries Gruffanuff, skipping up, "I knew, I knew I could trust thee—I knew that my Prince was the soul of honour. Jump into your carriages, ladies and gentlemen, and let us go to church at once; and as for dying, dear Giglio, no, no:—thou wilt forget that insignificant little chambermaid of a Queen—thou wilt live to be consoled by thy Barbara! She wishes to be a Queen, and not a Queen Dowager, my gracious Lord!" And hanging upon poor Giglio's arm, and leering and grinning in his face in the most disgusting manner, this old wretch tripped off in her white satin shoes, and jumped into the very carriage which had been got ready to convey Giglio and Rosalba to church. The cannons roared again, the bells pealed triple-bobmajors, the people came out flinging flowers upon the path of the royal bride and bridegroom, and Gruff looked out of the gilt coach window and bowed and grinned to them. Phoo ! the horrid old wretch !

XIX

And Now We Come to the Last Scene in the Pantomime

T H E M A N Y ups and downs of her life had given the Princess Rosalba prodigious strength of mind, and that highly principled young woman presently recovered from her fainting-fit, out of which Fairy Blackstick, by a precious essence which the Fairy always carried in her pocket, awakened her. Instead of tearing her hair, crying, and bemoaning herself, and fainting again, as many young women would have done, Rosalba remembered that she owed an example of firmness to her subjects ; and though she loved Giglio more than her life, was determined, as she told the Fairy, not to interfere between him and justice, or to cause him to break his royal word.

" I cannot marry him, but I shall love him always," says she to Blackstick ; " I will go and be present at his marriage with the Countess, and sign the book, and wish them happy with all my heart. I will see, when I get home, whether I cannot make the new Queen some handsome presents. The Crim Tartary crown diamonds are uncommonly fine, and I shall never have any use for them. I will live and die unmarried like Queen Elizabeth, and, of course, I shall leave my crown to Giglio when I quit this world. Let us go and see them married, my dear Fairy, let me say one last farewell to him ; and then, if you please, I will return to my own dominions."

So the Fairy kissed Rosalba with peculiar tenderness, and at once changed her wand into a very comfortable coach-and-four, with a steady coachman, and two respectable footmen behind, and the Fairy and Rosalba got into the coach, which Angelica and Bulbo entered after them. As for honest

Bulbo, he was blubbering in the most pathetic manner, quite overcome by Rosalba's misfortune. She was touched by the honest fellow's sympathy, promised to restore to him the confiscated estates of Duke Padella his father, and created him, as he sat there in the coach, Prince, Highness, and First Grandee of the Crim Tartar Empire. The coach moved on, and, being a fairy coach, soon came up with the bridal procession.

Before the ceremony at church it was the custom in Paflagonia, as it is in other countries, for the bride and bridegroom to sign the Contract of Marriage, which was to be witnessed by the Chancellor, Minister, Lord Mayor, and principal officers of state. Now, as the royal palace was being painted and furnished anew, it was not ready for the reception of the King and his bride, who proposed at first to take up their residence at the Prince's palace, that one which Valoroso occupied when Angelica was born, and before he usurped the throne.

So the marriage party drove up to the palace : the dignitaries got out of their carriages and stood aside : poor Rosalba stepped out of her coach, supported by Bulbo, and stood almost fainting up against the railings so as to have a last look of her dear Giglio. As for Blackstick, she, according to her custom, had flown out of the coach window in some inscrutable manner, and was now standing at the palace door.

Giglio came up the steps with his horrible bride on his arm, looking as pale as if he was going to execution. He only frowned at the Fairy Blackstick—he was angry with her, and thought she came to insult his misery.

" Get out of the way, pray," says Gruffanuff haughtily. " I wonder why you are always poking your nose into other people's affairs ? "

" Are you determined to make this poor young man unhappy ? " says Blackstick.

" To marry him, yes ! What business is it of yours ? Pray, madam, don't say ' you ' to a Queen," cries Gruffanuff.

" You won't take the money he offered you ? "

" No."

" You won't let him off his bargain, though you know you cheated him when you made him sign the paper ? "

" Impudence ! Policemen, remove this woman ! " cries Gruffanuff. And the policemen were rushing forward, but with a wave of her wand the Fairy struck them all like so many statues in their places.

MADAM GRUFFANUFF FINDS A HUSBAND

" You won't take anything in exchange for your bond, Mrs. Gruffanuff," cries the Fairy, with awful severity. " I speak for the last time."

" No ! " shrieks Gruffanuff, stamping with her foot. " I'll have my husband, my husband, my husband ! "

" You SHALL HAVE YOUR HUSBAND ! " the Fairy Blackstick cried ; and advancing a step, laid her hand upon the nose of the KNOCKER.

As she touched it, the brass nose seemed to elongate, the open mouth opened still wider, and uttered a roar which made everybody start. The eyes rolled wildly ; the arms and legs uncurled themselves, writhed about, and seemed to lengthen with each twist ; the knocker expanded into a figure in yellow livery, six feet high ; the screws by which it was fixed to the door unloosed themselves, and JENKINS GRUFFANUFF once more trod the threshold off which he had been lifted more than twenty years ago !

"Master's not at home," says Jenkins, just in his old voice ; and Mrs. Jenkins, giving a dreadful *youp*, fell down in a fit, in which nobody minded her.

For everybody was shouting, "Huzzay ! huzzay ! " "Hip, hip, hurray ! " " Long live the King and Queen ! " "Were such things ever seen ? " " No, never, never, never ! " " The Fairy Blackstick for ever ! "

The bells were ringing double peals, the guns roaring and banging most prodigiously. Bulbo was embracing everybody ; the Lord Chancellor was flinging up his wig and shouting like a madman ; Hedzoff had got the Archbishop round the waist, and they were dancing a jig for joy ; and as for Giglio, I leave you to imagine what *he* was doing, and if he kissed Rosalba once, twice—twenty thousand times, I'm sure I don't think he was wrong.

So Gruffanuff opened the hall door with a low bow, just as he had been accustomed to do, and they all went in and signed the book, and then they went to church and were married, and the Fairy Blackstick sailed away on her cane, and was never more heard of in Paflagonia.

And here ends the Fireside Pantomime

TRAVELS OF BARON MUNCHAUSEN

Some years before my beard announced approaching manhood, or, in other words, when I was neither man nor boy, but between both, I expressed in repeated conversations a strong desire of seeing the world, from which I was discouraged by my parents, though my father had been no inconsiderable traveller himself, as will appear before I have reached the end of my singular, and, I may add, interesting adventures. A cousin, by my mother's side, took a liking to me, often said I was a fine forward youth, and was much inclined to gratify my curiosity. His eloquence had more effect than mine, for my father consented to my accompanying him in a voyage to the island of Ceylon, where his uncle had resided as governor many years.

We sailed from Amsterdam with despatches from their High Mightinesses the States of Holland. The only circumstance which happened on our voyage worth relating was the wonderful effects of a storm, which had torn up by the roots a great number of trees of enormous bulk and height, in an island where we lay at anchor to take in wood and water; some of these trees weighed many tons, yet they were carried by the wind so amazingly high, that they appeared like the feathers of small birds floating in the air, for they were at least five miles above the earth : however, as soon as the storm subsided they all fell perpendicularly into their respective places, and took root again, except the largest which happened, when it was blown into the air, to have a man and his wife, a very honest old couple, upon its branches, gathering cucumbers (in this part of the globe that useful vegetable grows upon trees) : the weight of this couple, as the tree descended, over-balanced the trunk, and brought it down in an horizontal position : it fell upon the chief man of the island, and killed him on the spot ; he had quitted his house in the storm, under an apprehension of its falling upon him, and was returning through his own garden when this fortunate accident happened. The word fortunate, here, requires some explanation. This chief was a man of a very avaricious and oppressive disposition, and though he had no family, the natives of the island were half-starved by his oppressive and infamous impositions.

The very goods which he had thus taken from them were spoiling in his stores, while the poor wretches from whom they were plundered were pining in poverty. Though the destruction of this tyrant was accidental, the people chose the cucumber-gatherers for their governors, as a mark of their gratitude for destroying, though accidentally, their late tyrant.

After we had repaired the damages we sustained in this remarkable storm, and taken leave of the new governor and his lady, we sailed with a fair wind for the object of our voyage.

In about six weeks we arrived at Ceylon, where we were received with great marks of friendship and true politeness. The following singular adventures may not prove unentertaining.

After we had resided at Ceylon about a fortnight I accompanied one of the governor's brothers upon a shooting party. He was a strong, athletic man, and being used to that climate (for he had resided there some years), he bore the violent heat of the sun much better than I could ; in our excursion he had made a considerable progress through a thick wood when I was only at the entrance.

Near the banks of a large piece of water, which had engaged my attention, I thought I heard a rustling noise behind ; on turning about I was almost petrified (as who would not ?) at the sight of a lion, which was evidently approaching with the intention of satisfying his appetite with my poor carcase, and that without asking my consent. What was to be done in this horrible dilemma ? I had not even a moment for reflection ; my piece was only charged with swan-shot, and I had no other about me : however, though I could have no idea of killing such an animal with that weak kind of ammunition, yet I had some hopes of frightening him by the report, and perhaps of wounding him also. I immediately let fly, without waiting till he was within reach, and the report did but enrage him, for he now quickened his pace, and seemed to approach me full speed : I attempted to escape, but that only added (if an addition could be made) to my distress ; for the moment I turned about I found a large crocodile, with his mouth extended almost ready to receive me. On my right hand was the piece of water before mentioned, and on my left a deep precipice, said to have, as I have since learned, a receptacle at the bottom for venomous creatures : in short I gave myself up as lost, for the lion was now upon his hind-legs, just in the act of seizing me ; I fell involuntarily to the ground with fear, and, as it afterwards appeared, he sprang over me. I lay some time in a situation which no language can describe, expecting to feel his teeth or talons in some part of me every moment : after waiting in this prostrate situation a few seconds I heard a violent but unusual noise, different from any sound that had ever before assailed my ears ; nor is it at all to be wondered at, when I inform you from whence it proceeded : after listening for some time, I ventured to raise my head and look round, when, to my unspeakable joy, I perceived the lion had, by the eagerness with which he sprung at me, jumped forward, as I fell, into the crocodile's mouth ! which, as before observed, was wide open ; the head of the one stuck in the throat of the other ! and they were struggling to extricate themselves ! I fortunately recollected my hunting-knife, which was by my side ; with this instrument I severed the lion's head at one blow, and the body fell at my feet ! I then, with the butt-end of my fowling-piece, rammed the head farther into the throat of the crocodile, and destroyed him by suffocation, for he could neither gorge nor eject it.

Soon after I had thus gained a complete victory over my two powerful adversaries my companion arrived in search of me ; for finding I did not follow him into the wood, he returned, apprehending I had lost my way, or met with some accident.

After mutual congratulations, we measured the crocodile, which was just forty feet in length.

As soon as we had related this extraordinary adventure to the governor, he sent a wagon and servants, who brought home the two carcases. The lion's skin was properly preserved, with its hair on, after which it was made into tobacco-pouches, and presented by me, upon our return to Holland, to the burgomasters, who, in return, requested my acceptance of a thousand ducats.

The skin of the crocodile was stuffed in the usual manner, and makes a capital article in their public museum at Amsterdam, where the exhibitor relates the whole story to each spectator, with such additions as he thinks proper.

Some years after this I set off to Russia, in the midst of winter, from a just notion that frost and snow must of course mend the roads, which every traveller had described as uncommonly bad through the northern parts of Germany, Poland, Courland, and Livonia. I went on horseback, as the most convenient manner of travelling ; I was but lightly clothed, and of this I felt the inconvenience the more I advanced north-east. What must not a poor old man have suffered in that severe weather and climate, whom I saw on a bleak common in Poland, lying on the road, helpless, shivering, and hardly having wherewithal to cover his nakedness ? I pitied the poor soul : though I felt the severity of the air myself, I threw my mantle over him, and immediately I heard a voice from the heavens, blessing me for that piece of charity, saying,

" You will be rewarded, my son, for this in time."

I went on : night and darkness overtook me. No village

was to be seen. The country was covered with snow, and I was unacquainted with the road.

Tired, I alighted, and fastened my horse to something like a pointed stump of a tree, which appeared above the snow ; for the sake of safety I placed my pistols under my arm, and lay down on the snow, where I slept so soundly that I did not open my eyes till full daylight. It is not easy to conceive my astonishment to find myself in the midst of a village, lying in a churchyard ; nor was my horse to be seen, but I heard him soon after neigh somewhere above me. On looking upwards I beheld him hanging by his bridle to the weather-cock of the steeple. Matters were now very plain to me : the village had been covered with snow overnight ; a sudden change of weather had taken place ; I had sunk down to the churchyard whilst asleep, gently, and in the same proportion as the snow had melted away ; and what in the dark I had taken to be a stump of a little tree appearing above the snow, to which I had tied my horse, proved to have been the cross or weather-cock of the steeple!

Without long consideration I took one of my pistols, shot the bridle in two, brought down the horse, and proceeded on my journey. [Here the Baron seems to have forgot his feelings ; he should certainly have ordered his horse a feed of corn, after fasting so long.]

He carried me well—advancing into the interior parts of Russia. I found travelling on horseback rather unfashionable in winter, therefore I submitted, as I always do, to the custom of the country, took a single horse sledge, and drove briskly towards St. Petersburg. I do not exactly recollect whether it was in Eastland or Jugemanland but I remember that in the midst of a dreary forest I spied a terrible wolf making after me, with all the speed of ravenous winter hunger. He soon overtook me. There was no possibility of escape. Mechanically I laid myself down flat in the sledge, and let my horse run for our safety. What I wished, but hardly hoped or expected, happened immediately after. The wolf did not mind me in the least, but took a leap over me, and falling furiously on the horse, began instantly to tear and devour the hind-part of the poor animal, which ran the faster for his pain and terror. Thus unnoticed and safe myself, I lifted my head slyly up, and with horror I beheld that the wolf had ate his way into the horse's body ; it was not long before he had fairly forced himself into it, when I took my advantage, and fell upon him with the butt-end of my whip. This unexpected attack in his rear frightened him so much, that he leaped forward with all his might : the horse's carcase dropped on the ground, but in his place the wolf was in the harness, and I on my part whipping him continually : we both arrived in full career safe to St. Petersburg, contrary to our respective expectations, and very much to the astonishment of the spectators.

It was some time before I could obtain a commission in the army, and for several months I was perfectly at liberty to sport away my time and money in the most gentleman-like manner. You may easily imagine that I spent much of both out of town with such gallant fellows as knew how to make the most of an open forest country. The very recollection of those amusements gives me fresh spirits, and creates a warm wish for a repetition of them. One morning I saw, through the windows of my bedroom, that a large pond not far off was covered with wild ducks. In an instant I took my gun from the corner, ran downstairs and out of the house in such a hurry, that I imprudently struck my face against the doorpost. Fire flew out of my eyes, but it did not prevent my intention ; I soon came within shot, when, levelling my piece, I observed to my sorrow, that even the flint had sprung from the cock by the violence of the shock I had just received. There was no time to be lost. I presently remembered the effect it had on my eyes, therefore opened the pan, levelled my piece against the wild fowls, and my fist against one of my eyes. [The Baron's eyes have retained fire ever since, and appear particularly illuminated when he relates this anecdote.] A hearty blow drew sparks again ; the shot went off, and I killed fifty brace of ducks, twenty widgeons, and three couple of teals. Presence of mind is the soul of manly exercises.

Chance and good luck often correct our mistakes ; of this I had a singular instance soon after, when, in the depth of a forest, I saw a wild pig and sow running close behind each other. My ball had missed them, yet the foremost pig only ran away, and the sow stood motionless, as fixed to the ground. On examining into the matter, I found the latter one to be an old sow, blind with age, which had taken hold of her pig's tail, in order to be led along by filial duty. My ball, having passed between the two, had cut his leading-string, which the old sow continued to hold in her mouth ; and as her former guide did not draw her on any longer, she had stopped of course ; I therefore laid hold of the remaining end of the pig's tail, and led the old beast home without any farther trouble on my part, and without any reluctance or apprehension on the part of the helpless old animal.

Terrible as these wild sows are, yet more fierce and dangerous are the boars, one of which I had once the misfortune to meet in a forest, unprepared for attack or defence. I retired behind an oak-tree just when the furious animal levelled a side-blow at me, with such force, that his tusks pierced through the tree, by which means he could neither repeat the blow nor retire. Ho, ho ! thought I, I shall soon have you now ! and immediately I laid hold of a stone, wherewith I hammered and bent his tusks in such a manner, that he could not retreat by any means, and must wait my return from the next village, whither I went for ropes and a cart, to secure him properly, and to carry him off safe and alive, in which I perfectly succeeded.

Having one day spent all my shot, I found myself unexpectedly in presence of a stately stag, looking at me as unconcernedly as if he had known of my empty pouches. I charged immediately with powder, and upon it a good handful of cherry-stones, for I had sucked the fruit as far as the hurry would permit. Thus I let fly at him, and hit him just on the middle of the forehead, between his antlers ; it stunned him—he staggered—yet he made off. A year or two after, being with a party in the same forest, I beheld a noble stag with a fine full grown cherry-tree above ten feet high between his antlers. I immediately recollected my former adventure, looked upon him as my property, and brought him to the ground by one shot, which at once gave me the haunch and cherry-sauce ; for the tree was covered with the richest fruit, the like I had never tasted before.

All these narrow and lucky escapes, gentlemen, were chances turned to advantage by presence of mind and vigorous exertions, which, taken together, as everybody knows, make the fortunate sportsman, sailor, and soldier ; but he would be a very blamable and imprudent sports- man, admiral, or general, who would always depend upon chance and his stars, without troubling himself about those arts which are their particular pursuits, and without pro- viding the very best implements, which insure success.

I remember with pleasure and tenderness a superb Lithuanian horse, which no money could have bought. He became mine by an accident, which gave me an opportunity of showing my horsemanship to a great advantage. I was at Count Przobossky's noble country-seat in Lithuania, and remained with the ladies at tea in the drawing-room, while the gentlemen were down in the yard, to see a young horse of blood which had just arrived from the stud. We suddenly heard a noise of distress ; I hastened downstairs, and found the horse so unruly, that nobody durst approach or mount him. The most resolute horsemen stood dismayed and aghast ; despondency was expressed in every countenance, when, in one leap, I was on his back, took him by surprise, and worked him quite into gentleness and obedience, with the best display of horsemanship I was master of. Fully to show this to the ladies, and save them unnecessary trouble, I forced him to leap in at one of the open windows of the tea-room, walked round several times, pace, trot, and gallop, and at last made him mount the tea-table, there to repeat his lessons in a pretty style of miniature which was exceedingly pleasing to the ladies, for he performed them amazingly well, and did not break either cup or saucer. It placed me so high in their opinion, and so well in that of the noble lord, that, with his usual politeness, he begged I would accept of this young horse, and ride him full career to conquest and honour in the campaign against the Turks, which was soon to be opened, under the command of Count Munich.

We made a terrible havoc amongst them, and drove them not only back to a walled town in their rear, but even through it, contrary to our most sanguine expectations. The swiftness of my Lithuanian enabled me to be foremost in the pursuit ; and seeing the enemy fairly flying through the opposite gate, I thought it would be prudent to stop in the market-place, to order the men to rendezvous. I stopped, gentlemen ; but judge of my astonishment when in this market-place I saw not one of my hussars about me ! Are they scouring the other streets ? or what is become of them ? They could not be far off, and must, at all events, soon join me. In that expectation I walked my panting Lithuanian to a spring in this market-place, and let him drink. He drank uncommonly, with an eagerness not to be satisfied, but natural enough ; for when I looked round for my men, what should I see, gentlemen ! the hind part of the poor creature—croup and legs were missing, as if he had been cut in two, and the water ran out as it came in, without refreshing or doing him any good ! How it could have happened was quite a mystery to me, till I returned with him to the town-gate. There I saw, that when I rushed in pell-mell with the flying enemy, they had dropped the portcullis (a heavy falling door, with sharp spikes at the bottom, let down suddenly to prevent the entrance of an enemy into a fortified town) unperceived by me, which had totally cut off his hind part, that still lay quivering on the outside of the gate. It would have been an irreparable loss, had not our farrier contrived to bring both parts together while hot. He sewed them up with sprigs and young shoots of laurels that were at hand ; the wound healed, and, what could not have happened but to so glorious a horse, the sprigs took root in his body, grew up, and formed a bower over me ; so that afterwards I could go upon many other expeditions in the shade of my own and my horse's laurels.

I was not always successful. I had the misfortune to be overpowered by numbers, to be made prisoner of war ; and, what is worse, but always usual among the Turks, to be sold for a slave. [The Baron was afterwards in great favour with the Grand Seignior, as will appear hereafter.] In that state of humiliation my daily task was not very hard and laborious, but rather singular and irksome. It was to drive the Sultan's bees every morning to their pasture-grounds, to attend them all the day long, and against night to drive them back to their hives. One evening I missed a bee, and soon observed that two bears had fallen upon her to tear her to pieces for the honey she carried. I had nothing like an offensive weapon in my hands but the silver hatchet, which is the badge of the Sultan's gardeners and farmers. I threw it at the robbers, with an intention to frighten them away, and set the poor bee at liberty ; but, by an unlucky turn of my arm, it flew upwards, and continued rising till it reached the moon. How should I recover it ? how fetch it down again ? I recollected that Turkey-beans grow very quick, and run up to an astonishing height. I planted one immediately ; it grew, and actually fastened itself to one of the moon's horns. I had no more to do now but to climb up by it into the moon, where I safely arrived, and had a troublesome piece of business before I could find my silver hatchet, in a place where every thing has the brightness of silver ; at last, however, I found it in a heap of chaff and chopped straw. I was now for returning : but, alas ! the heat of the sun had dried up my bean ; it was totally useless for my descent : so I fell to work, and twisted me a rope of that chopped straw, as long and as well as I could make it. This I fastened to one of the moon's horns, and slid down to the end of it. Here I held myself fast with the left hand, and with the hatchet in my right, I cut the long, now useless end of the upper part, which, when tied to the lower end, brought me a good deal lower : this repeated splicing and tying of the rope did not improve its quality, or bring me down to the Sultan's farm. I was four or five miles from the earth at least when it broke ; I fell to the ground with such amazing violence, that I found myself stunned, and in a hole nine fathoms deep at least, made by the weight of my body falling from so great a height : I recovered, but knew not how to get out again ; however, I dug slopes or steps with my finger-nails (the Baron's nails were then of forty years' growth), and easily accomplished it.

Peace was soon after concluded with the Turks, and gaining my liberty, I left St. Petersburg at the time of that singular revolution, when the emperor in his cradle, his mother, the Duke of Brunswick, her father, Field-Marshal Munich, and many others were sent to Siberia. The winter was then so uncommonly severe all over Europe, that ever since the sun seems to be frostbitten. At my return to this place, I felt on the road greater inconveniences than those I had experienced on my setting out.

I travelled post, and finding myself in a narrow lane, bid the postilion give a signal with his horn, that other travellers might not meet us in the narrow passage. He blew with all his might ; but his endeavours were in vain, he could not make the horn sound, which was unaccountable, and rather unfortunate, for soon after we found ourselves in the presence of another coach coming the other way : there was no proceeding ; however, I got out of my carriage, and being pretty strong, placed it, wheels and all, upon my head : I then jumped over a hedge about nine feet high (which, considering the weight of the coach, was rather difficult) into a field, and came out again by another jump into the road beyond the other carriage : I then went back for the horses, and placing one upon my head, and the other under my left arm, by the same means brought them to my coach, put to, and proceeded to an inn at the end of our stage. I should have told you that the horse under my arm was very spirited, and not above four years old ; in making my second spring over the hedge, he expressed great dislike to that violent kind of motion by kicking and snorting ; however, I confined his hind legs by putting them into my coat pocket. After we arrived at the inn my postilion and I refreshed ourselves : he hung his horn on a peg near the kitchen fire ; I sat on the other side.

Suddenly we heard a *tereng ! tereng ! teng ! teng !* We looked round, and now found the reason why the postilion had not been able to sound his horn ; his tunes were frozen up in the horn, and came out now by thawing, plain enough, and much to the credit of the driver ; so that the honest fellow entertained us for some time with a variety of tunes, without putting his mouth to the horn—The King of Prussia's March—Over the Hill and over the Dale—with many other favourite tunes ; at length the thawing entertainment concluded, as I shall this short account of my Russian travels.

CAUTIONARY TALES

GREEDY RICHARD

by JANE TAYLOR

" I THINK I want some pies this morning,"
Said Dick, stretching himself and yawning ;
So down he threw his slate and books,
And saunter'd to the pastry-cook's.

And there he cast his greedy eyes
Round on the jellies and the pies,
So to select, with anxious care,
The very nicest that was there.

At last the point was thus decided,
As his opinion was divided
'Twixt pie and jelly, he was loath
Either to leave, so took them both.

Now Richard never could be pleas'd
To stop when hunger was appeas'd,
But would go on to eat and stuff,
Long after he had had enough.

" I shan't take any more," said Dick :
" Dear me, I feel extremely sick :
I cannot eat this other bit ;
I wish I had not tasted it."

Then slowly rising from his seat,
He threw the cheesecake in the street,
And left the tempting pastry-cook's,
With very discontented looks.

Just then a man with wooden leg
Met Dick, and held his hat to beg ;
And while he told his mournful case,
Look'd at him with imploring face.

Dick, wishing to relieve his pain,
His pockets search'd, but search'd in vain,
And so at last he did declare,
He had not got a farthing there.

The beggar turn'd with face of grief,
And look of patient unbelief,
While Richard, now completely tam'd,
Felt inconceivably asham'd.

" I wish," said he (but wishing's vain)
" I had my money back again,
And had not spent my last, to pay
For what I only threw away.

" Another time I'll take advice,
And not buy things because they're nice ;
But rather save my little store,
To give poor folks, who want it more."

THE WATCHFULNESS OF PAPA

by JANE AND ANNE TAYLOR

MAMA HAD ordered Anne the maid
　　Miss Caroline to wash,
And put on with her nice clean frock
　　A handsome muslin sash.

But Caroline quite naughty grew,
　　For what I cannot think,
And said, "Oh that's a nasty sash,
　　I'll wear my pretty pink."

Papa, who in the parlour sat
　　And heard her make that rout,
That instant went to Caroline,—
　　To whip her there's no doubt.

MATILDA

Who Told Lies and was Burned to Death

by HILAIRE BELLOC

MATILDA told such Dreadful Lies,

It made one Gasp and Stretch one's Eyes !
Her Aunt, who, from her Earliest Youth,
Had kept a Strict Regard for Truth,

Attempted to Believe Matilda :
The effort very nearly killed her,
And would have done so, had not She
Discovered this Infirmity.
For once, towards the Close of Day,
Matilda, growing tired of play,

And finding she was left alone.
Went tiptoe

      to

          the Telephone
And summoned the Immediate Aid
Of London's Noble Fire-Brigade.
Within an hour the Gallant Band
Were pouring in on every hand,
From Putney, Hackney Downs, and Bow
With Courage high and Hearts a-glow
They galloped, roaring through the Town,

"Matilda's House is Burning Down!"
Inspired by British Cheers and Loud
Proceeding from the Frenzied Crowd,
They ran their ladders through a score
Of windows on the Ball Room Floor!
And took Peculiar Pains to Souse
The Pictures up and down the House,

Until Matilda's Aunt succeeded
In showing them they were not needed;
And even then she had to pay
To get the Men to go away!

.　　.　　.　　.　　.

It happened that a few Weeks later
Her Aunt was off to the Theatre
To see that Interesting Play

The Second Mrs. Tanqueray.

She had refused to take her Niece
To hear this Entertaining Piece :
A Deprivation Just and Wise
To Punish her for Telling Lies.
That Night a Fire *did* break out—
You should have heard Matilda Shout !
You should have heard her Scream and Bawl,

And throw the window up and call
To People passing in the Street—
(The rapidly increasing Heat
Encouraging her to obtain
Their confidence)—but all in vain !
For every time She shouted " Fire ! "

They only answered " Little Liar ! "
And therefore when her Aunt returned,

Matilda, and the House, were Burned.

FRANKLIN HYDE

Who Caroused in the Dirt and was corrected by His Uncle

by HILAIRE BELLOC

HIS UNCLE came on Franklin Hyde
Carousing in the Dirt.
He Shook him hard from Side to Side
And

Hit him till it Hurt,

Exclaiming, with a Final Thud,

" Take

that ! Abandoned Boy !
For Playing with Disgusting Mud
As though it were a Toy ! "

MORAL

From Franklin Hyde's adventure, learn
To pass your Leisure Time

In Cleanly Merriment, and turn
From Mud and Oose and Slime
And every form of Nastiness—
But, on the other Hand,
Children in ordinary Dress
May always play with Sand.

JOHN GILPIN

by WILLIAM COWPER

JOHN GILPIN was a citizen
  Of credit and renown,
A train-band captain eke was he
  Of famous London town.

John Gilpin's spouse said to her dear,
  " Though wedded we have been
These twice ten tedious years, yet we
  No holiday have seen.

" To-morrow is our wedding-day,
  And we will then repair
Unto ' The Bell ' at Edmonton,
  All in a chaise and pair.

" My sister and my sister's child,
  Myself and children three,
Will fill the chaise ; so you must ride
  On horseback after we."

He soon replied, " I do admire
  Of womankind but one,
And you are she, my dearest dear,
  Therefore it shall be done.

" I am a linen-draper bold,
  As all the world doth know,
And my good friend the Calender
  Will lend his horse to go."

Quoth Mistress Gilpin, " That's well said ;
   And, for that wine is dear,
We will be furnished with our own,
   Which is both bright and clear."

John Gilpin kissed his loving wife ;
   O'erjoyed was he to find
That though on pleasure she was bent,
   She had a frugal mind.

The morning came, the chaise was brought,
   But yet was not allowed
To drive up to the door, lest all
   Should say that she was proud.

So three doors off the chaise was stayed,
   Where they did all get in ;
Six precious souls, and all agog
   To dash through thick and thin.

Smack went the whip, round went the wheels
   Were never folk so glad ;
The stones did rattle underneath
   As if Cheapside were mad.

John Gilpin at his horse's side
   Seized fast the flowing mane,
And up he got, in haste to ride,
   But soon came down again ; ·

For saddle-tree scarce reached had he,
   His journey to begin,
When, turning round his head, he saw
   Three customers come in.

So down he came ; for loss of time,
   Although it grieved him sore,
Yet loss of pence, full well he knew,
   Would trouble him much more.

'Twas long before the customers
   Were suited to their mind,
When Betty, screaming, came down stairs,
   " The wine is left behind ! "

" Good lack ! " quoth he ; " yet bring it me,
   My leathern belt likewise,
In which I bear my trusty sword,
   When I do exercise."

Now Mistress Gilpin (careful soul !)
   Had two stone bottles found,
To hold the liquor that she loved,
   And keep it safe and sound.

Each bottle had a curling ear,
   Through which the belt he drew,
And hung a bottle on each side,
   To make his balance true.

Then over all, that he might be
   Equipped from top to toe,
His long red cloak, well brushed and neat,
   He manfully did throw.

Now see him mounted once again
   Upon his nimble steed,
Full slowly pacing o'er the stones
   With caution and good heed !

But, finding soon a smoother road
   Beneath his well-shod feet,
The snorting beast began to trot,
   Which galled him in his seat.

So, " Fair and softly," John he cried,
   But John he cried in vain ;
That trot became a gallop soon,
   In spite of curb and rein.

So stooping down, as needs he must
   Who cannot sit upright,
He grasped the mane with both his hands,
   And eke with all his might.

His horse, who never in that sort
   Had handled been before,
What thing upon his back had got
   Did wonder more and more.

Away went Gilpin, neck or naught ;
   Away went hat and wig ;
He little dreamt, when he set out,
   Of running such a rig.

The wind did blow, the cloak did fly,
   Like streamer long and gay,
Till, loop and button failing both,
   At last it flew away.

Then might all people well discern
   The bottles he had slung ;
A bottle swinging at each side,
   As hath been said or sung.

The dogs did bark, the children screamed,
  Up flew the windows all ;
And every soul cried out, " Well done ! "
  As loud as he could bawl.

Away went Gilpin—who but he ?
  His fame soon spread around—
He carries weight ! he rides a race !
  'Tis for a thousand pound !

And still, as fast as he drew near,
  'Twas wonderful to view
How in a trice the turnpike men
  Their gates wide open threw.

And now, as he went bowing down
  His reeking head full low,
The bottles twain behind his back
  Were shattered at a blow.

Down ran the wine into the road,
  Most piteous to be seen,
Which made his horse's flanks to smoke
  As they had basted been.

But still he seemed to carry weight,
  With leathern girdle braced ;
For all might see the bottle-necks
  Still dangling at his waist.

Thus all through merry Islington
  These gambols he did play,
And till he came unto the Wash
  Of Edmonton so gay.

And there he threw the wash about
  On both sides of the way,
Just like unto a trundling mop,
  Or a wild goose at play.

At Edmonton, his loving wife
  From the balcóny spied
Her tender husband, wondering much
  To see how he did ride.

" Stop, stop, John Gilpin !—here's the house ! "
  They all at once did cry ;
" The dinner waits, and we are tired."
  Said Gilpin, " So am I ! "

But yet his horse was not a whit
  Inclined to tarry there ;
For why ?—his owner had a house
  Full ten miles off, at Ware.

So like an arrow swift he flew,
  Shot by an archer strong ;
So did he fly—which brings me to
  The middle of my song.

Away went Gilpin, out of breath,
  And sore against his will,
Till at his friend the Calender's
  His horse at last stood still.

The Calender, amazed to see
  His neighbour in such trim,
Laid down his pipe, flew to the gate,
  And thus accosted him :—

"What news? what news? your tidings tell :
  Tell me you must and shall—
Say why bareheaded you are come,
  Or why you come at all."

Now Gilpin had a pleasant wit,
  And loved a timely joke ;
And thus unto the Calender
  In merry guise he spoke :

"I came because your horse would come ;
  And, if I well forebode,
My hat and wig will soon be here ;
  They are upon the road."

The Calender, right glad to find
  His friend in merry pin,
Returned him not a single word,
  But to the house went in ;

Whence straight he came with hat and wig
  A wig that flowed behind,
A hat not much the worse for wear,
  Each comely in its kind.

He held them up, and, in his turn,
  Thus showed his ready wit,—
"My head is twice as big as yours ;
  They therefore needs must fit.

"But let me scrape the dirt away
  That hangs upon your face ;
And stop and eat, for well you may
  Be in a hungry case."

Says John, " It is my wedding-day,
  And all the world would stare,
If wife should dine at Edmonton,
  And I should dine at Ware."

So turning to his horse, he said,
  " I am in haste to dine ;
'Twas for your pleasure you came here,
  You shall go back for mine."

Ah, luckless speech, and bootless boast !
  For which he paid full dear ;
For while he spake, a braying ass
  Did sing most loud and clear ;

Whereat his horse did snort as he
  Had heard a lion roar,
And galloped off with all his might,
  As he had done before.

Away went Gilpin, and away
  Went Gilpin's hat and wig ;
He lost them sooner than at first,
  For why ?—they were too big.

Now Mistress Gilpin, when she saw
  Her husband posting down
Into the country far away,
  She pulled out half-a-crown.

And thus unto the youth she said,
  That drove them to " The Bell,"
" This shall be yours when you bring back
  My husband safe and well."

The youth did ride, and soon did meet
　　John coming back amain,
Whom in a trice he tried to stop
　　By catching at his rein ;

But not performing what he meant,
　　And gladly would have done,
The frighted steed he frighted more,
　　And made him faster run.

Away went Gilpin, and away
　　Went postboy at his heels,
The postboy's horse right glad to miss
　　The lumbering of the wheels.

Six gentlemen upon the road
　　Thus seeing Gilpin fly,
With postboy scampering in the rear,
　　They raised the hue and cry :

" Stop thief ! stop thief !—a highwayman ! "
　　Not one of them was mute ;
And all and each that passed that way
　　Did join in the pursuit.

And now the turnpike gates again
　　Flew open in short space,
The tollmen thinking, as before,
　　That Gilpin rode a race.

And so he did, and won it too,
　　For he got first to town ;
Nor stopped till where he had got up
　　He did again get down.

Now let us sing, " Long live the king,
  And Gilpin, long live he ;
And when he next doth ride abroad,
  May I be there to see ! "

THE JACKDAW OF RHEIMS

by THOMAS INGOLDSBY
(Rev. R. H. Barham)

THE JACKDAW sat on the Cardinal's chair !
Bishop and abbot, and prior were there ;
 Many a monk, and many a friar,
 Many a knight, and many a squire,
With a great many more of lesser degree,—
In sooth, a goodly company ;
And they served the Lord Primate on bended knee.
 Never, I ween, Was a prouder seen,
Read of in books, or dreamt of in dreams,
Than the Cardinal Lord Archbishop of Rheims !

 In and out Through the motley rout,
That little Jackdaw kept hopping about ;
 Here and there, Like a dog in a fair,
 Over comfits and cates, And dishes and plates,
Cowl and cope, and rochet and pall,
Mitre and crosier ! he hopp'd upon all !
 With a saucy air, He perch'd on the chair
Where, in state, the great Lord Cardinal sat
In the great Lord Cardinal's great red hat ;
 And he peer'd in the face Of his Lordship's Grace,
With a satisfied look, as if he would say,
" We Two are the greatest folks here to-day ! "
 And the priests, with awe, As such freaks they saw,
Said, " The Devil must be in that little Jackdaw ! ! "

The feast was over, the board was clear'd,
The flawns and the custards had all disappear'd,
And six little Singing-boys,—dear little souls !
In nice clean faces, and nice white stoles,
      Came, in order due, Two by two,
Marching that grand refectory through !
A nice little boy held a golden ewer,
Emboss'd and fill'd with water as pure
As any that flows between Rheims and Namur,
Which a nice little boy stood ready to catch
In a fine golden hand-basin made to match.
Two nice little boys, rather more grown,
Carried lavender-water, and eau de Cologne ;
And a nice little boy had a nice cake of soap,
Worthy of washing the hands of the Pope.
      One little boy more A napkin bore,
Of the best white diaper, fringed with pink,
And a Cardinal's Hat mark'd in " permanent ink."

The great Lord Cardinal turns at the sight
Of these nice little boys dress'd all in white :
      From his finger he draws His costly turquoise ;
And, not thinking at all about little Jackdaws,
      Deposits it straight By the side of his plate,
While the nice little boys on his Eminence wait ;
Till, when nobody's dreaming of any such thing,
That little Jackdaw hops off with the ring !

           .   .   .   .

      There's a cry and a shout, And a deuce of a rout,
And nobody seems to know what they're about,
But the monks have their pockets all turn'd inside out ;
      The friars are kneeling, And hunting, and feeling
The carpet, the floor, and the walls, and the ceiling.
      The Cardinal drew Off each plum-colour'd shoe,
And left his red stockings exposed to the view ;

He peeps, and he feels In the toes and the heels ;
They turn up the dishes,—they turn up the plates,—
They take up the poker and poke out the grates,
   —They turn up the rugs, They examine the mugs :—
   But, no !—no such thing ;— They can't find THE RING !
And the Abbot declared that, " when nobody twigg'd it,
Some rascal or other had popp'd in, and prigg'd it ! "

The Cardinal rose with a dignified look,
He call'd for his candle, his bell, and his book !
   In holy anger, and pious grief,
   He solemnly cursed that rascally thief !
   He cursed him at board, he cursed him in bed ;
   From the sole of his foot to the crown of his head ;
   He cursed him in sleeping, that every night
   He should dream of the devil, and wake in a fright ;
   He cursed him in eating, he cursed him in drinking,
   He cursed him in coughing, in sneezing, in winking ;
   He cursed him in sitting, in standing, in lying ;
   He cursed him in walking, in riding, in flying,
   He cursed him in living, he cursed him dying !—
Never was heard such a terrible curse ! !
   But what gave rise To no little surprise,
Nobody seem'd one penny the worse !

The day was gone. The night came on,
The Monks and the Friars they search'd till dawn ;
   When the Sacristan saw, On crumpled claw,
Come limping a poor little lame Jackdaw !
   No longer gay, As on yesterday ;
His feathers all seem'd to be turn'd the wrong way ;—
His pinions droop'd—he could hardly stand,—
His head was as bald as the palm of your hand ;
   His eye so dim, So wasted each limb,
That, heedless of grammar, they all cried, " THAT HIM !—

That's the scamp that has done this scandalous thing !
That's the thief that has got my Lord Cardinal's Ring ! "
    The poor little Jackdaw, When the monks he saw,
Feebly gave vent to the ghost of a caw ;
And turn'd his bald head, as much as to say,
" Pray, be so good as to walk this way ! "
    Slower and slower He limp'd on before,
Till they came to the back of the belfry-door,
    Where the first thing they saw, Midst the sticks and
      the straw,
Was the RING, in the nest of that little Jackdaw !

Then the great Lord Cardinal call'd for his book,
And off that terrible curse he took ;
    The mute expression Served in lieu of confession,
And, being thus coupled with full restitution,
The Jackdaw got plenary absolution !
    —When those words were heard, That poor little bird
Was so changed in a moment, 'twas really absurd,
    He grew sleek, and fat ; In addition to that,
A fresh crop of feathers came thick as a mat !
    His tail waggled more Even than before ;
But no longer it wagg'd with an impudent air,
No longer he perch'd on the Cardinal's chair.
    He hopp'd now about With a gait devout ,
At Matins, at Vespers, he never was out ;
And, so far from any more pilfering deeds,
He always seem'd telling the Confessor's beads.
If any one lied,—or if any one swore,—
Or slumber'd in pray'r-time and happen'd to snore,
    That good Jackdaw Would give a great " Caw ! "
As much as to say, " Don't do so any more ! "
While many remark'd, as his manners they saw,
That they " never had known such a pious Jackdaw ! "
    He long lived the pride Of that country side,
And at last in the odour of sanctity died ;

When, as words were too faint His merits to paint
The Conclave determined to make him a Saint ;
And on newly-made Saints and Popes, as you know,
It's the custom, at Rome, new names to bestow,
So they canonised him by the name of Jem Crow !

THE PIED PIPER OF
HAMELIN

by ROBERT BROWNING

I

Hamelin Town's in Brunswick,
  By famous Hanover city ;
The river Weser, deep and wide,
Washes its wall on the southern side ;
A pleasanter spot you never spied ;
  But, when begins my ditty,
Almost five hundred years ago,
To see the townsfolk suffer so
  From vermin, was a pity.

II

  Rats !
They fought the dogs and killed the cats,
  And bit the babies in the cradles,
And ate the cheeses out of the vats,
  And licked the soup from the cook's own ladles,
Split open the kegs of salted sprats,
Made nests inside men's Sunday hats,
And even spoiled the women's chats
      By drowning their speaking
      With shrieking and squeaking
In fifty different sharps and flats.

III

At last the people in a body
    To the Town Hall came flocking :
" 'Tis clear," cried they, " our Mayor's a noddy ;
    " And as for our Corporation—shocking
" To think we buy gowns lined with ermine
" For dolts that can't or won't determine
" What's best to rid us of our vermin !
" You hope, because you're old and obese,
" To find in the furry civic robe ease ?
" Rouse up, sirs ! Give your brains a racking
" To find the remedy we're lacking,
" Or, sure as fate, we'll send you packing ! "
At this the Mayor and Corporation
Quaked with a mighty consternation.

IV

An hour they sat in council,
    At length the Mayor broke silence :
" For a guilder I'd my ermine gown sell,
    " I wish I were a mile hence !
" It's easy to bid one rack one's brain—
" I'm sure my poor head aches again
" I've scratched it so, and all in vain.
" Oh for a trap, a trap, a trap ! "
Just as he said this, what should hap
At the chamber door but a gentle tap ?
" Bless us," cried the Mayor, " what's that ? "
(With the Corporation as he sat,
Looking little though wondrous fat ;
Nor brighter was his eye, nor moister
Than a too-long-opened oyster,
Save when at noon his paunch grew mutinous
For a plate of turtle green and glutinous)

" Only a scraping of shoes on the mat ?
" Anything like the sound of a rat
" Makes my heart go pit-a-pat ! "

V

" Come in ! "—the Mayor cried, looking bigger :
And in did come the strangest figure !
His queer long coat from heel to head
Was half of yellow and half of red,
And he himself was tall and thin,
With sharp blue eyes, each like a pin,
And light loose hair, yet swarthy skin,
No tuft on cheek nor beard on chin,
But lips where smiles went out and in—
There was no guessing his kith and kin !
And nobody could enough admire
The tall man and his quaint attire :
Quoth one : " It's as my great grandsire,
" Starting up at the Trump of Doom's tone,
" Had walked this way from his painted tombstone ! "

VI

He advanced to the council table :
And, " Please your honours," said he, " I'm able,
" By means of a secret charm, to draw
    " All creatures living beneath the sun,
    " That creep or swim or fly or run,
" After me so as you never saw !
" And I chiefly use my charm
" On creatures that do people harm,
" The mole, and toad, and newt, and viper ;
" And people call me the Pied Piper."
(And here they noticed round his neck
    A scarf of red and yellow stripe,
To match with his coat of the self-same cheque ;
    And at the scarf's end hung a pipe ;

And his fingers, they noticed, were ever straying
As if impatient to be playing
Upon this pipe, as low it dangled
Over his vesture so old-fangled.)
" Yet," said he, " poor piper as I am,
" In Tartary I freed the Cham,
    " Last June, from his huge swarms of gnats ;
" I eased in Asia the Nizam
    " Of a monstrous brood of vampyre-bats :
" And as for what your brain bewilders,
    " If I can rid your town of rats
" Will you give me a thousand guilders ? "
" One ? fifty thousand ! "—was the exclamation
Of the astonished Mayor and Corporation.

VII

Into the street the Piper stept,
    Smiling first a little smile,
As if he knew what magic slept
    In his quiet pipe the while ;
Then, like a musical adept,
To blow the pipe his lips he wrinkled,
And green and blue his sharp eyes twinkled,
Like a candle-flame where salt is sprinkled ;
And ere three shrill notes the pipe uttered,
You heard as if an army muttered ;
And the muttering grew to a grumbling ;
And the grumbling grew to a mighty rumbling ;
And out of the houses the rats came tumbling.
Great rats, small rats, lean rats, brawny rats,
Brown rats, black rats, grey rats, tawny rats,
Grave old plodders, gay young friskers,
    Fathers, mothers, uncles, cousins,
Cocking tails and pricking whiskers,
    Families by tens and dozens,

Brothers, sisters, husbands, wives—
Followed the Piper for their lives.
From street to street he piped advancing,
And step for step they followed dancing,
Until they came to the river Weser,
    Wherein all plunged and perished !
—Save one who, stout as Julius Cæsar,
Swam across and lived to carry
    (As he, the manuscript he cherished)
To Rat-land home his commentary :
Which was, " At the first shrill notes of the pipe,
" I heard a sound as of scraping tripe,
" And putting apples, wondrous ripe,
" Into a cider-press's gripe :
" And a moving away of pickle-tub-boards,
" And leaving ajar of conserve-cupboards,
" And a drawing the corks of train-oil-flasks,
" And a breaking the hoops of butter-casks :
" And it seemed as if a voice
    (" Sweeter far than by harp or by psaltery
" Is breathed) called out, ' Oh rats, rejoice !
    " ' The world is grown to one vast drysaltery !
" ' So munch on, crunch on, take your nuncheon,
" ' Breakfast, supper, dinner, luncheon ! '
" And just as a bulky sugar-puncheon,
" All ready staved, like a great sun shone
" Glorious scarce an inch before me,
" Just as methought it said, ' Come, bore me ! '
" —I found the Weser rolling o'er me."

VIII

You should have heard the Hamelin people
Ringing the bells till they rocked the steeple ;
" Go," cried the Mayor, " and get long poles,
" Poke out the nests and block up the holes !

" Consult with carpenters and builders,
" And leave in our town not even a trace
" Of the rats ! "—when suddenly, up the face
Of the Piper perked in the market-place,
With a, " First, if you please, my thousand guilders ! "

IX

A thousand guilders ! The Mayor looked blue ;
So did the Corporation too.
For council dinners made rare havoc
With Claret, Moselle, Vin-de-Grave, Hock ;
And half the money would replenish
Their cellar's biggest butt with Rhenish.
To pay this sum to a wandering fellow
With a gipsy coat of red and yellow !
" Besides," quoth the Mayor with a knowing wink,
" Our business was done at the river's brink ;
" We saw with our eyes the vermin sink,
" And what's dead can't come to life, I think.
" So, friend, we're not the folks to shrink
" From the duty of giving you something for drink,
" And a matter of money to put in your poke :
" But as for the guilders, what we spoke
" Of them, as you very well know, was in joke.
" Besides, our losses have made us thrifty ;
" A thousand guilders ! Come, take fifty ! "

X

The Piper's face fell, and he cried
" No trifling ! I can't wait, beside !
" I've promised to visit by dinnertime
" Bagdat, and accept the prime
" Of the Head-Cook's pottage, all he's rich in,
" For having left, in the Caliph's kitchen,

" Of a nest of scorpions no survivor—
" With him I proved no bargain-driver,
" With you, don't think I'll bate a stiver !
" And folks who put me in a passion
" May find me pipe to another fashion."

XI

" How ? " cried the Mayor, " d'ye think I'll brook
" Being worse treated than a Cook ?
" Insulted by a lazy ribald
" With idle pipe and vesture piebald ?
" You threaten us, fellow ? Do your worst,
" Blow your pipe there till you burst ! "

XII

Once more he stept into the street
   And to his lips again
   Laid his long pipe of smooth straight cane ;
And ere he blew three notes (such sweet
Soft notes as yet musician's cunning
   Never gave the enraptured air)
There was a rustling that seemed like a bustling
Of merry crowds justling at pitching and hustling,
Small feet were pattering, wooden shoes clattering,
Little hands clapping, and little tongues chattering,
And, like fowls in a farm-yard when barley is scattering,
Out came the children running.
All the little boys and girls,
With rosy cheeks and flaxen curls,
And sparkling eyes and teeth like pearls,
Tripping and skipping, ran merrily after
The wonderful music with shouting and laughter.

XIII

The Mayor was dumb, and the Council stood
As if they were changed into blocks of wood,

Unable to move a step, or cry
To the children merrily skipping by—
And could only follow with the eye
That joyous crowd at the Piper's back.
But how the Mayor was on the rack,
And the wretched Council's bosoms beat,
As the Piper turned from the High Street
To where the Weser rolled its waters
Right in the way of their sons and daughters !
However he turned from South to West,
And to Koppelberg Hill his steps addressed,
And after him the children pressed ;
Great was the joy in every breast.
" He never can cross that mighty top !
" He's forced to let the piping drop,
" And we shall see our children stop ! "
When, lo, as they reached the mountain's side,
A wondrous portal opened wide,
As if a cavern was suddenly hollowed ;
And the Piper advanced and the children followed,
And when all were in to the very last,
The door in the mountain-side shut fast.
Did I say, all ? No ! One was lame,
  And could not dance the whole of the way ;
And in after years, if you would blame
  His sadness, he was used to say,—
" It's dull in our town since my playmates left !
" I can't forget that I'm bereft
" Of all the pleasant sights they see,
" Which the Piper also promised me.
" For he led us, he said, to a joyous land,
" Joining the town, and just at hand,
" Where waters gushed and fruit-trees grew,
" And flowers put forth a fairer hue,
" And everything was strange and new ;
" The sparrows were brighter than peacocks here,
" And their dogs outran our fallow deer,

" And honey-bees had lost their stings,
" And horses were born with eagles' wings :
" And just as I became assured
" My lame foot would be speedily cured,
" The music stopped and I stood still,
" And found myself outside the hill,
" Left alone against my will,
" To go now limping as before,
" And never hear of that country more ! "

XIV

Alas, alas for Hamelin !
    There came into many a burgher's pate
    A text which says, that Heaven's Gate
    Opes to the rich at as easy rate
As the needle's eye takes a camel in !
The mayor sent East, West, North and South,
To offer the Piper by word of mouth,
    Wherever it was men's lot to find him,
Silver and gold to his heart's content,
If he'd only return the way he went,
    And bring the children behind him.
But when they saw 'twas a lost endeavour,
And Piper and dancers were gone for ever,
They made a decree that lawyers never
    Should think their records dated duly
If, after the day of the month and year,
These words did not as well appear,
" And so long after what happened here
    " On the Twenty-second of July,
" Thirteen hundred and seventy-six : "
And the better in memory to fix
The place of the children's last retreat,
They called it, the Pied Piper's Street—
Where any one playing on pipe or tabor
Was sure for the future to lose his labour.

Nor suffered they hostelry or tavern
　　To shock with mirth a street so solemn ;
But opposite the place of the cavern
　　They wrote the story on a column,
And on the great church-window painted
The same, to make the world acquainted
How their children were stolen away ;
And there it stands to this very day.
And I must not omit to say
That in Transylvania there's a tribe
Of alien people who ascribe
The outlandish ways and dress
On which their neighbours lay such stress,
To their fathers and mothers having risen
Out of some subterraneous prison
Into which they were trepanned
Long time ago in a mighty band
Out of Hamelin town in Brunswick land,
But how or why, they don't understand.

XV

So, Willy, let you and me be wipers
Of scores out with all men—especially pipers :
And, whether they pipe us free from rats or from mice,
If we've promised them aught, let us keep our promise !

THE FAIRIES

by WILLIAM ALLINGHAM

Up the airy mountain,
  Down the rushy glen,
We daren't go a-hunting
  For fear of little men ;
Wee folk, good folk,
  Trooping all together ;
Green jacket, red cap,
  And white owl's feather !

Down along the rocky shore
  Some make their home,
They live on crispy pancakes
  Of yellow tide-foam ;
Some in the reeds
  Of the black mountain lake,
With frogs for their watch-dogs,
  All night awake.

High on the hill-top
  The old King sits ;
He is now so old and grey
  He's nigh lost his wits.
With a bridge of white mist
  Columbkill he crosses,
On his stately journeys
  From Slieveleague to Rosses ;
Or going up with music
  On cold starry nights,
To sup with the Queen
  Of the gay Northern Lights.

They stole little Bridget
  For seven years long ;
When she came down again
  Her friends were all gone.
They took her lightly back,
  Between the night and morrow,
They thought that she was fast asleep,
  But she was dead with sorrow.
They have kept her ever since
  Deep within the lake,
On a bed of flag-leaves,
  Watching till she wake.

By the craggy hill-side,
  Through the mosses bare,
They have planted thorn-trees
  For pleasure here and there.
Is any man so daring
  As dig them up in spite,
He shall find their sharpest thorns
  In his bed at night.

Up the airy mountain,
  Down the rushy glen,
We daren't go a-hunting
  For fear of little men ;
Wee folk, good folk,
  Trooping all together ;
Green jacket, red cap,
  And white owl's feather !

THE SNOW QUEEN

by HANS ANDERSEN

In Seven Stories

STORY THE FIRST

You MUST attend to the beginning of this story, for when we get to the end we shall know more than we do now about a very wicked hobgoblin ; he was one of the very worst, for he was a real demon. One day, when he was in a merry mood, he made a looking-glass which had the power of making everything good or beautiful that was reflected in it almost shrink to nothing, while everything that was worthless and bad looked increased in size and worse than ever. The most lovely landscapes appeared like boiled spinach, and the people became hideous, and looked as if they stood on their heads and had no bodies. Their countenances were so distorted that no one could recognise them, and even one freckle on the face appeared to spread over the whole of the nose and mouth. The demon said this was very amusing. When a good or pious thought passed through the mind of any one it was misrepresented in the glass ; and then how the demon laughed at his cunning invention. All who went to the demon's school—for he kept a school—talked everywhere of the wonders they had seen, and declared that people could now, for the first time, see what the world and mankind were really like. They carried the glass about everywhere, till at last there was not a land nor a people who had not been looked at through this distorted mirror. They wanted even to fly with it up to heaven to see the angels, but the higher they flew the more slippery the glass became, and they could scarcely hold it, till at last it slipped from their hands, fell to the earth, and was broken into millions of pieces. But now the looking-glass caused more unhappiness than ever, for some of the fragments were not so large as a grain of sand, and they flew about the world into every country. When one of these tiny atoms flew into a person's eye, it stuck there unknown to him, and from that moment he saw everything through a distorted medium, or could see only the worst side of what he looked at, for even the smallest fragment retained the same power which had belonged to the whole mirror. Some few persons even got a fragment of the looking-glass in their hearts, and this was very terrible, for their hearts became cold like a lump of ice. A few of the pieces were so large that they could be used as window-panes ; it would have been a sad thing to look at our friends through them. Other pieces were made into spectacles ; this was dreadful for those who wore them, for they could see nothing either rightly or justly. At all this the wicked demon laughed till his sides shook—it tickled him so to see the mischief he had done. There were still a number of these little fragments of glass floating about in the air, and now you shall hear what happened with one of them.

SECOND STORY

A LITTLE BOY AND A LITTLE GIRL

IN A LARGE town, full of houses and people, there is not room for everybody to have even a little garden, therefore they are obliged to be satisfied with a few flowers in flower-pots. In one of these large towns lived two poor children who had a garden something larger and better than a few flower-pots. They were not brother and sister, but they loved each other almost as much as if they had been. Their parents lived opposite to each other in two garrets, where the roofs of neighbouring houses projected out towards each other, and the water-pipe ran between them. In each house was a little window, so that any one could step across the gutter from one window to the other. The parents of these children had each a large wooden box in which they culti- vated kitchen herbs for their own use, and a little rose-bush in each box, which grew splendidly. Now after a while the parents decided to place these two boxes across the water- pipe, so that they reached from one window to the other and looked like two banks of flowers. Sweet peas dropped over the boxes, and the rose-bushes shot forth long branches, which were trained round the windows and clustered together almost like a triumphal arch of leaves and flowers. The boxes were very high, and the children knew they must not climb upon them without permission, but they were often, however, allowed to step out together and sit upon their little stools under the rose-bushes, or play quietly. In winter all this pleasure came to an end, for the windows were sometimes quite frozen over. But then they would warm copper pennies on the stove, and hold the warm pennies against the frozen pane ; there would be very soon a little round hole through which they could peep, and the soft bright eyes of the little boy and girl would beam through the hole at each window as they looked at each other. Their names were Kay and Gerda. In summer they could be together with one jump from the window, but in winter they had to go up and down the long staircase and out through the snow before they could meet.

" See there are the white bees swarming," said Kay's old grandmother one day when it was snowing.

" Have they a queen bee ? " asked the little boy, for he knew that the real bees always had a queen.

" To be sure they have," said the grandmother. " She is flying there where the swarm is thickest. She is the largest of them all, and never remains on the earth, but flies up to the dark clouds. Often at midnight she flies through the streets of the town, and looks in at the windows, then the ice freezes on the panes into wonderful shapes, that look like flowers and castles."

" Yes, I have seen them," said both the children, and they knew it must be true.

" Can the Snow Queen come in here ? " asked the little girl.

" Only let her come," said the boy, " I'll set her on the stove and then she'll melt."

Then the grandmother smoothed his hair and told him some more tales. One evening, when little Kay was at home, half undressed, he climbed on a chair by the window and peeped out through the little hole. A few flakes of snow were falling, and one of them, rather larger than the rest, alighted on the edge of one of the flower-boxes. This snow-flake grew larger and larger till at last it became the figure of a woman, dressed in garments of white gauze, which looked like millions of starry snow-flakes linked together. She was fair and beautiful, but made of ice— shining and glittering ice. Still she was alive and her eyes sparkled like bright stars, but there was neither peace nor rest in their glance. She nodded towards the window, and waved her hand. The little boy was frightened and sprang from the chair ; at the same moment it seemed as if a large bird flew by the window. On the following day there was a clear frost, and very soon came the spring. The sun shone ; the young green leaves burst forth ; the swallows built their nests ; windows were opened, and the children sat once more in the garden on the roof, high above all the other rooms. How beautifully the roses blossomed this summer. The little girl had learnt a hymn in which roses were spoken of, and then she thought of their own roses, and she sang the hymn to the little boy, and he sang too :—

> " *Roses bloom and cease to be,*
> *But we shall the Christ-child see.*"

Then the little ones held each other by the hand, and kissed the roses, and looked at the bright sunshine, and spoke to it as if the Christ-child were there. Those were splendid summer days. How beautiful and fresh it was out among the rose-bushes, which seemed as if they would never leave off blooming. One day Kay and Gerda sat looking at a book full of pictures of animals and birds, and then just as the clock in the church tower struck twelve, Kay said, " Oh ! something has struck my heart ! " and soon after, " There is something in my eye."

The little girl put her arm round his neck, and looked into his eye, but she could see nothing.

" I think it is gone," he said. But it was not gone ; it was one of those bits of the looking-glass—that magic mirror, of which we have spoken—the ugly glass which made everything great and good appear small and ugly, while all that was wicked and bad became more visible, and every little fault could be plainly seen. Poor little Kay had also received a small grain in his heart, which quickly turned to a lump of ice. He felt no more pain, but the glass was there still. " Why do you cry ? " said he at last ; " it makes you look ugly. There is nothing the matter with me now. Oh ! see," he cried suddenly, " that rose is worm-eaten, and this one is quite crooked. After all, they are ugly roses, just like the box in which they stand." And then he kicked the boxes with his foot, and pulled off the two roses.

" Kay, what are you doing ? " cried the little girl ; and then, when he saw how frightened she was, he tore off another rose, and jumped through his own window away from sweet little Gerda.

When she afterwards brought out the picture book, he said, " It was only fit for babies in long clothes," and when grandmother told any stories, he would interrupt her with " but " ; or, when he could manage it, he would get behind her chair, put on a pair of spectacles, and imitate her very cleverly, to make people laugh. By-and-by he began to mimic the speech and gait of persons in the street. All that was peculiar or disagreeable in a person he would imitate directly, and people said, " That boy will be very clever ; he has a remarkable genius." But it was the piece of glass in his eye, and the coldness in his heart, that made him behave like this. He would even tease little Gerda, who loved him with all her heart. His games, too, were quite different ; they were not so childish. One winter's day, when it snowed, he brought out a burning-glass, then he held out the tail of his blue coat, and let the snow-flakes fall upon it. " Look in this glass, Gerda," said he ; and she saw how every flake of snow was magnified, and looked like a beautiful flower or a glittering star. " Is it not clever ? " said Kay, " and much more interesting than looking at real flowers. There is not a single fault in it, and the snow-flakes are quite perfect till they begin to melt."

Soon after, Kay made his appearance in large thick gloves, and with his sledge at his back. He called upstairs to Gerda, " I've got leave to go into the great square, where the other boys play and ride." And away he went.

In the great square, the boldest among the boys would often tie their sledges to country people's carts, and go with them a good way. This was capital. But while they were all amusing themselves, and Kay with them, a great sledge came by ; it was painted white, and in it sat someone wrapped in a rough white fur, and wearing a white cap. The sledge drove twice round the square, and Kay fastened his own little sledge to it, so that when it went away, he followed with it. It went faster and faster right through the next street, and then the person who drove turned round and nodded pleasantly to Kay, just as if they were acquainted with each other, but whenever Kay wished to loosen his little sledge the driver nodded again, so Kay sat still, and they drove out through the town gate. Then the snow began to fall so heavily that the little boy could not see a hand's breadth before him, but still they drove on ; then he suddenly loosened the cord so that the large sledge might go on without him, but it was of no use, his little carriage held fast, and away they went like the wind. Then he called out loudly, but nobody heard him, while the snow beat upon him, and the sledge flew onwards. Every now and then it gave a jump as if they were going over hedges and ditches. The boy was frightened, and tried to say a prayer, but he could remember nothing but the multiplication table.

The snow-flakes became larger and larger till they appeared like great white chickens. All at once they sprang on one side, the great sledge stopped, and the person who had driven it rose up. The fur and the cap, which were made entirely of snow, fell off, and he saw a lady, tall and white : it was the Snow Queen.

" We have driven well," said she, " but why do you tremble ? Here, creep into my warm fur." Then she seated him beside her in the sledge, and as she wrapped the fur round him he felt as if he was sinking into a snow-drift.

" Are you still cold ? " she asked, as she kissed him on the forehead. The kiss was colder than ice ; it went quite through to his heart, which was already almost a lump of ice ; he felt as if he were going to die, but only for a moment ; he soon seemed quite well again, and did not notice the cold all around him.

" My sledge ! don't forget my sledge," was his first thought, and then he looked and saw that it was bound fast to one of the white chickens, which flew behind him with the sledge at its back. The Snow Queen kissed little Kay again, and by this time he had forgotten little Gerda, his grandmother, and all at home.

" Now you must have no more kisses," she said, " or I should kiss you to death."

Kay looked at her, and saw that she was so beautiful, he could not imagine a more intelligent and lovely face ; she did not now seem to be made of ice, as when he had seen her through his window, and she had nodded to him. In his eyes she was perfect, and he did not feel at all afraid. He told her he could do mental arithmetic, as far as fractions, and that he knew the number of square miles and the number of inhabitants in the country. And she always smiled so that he thought he did not know enough yet, and looked round the vast expanse as she flew higher and higher with him upon a black cloud, while the storm blew and howled as if it were singing old songs. They flew over woods and lakes, over sea and land ; below them roared the wild wind ; the wolves howled and the snow crackled ; over them flew the black screaming crows, and above all shone the moon, clear and bright ; and so Kay passed through the long winter's night, and by day he slept at the feet of the Snow Queen.

THIRD STORY

THE FLOWER GARDEN OF THE WOMAN WHO COULD CONJURE

BUT HOW fared little Gerda during Kay's absence? What had become of him, no one knew, nor could anyone give the slightest information, excepting the boys, who said that he had tied his sledge to another very large one, which had driven through the street, and out of the town gate. Nobody knew where it went ; many tears were shed for him, and little Gerda wept bitterly for a long time. She said she knew he must be dead, that he was drowned in the river which flowed close by the school. Oh, indeed, those long winter days were very dreary. But at last spring came, and warm sunshine. " Kay is dead and gone," said little Gerda.

" I don't believe it," said the sunshine.

" He is dead and gone," she said to the sparrows.

" We don't believe it," they replied ; and at last little Gerda began to doubt it herself. " I will put on my new red shoes," she said one morning, " those that Kay has never seen, and then I will go down to the river, and ask for him." It was quite early when she kissed her old grandmother, who was still asleep ; then she put on her red shoes, and went quietly alone out of the town gates towards the **river.** " Is it true that you have taken my little playmate

away from me ? " she said to the river. " I will give you my
red shoes if you will give him back to me." And it seemed as
if the waves nodded to her in a strange manner. Then she
took off her red shoes, which she liked better than anything
else, and threw them both into the river, but they fell near
the bank, and the little waves carried them back to land,
just as if the river would not take from her what she loved
best, because they could not give her back little Kay. But
she thought the shoes had not been thrown out far enough.
Then she crept into a boat that lay among the reeds, and
threw the shoes again from the farther end of the boat into
the water, but it was not fastened, and her movement sent
it gliding away from the land. When she saw this, she
hastened to reach the end of the boat, but before she could
do so, it was more than a yard from the bank, and drifting
away faster than ever. Then little Gerda was very much
frightened, and began to cry, but no one heard her except
the sparrows, and they could not carry her to land, but
they flew along by the shore, and sang, as if to comfort her,
" Here we are ! Here we are ! " The boat floated with the
stream ; little Gerda sat quite still with only her stockings
on her feet ; the red shoes floated after her, but she could
not reach them because the boat kept so much in advance.
The banks on each side of the river were very pretty. There
were beautiful flowers, old trees, sloping fields, in which
cows and sheep were grazing, but not a man to be seen.
Perhaps the river will carry me to little Kay, thought
Gerda, and then she became more cheerful, and raised
her head, and looked at the beautiful green banks ; and so
the boat sailed on for hours. At length she came to a large
cherry orchard, in which stood a small house with strange
red and blue windows. It had also a thatched roof, and
outside, were two wooden soldiers, that presented arms to
her as she sailed past. Gerda called out to them, for she
thought they were alive, but of course they did not answer ;
and as the boat drifted nearer to the shore, she saw what
they really were. Then Gerda called still louder, and there

came a very old woman out of the house, leaning on a crutch. She wore a large hat to shade her from the sun, and on it were painted all sorts of pretty flowers. " You poor little child," said the old woman, " how did you manage to come all this distance into the wide world on such a rapid rolling stream ? " And then the old woman walked into the water, seized the boat with her crutch, drew it to land, and lifted little Gerda out. And Gerda was glad to feel herself again on dry ground, although she was rather afraid of the strange old woman. " Come and tell me who you are," said she, " and how you came here."

Then Gerda told her everything, while the old woman shook her head, and said, " Hem-hem " ; and when she had finished, Gerda asked if she had not seen little Kay, and the old woman told her he had not passed by that way, but he very likely would come. So she told Gerda not to be sorrowful, but to taste the cherries and look at the flowers ; they were better than any picture-book, for each of them could tell a story. Then she took Gerda by the hand, and led her into the little house, and the old woman closed the door. The windows were very high, and as the panes were red, blue, and yellow, the daylight shone through them in all sorts of singular colours. On the table stood some beautiful cherries, and Gerda had permission to eat as many as she would. While she was eating them, the old woman combed out her long flaxen ringlets with a golden comb, and the glossy curls hung down on each side of the little round pleasant face, which looked fresh and blooming as a rose. " I have long been wishing for a dear little maiden like you," said the old woman, " and now you must stay with me and see how happily we shall live together." And while she went on combing little Gerda's hair, she thought less and less about her adopted brother Kay, for the old woman could conjure, although she was not a wicked witch ; she conjured only a little for her own amusement, and now, because she wanted to keep Gerda. Therefore she went into the garden, and stretched out her crutch towards all the rose-trees, beautiful though they were, and they immediately sunk into the dark earth, so that no one could tell where they had once stood. The old woman was afraid that if little Gerda saw roses, she would think of those at home, and then remember little Kay, and run away. Then she took Gerda into the flower-garden. How fragrant and beautiful it was ! Every flower that could be thought of for every season of the year was here in full bloom ; no picture-book could have more beautiful colours. Gerda jumped for joy, and played till the sun went down behind the tall cherry-trees ; then she slept in an elegant bed with red silk pillows, embroidered with coloured violets ; and then she dreamed as pleasantly as a queen on her wedding-day. The next day, and for many days after, Gerda played with the flowers in the warm sunshine. She knew every flower, and yet, although there were so many of them, it seemed as if one were missing, but which it was she could not tell. One day, however, as she sat looking at the old woman's hat with the painted flowers on it, she saw that the prettiest of them all was a rose. The old woman had forgotten to take it from her hat when she made all the roses sink into the earth. But it is difficult to keep the thoughts together in everything ; one little mistake upsets all our arrangements.

" What, are there no roses here ? " cried Gerda · and she ran out into the garden, and examined all the beds, and searched and searched. There was not one to be found. Then she sat down and wept, and her tears fell just on the place where one of the rose-trees had sunk down. The warm tears moistened the earth, and the rose-tree sprouted up at once, as blooming as when it had sunk ; and Gerda embraced it, and kissed the roses, and thought of the beautiful roses at home, and, with them, of little Kay.

" Oh, how I have been detained ! " said the little maiden. " I wanted to seek for little Kay. Do you know where he is ? " she asked the roses ; " do you think he is dead ? "

And the roses answered, " No, he is not dead. We have

been in the ground where all the dead lie ; but Kay is not there."

" Thank you," said little Gerda, and then she went to the other flowers, and looked into their little cups, and asked, " Do you know where little Kay is ? " But each flower, as it stood in the sunshine, dreamed only of its own little fairy tale or history. Not one knew anything of Kay. Gerda heard many stories from the flowers, as she asked them one after another about him.

And what said the tiger-lily ? " Hark, do you hear the drum ?—' tum, tum,'—there are only two notes always, ' tum, tum.' Listen to the women's song of mourning ! Hear the cry of the priest ! In her long red robe stands the Hindoo widow by the funeral pile. The flames rise around her as she places herself on the dead body of her husband ; but the Hindoo woman is thinking of the living one in that circle ; of him, her son, who lighted those flames. Those shining eyes trouble her heart more painfully than the flames which will soon consume her body to ashes. Can the fire of the heart be extinguished in the flames of a funeral pile ? "

" I don't understand that at all," said little Gerda.

" That is my story," said the tiger-lily.

What says the convolvulus ? " Near yonder narrow road stands an old knight's castle ; thick ivy creeps over the old ruined walls, leaf over leaf, even to the balcony, in which stands a beautiful maiden. She bends over the balustrades, and looks up the road. No rose on its stem is fresher than she ; no apple-blossom, wafted by the wind, floats more lightly than she moves. Her rich silk rustles as she bends over and exclaims, ' Will he not come ? ' "

" Is it Kay you mean ? " asked Gerda.

" I am only speaking of a story of my dream," replied the flower.

What said the little snowdrop ? " Between two trees a rope is hanging ; there is a piece of board upon it ; it is a swing. Two pretty little girls, in dresses white as snow, and with long green ribbons fluttering from their hats, are sitting upon it, swinging. Their brother, who is taller than they are, stands in the swing ; he has one arm round the rope, to steady himself ; in one hand he holds a little bowl, and in the other a clay pipe ; he is blowing bubbles. As the swing goes on, the bubbles fly upward, reflecting the most beautiful varying colours. The last still hangs from the bowl of the pipe, and sways in the wind. On goes the swing ; and then a little black dog comes running up. He is almost as light as the bubble, and he raises himself on his hind legs, and wants to be taken into the swing ; but it does not stop, and the dog falls ; then he barks, and gets angry. The children stoop towards him, and the bubble bursts. A swinging plank, a light sparkling foam picture,— that is my story."

" It may be all very pretty what you are telling me," said little Gerda ; " but you speak so mournfully, and you do not mention little Kay at all."

What do the hyacinths say ? " There were three beautiful sisters, fair and delicate. The dress of one was red, of the second blue, and of the third pure white. Hand in hand, they danced in the bright moonlight, by the calm lake ; but they were human beings, not fairy elves. The sweet fragrance attracted them, and they disappeared in the wood ; here the fragrance became stronger. Three coffins, in which lay three beautiful maidens, glided from the thickest part of the forest across the lake. The fire-flies flew lightly over them, like little floating torches. Do the dancing maidens sleep, or are they dead ? The scent of the flowers says that they are corpses. The evening bell tolls their knell."

" You make me quite sorrowful," said little Gerda ; " your perfume is so strong, you make me think of the dead maidens. Ah ! is little Kay really dead then ? The roses have been in the earth, and they say no."

" Cling, clang," tolled the hyacinth bells. " We are not tolling for little Kay ; we do not know him. We sing our song, the only one we know."

N *

Then Gerda went to the buttercups that were glittering amongst the bright green leaves.

" You are little bright suns," said Gerda ; " tell me if you know where I can find my playfellow."

And the buttercups sparkled gaily, and looked again at Gerda. What song could the buttercups sing ? It was not about Kay.

" The bright warm sun shone on a little court, on the first warm day of spring. His white beams rested on the white walls of the neighbouring house ; and close by bloomed the first yellow flower of the season, glittering like gold in the sun's warm ray. An old woman sat in her arm-chair at the house-door, and her grand-daughter, a poor and pretty servant-maid, came to see her for a short visit. When she kissed her grandmother, there was gold every-where : the gold of the heart in that holy kiss ; it was a golden morning ; there was gold in the beaming sunlight, gold in the leaves of the lowly flower, and on the lips of the maiden. There, that is my story," said the buttercup.

" My poor old grandmother ! " sighed Gerda ; " she is longing to see me, and grieving for me as she did for little Kay ; but I shall soon go home now, and take little Kay with me. It is no use asking the flowers ; they know only their own songs, and can give me no information."

And then she tucked up her little dress, that she might run faster ; but the narcissus caught her by the leg as she was jumping over it ; so she stopped and looked at the tall yellow flower, and said, " Perhaps you may know something."

Then she stooped down quite close to the flower, and listened ; and what did it say ?

" I can see myself, I can see myself," said the narcissus. " Oh, how sweet is my perfume ! Up in a little room with a bow window, stands a little dancing girl, half undressed ; she stands sometimes on one leg, and sometimes on both, and looks as if she would tread the whole world under her feet. She is nothing but a delusion. She is pouring water out of a tea·pot on a piece of stuff which she holds in her hand ; it is her bodice. ' Cleanliness is a good thing,' she says. Her white dress hangs on a peg ; it has also been washed in the tea-pot, and dried on the roof. She puts it on, and ties a saffron-coloured handkerchief round her neck, which makes the dress look whiter. See how she stretches out her legs, as if she were showing off on a stem. I can see myself, I can see myself."

" What do I care for all that," said Gerda, " you need not tell me such stuff." And then she ran to the other end of the garden. The door was fastened, but she pressed against the rusty latch, and it gave way. The door sprang open, and little Gerda ran out with bare feet into the wide world. She looked back three times, but no one seemed to be following her. At last she could run no longer, so she sat down to rest on a great stone, and when she looked round she saw that the summer was over, and autumn very far advanced. She had known nothing of this in the beautiful garden, where the sun shone and the flowers grew all the year round.

" Oh, how I have wasted my time ! " said little Gerda ; " it is autumn. I must not rest any longer," and she rose up to go on. But her little feet were wounded and sore, and everything around her looked so cold and bleak. The long willow-leaves were quite yellow. The dew-drops fell like water, leaf after leaf dropped from the tree, the sloe-thorn alone still bore fruit, but the sloes were sour, and set the teeth on edge. Oh, how dark and weary the whole world appeared !

FOURTH STORY

THE PRINCE AND PRINCESS

GERDA was obliged to rest again, and just opposite the place where she sat, she saw a great crow come hopping across the snow towards her. He stood looking at her for some time, and then he wagged his head and said, " Caw, caw ; good-day, good-day." He pronounced the words as plainly as he could, because he meant to be kind to the little girl ; and then he asked her where she was going all alone in the wide world.

The word *alone* Gerda understood very well, and knew how much it expressed. So then she told the crow the whole story of her life and adventures, and asked him if he had seen little Kay.

The crow nodded his head very gravely, and said, " Perhaps I have—it may be."

" No ! Do you think you have ? " cried little Gerda, and she kissed the crow, and hugged him almost to death with joy.

" Gently, gently," said the crow. " I believe I know. I think it may be little Kay ; but he has certainly forgotten you by this time for the princess."

" Does he live with a princess ? " asked Gerda.

" Yes, listen," replied the crow ; " but it is so difficult to speak your language. If you understand the crows' language[1] then I can explain it better. Do you ? "

" No, I have never learnt it," said Gerda, " but my grandmother understands it, and used to speak it to me. I wish I had learnt it."

" It does not matter," answered the crow ; " I will explain as well as I can, although it will be very badly done " ; and he told her what he had heard. " In this kingdom where we now are," said he, " there lives a princess, who is so wonderfully clever that she has read all the newspapers in the world, and forgotten them too, although she is so clever. A short time ago, as she was sitting on her throne, which people say is not such an agreeable seat as is often supposed, she began to sing a song which commences in these words :

---

[1] Children have a kind of language, or gibberish which is sometimes called " crows language " ; it is formed by adding letters or syllables to every word.

' Why should I not be married ?

' Why not indeed ? ' said she, and so she determined to marry if she could find a husband who knew what to say when he was spoken to, and not one who could only look grand, for that was so tiresome. Then she assembled all her court ladies together at the beat of the drum, and when they heard of her intentions they were very much pleased. ' We are so glad to hear it,' said they ' we were talking about it ourselves the other day.' You may believe that every word I tell you is true," said the crow, " for I have a tame sweetheart who goes freely about the palace, and she told me all this."

Of course his sweetheart was a crow, for " birds of a feather flock together," and one crow always chooses another crow.

" Newpapers were published immediately, with a border of hearts, and the initials of the princess among them. They gave notice that every young man who was handsome was free to visit the castle and speak with the princess ; and those who could reply loud enough to be heard when spoken to, were to make themselves quite at home at the palace ; but the one who spoke best would be chosen as a husband for the princess. Yes, yes, you may believe me, it is all as true as I sit here," said the crow. " The people came in crowds. There was a great deal of crushing and running about, but no one succeeded either on the first or the second day. They could all speak very well while they were outside in the streets, but when they entered the palace gates, and saw the guards in silver uniforms, and the footmen in their golden livery on the staircase, and the great halls lighted up, they became quite confused. And when they stood before the throne on which the princess sat, they could do nothing but repeat the last words she had said ; and she had no particular wish to hear her own words over again. It was just as if they had all taken something to make them sleepy while they were in the palace, for they did not recover themselves nor speak till they got back again into the street. There was quite a long line of them reaching from the town gate to the palace. I went myself to see them," said the crow. " They were hungry and thirsty, for at the palace they did not get even a glass of water. Some of the wisest had taken a few slices of bread and butter with them, but they did not share it with their neighbours ; they thought if they went in to the princess looking hungry, there would be a better chance for themselves."

" But Kay ! tell me about little Kay ! " said Gerda, " was he amongst the crowd ? "

" Stop a bit, we are just coming to him. It was on the third day, there came marching cheerfully along to the palace a little personage, without horses or carriage, his eyes sparkling like yours ; he had beautiful long hair, but his clothes were very poor."

" That was Kay ! " said Gerda joyfully. " Oh, then I have found him " ; and she clapped her hands.

" He had a little knapsack on his back," added the crow.

" No it must have been his sledge," said Gerda ; " for he went away with it."

" It may have been so," said the crow ; " I did not look at it very closely. But I know from my tame sweetheart that he passed through the palace gates, saw the guards in their silver uniforms, and the servants in their liveries of gold on the stairs, but he was not in the least embarrassed. ' It must be very tiresome to stand on the stairs,' he said. ' I prefer to go in.' The rooms were blazing with light. Councillors and ambassadors walked about with bare feet, carrying golden vessels ; it was enough to make anyone feel serious. His boots creaked loudly as he walked, and yet he was not at all uneasy."

" It must be Kay," said Gerda, " I know he had new boots on, I have heard them creak in grandmother's room."

" They really did creak," said the crow, "yet he went

boldly up to the princess herself, who was sitting on a pearl as large as a spinning wheel, and all the ladies of the court were present with their maids, and all the cavaliers with their servants ; and each of the maids had another maid to wait upon her, and the cavaliers' servants had their own servants as well as a page each. They all stood in circles round the princess, and the nearer they stood to the door, the prouder they looked. The servants' pages, who always wore slippers, could hardly be looked at, they held themselves up so proudly by the door."

" It must be quite awful," said little Gerda, " but did Kay win the princess ? "

" If I had not been a crow," said he, " I would have married her myself, although I am engaged. He spoke just as well as I do, when I speak the crows' language, so I heard from my tame sweetheart. He was quite free and agreeable, and said he had not come to woo the princess, but to hear her wisdom ; and he was as pleased with her as she was with him."

" Oh, certainly that was Kay," said Gerda, " he was so clever ; he could work mental arithmetic and fractions. Oh, will you take me to the palace ? "

" It is very easy to ask that," replied the crow, " but how are we to manage it. However, I will speak about it to my tame sweetheart, and ask her advice ; for I must tell you it will be very difficult to gain permission for a little girl like you to enter the palace."

" Oh, yes ; but I shall gain permission easily," said Gerda, " for when Kay hears that I am here, he will come out and fetch me in immediately."

" Wait for me here by the palings," said the crow, wagging his head as he flew away.

It was late in the evening before the crow returned. " Caw, caw," he said, "she sends you greeting, and here is a little roll which she took from the kitchen for you ; there is plenty of bread there, and she thinks you must be hungry. It is not possible for you to enter the palace by the front entrance. The guards in silver uniform and the servants in gold livery would not allow it. But do not cry, we will manage to get you in ; my sweetheart knows a little back-staircase that leads to the sleeping apartments, and she knows where to find the key."

Then they went into the garden through the great avenue, where the leaves were falling one after another, and they could see the lights in the palace being put out in the same manner. And the crow led little Gerda to a back door, which stood ajar. Oh ! how little Gerda's heart beat with anxiety and longing ; it was just as if she were going to do something wrong, and yet she only wanted to know where little Kay was. " It must be he," she thought, " with those clear eyes, and that long hair." She could fancy she saw him smiling at her, as he used to at home, when they sat among the roses. He would certainly be glad to see her, and to hear what a long distance she had come for his sake, and to know how sorry they had all been at home because he did not come back. Oh, what joy and yet fear she felt ! They were now on the stairs, and in a small closet at the top a lamp was burning. In the middle of the floor stood the tame crow, turning her head from side to side, and gazing at Gerda, who curtsied as her grandmother had taught her to do.

" My betrothed has spoken so very highly of you, my little lady," said the tame crow, " your life-history, *Vita*, as it may be called, is very touching. If you will take the lamp, I will walk before you. We will go straight along this way, then we shall meet no one."

" It seems to me as if somebody were behind us," said Gerda, as something rushed by her like a shadow on the wall, and then horses with flying manes and thin legs, hunters, ladies and gentlemen on horseback, glided by her, like shadows on the wall.

" They are only dreams," said the crow ; " they are coming to fetch the thoughts of the great people out hunting."

" All the better, for we shall be able to look at them in their beds more safely. I hope that when you rise to honour and favour, you will show a grateful heart."

" You may be quite sure of that," said the crow from the forest.

They now came into the first hall, the walls of which were hung with rose-coloured satin, embroidered with artificial flowers. Here the dreams again flitted by them, but so quickly that Gerda could not distinguish the royal persons. Each hall appeared more splendid than the last, it was enough to bewilder anyone. At length they reached a bed-room. The ceiling was like a great palm-tree, with glass-leaves of the most costly crystal, and over the centre of the floor two beds, each resembling a lily, hung from a stem of gold. One, in which the princess lay, was white, the other was red, and in this Gerda had to seek for little Kay. She pushed one of the red leaves aside, and saw a little brown neck. Oh, that must be Kay ! She called his name out quite loud, and held the lamp over him. The dreams rushed back into the room on horseback. He woke, and turned his head round ; it was not little Kay ! The prince was only like him in the neck, still he was young and pretty. Then the princess peeped out of her white-lily bed, and asked what was the matter. Then little Gerda wept and told her story, and all that the crows had done to help her.

" You poor child," said the prince and princess ; then they praised the crows, and said they were not angry with them for what they had done, but that it must not happen again, and this time they should be rewarded.

" Would you like to have your freedom ? " asked the princess, " or would you prefer to be raised to the position of court crows, with all that is left in the kitchen for your-selves ? "

Then both the crows bowed, and begged to have a fixed appointment, for they thought of their old age, and said it would be so comfortable to feel that they had provision for their old days, as they called it. And then the prince

got out of his bed, and gave it up to Gerda,—he could not
do more ; and she lay down. She folded her little hands,
and thought, " How good everybody is to me, men and
animals too " ; then she closed her eyes and fell into a
sweet sleep. All the dreams came flying back again to her,
and they looked like angels, and one of them drew a little
sledge, on which sat Kay, and nodded to her. But all this
was only a dream, and vanished as soon as she awoke.

The following day she was dressed from head to foot in
silk and velvet, and they invited her to stay at the palace
for a few days, and enjoy herself ; but she only begged for
a pair of boots, and a little carriage, and a horse to draw it,
so that she might go out into the wide world to seek for
Kay. And she obtained, not only boots, but also a muff,
and she was neatly dressed ; and when she was ready to go,
there, at the door, she found a coach, made of pure gold,
with the coat-of-arms of the prince and princess shining
upon it like a star, and the coachman, footman, and out-
riders all wearing golden crowns on their heads. The
prince and princess themselves helped her into the coach,
and wished her success. The forest crow, who was now
married, accompanied her for the first three miles ; he sat
by Gerda's side, as he could not bear riding backwards.
The tame crow stood in the doorway flapping her wings.
She could not go with them, because she had been suffering
from headache ever since the new appointment, no doubt
from eating too much. The coach was well stored with sweet
cakes, and under the seat were fruit and gingerbread nuts.
" Farewell, farewell," cried the prince and princess, and
little Gerda wept, and the crow wept ; and then, after a
few miles, the crow also said " Farewell," and this was the
saddest parting. However, he flew to a tree, and stood
flapping his black wings as long as he could see the coach,
which glittered in the bright sunshine.

THE LITTLE ROBBER GIRL

THE COACH drove on through a thick forest, where it lighted up the way like a torch, and dazzled the eyes of some robbers, who could not bear to let it pass them unmolested.

" It is gold ! it is gold ! " cried they, rushing forward, and seizing the horses. Then they struck the little jockeys, the coachman, and the footmen dead, and pulled little Gerda out of the carriage.

" She is fat and pretty, and she has been fed with the kernels of nuts," said the old robber-woman, who had a long beard and eye-brows that hung over her eyes. " She is as good as a little lamb ; how nice she will taste ! " and as she said this, she drew forth a shining knife, that glittered horribly. " Oh ! " screamed the old woman at the same moment ; for her own daughter, who held her back, had bitten her in the ear. She was a wild and naughty girl, and the mother called her an ugly thing, and had not time to kill Gerda.

" She shall play with me," said the little robber-girl ; " she shall give me her muff and her pretty dress, and sleep with me in my bed." And then she bit her mother again, and made her spring in the air, and jump about ; and all the robbers laughed, and said, " See how she is dancing with her young cub."

" I will have a ride in the coach," said the little robber-girl ; and she would have her own way ; for she was so self-willed and obstinate.

She and Gerda seated themselves in the coach, and drove away, over stumps and stones, into the depths of the forest. The little robber-girl was about the same size as Gerda, but stronger ; she had broader shoulders and a darker skin ; her eyes were quite black, and she had a mournful look. She clasped little Gerda round the waist, and said,—

" They shall not kill you as long as you don't make me vexed with you. I suppose you are a princess."

" No," said Gerda ; and then she told her all her history, and how fond she was of little Kay.

The robber-girl looked earnestly at her, nodded her head slightly, and said, " They sha'n't kill you, even if I do get angry with you ; for I will do it myself." And then she wiped Gerda's eyes, and stuck her own hands in the beautiful muff which was so soft and warm.

The coach stopped in the courtyard of a robber's castle, the walls of which were cracked from top to bottom. Ravens and crows flew in and out of the holes and crevices while great bull-dogs, either of which looked as if it could swallow a man, were jumping about ; but they were not allowed to bark. In the large old smoky hall a bright fire was burning on the stone floor. There was no chimney ; so the smoke went up to the ceiling, and found a way out for itself. Soup was boiling in a large cauldron, and hares and rabbits were roasting on the spit.

" You shall sleep with me and all my little animals to-night," said the robber-girl, after they had had something to eat and drink. So she took Gerda to a corner of the hall, where some straw and carpets were laid down. Above them, on laths and perches, were more than a hundred pigeons, who all seemed to be asleep, although they moved slightly when the two little girls came near them. " These all belong to me," said the robber-girl ; and she seized the nearest to her, held it by the feet, and shook it till it flapped its wings. " Kiss it," cried she, flapping it in Gerda's face. " There sit the wood-pigeons," continued she, pointing to a number of laths and a cage which had been fixed into the walls, near one of the openings. " Both rascals would fly away directly, if they were not closely locked up. And here is my old sweetheart ' Ba '"; and she dragged out a reindeer by the horn ; he wore a bright copper ring round his neck, and was tied up. " We are obliged to hold him tight too, or else he would run away from us also. I tickle his neck every evening with my sharp knife, which frightens him very much." And then the robber-girl drew a long knife from a chink in the wall, and let it slide gently over the reindeer's neck. The poor animal began to kick, and the little robber-girl laughed, and pulled down Gerda into bed with her.

"Will you have that knife with you while you are asleep?" asked Gerda, looking at it in great fright.

"I always sleep with the knife by me," said the robber-girl. "No one knows what may happen. But now tell me again all about little Kay, and why you went out into the world."

Then Gerda repeated her story over again, while the wood-pigeons in the cage over her cooed, and the other pigeons slept. The little robber-girl put one arm across Gerda's neck, and held the knife in the other, and was soon fast asleep and snoring. But Gerda could not close her eyes at all; she knew not whether she was to live or die. The robbers sat round the fire, singing and drinking, and the old woman stumbled about. It was a terrible sight for a little girl to witness.

Then the wood-pigeons said, "Coo-coo; we have seen little Kay. A white fowl carried his sledge, and he sat in the carriage of the Snow Queen, which drove through the wood while we were lying in our nest. She blew upon us, and all the young ones died excepting us two. Coo, coo."

"What are you saying up there?" cried Gerda. "Where was the Snow Queen going? Do you know anything about it?"

"She was most likely travelling to Lapland, where there is always snow and ice. Ask the reindeer that is fastened up there with a rope."

"Yes, there is always snow and ice," said the reindeer; "and it is a glorious place; you can leap and run about freely on the sparkling icy plains. The Snow Queen has her summer tent there, but her strong castle is at the North Pole, on an island called Spitzbergen."

" Oh, Kay, little Kay ! " sighed Gerda.

" Lie still," said the robber-girl, " or I shall run my knife into your body."

In the morning Gerda told her all that the wood-pigeon had said ; and the little robber-girl looked quite serious, and nodded her head, and said, " That is all talk, that is all talk. Do you know where Lapland is ? " she asked the reindeer.

" Who should know better than I do ? " said the animal, while his eyes sparkled. " I was born and brought up there, and used to run about the snow-covered plains."

" Now listen," said the robber-girl ; " all our men are gone away,—only mother is here, and here she will stay ; but at noon she always drinks out of a great bottle, and afterwards sleeps for a little while ; and then I'll do something for you." Then she jumped out of bed, clasped her mother round the neck, and pulled her by the beard, crying, " My own little nanny-goat, good morning." Then her mother filliped her nose till it was quite red ; yet she did it all for love.

When the mother had drunk out of the bottle, and was gone to sleep, the little robber-maiden went to the reindeer, and said, " I should like very much to tickle your neck a few times more with my knife, for it makes you look so funny ; but never mind,—I will untie your cord, and set you free, so that you may run away to Lapland ; but you must make good use of your legs, and carry this little maiden to the castle of the Snow Queen where her playfellow is. You have heard what she told me, for she spoke loud enough, and you were listening."

Then the reindeer jumped for joy ; and the little robber-girl lifted Gerda on his back, and had the forethought to tie her on, and even to give her her own little cushion to sit on.

" Here are your fur boots for you," said she ; " for it will be very cold ; but I must keep the muff ; it is so pretty. However, you shall not be frozen for the want of it ; here are my mother's large warm mittens ; they will reach up to your elbows. Let me put them on. There, now your hands look just like my mother's."

But Gerda wept for joy.

" I don't like to see you fret," said the little robber-girl ; " you ought to look quite happy now ; and here are two loaves and a ham, so that you need not starve." These were fastened on the reindeer, and then the little robber-maiden opened the door, coaxed in all the great dogs, and then cut the string with which the reindeer was fastened, with her sharp knife, and said, " Now run, but mind you take good care of the little girl." And then Gerda stretched out her hand, with the great mitten on it, towards the little robber-girl, and said, " Farewell," and away flew the reindeer, over stumps and stones, through the great forest, over marshes and plains, as quickly as he could. The wolves howled, and the ravens screamed ; while up in the sky quivered red lights like flames of fire. " There are my old northern lights," said the reindeer ; " see how they flash." And he ran on day and night still faster and faster, but the loaves and the ham were all eaten by the time they reached Lapland.

SIXTH STORY

THE LAPLAND WOMAN AND THE FINLAND WOMAN

They stopped at a little hut; it was very mean looking; the roof sloped nearly down to the ground, and the door was so low that the family had to creep in on their hands and knees, when they went in and out. There was no one at home but an old Lapland woman, who was cooking fish by the light of a train-oil lamp. The reindeer told her all about Gerda's story, after having first told his own, which seemed to him the most important, but Gerda was so pinched with the cold that she could not speak. " Oh, you poor things," said the Lapland woman, " you have a long way to go yet. You must travel more than a hundred miles farther, to Finland. The Snow Queen lives there now, and she burns Bengal lights every evening. I will write a few words on a dried stock-fish, for I have no paper, and you can take it from me to the Finland woman who lives there ; she can give you better information than I can." So when Gerda was warmed, and had taken something to eat and drink, the woman wrote a few words on the dried fish, and told Gerda to take great care of it. Then she tied her again on the reindeer, and he set off at full speed. Flash, flash, went the beautiful blue northern lights in the air the whole night long. And at length they reached Finland, and knocked at the chimney of the Finland woman's hut, for it had no door above the ground. They crept in, but it was so terribly hot inside that the woman wore scarcely any clothes ; she was small and very dirty looking. She loosened little Gerda's dress, and took off the fur boots and the mittens, or Gerda would have been unable to bear the heat ; and then she placed a piece of ice on the reindeer's head, and read what was written on the dried fish. After she had read it three times, she knew it by heart, so she popped the fish into the soup saucepan, as she knew it was good to eat, and she never wasted anything. The reindeer told his own story first, and then little Gerda's, and the Finlander twinkled with her clever eyes, but she said nothing. " You are so clever," said the reindeer ; " I know you can tie all the winds of the world with a piece of twine. If a sailor unties one knot, he has a fair wind ; and when he unties the second it blows hard ; but if the third and fourth are loosened, then comes a storm, which will root up whole forests. Cannot you give this little maiden something which will make her as strong as twelve men, to overcome the Snow Queen ? "

" The power of twelve men ! " said the Finland woman ; " that would be of very little use." But she went to a shelf and took down and unrolled a large skin, on which were inscribed wonderful characters, and she read till the perspiration ran down from her forehead. But the reindeer begged so hard for little Gerda, and Gerda looked at the Finland woman with such beseeching tearful eyes, that her own eyes began to twinkle again ; so she drew the reindeer into a corner, and whispered to him while she laid a fresh piece of ice on his head, " Little Kay is really with the Snow Queen, but he finds everything there so much to his taste and his liking, that he believes it is the finest place in the world ; but this is because he has a piece of broken glass in his heart, and a little piece of glass in his eye. These must be taken out, or he will never be a human being again, and the Snow Queen will retain her power over him."

" But can you not give little Gerda something to help her to conquer this power ? "

" I can give her no greater power than she has already," said the woman, " don't you see how strong that is ? How men and animals are obliged to serve her, and how well she has got through the world, barefooted as she is. She cannot receive any power from me greater than she now has, which consists in her own purity and innocence of heart. If she cannot herself obtain access to the Snow Queen, and remove the glass fragments from little Kay, we can do nothing to help her. Two miles from here the Snow Queen's garden begins ; you can carry the little girl so far, and set her down by the large bush which stands in the snow, covered with red berries. Do not stay gossiping, but come back here as quickly as you can." Then the Finland woman lifted little Gerda upon the reindeer, and he ran away with her as quickly as he could.

" Oh, I have forgotten my boots and my mittens," cried little Gerda, as soon as she felt the cutting cold, but the reindeer dared not stop ; so he ran on till he reached the bush with the red berries ; here he sat Gerda down, and he kissed her, and the great bright tears trickled over the animal's cheeks ; then he left her and ran back as fast as he could.

There stood poor Gerda, without shoes, without gloves, in the midst of cold, dreary, ice-bound Finland. She ran forwards as quickly as she could, when a whole regiment of snow-flakes came round her ; they did not, however, fall from the sky, which was quite clear and glittering with the northern lights. The snow-flakes ran along the ground, and the nearer they came to her, the larger they appeared. Gerda remembered how large and beautiful they looked through the burning glass. But these were really larger and much more terrible, for they were alive, and were the guards of the Snow Queen, and had the strangest shapes. Some were like great porcupines, others like twisted serpents with their heads stretching out, and some few were like little fat bears with their hair bristled ; but all were dazzlingly white, and were all living snow-flakes. Then little Gerda, repeated the Lord's Prayer, and the cold was so great that she could see her own breath come out of her mouth like steam as she uttered the words. The steam appeared to increase, as she continued her prayer, till it took the shape of little angels, who grew larger the moment they touched the earth. They all wore helmets on their heads, and carried spears and shields. Their number continued to increase more and more ; and by the time Gerda had finished her prayers, a whole legion stood around her. They thrust their spears into the terrible snow-flakes, so that they shivered into a hundred pieces, and little Gerda could go forward with courage and safety. The angels stroked her hands and feet, so that she felt the cold less, and she hastened on to the Snow Queen's castle.

But now we must see what Kay is doing. In truth he thought not of little Gerda, and never supposed she could be standing in the front of the palace.

OF THE PALACE OF THE SNOW QUEEN, AND WHAT HAPPENED THERE AT LAST

THE WALLS of the palace were formed of drifted snow, and the windows and doors of the cutting winds. There were more than a hundred rooms in it, all as if they had been formed with snow blown together. The largest of them extended for several miles ; they were all lighted up by the vivid light of the aurora, and they were so large and empty, so icy cold and glittering ! There were no amusements here, not even a little bear's ball, when the storm might have been the music, and the bears could have danced on their hind legs, and shown their good manners. There were no pleasant games of snap-dragon, or touch, or even a gossip over the tea-table, for the young-lady foxes. Empty, vast, and cold were the halls of the Snow Queen. The flickering flame of the northern lights could be plainly seen, whether they rose high or low in the heavens, from every part of the castle. In the midst of this empty, endless hall of snow was a frozen lake, broken on its surface into a thousand forms ; each piece resembled another, from being in itself perfect as a work of art, and in the centre of this lake sat the Snow Queen, when she was at home. She called the lake "The Mirror of Reason," and said that it was the best, and indeed the only one in the world.

Little Kay was quite blue with cold, indeed almost black, but he did not feel it, for the Snow Queen had kissed away the icy shiverings, and his heart was already a lump of ice. He dragged some sharp, flat pieces of ice to and fro, and placed them together in all kinds of positions, as if he wished to make something out of them ; just as we try to form various figures with little tablets of wood which we call a "Chinese puzzle." Kay's figures were very artistic ; it was the icy game of reason at which he played, and in his eyes the figures were very remarkable, and of the highest importance ; this opinion was owing to the piece of glass still sticking in his eye. He composed many complete figures, forming different words, but there was one word he never could manage to form, although he wished it very much. It was the word " Eternity." The Snow Queen had said to him, " When you can find out this, you shall be your own master, and I will give you the whole world and a new pair of skates." But he could not accomplish it.

" Now I must hasten away to warmer countries," said the Snow Queen. " I will go and look into the black craters of the tops of burning mountains, Etna and Vesuvius, as they are called—I shall make them look white, which will be good for them, and for the lemons and the grapes." And away flew the Snow Queen, leaving little Kay quite alone in the great hall which was so many miles in length ; so he sat and looked at his pieces of ice, and was thinking so deeply, and sat so still that anyone might have supposed he was frozen.

Just at this moment it happened that little Gerda came through the great door of the castle. Cutting winds were raging around her, but she offered up a prayer and the winds sank down as if they were going to sleep ; and she went on till she came to the large empty hall, and caught sight of Kay ; she knew him directly ; she flew to him and threw her arms round his neck, and held him fast, while she exclaimed, " Kay, dear little Kay, I have found you at last."

But he sat quite still, stiff and cold.

Then little Gerda wept hot tears, which fell on his breast, and penetrated into his heart, and thawed the lump of ice, and washed away the little pieces of glass which had stuck there. Then he looked at her, and she sang—

> " Roses bloom and cease to be,
> But we shall the Christ-child see."

Then Kay burst into tears, and he wept so that the splinter of glass swam out of his eye. Then he recognised

Gerda, and said, joyfully, "Gerda, dear little Gerda, where have you been all this time, and where have I been?" And he looked all around him, and said, "How cold it is, and how large and empty it all looks," and he clung to Gerda, and she laughed and wept for joy. It was so pleasing to see them that the pieces of ice even danced about; and when they were tired and went to lie down, they formed themselves into the letters of the word which the Snow Queen had said he must find out before he could be his own master, and have the whole world and a pair of new skates. Then Gerda kissed his cheeks, and they became blooming; and she kissed his eyes, and they shone like her own; she kissed his hands and his feet, and then he became quite healthy and cheerful. The Snow Queen might come home now when she pleased, for there stood his certainty of freedom, in the word she wanted, written in shining letters of ice.

Then they took each other by the hand, and went forth from the great palace of ice. They spoke of the grandmother, and of the roses on the roof, and as they went on the winds were at rest, and the sun burst forth. When they arrived at the bush with red berries, there stood the reindeer waiting for them, and he had brought another young reindeer with him, whose udders were full, and the children drank her warm milk and kissed her on the mouth. Then they carried Kay and Gerda first to the Finland woman, where they warmed themselves thoroughly in the hot room, and she gave them directions about their journey home. Next they went to the Lapland woman, who had made some new clothes for them, and put their sleighs in order. Both the reindeer ran by their side, and followed them as far as the boundaries of the country, where the first green leaves were budding. And here they took leave of the two reindeer and the Lapland woman, and all said—Farewell. Then the birds began to twitter, and the forest too was full of green young leaves; and out of it came a beautiful horse, which Gerda remembered, for it was one which had drawn the golden coach. A young girl was riding upon it, with a shining red cap on her head, and pistols in her belt. It was the little robber maiden, who had got tired of staying at home ; she was going first to the north, and if that did not suit her, she meant to try some other part of the world. She knew Gerda directly, and Gerda remembered her ; it was a joyful meeting.

" You are a fine fellow to go gadding about in this way," said she to little Kay, " I should like to know whether you deserve that anyone should go to the end of the world to find you."

But Gerda patted her cheeks, and asked after the prince and princess.

" They are gone to foreign countries," said the robber-girl.

" And the crow ? " asked Gerda.

" Oh, the crow is dead," she replied ; " his tame sweet-heart is now a widow, and wears a bit of black worsted round her leg. She mourns very pitifully, but it is all stuff. But now tell me how you managed to get him back."

Then Gerda and Kay told her all about it.

" Snip, snap, snare ! it's all right at last," said the robber-girl.

Then she took both their hands, and promised that if ever she should pass through the town, she would call and pay them a visit. And then she rode away into the wide world. But Gerda and Kay went hand-in-hand towards home ; and as they advanced, spring appeared more lovely with its green verdure and its beautiful flowers. Very soon they recognised the large town where they lived, and the tall steeples of the churches, in which the sweet bells were ringing a merry peal as they entered it, and found their way to their grandmother's door. They went upstairs into the little room, where all looked just as it used to do. The old clock was going " tick, tick," and the hands pointed to the time of day, but as they passed through the door into the room, they perceived that they were both grown up, and become a man and woman. The roses out on the roof were in full bloom, and peeped in at the window ; and there stood the little chairs, on which they had sat when children ; and Kay and Gerda seated themselves each on their own chair, and held each other by the hand, while the cold empty grandeur of the Snow Queen's palace vanished from their memories like a painful dream. The grandmother sat in God's bright sunshine, and she read aloud from the Bible, " Except ye become as little children, ye shall in no wise enter into the kingdom of God.'' And Kay and Gerda looked into each other's eyes, and all at once understood the words of the old song,

> *Roses bloom and cease to be,*
> *But we shall the Christ-child see.*

And they both sat there, grown up, yet children at heart ; and it was summer,—warm, beautiful summer.

THE BRAVE LITTLE TAILOR

by GRIMM

A LITTLE tailor was sitting near his window one summer's morning, plying his needle cheerfully, when by came a woman, crying, " Jam to sell, good jam to sell ! " The tailor thought he would like some jam, so he put his head out of the window, called the woman to him, and purchased a small pot. It made his mouth water to see it, it was so red, so clear, so delicious looking. He could hardly wait to eat it. He cut himself a slice of bread, and spread the jam upon it ; but he thought he had better finish the coat he was making before he made his fingers sticky with bread and jam, so he laid it beside him. While he was stitching away as fast as he could, taking bigger and bigger stitches, to get at the jam the sooner, the flies were attracted by the jam, and down they came in a swarm and buzzed about it. " Get away, get away," said the little tailor, stopping in his work to brush them away. But vainly he waved them off. They continued to buzz round the jam as before in greater numbers than ever, till the tailor was so exasperated that he snatched up a cloth and struck a great blow at the bread and jam so that seven flies lay dead on the spot. " Oh, ho," said he, " am I as bold a fellow as all that ? Seven at one blow ! The whole town shall hear of it." And the little tailor forthwith cut himself out a belt, on which he worked, in large letters, the words : " Seven at one blow." " The town shall hear of it," he cried, " Nay, the whole world shall hear of it."

So he put on the belt, and sallied forth into the wide world, as his workshop was too narrow a field for his valour. Before he went, he looked to see what he could take with him ; but he found only a small cheese, which he put into his pocket. After passing through the gates of the town, he perceived a bird entangled in a bush, and this he caught and put into his other pocket, after which he pursued his way rapidly enough, for he was so light and nimble that he scarcely felt the least fatigue. The road he followed led over a mountain, and, on reaching its highest summit, he found a powerful giant sitting looking about him, at the landscape around. The little tailor went up to him boldly, and said, in a cheerful voice : " Good morning, comrade ; so you are looking at the wide world, are you ? I am just going into it. Now, what say you to accompanying me ? "

The giant looked at the tailor with the utmost contempt, and said in a voice of thunder : " You miserable little whipper-snapper ! " " Miserable little whipper-snapper, indeed ! " rejoined the little tailor, unbuttoning his coat, and pointing to his belt, " only read, and see what sort of a man I am." The giant read, " Seven at one blow," and, concluding it meant seven men that the tailor had killed, began to entertain a greater degree of respect for the little fellow. Nevertheless, being desirous of putting him to the proof, he picked up a stone, and squeezed it till the water dropped out of it. " Now do the same," said the giant, " if you have strength enough." " Is that all ? " cried the little tailor ; " that's a mere joke for me." And, putting his hand into his pocket, he drew out the cheese, and squeezed it till the whey oozed out. " This is better still, I think," said he. The giant did not know what to think or to say ; so he picked up another stone, and threw it upwards to such a height that no eye could follow it. " There ! " cried he ; " do as much, if you can, my little fellow." " It's a good throw," returned the tailor, " but the stone must needs fall to earth again somewhere or other ; now I'll throw something that won't come back." And, drawing forth the bird from his pocket, he cast it into the air. Delighted at regaining its liberty, the bird flew away and did not return. " What say you to that ? " asked the tailor. " It's a good throw," replied the giant ; " but now let's see what weight you can carry." He then led the little tailor to a spot where lay a felled oak of great size, and bid him to carry it out of the forest. " Willingly," said the little man : " and if you do but place the trunk on your shoulder, I will lift up the branches, which are the heavier of the two." The giant accordingly shouldered the trunk of the tree, and no sooner was it on his shoulder and his back turned than nimbly the tailor sat down on one of the branches, and, as the giant could not look round, he was tricked into carrying not only the whole tree, but the tailor into the bargain. Merrily whistled the little tailor as they went along, as though the burden were light as a feather. After they had gone a few yards, the giant could bear the weight no longer, and let the tree fall from his shoulder, while the tailor quickly jumped down and pretended to be holding the branches, and laughed at the giant for being unable to carry a tree, though he was such a big fellow. They went further along the road then, and presently they came to a cherry-tree. When they reached it, the giant bent down the top, and, placing it in the tailor's hands, bade him eat of the fruit. Now the tailor was much too weak to hold the branches, and when the giant let them go, they carried the tailor off his feet and lifted him up into the air as they rebounded. " So ! " cried the giant. " You have not even the strength to hold such a twig as that ? " " Oh," returned the tailor, " it is not the strength that fails me, but there is a sportsman shooting in yonder bush, and I had a mind to get out of his way. Jump after me, if you can." The giant tried, but he could not manage to clear the tree, and remained hanging midway on one of the branches, so that the little tailor got the best of it this time too.

" Since you are such a brave fellow," said the giant, " come and spend the night in our cavern." The little tailor made no objection to follow him, and they reached the cavern, where they found several other giants sitting by the fire, each eating a whole roast lamb for his supper. The giant then pointed to a bed, and told the tailor he might turn in and sleep there to his heart's content. But the bed was so large that the little man preferred creeping into a corner of the cavern. Towards midnight, when the giant thought he must be fast asleep, he took an iron club and shivered the bed at a single blow, making sure that the little fellow who lay in it must be crushed to pulp. The next morning, the giants woke up and sallied out into the forest, and they had forgotten all about their little visitor of the night before. What was their astonishment when up he came, looking as cheerful and bold as ever. The giants were frightened, and set about to find out how he had escaped the blow of the club. " Did you sleep well," they asked him. " Oh, yes, thank you," replied the tailor, " I never slept better." " Did nothing disturb you at all in the night? " asked the giants. The little tailor pretended to recollect something. " Ah, yes," he said, " now I come to think of it, I did feel something ; but it was only a moth striking against the bedclothes." At this the giants were so frightened, lest he should wish to avenge himself for their treachery, that they took to their heels as fast as they could.

As to the little tailor, he continued his journey. After wandering a considerable way, he reached the court-yard of a royal palace, when, feeling tired, he stretched himself on the grass, and fell asleep. Some persons, who happened to see him, read the legend on his belt, " Seven at one blow," and immediately concluded he was a mighty warrior. So they hastened to inform the king of his arrival, observing that it would be well to secure the services of such a man in case war were to break out again. The king therefore sent one of his courtiers to invite the stranger to enter his army, as soon as he should awake. The courtier having delivered his message, the tailor replied : " I came with the express intention of offering my services to his majesty." He was accordingly received with all honours and given a splendid house to live in.

The soldiers were jealous of the little tailor's promotion, and after a time they went to the king and begged him to release them from further service. This put the king into a difficult position, for he could not bear the idea of losing his faithful generals, yet he did not dare to offend the powerful newcomer, lest he should kill both him and his people, and take possession of the kingdom. So after a good deal of thought, he sent to the tailor, to say, that, as he was such a hero, he wanted him to rid the land of a couple of giants who lived in a neighbouring forest, promising that, if he succeeded, he would give him his only daughter in marriage, and half his kingdom. The king added, that a hundred horse soldiers should lend him their assistance. The little tailor thought it would be a fine thing to marry a beautiful princess, so he sent back word that he would soon tame the giants, and that he wanted no help, for he who could kill seven at a blow was not to be daunted by two.

The little tailor then set out, followed by a hundred horse soldiers ; but, on reaching the forest, he told them to wait till he returned, as he meant to fight the giants alone. He then entered the thicket, and, advancing cautiously on tip-toe, at last discovered the two giants asleep under a tree. The little tailor lost no time in filling his pockets with stones, and then climbed into the tree and ensconced himself in its branches. From there, with great precision, he let fall several stones, one after another, right on top of one of the giants, who at length awoke, and, turning to his companion, asked angrily why he struck him ? " You are dreaming," said the other : " I didn't touch you." They went to sleep again, when the tailor threw down a stone that hit the other giant. " What are you hitting me for ? " said the latter. " Nonsense, you are dreaming," said the other. But after quarrelling awhile, as they were both tired, they presently fell asleep again. The tailor then chose a very heavy stone, and hurled it with all his might at the first giant. " This is too bad ! " cried he, rising in a fury and attacking his companion. The other giant quickly began to hit back, and such was their rage that they tore up whole trees, and never ceased striking each other till they both lay dead on the ground. The tailor now came down, and, drawing his sword, plunged it into the breast of each of the dead giants in turn, and then returned to the horse soldiers, and told them he had overcome the giants. " It was hard work," added he, " for they tore up trees to defend themselves ; but what could they do against a man who can kill seven at a blow ? " The soldiers, however, would not believe him, till they had ridden into the forest and seen the uprooted trees and the giants lying dead in their blood.

The king, after he had got rid of the giants, was not much pleased at the thoughts of giving up half his kingdom to the stranger ; so he said : " You have not yet done : in the palace courtyard lies a bear, with whom you must pass the night, and if, when I rise in the morning, I find you still living, you shall then have your reward." " Very well," said the tailor, " I am willing."

So when evening came, our little tailor was led out and shut up in a courtyard with the bear, who rose at once and came towards him with his paw uplifted to strike. " Softly, softly, my friend," said the little tailor, " I know a better game than that." Then, pulling out of his pocket some fine walnuts, he cracked them, and ate the kernels. When the bear saw this, he longed for some too ; so the tailor felt in his pocket and gave him a handful, not of walnuts, but nice round pebbles. The bear snapped them up, but could not crack one of them, do what he would. Then said he to the tailor : " Friend, pray crack me the nuts." " Why, what a duffer you are," said the tailor, " to have such a jaw as that, and not to be able to crack a little nut ! " So he took the stones, and, slyly changing them for nuts, put them into his mouth, and crack ! they went. " Oh ! " said the bear, " now I see the way to do it. I am sure I can do it myself." Then the tailor gave him the pebbles again, and the bear chewed away as hard as he could, till he lay down quite exhausted.

But the little tailor thought this would not last long ; so he pulled a fiddle out from under his coat, and played the bear a tune. As soon as the bear heard it, he could not help jumping up and beginning to dance ; and when he had jigged away for awhile, he said, " Tell me, friend, is the fiddle hard to play upon ? " " No, not at all ! " said the little tailor. " Will you teach me to play the fiddle ? " said the bear, " so that I may have music whenever I want to dance." " With all my heart ; but let me look at your claws : they are so very long that I must first clip your nails a bit." Then the tailor pretended that he could not cut the nails unless the bear's paws were tied tight. " Very well," said the bear, so he lifted up his paws one after another, and the tailor tied them down tight. " Now," said the tailor, " wait till I come with my scissors." So he left the bear to growl as loud as he liked, and laid himself down on a heap of straw in the corner, and slept soundly. In the morning when the king came, he found the tailor sitting comfortably at breakfast, and could no longer help keeping his word, but was obliged, willy-nilly, to give him his daughter and half his kingdom. So the wedding was celebrated with much pomp, though with little joy, and the tailor became a king. As for the bear, it became a great pet and danced at the wedding.

ÆSOP'S FABLES[1]

The Fox and the Crow

A CROW had snatched a goodly piece of cheese out of a window, and flew with it into a high tree, intent to enjoy her prize. A Fox spied the dainty morsel, and thus he planned his approaches. " O Crow," said he, " how beautiful are thy wings, how bright thine eye ! how graceful thy neck ! thy breast is the breast of an eagle ! thy claws—I beg pardon—thy talons, are a match for all the beasts of the field. O ! that such a bird should be dumb, and want only a voice ! " The Crow, pleased with the flattery, and chuckling to think how she would surprise the Fox with her caw, opened her mouth :—down dropped the cheese ! which the Fox snapping up, observed, as he walked away, " that whatever he had remarked of her beauty, he had said nothing yet of her brains."

The Wolf in Sheep's Clothing

A WOLF, once upon a time, resolved to disguise himself, thinking that he should thus gain an easier livelihood. Having, therefore, clothed himself in a sheep's skin, he contrived to get among a flock of Sheep, and feed along with them, so that even the Shepherd was deceived by the imposture. When night came and the fold was closed, the Wolf was shut up with the Sheep, and the door made fast. But the Shepherd, wanting something for his supper, and going in to fetch out a sheep, mistook the Wolf for one of them, and killed him on the spot.

---

[1] These fables are from the volume in Everyman's Library published by Messrs. Dent, and edited by Mr. Ernest Rhys.

The Shepherd-Boy and the Wolf

A SHEPHERD-BOY, who tended his flock not far from a village, used to amuse himself at times in crying out " Wolf ! Wolf ! " Twice or thrice his trick succeeded. The whole village came running out to his assistance ; when all the return they got was to be laughed at for their pains. At last one day the Wolf came indeed. The Boy cried out in earnest. But his neighbours, supposing him to be at his old sport, paid no heed to his cries, and the Wolf devoured the Sheep. So the Boy learned, when it was too late, that liars are not believed even when they tell the truth.

The Wolf and the Lamb

AS A WOLF was lapping at the head of a running brook, he spied a stray Lamb paddling, at some distance, down the stream. Having made up his mind to seize her, he bethought himself how he might justify his violence. " Villain ! " said he, running up to her, " how dare you muddle the water that I am drinking ? " " Indeed," said the Lamb humbly, " I do not see how I can disturb the water, since it runs from you to me, not from me to you." " Be that as it may," replied the Wolf, " it was but a year ago that you called me many ill names." " Oh, Sir ! " said the Lamb, trembling, " a year ago I was not born." " Well," replied the Wolf, " if it was not you, it was your father, and that is all the same ; but it is no use trying to argue me out of my supper "—and without another word he fell upon the poor helpless Lamb and tore her to pieces.

A tyrant never wants a plea. And they have little chance of resisting the injustice of the powerful whose only weapons are innocence and reason.

The Fox and the Grapes

A HUNGRY Fox stole one day into a vineyard where many bunches of Grapes hung ripe and ready for eating.

R*

But as luck would have it, they were fastened upon a tall trellis, just too high for Reynard to reach. He jumped, and paused, and jumped again, in the attempt to get at them. But it was all in vain. At last he was fairly tired out, and thereupon, " Take them who will," he cried, " THE GRAPES ARE SOUR ! "

The Boy and the Nettle

A BOY playing in the fields got stung by a Nettle. He ran home to his mother, telling her that he had but touched that nasty weed, and it had stung him. " It was just your touching it, my boy," said the mother, " that caused it to sting you ; the next time you meddle with a Nettle, grasp it tightly, and it will do you no hurt."

The Mice in Council

ONCE UPON a time the Mice being sadly distressed by the persecution of the Cat, resolved to call a meeting, to decide upon the best means of getting rid of this continual annoyance. Many plans were discussed and rejected ; at last a young Mouse got up and proposed that a Bell should be hung round the Cat's neck, that they might for the future always have notice of her coming, and so be able to escape. This proposition was hailed with the greatest applause, and was agreed to at once unanimously. Upon which an old Mouse, who had sat silent all the while, got up and said that he considered the contrivance most ingenious, and that it would, no doubt, be quite successful ; but he had only one short question to put, namely, which of them it was who would Bell the Cat ?

It is one thing to propose, another to execute.

The Ant and the Grasshopper

ON A COLD frosty day an Ant was dragging out some of the corn which he had laid up in summer time, to dry it. A Grasshopper, half-perished with hunger, besought the Ant to give him a morsel of it to preserve his life. " What were you doing," said the Ant, " this last summer ? " " Oh," said the Grasshopper, " I was not idle. I kept singing all the summer long." Said the Ant, laughing and shutting up his granary, " Since you could sing all summer, you may dance all winter."

The Fox Without a Tail

A Fox being caught in a trap, was glad to compound for his neck by leaving his tail behind him ; but upon coming abroad into the world, he began to be so sensible of the disgrace such a defect would bring upon him, that he almost wished he had died rather than come away without it. However, resolving to make the best of a bad matter, he called a meeting of the rest of the Foxes, and proposed that all should follow his example. " You have no notion," said he, " of the ease and comfort with which I now move about : I could never have believed it if I had not tried it myself ; but really when one comes to reason upon it, a tail is such an ugly, inconvenient, unnecessary appendage, that the only wonder is that, as Foxes, we could have put up with it so long. I propose, therefore, my worthy brethren, that you all profit by the experience that I am most willing to afford you, and that all Foxes from this day forward cut off their tails." Upon this one of the oldest stepped forward, and said, " I rather think, my friend, that you would not have advised us to part with our tails, if there were any chance of recovering your own."

The Ass in the Lion's Skin

AN ASS having put on a Lion's skin, roamed about, frightening all the silly animals he met with, and, seeing a Fox, he tried to alarm him also. But Reynard, having heard his voice, said, " Well, to be sure ! and I should have been frightened too, if I had not heard you bray."

The Dog and the Shadow

A Dog had stolen a piece of meat out of a butcher's shop, and was crossing a river on its way home, when he saw his own shadow reflected in the stream below. Thinking that it was another dog with another piece of meat, he resolved to make himself master of that also ; but in snapping at the supposed treasure, he dropped the bit he was carrying, and so lost all.

Grasp at the shadow and lose the substance—the common fate of those who hazard a real blessing for some visionary good.

The Oak and the Reed

A GREAT Oak would never bow him for no wind, and a Reed which was at his foot bowed himself as much as the wind would. And the Oak said to him, " Why dost thou not abide still as I do ? " And the Reed answered, " I have not the might which thou hast." And the Tree said to the Reed proudly, " Then have I more strength than thou."

And anon after came a great wind which threw down to the ground the said great Tree, and the Reed abode in his own being.

AN ELEGY ON THE GLORY OF HER SEX, MADAM MARY BLAIZE

by OLIVER GOLDSMITH

GOOD PEOPLE all, with one accord,
   Lament for Madam Blaize,
Who never wanted a good word—
   From those who spoke her praise.

The needy seldom pass'd her door,
   And always found her kind ;
She freely lent to all the poor—
   Who left a pledge behind.

She strove the neighbourhood to please
   With manners wondrous winning ;
And never follow'd wicked ways—
   Unless when she was sinning.

At church, in silks and satins new,
   With hoop of monstrous size,
She never slumber'd in her pew—
   But when she shut her eyes.

Her love was sought, I do aver,
   By twenty beaux and more ;
The King himself has follow'd her—
   When she has walk'd before.

But now, her wealth and finery fled,
   Her hangers-on cut short-all :
The Doctors found, when she was dead—
   Her last disorder mortal.

Let us lament, in sorrow sore,
   For Kent Street well may say,
That had she lived a twelvemonth more,—
   She had not died to-day.

OLD SAWS

I

THREE children sliding on the ice
   Upon a summer's day,
As it fell out, they all fell in,
   The rest they ran away.

Now had these children been at home,
   Or sliding on dry ground,
Ten thousand pounds to one penny
   They had not all been drown'd.

You parents all that children have,
   And you that have got none,
If you would have them safe abroad,
   Pray keep them safe at home.

2

There was a man, and he had nought,
   And robbers came to rob him ;
He crept up to the chimney-pot,
   And then they thought they had him.

But he got down on t'other side,
   And then they could not find him.
He ran fourteen miles in fifteen days,
   And never looked behind him.

3

The man in the wilderness asked me,
   How many strawberries grew in the sea.
I answered him as I thought good,
As many as red herrings grew in the wood.

4

I saw a peacock with a fiery tail,
I saw a blazing comet drop down hail,
I saw a cloud wrapped with ivy round,
I saw an oak creep upon the ground,
I saw a pismire swallow up a whale,
I saw the sea brimful of ale,
I saw a Venice glass full fifteen feet deep,
I saw a well full of men's tears that weep,
I saw red eyes all of a flaming fire,
I saw a house bigger than the moon and higher,
I saw the sun at twelve o'clock at night,
I saw the man that saw this wondrous sight.

ALICE'S ADVENTURES IN WONDERLAND

by LEWIS CARROLL

CHAPTER I

Down the Rabbit-Hole

ALICE was beginning to get very tired of sitting by her sister on the bank, and of having nothing to do : once or twice she had peeped into the book her sister was reading, but it had no pictures or conversations in it, " and what is the use of a book," thought Alice, " without pictures or conversations ? "

So she was considering in her own mind (as well as she could, for the hot day made her feel very sleepy and stupid) whether the pleasure of making a daisy-chain would be worth the trouble of getting up and picking the daisies, when suddenly a White Rabbit with pink eyes ran close by her.

There was nothing so *very* remarkable in that ; nor did Alice think it so *very* much out of the way to hear the Rabbit say to itself, " Oh dear ! Oh dear ! I shall be too late ! " (when she thought it over afterwards, it occurred to her that she ought to have wondered at this, but at the time it all seemed quite natural) ; but when the Rabbit actually *took a watch out of its waistcoat-pocket*, and looked at it, and then hurried on, Alice started to her feet, for it flashed across her mind that she had never before seen a rabbit with either a waistcoat-pocket, or a watch to take out of it, and burning with curiosity, she ran across the field after it, and was just in time to see it pop down a large rabbit-hole under the hedge.

In another moment down went Alice after it, never once considering how in the world she was to get out again.

The rabbit-hole went straight on like a tunnel for some way, and then dipped suddenly down, so suddenly that Alice had not a moment to think about stopping herself before she found herself falling down what seemed to be a very deep well.

Either the well was very deep, or she fell very slowly, for she had plenty of time as she went down to look about her, and to wonder what was going to happen next. First, she tried to look down and make out what she was coming to, but it was too dark to see anything ; then she looked at the sides of the well, and noticed that they were filled with cupboards and book-shelves : here and there she saw maps and pictures hung upon pegs. She took down a jar from one of the shelves as she passed ; it was labelled " ORANGE MARMALADE," but to her great disappointment it was empty : she did not like to drop the jar for fear of killing somebody underneath, so managed to put it into one of the cupboards as she fell past it.

" Well ! " thought Alice to herself. " After such a fall as this, I shall think nothing of tumbling down stairs ! How brave they'll all think me at home ! Why, I wouldn't say anything about it, even if I fell off the top of the house ! " (Which was very likely true.)

Down, down, down. Would the fall *never* come to an end ? " I wonder how many miles I've fallen by this time ? " she said aloud. " I must be getting somewhere near the centre of the earth. Let me see : that would be four thous-and miles down. I think——" (for, you see, Alice had learnt several things of this sort in her lessons in the schoolroom, and though this was not a *very* good opportunity for show-ing off her knowledge, as there was no one to listen to her, still it was good practice to say it over) " —yes, that's about the right distance—but then I wonder what Latitude or Longitude I've got to ? " (Alice had no idea what Latitude was, or Longitude either, but thought they were nice grand words to say.)

Presently she began again. " I wonder if I shall fall right *through* the earth ! How funny it'll seem to come out among the people that walk with their heads downwards ! The Antipathies, I think——" (she was rather glad there *was* no one listening, this time, as it didn't sound at all the right word) " —but I shall have to ask them what the name of the country is, you know. Please, Ma'am, is this New Zealand or Australia ? " (and she tried to curtsey as she spoke —fancy *curtseying* as you're falling through the air ! Do you think you could manage it?) " And what an ignorant little girl she'll think me ! No, it'll never do to ask ; perhaps I shall see it written up somewhere."

Down, down, down. There was nothing else to do, so Alice soon began talking again. " Dinah'll miss me very much to-night, I should think ! " (Dinah was the cat.) " I hope they'll remember her saucer of milk at tea-time. Dinah, my dear, I wish you were down here with me ! There are no mice in the air, I'm afraid, but you might catch a bat, and that's very like a mouse, you know. But do cats eat bats, I wonder ? " And here Alice began to get rather sleepy, and went on saying to herself, in a dreamy sort of way, " Do cats eat bats ? Do cats eat bats ? " and sometimes, " Do bats eat cats ? " for, you see, as she couldn't answer either question, it didn't much matter which way she put it. She felt that she was dozing off, and had just begun to dream that she was walking hand in hand with Dinah, and saying to her very earnestly, " Now, Dinah, tell me the truth : did you ever eat a bat ? " when suddenly, thump ! thump ! down she came upon a heap of sticks and dry leaves, and the fall was over.

Alice was not a bit hurt, and she jumped up on to her feet in a moment : she looked up, but it was all dark overhead ; before her was another long passage, and the White Rabbit was still in sight, hurrying down it. There was not a moment to be lost : away went Alice like the wind, and was just in time to hear it say, as it turned the corner, " Oh my ears and whiskers, how late it's getting ! " She was close behind it when she turned the corner, but the Rabbit was no longer to be seen : she found herself in a long, low hall, which was lit up by a row of lamps hanging from the roof.

There were doors all round the hall, but they were all locked ; and when Alice had been all the way down one side and up the other, trying every door, she walked sadly down the middle, wondering how she was ever to get out again.

Suddenly she came upon a little three-legged table, all made of solid glass ; there was nothing on it but a tiny golden key, and Alice's first idea was that this might belong to one of the doors of the hall ; but, alas ! either the locks were too large, or the key was too small, but at any rate it would not open any of them. However, on the second time round, she came upon a low curtain she had not noticed before, and behind it was a little door about fifteen inches high : she tried the little golden key in the lock, and to her great delight it fitted !

Alice opened the door and found that it led into a small passage, not much larger than a rat-hole ; she knelt down and looked along the passage into the loveliest garden you ever saw. How she longed to get out of that dark hall, and wander about among those beds of bright flowers and those cool fountains, but she could not even get her head through the doorway ; " and even if my head would go through," thought poor Alice, " it would be of very little use without my shoulders. Oh, how I wish I could shut up like a telescope! I think I could, if I only knew how to begin." For, you see, so many out-of-the-way things had happened lately, that Alice had begun to think that very few things indeed were really impossible.

There seemed to be no use in waiting by the little door, so she went back to the table, half hoping she might find another key on it, or at any rate a book of rules for shutting people up like telescopes : this time she found a little bottle on it, (" which certainly was not here before," said Alice,) and tied round the neck of the bottle was a paper label, with the words " DRINK ME " beautifully printed on it in large letters.

It was all very well to say " Drink me," but the wise little Alice was not going to do *that* in a hurry. " No, I'll look first," she said, " and see whether it's marked ' *poison* ' or not " ; for she had read several nice little stories about children who had got burnt, and eaten up by wild beasts and other unpleasant things, all because they *would* not remember the simple rules their friends had taught them : such as, that a red-hot poker will burn you if you hold it too long ; and that if you cut your finger *very* deeply with a knife, it usually bleeds ; and she had never forgotten that, if you drink much from a bottle marked " poison," it is most certain to disagree with you sooner or later.

However, this bottle was not marked " poison," so Alice ventured to taste it, and finding it very nice (it had, in fact, a sort of mixed flavour of cherry-tart, custard, pine-apple, roast turkey, toffee, and hot buttered toast,) she very soon finished it off.

*   *   *   *   *   *   *

" What a curious feeling ! " said Alice. " I must be shutting up like a telescope."

And so it was indeed : she was now only ten inches high, and her face brightened up at the thought that she was now the right size for going through the little door into that lovely garden. First, however, she waited for a few minutes to see if she was going to shrink any further : she felt a little nervous about this ; " for it might end, you know," said Alice to herself, " in my going out altogether, like a candle. I wonder what I should be like then ? " And she tried to fancy what the flame of a candle looks like after the candle is blown out, for she could not remember ever having seen such a thing.

After a while, finding that nothing more happened, she decided on going into the garden at once ; but, alas for poor Alice ! when she got to the door, she found she had forgotten the little golden key, and when she went back to the table for it, she found she could not possibly reach it : she could see it quite plainly through the glass, and she tried her best to climb up one of the legs of the table, but it was too slippery ; and when she had tired herself out with trying, the poor little thing sat down and cried.

" Come, there's no use in crying like that ! " said Alice to herself, rather sharply. " I advise you to leave off this minute ! " She generally gave herself very good advice (though she very seldom followed it), and sometimes she scolded herself so severely as to bring tears into her eyes ; and once she remembered trying to box her own ears for having cheated herself in a game of croquet she was playing against herself, for this curious child was very fond of pretending to be two people. " But it's no use now," thought poor Alice, " to pretend to be two people ! Why, there's hardly enough of me left to make *one* respectable person ! "

Soon her eye fell on a little glass box that was lying under the table : she opened it, and found in it a very small cake, on which the words " EAT ME " were beautifully marked in currants. " Well, I'll eat it," said Alice, " and if it makes me grow larger, I can reach the key ; and if it makes me grow smaller, I can creep under the door ; so either way I'll get into the garden, and I don't care which happens ! "

She ate a little bit, and said anxiously to herself, " Which way ? Which way ? " holding her hand on the top of her head to feel which way it was growing, and she was quite surprised to find that she remained the same size ; to be sure, this is what generally happens when one eats cake, but Alice had got so much into the way of expecting nothing but out-of-the-way things to happen, that it seemed quite dull and stupid for life to go on in the common way.

So she set to work, and very soon finished off the cake.

*   *   *   *   *   *   *

CHAPTER II

The Pool of Tears

" CURIOUSER and curiouser ! " cried Alice (she was so much surprised, that for the moment she quite forgot how to speak good English) ; " now I'm opening out like the largest telescope that ever was ! Good-bye, feet ! " (for when she looked down at her feet, they seemed to be almost out of sight, they were getting so far off). " Oh, my poor little feet, I wonder who will put on your shoes and stockings for you now, dears ? I'm sure *I* shan't be able ! I shall be a great deal too far off to trouble myself about you : you must manage the best way you can—but I must be kind to them," thought Alice, " or perhaps they won't walk the way I want to go ! Let me see : I'll give them a new pair of boots every Christmas."

And she went on planning to herself how she would manage it. " They must go by the carrier," she thought ; " and how funny it'll seem, sending presents to one's own feet ! And how odd the directions will look !

> *Alice's Right Foot, Esq.*
> *Hearthrug,*
> *near the Fender,*
> (*with Alice's love*).

Oh dear, what nonsense I'm talking ! "

Just then her head struck against the roof of the hall : in fact she was now rather more than nine feet high, and she at once took up the little golden key and hurried off to the garden door.

Poor Alice ! It was as much as she could do, lying down on one side, to look through into the garden with one eye ; but to get through was more hopeless than ever : she sat down and began to cry again.

" You ought to be ashamed of yourself," said Alice, " a great girl like you," (she might well say this,) " to go on

crying in this way ! Stop this moment, I tell you ! " But
she went on all the same, shedding gallons of tears, until
there was a large pool all round her, about four inches deep
and reaching half down the hall.

After a time she heard a little pattering of feet in the
distance, and she hastily dried her eyes to see what was
coming. It was the White Rabbit returning, splendidly
dressed, with a pair of white kid gloves in one hand and a
large fan in the other : he came trotting along in a great
hurry, muttering to himself as he came, " Oh ! the Duchess,
the Duchess ! Oh ! won't she be savage if I've kept her
waiting ! " Alice felt so desperate that she was ready to
ask help of anyone ; so, when the Rabbit came near her,
she began, in a low, timid voice, " If you please, sir——"
The Rabbit started violently, dropped the white kid gloves
and the fan, and skurried away into the darkness as hard
as he could go.

Alice took up the fan and gloves, and, as the hall was very
hot, she kept fanning herself all the time she went on talking : " Dear, dear ! How queer everything is to-day ! And
yesterday things went on just as usual. I wonder if I've
been changed in the night ? Let me think : *was* I the same
when I got up this morning ? I almost think I can remember
feeling a little different. But if I'm not the same, the next
question is, Who in the world am I ? Ah, *that's* the great
puzzle ! " And she began thinking over all the children she
knew that were of the same age as herself, to see if she could
have been changed for any of them.

" I'm sure I'm not Ada," she said, " for her hair goes in
such long ringlets, and mine doesn't go in ringlets at all ;
and I'm sure I can't be Mabel, for I know all sorts of things,
and she, oh ! she knows such a very little ! Besides, *she's*
she, and *I'm* I, and—oh dear, how puzzling it all is ! I'll
try if I know all the things I used to know. Let me see :
four times five is twelve, and four times six is thirteen, and
four times seven is—oh dear ! I shall never get to twenty at
that rate ! However, the Multiplication Table doesn't

signify : let's try Geography. London is the capital of Paris, and Paris is the capital of Rome, and Rome—no, *that's* all wrong, I'm certain ! I must have been changed for Mabel ! I'll try and say ' *How doth the little—* ' " and she crossed her hands on her lap as if she were saying lessons, and began to repeat it, but her voice sounded hoarse and strange, and the words did not come the same as they used to do :—

> " *How doth the little crocodile*
> *Improve his shining tail,*
> *And pour the waters of the Nile*
> *On every golden scale !*
>
> " *How cheerfully he seems to grin,*
> *How neatly spread his claws,*
> *And welcomes little fishes in,*
> *With gently smiling jaws !* "

" I'm sure those are not the right words," said poor Alice, and her eyes filled with tears again as she went on. " I must be Mabel, after all, and I shall have to go and live in that poky little house, and have next to no toys to play with and oh ! ever so many lessons to learn ! No, I've made up my mind about it ; if I'm Mabel, I'll stay down here ! It'll be no use their putting their heads down and saying, ' Come up again, dear ! ' I shall only look up and say ' Who am I, then ? Tell me that first, and then, if I like being that person, I'll come up : if not, I'll stay down here till I'm somebody else '—but, oh dear ! " cried Alice, with a sudden burst of tears, " I do wish they *would* put their heads down ! I am so *very* tired of being all alone here ! "

As she said this she looked down at her hands, and was surprised to see that she had put on one of the Rabbit's little white kid gloves while she was talking. " How *can* I have done that ? " she thought. " I must be growing small again." She got up and went to the table to measure herself by it, and found that, as nearly as she could guess, she was now about two feet high, and was going on shrinking rapidly : she soon found out that the cause of this was the fan she was holding, and she dropped it hastily just in time to avoid shrinking away altogether.

" That *was* a narrow escape ! " said Alice, a good deal frightened at the sudden change, but very glad to find herself still in existence ; " and now for the garden ! " and she ran with all her speed back to the little door : but, alas ! the little door was shut again, and the little golden key was lying on the glass table as before, " and things are worse than ever," thought the poor child, " for I never was so small as this before, never ! And I declare it's too bad, that it is ! "

As she said these words her foot slipped, and in another moment, splash ! she was up to her chin in salt water. Her first idea was that she had somehow fallen into the sea, " and in that case I can go back by railway," she said to herself. (Alice had been to the seaside once in her life, and had come to the general conclusion, that wherever you go to on the English coast you find a number of bathing machines in the sea, some children digging in the sand with wooden spades, then a row of lodging houses, and behind them a railway station.) However, she soon made out that she was in the pool of tears which she had wept when she was nine feet high.

" I wish I hadn't cried so much ! " said Alice, as she swam about, trying to find her way out. " I shall be punished for it now, I suppose, by being drowned in my own tears ! That *will* be a queer thing, to be sure ! However, everything is queer to-day."

Just then she heard something splashing about in the pool a little way off, and she swam nearer to make out what it was : at first she thought it must be a walrus or hippopotamus, but then she remembered how small she was now, and she soon made out that it was only a mouse that had slipped in like herself.

" Would it be of any use now," thought Alice, " to speak to this mouse ? Everything is so out-of-the-way down here, that I should think very likely it can talk : at any rate, there's no harm in trying." So she began : " O Mouse, do you know the way out of this pool? I am very tired of swimming about here, O Mouse ! " (Alice thought this must be the right way of speaking to a mouse : she had never done such a thing before, but she remembered having seen in her brother's Latin Grammar, " A mouse—of a mouse—to a mouse—a mouse—O mouse ! ") The Mouse looked at her rather inquisitively, and seemed to her to wink with one of its little eyes, but it said nothing.

" Perhaps it doesn't understand English," thought Alice ; " I daresay it's a French mouse, come over with William the Conqueror." (For, with all her knowledge of history, Alice had no very clear notion how long ago anything had happened.) So she began again : " Où est ma chatte ? " which was the first sentence in her French lesson-book. The Mouse gave a sudden leap out of the water, and seemed to quiver all over with fright. " Oh, I beg your pardon ! " cried Alice hastily, afraid that she had hurt the poor animal's feelings. " I quite forgot you didn't like cats."

" Not like cats ! " cried the Mouse, in a shrill, passionate voice. " Would *you* like cats if you were me ? "

" Well, perhaps not," said Alice in a soothing tone : " don't be angry about it. And yet I wish I could show you our cat Dinah : I think you'd take a fancy to cats if you could only see her. She is such a dear quiet thing," Alice went on, half to herself, as she swam lazily about in the pool, " and she sits purring so nicely by the fire, licking her paws and washing her face—and she is such a nice soft thing to nurse—and she's such a capital one for catching mice——oh, I beg your pardon ! " cried Alice again, for this time the Mouse was bristling all over, and she felt certain it must be really offended. " We won't talk about her any more if you'd rather not."

" We, indeed ! " cried the Mouse, who was trembling down to the end of his tail. " As if *I* would talk on such a subject ! Our family always *hated* cats : nasty, low, vulgar things ! Don't let me hear the name again ! "

" I won't indeed ! " said Alice, in a great hurry to change the subject of conversation. " Are you—are you fond—of—of dogs ? " The Mouse did not answer, so Alice went on eagerly : " There is such a nice little dog near our house I should like to show you ! A little bright-eyed terrier, you know, with oh, such long curly brown hair ! And it'll fetch things when you throw them, and it'll sit up and beg for its dinner, and all sorts of things—I can't remember half of them—and it belongs to a farmer, you know, and he says it's so useful, it's worth a hundred pounds ! He says it kills all the rats and—oh dear ! " cried Alice in a sorrowful tone, " I'm afraid I've offended it again ! " For the Mouse was swimming away from her as hard as it could go, and making quite a commotion in the pool as it went.

So she called softly after it, " Mouse, dear ! Do come back again, and we won't talk about cats or dogs either, if you don't like them ! " When the Mouse heard this, it turned round and swam slowly back to her : its face was quite pale (with passion, Alice thought), and it said in a low trembling voice, " Let us get to the shore, and then I'll tell you my history, and you'll understand why it is I hate cats and dogs."

It was high time to go, for the pool was getting quite crowded with the birds and animals that had fallen into it : there were a Duck and a Dodo, a Lory and an Eaglet, and several other curious creatures. Alice led the way, and the whole party swam to the shore.

CHAPTER III

A Caucus-race and a Long Tale

THEY WERE indeed a queer-looking party that assembled on the bank—the birds with draggled feathers, the animals with their fur clinging close to them, and all dripping wet, cross, and uncomfortable.

The first question of course was, how to get dry again : they had a consultation about this, and after a few minutes it seemed quite natural to Alice to find herself talking familiarly with them, as if she had known them all her life. Indeed, she had quite a long argument with the Lory, who at last turned sulky, and would only say " I am older than you, and must know better " ; and this Alice would not allow without knowing how old it was, and, as the Lory positively refused to tell its age, there was no more to be said.

At last the Mouse, who seemed to be a person of authority among them, called out " Sit down, all of you, and listen to me ! *I'll* soon make you dry enough ! " They all sat down at once, in a large ring, with the Mouse in the middle. Alice kept her eyes anxiously fixed on it, for she felt sure she would catch a bad cold if she did not get dry very soon.

" Ahem ! " said the Mouse with an important air. " Are you all ready ? This is the driest thing I know. Silence all round, if you please ! ' William the Conqueror, whose cause was favoured by the pope, was soon submitted to by the English, who wanted leaders, and had been of late much accustomed to usurpation and conquest. Edwin and Morcar, the earls of Mercia and Northumbria——' "

" Ugh ! " said the Lory, with a shiver.

" I beg your pardon ! " said the Mouse, frowning, but very politely. " Did you speak ? "

" Not I ! " said the Lory hastily.

" I thought you did," said the Mouse. " —I proceed. ' Edwin and Morcar, the earls of Mercia and Northumbria, declared for him : and even Stigand, the patriotic archbishop of Canterbury, found it advisable—' "

" Found *what* ? " said the Duck.

" Found *it*," the Mouse replied rather crossly : " of course you know what ' it ' means."

" I know what ' it ' means well enough, when *I* find a thing," said the Duck ; " it's generally a frog or a worm. The question is, what did the archbishop find ? "

The Mouse did not notice this question, but hurriedly went on, " ' —found it advisable to go with Edgar Atheling to meet William and offer him the crown. William's conduct at first was moderate. But the insolence of his Normans—' How are you getting on now, my dear ? " it continued, turning to Alice as it spoke.

" As wet as ever," said Alice in a melancholy tone : " it doesn't seem to dry me at all."

" In that case," said the Dodo solemnly, rising to its feet, " I move that the meeting adjourn, for the immediate adoption of more energetic remedies——"

" Speak English ! " said the Eaglet. " I don't know the meaning of half those long words, and, what's more, I don't believe you do either ! " And the Eaglet bent down its head to hide a smile : some of the other birds tittered audibly.

" What I was going to say," said the Dodo in an offended tone, " was, that the best thing to get us dry would be a Caucus-race."

" What *is* a Caucas-race ? " said Alice ; not that she much wanted to know, but the Dodo had paused as if it thought that *somebody* ought to speak, and no one else seemed inclined to say anything.

" Why," said the Dodo, " the best way to explain it is to do it." (And, as you might like to try the thing yourself some winter day, I will tell you how the Dodo managed it.)

First it marked out a race-course, in a sort of circle, (" the exact shape doesn't matter," it said,) and then all the party were placed along the course, here and there. There was no " One, two, three, and away," but they began running when they liked, and left off when they liked, so that it was not easy to know when the race was over. However, when they had been running half an hour or so, and were quite dry again, the Dodo suddenly called out " The race is over ! " and they all crowded round it, panting, and asking " But who has won ? "

This question the Dodo could not answer without a great deal of thought, and it stood for a long time with one finger pressed upon its forehead (the position in which you usually see Shakespeare, in the pictures of him), while the rest waited in silence. At last the Dodo said, " *Everybody* has won, and *all* must have prizes."

" But who is to give the prizes ? " quite a chorus of voices asked.

" Why, *she*, of course," said the Dodo, pointing to Alice with one finger ; and the whole party at once crowded round her, calling out in a confused way, " Prizes ! Prizes ! "

Alice had no idea what to do, and in despair she put her hand in her pocket, and pulled out a box of comfits (luckily the salt water had not got into it), and handed them round as prizes. There was exactly one a-piece all round.

" But she must have a prize herself, you know," said the Mouse.

" Of course," the Dodo replied very gravely.

" What else have you got in your pocket ? " it went on, turning to Alice.

" Only a thimble," said Alice sadly.

" Hand it over here," said the Dodo.

Then they all crowded round her once more, while the Dodo solemnly presented the thimble, saying, " We beg your acceptance of this elegant thimble " ; and, when it had finished this short speech, they all cheered.

Alice thought the whole thing very absurd, but they all looked so grave that she did not dare to laugh ; and, as she could not think of anything to say, she simply bowed, and took the thimble, looking as solemn as she could.

The next thing was to eat the comfits ; this caused some noise and confusion, as the large birds complained that they could not taste theirs, and the small ones choked and had to be patted on the back. However, it was over at last, and they sat down again in a ring, and begged the Mouse to tell them something more.

" You promised to tell me your history, you know," said Alice, " and why it is you hate—C and D," she added in a whisper, half afraid that it would be offended again.

" Mine is a long and sad tale ! " said the Mouse, turning to Alice and sighing.

"It *is* a long tail, certainly," said Alice, looking down with wonder at the Mouse's tail ; "but why do you call it sad?" And she kept on puzzling about it while the Mouse was speaking, so that her idea of the tale was something like this :—

    " Fury said to

         a mouse, That
            he met ın the
              house, 'Let
                us both go
               to law: *I*
             will prose-
           cute *you*.—
          Come, I'll
         take no de-
        nial: We
      must have
     the trial;
   For really
   this morn-
  ing I've
nothing
to do.'
 Said the
   mouse to
     the cur,
      ' Such a
        trial, dear
         sir, With-
          no jurv
           or judge,
            would
           be wast-
          ing our
         breath.'
       'I'll be
     judge,
    I'll be
   jury,'
  said
cun-
ning
old
  Fury:
   'I'll
    try
     the
      whole
       cause,
       and
      con-
     demn
    you to
death'."

" You are not attending ! " said the Mouse to Alice severely. " What are you thinking of ? "

" I beg your pardon," said Alice very humbly : " you had got to the fifth bend, I think ? "

" I had *not* ! " cried the Mouse, angrily.

" A knot ! " said Alice, always ready to make herself useful, and looking anxiously about her. " Oh, do let me help to undo it ! "

" I shall do nothing of the sort," said the Mouse, getting up and walking away. " You insult me by talking such nonsense ! "

" I didn't mean it ! " pleaded poor Alice. " But you're so easily offended, you know ! "

The Mouse only growled in reply.

" Please come back and finish your story ! " Alice called after it. And the others all joined in chorus, " Yes, please do ! " but the Mouse only shook its head impatiently and walked a little quicker.

" What a pity it wouldn't stay ! " sighed the Lory, as soon as it was quite out of sight ; and an old Crab took the opportunity of saying to her daughter " Ah, my dear ! Let this be a lesson to you never to lose *your* temper ! " " Hold your tongue, Ma ! " said the young Crab, a little snappishly. " You're enough to try the patience of an oyster ! "

" I wish I had our Dinah here, I know I do ! " said Alice aloud, addressing nobody in particular. " She'd soon fetch it back ! "

" And who is Dinah, if I might venture to ask the question ? " said the Lory.

Alice replied eagerly, for she was always ready to talk about her pet : " Dinah's our cat. And she's such a capital one for catching mice, you can't think ! And oh, I wish you could see her after the birds ! Why, she'll eat a little bird as soon as look at it ! "

This speech caused a remarkable sensation among the party. Some of the birds hurried off at once ; one old

Magpie began wrapping itself up very carefully, remarking, " I really must be getting home ; the night-air doesn't suit my throat ! " and a Canary called out in a trembling voice to its children, " Come away, my dears ! It's high time you were all in bed ! " On various pretexts they all moved off, and Alice was soon left alone.

" I wish I hadn't mentioned Dinah ! " she said to herself in a melancholy tone. " Nobody seems to like her down here, and I'm sure she's the best cat in the world ! Oh, my dear Dinah ! I wonder if I shall ever see you any more ! " And here poor Alice began to cry again, for she felt very lonely and low-spirited. In a little while, however, she again heard a little pattering of footsteps in the distance, and she looked up eagerly, half hoping that the Mouse had changed his mind, and was coming back to finish his story.

CHAPTER IV
The Rabbit Sends in a Little Bill

IT WAS the White Rabbit, trotting slowly back again, and looking anxiously about as it went, as if it had lost something ; and she heard it muttering to itself, " The Duchess ! The Duchess ! Oh my dear paws ! Oh, my fur and whiskers ! She'll get me executed, as sure as ferrets are ferrets ! Where *can* I have dropped them, I wonder ? " Alice guessed in a moment that it was looking for the fan and the pair of white kid gloves, and she very good-naturedly began hunting about for them, but they were nowhere to be seen—everything seemed to have changed since her swim in the pool, and the great hall, with the glass table and the little door, had vanished completely.

Very soon the Rabbit noticed Alice, as she went hunting about, and called out to her in an angry tone, " Why, Mary Ann, what *are* you doing out here ? Run home this moment, and fetch me a pair of gloves and a fan ! Quick, now ! " And Alice was so much frightened that she ran off at once in the direction it pointed to, without trying to explain the mistake it had made.

"He took me for his housemaid," she said to herself as she ran. "How surprised he'll be when he finds out who I am! But I'd better take him his fan and gloves—that is, if I can find them." As she said this, she came upon a neat little house, on the door of which was a bright brass plate with the name W. RABBIT engraved upon it. She went in without knocking, and hurried upstairs, in great fear lest she should meet the real Mary Ann, and be turned out of the house before she had found the fan and gloves.

"How queer it seems," Alice said to herself, "to be going messages for a rabbit! I suppose Dinah'll be sending me on messages next!" And she began fancying the sort of thing that would happen: "'Miss Alice! Come here directly, and get ready for your walk!' 'Coming in a minute, nurse! But I've got to watch this mouse-hole till Dinah comes back, and see that the mouse doesn't get out.' Only I don't think," Alice went on, "that they'd let Dinah stop in the house if it began ordering people about like that!"

By this time she had found her way into a tidy little room with a table in the window, and on it (as she had hoped) a fan and two or three pairs of tiny white kid gloves: she took up the fan and a pair of the gloves, and was just going to leave the room, when her eye fell upon a little bottle that stood near the looking-glass. There was no label this time with the words "DRINK ME," but nevertheless she uncorked it and put it to her lips. "I know *something* interesting is sure to happen," she said to herself, "whenever I eat or drink anything; so I'll just see what this bottle does. I do hope it will make me grow large again, for really I'm quite tired of being such a tiny little thing!"

It did so indeed, and much sooner than she had expected: before she had drunk half the bottle, she found her head pressing against the ceiling, and had to stoop to save her neck from being broken. She hastily put down the bottle, saying to herself, "That's quite enough—I hope I shan't grow any more—As it is, I can't get out at the door—I do wish I hadn't drunk quite so much ! "

Alas ! it was too late to wish that ! She went on growing and growing, and very soon had to kneel down on the floor : in another minute there was not even room for this, and she tried the effect of lying down with one elbow against the door, and the other arm curled round her head. Still she went on growing, and, as a last resource she put one arm out of the window, and one foot up the chimney, and said to herself, " Now I can do no more, whatever happens. What *will* become of me ? "

Luckily for Alice, the little magic bottle had now had its full effect, and she grew no larger : still it was very uncomfortable, and, as there seemed to be no sort of chance of her ever getting out of the room again, no wonder she felt unhappy.

" It was much pleasanter at home," thought poor Alice, " when one wasn't always growing larger and smaller, and being ordered about by mice and rabbits. I almost wish I hadn't gone down that rabbit-hole—and yet—and yet—it's rather curious, you know, this sort of life ! I do wonder what *can* have happened to me ! When I used to read fairy-tales, I fancied that kind of thing never happened, and now here I am in the middle of one ! There ought to be a book written about me, that there ought ! And when I grow up, I'll write one—but I'm grown up now," she added in a sorrowful tone ; " at least there's no room to grow up any more *here*."

" But then," thought Alice, " shall I *never* get any older than I am now ? That'll be a comfort, one way—never to be an old woman—but then—always to have lessons to learn ! Oh, I shouldn't like *that* ! "

" Oh, you foolish Alice ! " she answered herself. " How can you learn lessons in here ? Why, there's hardly room for *you*, and no room at all for any lesson-books ! "

And so she went on, taking first one side and then the other, and making quite a conversation of it altogether ;

but after a few minutes she heard a voice outside, and stopped to listen.

" Mary Ann ! Mary Ann ! " said the voice. " Fetch me my gloves this moment ! " Then came a little pattering of feet on the stairs. Alice knew it was the Rabbit coming to look for her, and she trembled till she shook the house, quite forgetting that she was now about a thousand times as large as the Rabbit, and had no reason to be afraid of it.

Presently the Rabbit came up to the door, and tried to open it ; but as the door opened inwards, and Alice's elbow was pressed hard against it, that attempt proved a failure. Alice heard it say to itself " Then I'll go round and get in at the window."

" *That* you won't ! " thought Alice, and, after waiting till she fancied she heard the Rabbit just under the window, she suddenly spread out her hand, and made a snatch in the air. She did not get hold of anything, but she heard a little shriek and a fall, and a crash of broken glass, from which she concluded that it was just possible it had fallen into a cucumber frame, or something of the sort.

Next came an angry voice—the Rabbit's—" Pat ! Pat ! Where are you ? " And then a voice she had never heard before, " Sure then I'm here ! Digging for apples, yer honour ! "

" Digging for apples, indeed ! " said the Rabbit angrily. " Here ! Come and help me out of *this* ! " (Sounds of more broken glass.)

" Now tell me, Pat, what's that in the window ? "

" Sure, it's an arm, yer honour ! " (He pronounced it " arrum.")

" An arm, you goose ! Who ever saw one that size ? Why, it fills the whole window ! "

" Sure it does, yer honour : but it's an arm for all that."

" Well it's got no business there, at any rate : go and take it away ! "

There was a long silence after this, and Alice could only hear whispers now and then ; such as, " Sure, I don't like

it, yer honour, at all, at all ! " " Do as I tell you, you
coward ! " and at last she spread out her hand again, and
made another snatch in the air. This time there were *two*
little shrieks, and more sounds of broken glass. " What a
number of cucumber frames there must be ! " thought
Alice. " I wonder what they'll do next ! As for pulling me
out of the window, I only wish they *could* ! I'm sure *I* don't
want to stay in here any longer ! "

She waited for some time without hearing anything
more : at last came a rumbling of little cart-wheels, and the
sound of a good many voices all talking together : she made
out the words : " Where's the other ladder ?—Why I hadn't
to bring but one ; Bill's got the other—Bill ! Fetch it here,
lad !—Here, put 'em up at this corner—No, tie 'em together
first—they don't reach half high enough yet—Oh ! they'll
do well enough ; don't be particular—Here, Bill ! catch
hold of this rope—Will the roof bear ?—Mind that loose
slate—Oh, it's coming down ! Heads below ! " (a loud
crash)—" Now, who did that ?—It was Bill, I fancy—Who's
to go down the chimney ?—Nay, *I* shan't ! *You* do it !—
That I won't, then ! Bill's to go down—Here, Bill ! the
master says you've to go down the chimney ! "

" Oh ! So Bill's got to come down the chimney, has he ? "
said Alice to herself. " Why, they seem to put everything
upon Bill ! I wouldn't be in Bill's place for a good deal :
this fireplace is narrow, to be sure ; but I *think* I can kick
a little ! "

She drew her foot as far down the chimney as she could,
and waited till she heard a little animal (she couldn't guess
what sort it was) scratching and scrambling about in the
chimney close above her : then, saying to herself " This is
Bill," she gave one sharp kick, and waited to see what would
happen next.

The first thing she heard was a general chorus of " There
goes Bill ! " then the Rabbit's voice alone—" Catch him,
you by the hedge ! " then silence, and then another confusion of voices—" Hold up his head—Brandy now—Don't

choke him—How was it, old fellow ? What happened to you ? Tell us all about it ! "

At last came a little feeble, squeaking voice, (" That's Bill," thought Alice,) " Well, I hardly know—No more, thank ye ; I'm better now—but I'm a deal too flustered to tell you—all I know is, something comes at me like a Jack-in-the-box, and up I goes like a sky-rocket ! "

" So you did, old fellow ! " said the others.

" We must burn the house down ! " said the Rabbit's voice. And Alice called out as loud as she could, " If you do, I'll set Dinah at you ! "

There was a dead silence instantly, and Alice thought to herself " I wonder what they *will* do next ! If they had any sense, they'd take the roof off." After a minute or two they began moving about again, and Alice heard the Rabbit say " A barrowful will do, to begin with."

" A barrowful of *what* ? " thought Alice. But she had not long to doubt, for the next moment a shower of little pebbles came rattling in at the window, and some of them hit her in the face. " I'll put a stop to this," she said to herself, and shouted out " You'd better not do that again ! " which produced another dead silence.

Alice noticed with some surprise that the pebbles were all turning into little cakes as they lay on the floor, and a bright idea came into her head. " If I eat one of these cakes," she thought, " it's sure to make *some* change in my size ; and, as it can't possibly make me larger, it must make me smaller, I suppose."

So she swallowed one of the cakes, and was delighted to find that she began shrinking directly. As soon as she was small enough to get through the door, she ran out of the house, and found quite a crowd of little animals and birds waiting outside. The poor little Lizard, Bill, was in the middle, being held up by two guinea-pigs, who were giving it something out of a bottle. They all made a rush at Alice the moment she appeared ; but she ran off as hard as she could, and soon found herself safe in a thick wood.

" The first thing I've got to do," said Alice to herself, as she wandered about in the wood, " is to grow to my right size again ; and the second thing is to find my way into that lovely garden. I think that will be the best plan."

It sounded an excellent plan, no doubt, and very neatly and simply arranged ; the only difficulty was, that she had not the smallest idea how to set about it ; and, while she was peering about anxiously among the trees, a little sharp bark just over her head made her look up in a great hurry.

An enormous puppy was looking down at her with large round eyes, and feebly stretching out one paw, trying to touch her. " Poor little thing ! " said Alice, in a coaxing tone, and she tried hard to whistle to it ; but she was terribly frightened all the time at the thought that it might be hungry, in which case it would be very likely to eat her up in spite of all her coaxing.

Hardly knowing what she did, she picked up a little bit of stick, and held it out to the puppy ; whereupon the puppy jumped into the air off all its feet at once, with a yelp of delight, and rushed at the stick, and made believe to worry it ; then Alice dodged behind a great thistle to keep herself from being run over ; and the moment she appeared on the other side, the puppy made another rush at the stick, and tumbled head over heels in its hurry to get hold of it ; then Alice, thinking it was very like having a game of play with a cart-horse, and expecting every moment to be trampled under its feet, ran round the thistle again ; then the puppy began a series of short charges at the stick, running a very little way forwards each time and a long way back, and barking hoarsely all the while, till at last it sat down a good way off, panting, with its tongue hanging out of its mouth and its great eyes half shut.

This seemed to Alice a good opportunity for making her escape ; so she set off at once, and ran till she was quite tired and out of breath, and till the puppy's bark sounded quite faint in the distance.

" And yet what a dear little puppy it was ! " said Alice, as she leant against a buttercup to rest herself, and fanned herself with one of the leaves. " I should have liked teaching it tricks very much, if—if I'd only been the right size to do it ! Oh, dear ! I'd nearly forgotten that I've got to grow up again ! Let me see—how *is* it to be managed ? I suppose I ought to eat or drink something or other ; but the great question is, what ? "

The great question certainly was, what ? Alice looked all round her at the flowers and the blades of grass, but she could not see anything that looked like the right thing to eat or drink under the circumstances. There was a large mushroom growing near her, about the same height as herself ; and, when she had looked under it, and on both sides of it, and behind it, it occurred to her that she might as well look and see what was on the top of it.

She stretched herself up on tiptoe, and peeped over the edge of the mushroom, and her eyes immediately met those of a large blue caterpillar, that was sitting on the top with its arms folded, quietly smoking a long hookah, and taking not the smallest notice of her or of anything else.

CHAPTER V

Advice from a Caterpillar

THE CATERPILLAR and Alice looked at each other for some time in silence : at last the Caterpillar took the hookah out of its mouth, and addressed her in a languid, sleepy voice.

" Who are *you* ? " said the Caterpillar.

This was not an encouraging opening for a conversation. Alice replied, rather shyly, " I—I hardly know, sir, just at present—at least I know who I *was* when I got up this morning, but I think I must have been changed several times since then."

" What do you mean by that ? " said the Caterpillar sternly. " Explain yourself ! "

" I can't explain *myself*, I'm afraid, sir," said Alice, " because I'm not myself, you see."

" I don't see," said the Caterpillar.

" I'm afraid I can't put it more clearly," Alice replied very politely, " for I can't understand it myself to begin with ; and being so many different sizes in a day is very confusing."

" It isn't," said the Caterpillar.

" Well, perhaps you haven't found it so yet," said Alice, " but when you have to turn into a chrysalis—you will some day, you know—and then after that into a butterfly, I should think you'll feel it a little queer, won't you ? "

" Not a bit," said the Caterpillar.

" Well, perhaps your feelings may be different," said Alice ; " all I know is, it would feel very queer to *me*."

" You ! " said the Caterpillar contemptuously. " Who are *you* ? "

Which brought them back again to the beginning of the conversation. Alice felt a little irritated at the Caterpillar's making such *very* short remarks, and she drew herself up and said, very gravely, " I think you ought to tell me who *you* are, first."

" Why ? " said the Caterpillar.

Here was another puzzling question ; and as Alice could not think of any good reason, and as the Caterpillar seemed to be in a *very* unpleasant state of mind, she turned away.

" Come back ! " the Caterpillar called after her. " I've something important to say ! "

This sounded promising, certainly : Alice turned and came back again.

" Keep your temper," said the Caterpillar.

" Is that all ? " said Alice, swallowing down her anger as well as she could.

" No," said the Caterpillar.

Alice thought she might as well wait, as she had nothing else to do, and perhaps after all it might tell her something worth hearing. For some minutes it puffed away without speaking, but at last it unfolded its arms, took the hookah out of its mouth again, and said " So you think you're changed, do you ? "

" I'm afraid I am, sir," said Alice ; " I can't remember things as I used—and I don't keep the same size for ten minutes together ! "

" Can't remember *what* things ? " said the Caterpillar.

" Well, I've tried to say ' *How doth the little busy bee,*' but it all came different ! " Alice replied in a very melancholy voice.

" Repeat ' *You are old, Father William,*' " said the Caterpillar.

Alice folded her hands, and began :—

" *You are old, Father William,*" *the young man said,*
  " *And your hair has become very white ;*
And yet you incessantly stand on your head—
  *Do you think, at your age, it is right ? *"

" *In my youth,*" *Father William replied to his son,*
  " *I feared it might injure the brain ;*
But, now that I'm perfectly sure I have none
  Why, I do it again and again."

" *You are old,*" *said the youth, *" *as I mentioned before,*
  And have grown most uncommonly fat ;
Yet you turned a back-somersault in at the door—
  *Pray, what is the reason of that ? *"

" *In my youth,*" *said the sage, as he shook his grey locks,*
  " *I kept all my limbs very supple*
By the use of this ointment—one shilling the box—
  *Allow me to sell you a couple ? *"

" *You are old,*" *said the youth, *" *and your jaws are too weak*
  For anything tougher than suet ;
Yet you finished the goose, with the bones and the beak—
  *Pray, how did you manage to do it ? *"

" In my youth," said his father, " I took to the law,
  And argued each case with my wife ;
And the muscular strength, which it gave to my jaw,
  Has lasted the rest of my life."

" You are old," said the youth, " one would hardly suppose
  That your eye was as steady as ever ;
Yet you balance an ell on the end of your nose—
  What made you so awfully clever ? "

" I have answered three questions, and that is enough,"
  Said his father ; " don't give yourself airs !
Do you think I can listen all day to such stuff ?
  Be off, or I'll kick you down stairs ! "

" That is not said right," said the Caterpillar.

" Not *quite* right, I'm afraid," said Alice, timidly ; " some of the words have got altered."

" It is wrong from beginning to end," said the Caterpillar decidedly, and there was silence for some minutes.

The Caterpillar was the first to speak.

" What size do you want to be ? " it asked.

" Oh, I'm not particular as to size," Alice hastily replied : " only one doesn't like changing so often, you know."

" I *don't* know," said the Caterpillar.

Alice said nothing : she had never been so much contradicted in all her life before, and she felt that she was losing her temper.

" Are you content now ? " said the Caterpillar.

" Well, I should like to be a *little* larger, sir, if you wouldn't mind," said Alice : " three inches is such a wretched height to be."

" It is a very good height indeed ! " said the Caterpillar angrily, rearing itself upright as it spoke (it was **exactly** three inches high).

" But I'm not used to it ! " pleaded poor Alice in a

piteous tone. And she thought to herself, " I wish the creatures wouldn't be so easily offended ! "

" You'll get used to it in time," said the Caterpillar ; and it put the hookah into its mouth and began smoking again.

This time Alice waited patiently until it chose to speak again. In a minute or two the Caterpillar took the hookah out of its mouth and yawned once or twice, and shook itself. Then it got down off the mushroom, and crawled away into the grass, merely remarking as it went, " One side will make you grow taller, and the other side will make you grow shorter."

" One side of *what ?* The other side of *what ?* " thought Alice to herself.

" Of the mushroom," said the Caterpillar, just as if she had asked it aloud ; and in another moment it was out of sight.

Alice remained looking thoughtfully at the mushroom for a minute, trying to make out which were the two sides of it ; and as it was perfectly round, she found this a very difficult question. However, at last she stretched her arms round it as far as they would go, and broke off a bit of the edge with each hand.

" And now which is which ? " she said to herself, and nibbled a little of the right-hand bit to try the effect : the next moment she felt a violent blow underneath her chin : it had struck her foot !

She was a good deal frightened by this very sudden change, but she felt that there was no time to be lost, as she was shrinking rapidly ; so she set to work at once to eat some of the other bit. Her chin was pressed so closely against her foot, that there was hardly room to open her mouth ; but she did it at last, and managed to swallow a morsel of the left-hand bit.

* * * * * * *

" Come, my head's free at last ! " said Alice in a tone of delight, which changed into alarm in another moment, when she found that her shoulders were nowhere to be found : all she could see, when she looked down, was an immense length of neck, which seemed to rise like a stalk out of a sea of green leaves that lay far below her.

" What *can* all that green stuff be ? " said Alice. " And where *have* my shoulders got to ? And oh, my poor hands, how is it I can't see you ? " She was moving them about as she spoke, but no result seemed to follow, except a little shaking among the distant green leaves.

As there seemed to be no chance of getting her hands up to her head, she tried to get her head down to them, and was delighted to find that her neck would bend about easily in any direction, like a serpent. She had just succeeded in curving it down into a graceful zigzag, and was going to dive in among the leaves, which she found to be nothing but the tops of the trees under which she had been wandering, when a sharp hiss made her draw back in a hurry : a large pigeon had flown into her face, and was beating her violently with its wings.

" Serpent ! " screamed the Pigeon.

" I'm *not* a serpent ! " said Alice indignantly. " Let me alone."

" Serpent, I say again ! " repeated the Pigeon, but in a more subdued tone, and added with a kind of sob, " I've tried every way, and nothing seems to suit them ! "

" I haven't the least idea what you're talking about," said Alice.

" I've tried the roots of trees, and I've tried banks, and I've tried hedges," the Pigeon went on, without attending to her ; " but those serpents ! There's no pleasing them ! "

Alice was more and more puzzled, but she thought there was no use in saying anything more till the Pigeon had finished.

" As if it wasn't trouble enough hatching the eggs," said the Pigeon ; " but I must be on the look-out for serpents night and day ! Why, I haven't had a wink of sleep these three weeks ! "

"I'm very sorry you've been annoyed," said Alice, who was beginning to see its meaning.

"And just as I'd taken the highest tree in the wood," continued the Pigeon, raising its voice to a shriek, "and just as I was thinking I should be free of them at last, they must needs come wriggling down from the sky! Ugh, Serpent!"

"But I'm *not* a serpent, I tell you!" said Alice. "I'm a —— I'm a——"

"Well! *What* are you?" said the Pigeon. "I can see you're trying to invent something!"

"I—I'm a little girl," said Alice, rather doubtfully, as she remembered the number of changes she had gone through that day.

"A likely story indeed!" said the Pigeon in a tone of the deepest contempt. "I've seen a good many little girls in my time, but never *one* with such a neck as that! No, no! You're a serpent; and there's no use denying it. I suppose you'll be telling me next that you never tasted an egg!"

"I *have* tasted eggs, certainly," said Alice, who was a very truthful child; "but little girls eat eggs quite as much as serpents do, you know."

"I don't believe it," said the Pigeon; "but if they do, why then they're a kind of serpent, that's all I can say."

This was such a new idea to Alice, that she was quite silent for a minute or two, which gave the Pigeon the opportunity of adding "You're looking for eggs, I know *that* well enough; but what does it matter to me whether you're a little girl or a serpent?"

"It matters a good deal to *me*," said Alice hastily; "but I'm not looking for eggs, as it happens; and if I was, I shouldn't want *yours*: I don't like them raw."

"Well, be off, then!" said the Pigeon in a sulky tone, as it settled down again into its nest. Alice crouched down among the trees as well as she could, for her neck kept getting entangled among the branches, and every now and then she had to stop and untwist it. After a while she remembered that she still held the pieces of mushroom in her hands, and she set to work very carefully, nibbling first at one and then at the other, and growing sometimes taller and sometimes shorter, until she had succeeded in bringing herself down to her usual height.

It was so long since she had been anything near the right size, that it felt quite strange at first ; but she got used to it in a few minutes, and began talking to herself, as usual. " Come, there's half my plan done now ! How puzzling all these changes are ! I'm never sure what I'm going to be, from one minute to another ! However, I've got back to my right size : the next thing is, to get into that beautiful garden—how *is* that to be done, I wonder ? " As she said this, she came suddenly upon an open place, with a little house in it about four feet high. " Whoever lives there," thought Alice, " it'll never do to come upon them *this* size : why, I should frighten them out of their wits ! " So she began nibbling at the right-hand bit again, and did not venture to go near the house till she had brought herself down to nine inches high.

CHAPTER VI

Pig and Pepper

FOR A minute or two she stood looking at the house, and wondering what to do next, when suddenly a footman in livery came running out of the wood—(she considered him to be a footman because he was in livery : otherwise, judging by his face only, she would have called him a fish)—and rapped loudly at the door with his knuckles. It was opened by another footman in livery, with a round face and large eyes like a frog ; and both footmen, Alice noticed, had powdered hair that curled all over their heads. She felt very curious to know what it was all about, and crept a little way out of the wood to listen.

The Fish-Footman began by producing from under his arm a great letter, nearly as large as himself, and this he handed over to the other saying, in a solemn tone, " For the Duchess. An invitation from the Queen to play croquet." The Frog-Footman repeated, in the same solemn tone, only changing the order of the words a little, " From the Queen. An invitation for the Duchess to play croquet."

Then they both bowed low, and their curls got entangled together.

Alice laughed so much at this, that she had to run back into the wood for fear of their hearing her ; and, when she next peeped out, the Fish-Footman was gone, and the other was sitting on the ground near the door, staring stupidly up into the sky.

Alice went timidly up to the door and knocked.

" There's no sort of use in knocking," said the Footman, " and that for two reasons. First, because I'm on the same side of the door as you are ; secondly, because they're making such a noise inside, no one could possibly hear you." And certainly there was a most extraordinary noise going on within—a constant howling and sneezing, and every now and then a great crash, as if a dish or kettle had been broken to pieces.

" Please, then," said Alice, " how am I to get in ? "

" There might be some sense in your knocking," the Footman went on without attending to her, " if we had the door between us. For instance, if you were *inside*, you might knock, and I could let you out, you know." He was looking up into the sky all the time he was speaking, and this Alice thought decidedly uncivil. " But perhaps he can't help it," she said to herself ; " his eyes are so *very* nearly at the top of his head. But at any rate he might answer questions.— How am I to get in ? " she repeated, aloud.

" I shall sit here," the Footman remarked, " till to-morrow——"

At this moment the door of the house opened, and a large plate came skimming out, straight at the Footman's head :

it just grazed his nose, and broke to pieces against one of the trees behind him.

" ——or next day, maybe," the Footman continued in the same tone, exactly as if nothing had happened.

" How am I to get in ? " asked Alice again in a louder tone.

" *Are* you to get in at all ? " said the Footman. " That's the first question, you know."

It was, no doubt : only Alice did not like to be told so. " It's really dreadful," she muttered to herself, " the way all the creatures argue. It's enough to drive one crazy ! "

The Footman seemed to think this a good opportunity for repeating his remark, with variations. " I shall sit here," he said, " on and off, for days and days."

" But what am *I* to do ? " said Alice.

" Anything you like," said the Footman, and began whistling.

" Ho, there's no use in talking to him," said Alice desperately : " he's perfectly idiotic ! " And she opened the door and went in.

The door led right into a large kitchen, which was full of smoke from one end to the other : the Duchess was sitting on a three-legged stool in the middle, nursing a baby ; the cook was leaning over the fire, stirring a large cauldron which seemed to be full of soup.

" There's certainly too much pepper in that soup ! " Alice said to herself, as well as she could for sneezing.

There was certainly too much of it in the air. Even the Duchess sneezed occasionally ; and the baby was sneezing and howling alternately without a moment's pause. The only things in the kitchen that did not sneeze, were the cook, and a large cat which was sitting on the hearth and grinning from ear to ear.

" Please would you tell me," said Alice a little timidly, for she was not quite sure whether it was good manners for her to speak first, " why your cat grins like that ! "

" It's a Cheshire cat," said the Duchess, " and that's why. Pig ! "

She said the last word with such sudden violence that Alice quite jumped ; but she saw in another moment that it was addressed to the baby, and not to her, so she took courage, and went on again :—

" I didn't know that Cheshire cats always grinned ; in fact, I didn't know that cats *could* grin."

" They all can," said the Duchess ; " and most of 'em do."

" I don't know of any that do," Alice said very politely, feeling quite pleased to have got into a conversation.

" You don't know much," said the Duchess ; " and that's a fact."

Alice did not at all like the tone of this remark, and thought it would be as well to introduce some other subject of conversation. While she was trying to fix on one, the cook took the cauldron of soup off the fire, and at once set to work throwing everything within her reach at the Duchess and the baby—the fire-irons came first ; then followed a shower of saucepans, plates, and dishes. The Duchess took no notice of them even when they hit her ; and the baby was howling so much already, that it was quite impossible to say whether the blows hurt it or not.

" Oh, *please* mind what you're doing ! " cried Alice, jumping up and down in an agony of terror. " Oh, there goes his *precious* nose " ; as an unusually large saucepan flew close by it, and very nearly carried it off.

" If everybody minded their own business," the Duchess said in a hoarse growl, " the world would go round a deal faster than it does."

" Which would *not* be an advantage," said Alice, who felt very glad to get an opportunity of showing off a little of her knowledge. " Just think what work it would make with the day and night ! You see the earth takes twenty-four hours to turn round on its axis——"

" Talking of axes," said the Duchess, " chop off her head."

Alice glanced rather anxiously at the cook, to see if she meant to take the hint ; but the cook was busily engaged in stirring the soup, and did not seem to be listening, so she ventured to go on again : " Twenty-four hours, I *think* ; or is it twelve ? I——"

" Oh, don't bother *me*," said the Duchess ; " I never could abide figures ! " And with that she began nursing her child again, singing a sort of lullaby to it as she did so, and giving it a violent shake at the end of every line :

> "*Speak roughly to your little boy,*
> *And beat him when he sneezes ;*
> *He only does it to annoy,*
> *Because he knows it teases.*"

Chorus
(In which the cook and the baby joined) :—
" *Wow ! wow ! wow !* "

While the Duchess sang the second verse of the song, she kept tossing the baby violently up and down, and the poor little thing howled so, that Alice could hardly hear the words :—

> "*I speak severely to my boy,*
> *I beat him when he sneezes ;*
> *For he can thoroughly enjoy*
> *The pepper when he pleases !* "

Chorus
" *Wow ! wow ! wow !* "

" Here ! you may nurse it a bit, if you like ! " the Duchess said to Alice, flinging the baby at her as she spoke. " I must go and get ready to play croquet with the Queen," and she hurried out of the room. The cook threw a frying-pan after her as she went out, but it just missed her.

Alice caught the baby with some difficulty, as it was a

queer-shaped little creature, and held out its arms and legs in all directions, "just like a star-fish," thought Alice. The poor little thing was snorting like a steam-engine when she caught it, and kept doubling itself up and straightening itself out again, so that altogether, for the first minute or two, it was as much as she could do to hold it.

As soon as she had made out the proper way of nursing it (which was to twist it up into a sort of knot, and then keep tight hold of its right ear and left foot, so as to prevent its undoing itself), she carried it out into the open air. "If I don't take this child away with me," thought Alice, " they're sure to kill it in a day or two : wouldn't it be murder to leave it behind ? " She said the last words out loud, and the little thing grunted in reply (it had left off sneezing by this time). " Don't grunt," said Alice ; " that's not at all a proper way of expressing yourself."

The baby grunted again, and Alice looked very anxiously into its face to see what was the matter with it. There could be no doubt that it had a *very* turn-up nose, much more like a snout than a real nose ; also its eyes were getting extremely small for a baby : altogether Alice did not like the look of the thing at all. " But perhaps it was only sobbing," she thought, and looked into its eyes again, to see if there were any tears.

No, there were no tears. " If you're going to turn into a pig, my dear," said Alice, seriously, " I'll have nothing more to do with you. Mind now ! " The poor little thing sobbed again (or grunted, it was impossible to say which), and they went on for some while in silence.

Alice was just beginning to think to herself, " Now, what am I to do with this creature when I get it home ? " when it grunted again, so violently, that she looked down into its face in some alarm. This time there could be *no* mistake about it : it was neither more nor less than a pig, and she felt that it would be quite absurd for her to carry it any further.

So she set the little creature down, and felt quite relieved to see it trot quietly away into the wood. " If it had grown up," she said to herself, " it would have made a dreadfully ugly child : but it makes rather a handsome pig, I think." And she began thinking over other children she knew, who might do very well as pigs, and was just saying to herself, " if one only knew the right way to change them——" when she was a little startled by seeing the Cheshire Cat sitting on a bough of a tree a few yards off.

The Cat only grinned when it saw Alice. It looked good-natured, she thought : still it had *very* long claws and a great many teeth, so she felt that it ought to be treated with respect.

" Cheshire Puss," she began, rather timidly, as she did not at all know whether it would like the name : however, it only grinned a little wider. " Come, it's pleased so far," thought Alice, and she went on. " Would you tell me, please, which way I ought to go from here ? "

" That depends a good deal on where you want to get to," said the Cat.

" I don't much care where——" said Alice.

" Then it doesn't matter which way you go," said the Cat.

" ——so long as I get *somewhere*," Alice added as an explanation.

" Oh, you're sure to do that," said the Cat, " if you only walk long enough."

Alice felt that this could not be denied, so she tried another question. "What sort of people live about here ? "

" In *that* direction," the Cat said, waving its right paw round, " lives a Hatter : and in *that* direction," waving the other paw, " lives a March Hare. Visit either you like : they're both mad."

" But I don't want to go among mad people," Alice remarked.

" Oh, you can't help that," said the Cat : " we're all mad here. I'm mad. You're mad."

" How do you know I'm mad ? " said Alice.

" You must be," said the Cat, " or you wouldn't have come here."

Alice didn't think that proved it at all ; however, she went on. " And how do you know that you're mad ? "

" To begin with," said the Cat, " a dog's not mad. You grant that ? "

" I suppose so," said Alice.

" Well, then," the Cat went on, " you see a dog growls when it's angry, and wags its tail when it's pleased. Now *I* growl when I'm pleased, and wag my tail when I'm angry. Therefore I'm mad."

" *I* call it purring, not growling," said Alice.

" Call it what you like," said the Cat. " Do you play croquet with the Queen to-day ? "

" I should like it very much," said Alice, " but I haven't been invited yet."

" You'll see me there," said the Cat, and vanished.

Alice was not much surprised at this, she was getting so used to queer things happening. While she was looking at the place where it had been, it suddenly appeared again.

" By-the-bye, what became of the baby ? " said the Cat. " I'd nearly forgotten to ask."

" It turned into a pig," Alice quietly said, just as if it had come back in a natural way.

" I thought it would," said the Cat, and vanished again.

Alice waited a little, half expecting to see it again, but it did not appear, and after a minute or two she walked on in the direction in which the March Hare was said to live. " I've seen hatters before," she said to herself ; " the March Hare will be much the most interesting, and perhaps as this is May, it won't be raving mad—at least not so mad as it was in March." As she said this, she looked up, and there was the Cat again, sitting on a branch of a tree.

" Did you say pig, or fig ? " said the Cat.

" I said pig," replied Alice ; " and I wish you wouldn't keep appearing and vanishing so suddenly : you make one quite giddy."

" All right," said the Cat ; and this time it vanished quite slowly, beginning with the end of the tail, and ending with the grin, which remained some time after the rest of it had gone.

" Well ! I've often seen a cat without a grin," thought Alice, " but a grin without a cat ! It's the most curious thing I ever saw in all my life."

She had not gone much farther before she came in sight of the house of the March Hare : she thought it must be the right house, because the chimneys were shaped like ears and the roof was thatched with fur. It was so large a house, that she did not like to go nearer till she had nibbled some more of the left-hand bit of mushroom, and raised herself to about two feet high : even then she walked up towards it rather timidly, saying to herself " Suppose it should be raving mad after all ! I almost wish I'd gone to see the Hatter instead ! "

CHAPTER VII

A Mad Tea-Party

THERE was a table set out under a tree in front of the house, and the March Hare and the Hatter were having tea at it : a Dormouse was sitting between them, fast asleep, and the other two were using it as a cushion resting their elbows on it, and talking over its head. " Very uncomfortable for the Dormouse," thought Alice ; " only, as it's asleep, I suppose it doesn't mind."

The table was a large one, but the three were all crowded together at one corner of it. " No room ! No room ! " they cried out when they saw Alice coming. " There's *plenty* of room ! " said Alice indignantly, and she sat down in a large armchair at one end of the table.

" Have some wine," the March Hare said in an encouraging tone.

Alice looked all round the table, but there was nothing on it but tea. " I don't see any wine," she remarked.

" There isn't any," said the March Hare.

" Then it wasn't very civil of you to offer it," said Alice angrily.

" It wasn't very civil of you to sit down without being invited," said the March Hare.

" I didn't know it was *your* table," said Alice ; " it's laid for a great many more than three."

" Your hair wants cutting," said the Hatter. He had been looking at Alice for some time with great curiosity, and this was his first speech.

" You should learn not to make personal remarks," Alice said with some severity ; " it's very rude."

The Hatter opened his eyes very wide on hearing this ; but all he *said* was " Why is a raven like a writing-desk ? "

" Come, we shall have some fun now ! " thought Alice. " I'm glad they've begun asking riddles,—I believe I can guess that," she added aloud.

" Do you mean that you think you can find out the answer to it ? " said the March Hare.

" Exactly so," said Alice.

" Then you should say what you mean," the March Hare went on.

" I do," Alice hastily replied ; " at least—at least I mean what I say—that's the same thing, you know."

" Not the same thing a bit ! " said the Hatter. " Why, you might just as well say that ' I see what I eat ' is the same thing as ' I eat what I see ' ! "

" You might just as well say," added the March Hare, " that ' I like what I get ' is the same thing as ' I get what I like ' ! "

" You might just as well say," added the Dormouse, which seemed to be talking in his sleep, " that ' I breathe when I sleep ' is the same thing as ' I sleep when I breathe ' ! "

" It *is* the same thing with you," said the Hatter ; and here the conversation dropped, and the party sat silent for a minute, while Alice thought over all she could remember about ravens and writing-desks, which wasn't much.

The Hatter was the first to break the silence. " What day of the month is it ? " he said, turning to Alice : he had taken his watch out of his pocket, and was looking at it uneasily, shaking it every now and then, and holding it to his ear.

Alice considered a little, and then said " The fourth."

" Two days wrong ! " sighed the Hatter. " I told you butter wouldn't suit the works ! " he added, looking angrily at the March Hare.

" It was the *best* butter," the March Hare meekly replied.

" Yes, but some crumbs must have got in as well," the Hatter grumbled : " you shouldn't have put it in with the bread-knife."

The March Hare took the watch and looked at it gloomily : then he dipped it into his cup of tea, and looked at it again : but he could think of nothing better to say than his first remark, " It was the *best* butter, you know."

Alice had been looking over his shoulder with some curiosity. " What a funny watch ! " she remarked. " It tells the day of the month, and doesn't tell what o'clock it is ! "

" Why should it ? " muttered the Hatter. " Does *your* watch tell you what year it is ? "

" Of course not," Alice replied very readily : " but that's because it stays the same year for such a long time together."

" Which is just the case with *mine*," said the Hatter.

Alice felt dreadfully puzzled. The Hatter's remark seemed to have no meaning in it, and yet it was certainly English. " I don't quite understand," she said as politely as she could.

" The Dormouse is asleep again," said the Hatter, and he poured a little hot tea upon its nose.

The Dormouse shook its head impatiently, and said, without opening its eyes, " Of course, of course ; just what I was going to remark myself."

" Have you guessed the riddle yet ? " the Hatter said, turning to Alice again.

" No, I give it up," Alice replied : " what's the answer ? "

" I haven't the slightest idea," said the Hatter.

" Nor I," said the Hare.

Alice sighed wearily. " I think you might do something better with the time," she said, " than waste it asking riddles with no answers."

" If you knew Time as well as I do," said the Hatter, " you wouldn't talk about wasting *it*. It's *him*."

" I don't know what you mean," said Alice.

" Of course you don't ! " the Hatter said tossing his head contemptuously. " I dare say you never even spoke to Time ! "

" Perhaps not," Alice cautiously replied : " but I know I have to beat time when I learn music."

" Ah ! that accounts for it," said the Hatter. " He won't stand beating. Now, if you only kept on good terms with him, he'd do almost anything you liked with the clock. For instance, suppose it were nine o'clock in the morning, just time to begin lessons : you'd only have to whisper a hint to Time, and round goes the clock in a twinkling ! Half-past one, time for dinner ! "

(" I only wish it was," the March Hare said to itself in a whisper.)

" That would be grand, certainly," said Alice thoughtfully : " but then—I shouldn't be hungry for it, you know."

" Not at first, perhaps," said the Hatter : " but you could keep it to half-past one as long as you liked."

" Is that the way *you* manage ? " Alice asked.

The Hatter shook his head mournfully. " Not I ! " he replied. " We quarrelled last March—just before *he* went mad you know——" (pointing with his tea-spoon at the March Hare,) "——it was at the great concert given by the Queen of Hearts, and I had to sing

> ' *Twinkle, twinkle, little bat !*
> *How I wonder what you're at !* '

You know the song, perhaps ? "

" I've heard something like it," said Alice.

" It goes on, you know," the Hatter continued, " in this way :—

> ' *Up above the world you fly,*
> *Like a tea-tray in the sky.*
> *Twinkle, twinkle——*' "

Here the Dormouse shook itself, and began singing in its sleep " *Twinkle, twinkle, twinkle, twinkle——*" and went on so long that they had to pinch it to make it stop.

" Well, I'd hardly finished the first verse," said the Hatter, " when the Queen jumped up and bawled out ' He's murdering the time ! Off with his head ! ' "

" How dreadfully savage ! " exclaimed Alice.

" And ever since that," the Hatter went on in a mournful tone, " he won't do a thing I ask ! It's always six o'clock now."

A bright idea came into Alice's head. " Is that the reason so many tea-things are put out here ? " she asked.

" Yes, that's it," said the Hatter with a sigh : " it's always tea-time, and we've no time to wash the things between whiles."

" Then you keep moving round, I suppose ? " said Alice.

" Exactly so," said the Hatter : " as the things get used up."

" But what happens when you come to the beginning again ? " Alice ventured to ask.

" Suppose we change the subject," the March Hare interrupted, yawning. " I'm getting tired of this. I vote the young lady tells us a story."

" I'm afraid I don't know one," said Alice, rather alarmed at the proposal.

" Then the Dormouse shall ! " they both cried. " Wake up, Dormouse ! " And they pinched it on both sides at once.

The Dormouse slowly opened his eyes. " I wasn't asleep," he said in a hoarse, feeble voice : " I heard every word you fellows were saying."

" Tell us a story ! " said the March Hare.

" Yes, please do ! " pleaded Alice.

" And be quick about it," added the Hatter, " or you'll be asleep again before it's done."

" Once upon a time there were three little sisters," the Dormouse began in a great hurry ; " and their names were Elsie, Lacie, and Tillie ; and they lived at the bottom of a well——"

" What did they live on ? " said Alice, who always took a great interest in questions of eating and drinking.

" They lived on treacle," said the Dormouse, after thinking a minute or two.

" They couldn't have done that, you know," Alice gently remarked ; " they'd have been ill."

" So they were," said the Dormouse ; " *very* ill."

Alice tried a little to fancy to herself what such an extraordinary way of living would be like, but it puzzled her too much, so she went on : " But why did they live at the bottom of a well ? "

" Take some more tea," the March Hare said to Alice, very earnestly.

" I've had nothing yet," Alice replied in an offended tone, " so I can't take more."

" You mean you can't take *less*," said the Hatter : " it's very easy to take *more* than nothing."

" Nobody asked *your* opinion," said Alice.

" Who's making personal remarks now ? " the Hatter asked triumphantly.

Alice did not quite know what to say to this : so she helped herself to some tea and bread-and-butter, and then turned to the Dormouse, and repeated her question. " Why did they live at the bottom of a well ? "

The Dormouse again took a minute or two to think about it, and then said, " It was a treacle-well."

" There's no such thing ! " Alice was beginning very angrily, but the Hatter and the March Hare went " Sh ! sh ! " and the Dormouse sulkily remarked " If you can't be civil, you'd better finish the story for yourself."

" No, please go on ! " Alice said very humbly. " I won't interrupt you again. I dare say there may be *one*."

" One, indeed ! " said the Dormouse indignantly. However, he consented to go on. " And so these three little sisters —they were learning to draw, you know——"

" What did they draw ? " said Alice, quite forgetting her promise.

" Treacle," said the Dormouse, without considering at all this time.

" I want a clean cup," interrupted the Hatter : " let's all move one place on."

He moved on as he spoke, and the Dormouse followed him : the March Hare moved into the Dormouse's place, and Alice rather unwillingly took the place of the March Hare. The Hatter was the only one who got any advantage from the change : and Alice was a good deal worse off than before, as the March Hare had just upset the milk-jug into his plate.

Alice did not wish to offend the Dormouse again, so she began very cautiously : " But I don't understand. Where did they draw the treacle from ? "

" You can draw water out of a water-well," said the Hatter ; " so I should think you could draw treacle out of a treacle-well—eh, stupid ? "

" But they were *in* the well," Alice said to the Dormouse, not choosing to notice this last remark.

" Of course they were," said the Dormouse ; "——well in."

This answer so confused poor Alice, that she let the Dormouse go on for some time without interrupting it.

" They were learning to draw," the Dormouse went on, yawning and rubbing its eyes, for it was getting very sleepy ; " and they drew all manner of things—everything that begins with an M——"

" Why with an M ? " said Alice.

" Why not ? " said the March Hare.

Alice was silent.

The Dormouse had closed its eyes by this time, and was going off into a doze ; but, on being pinched by the Hatter, it woke up again with a little shriek, and went on : "——that begins with an M, such as mouse-traps, and the moon, and memory, and muchness—you know you say things are ' much of a muchness '—did you ever see such a thing as a drawing of a muchness ? "

" Really, now you ask me," said Alice, very much confused, " I don't think——"

" Then you shouldn't talk," said the Hatter.

This piece of rudeness was more than Alice could bear : she got up in great disgust, and walked off ; the Dormouse fell asleep instantly, and neither of the others took the least notice of her going, though she looked back once or twice, half hoping that they would call after her : the last time she saw them, they were trying to put the Dormouse into the teapot.

" At any rate I'll never go *there* again ! " said Alice as she picked her way through the wood. " It's the stupidest tea-party I ever was at in all my life ! "

Just as she said this, she noticed that one of the trees had a door leading right into it. " That's very curious ! " she thought. " But everything's curious to-day. I think I may as well go in at once." And in she went.

Once more she found herself in the long hall, and close to the little glass table. " Now, I'll manage better this time," she said to herself, and began by taking the little golden key, and unlocking the door that led into the garden. Then she set to work nibbling at the mushroom (she had kept a piece of it in her pocket) till she was about a foot high : then she walked down the little passage : and *then*—she found herself at last in the beautiful garden, among the bright flower-beds and the cool fountains.

CHAPTER VIII

The Queen's Croquet-Ground

A LARGE rose-tree stood near the entrance of the garden : the roses growing on it were white, but there were three gardeners at it busily painting them red. Alice thought this a very curious thing, and she went nearer to watch them, and just as she came up to them she heard one of them say, " Look out now, Five ! Don't go splashing paint over me like that ! "

" I couldn't help it," said Five in a sulky tone. " Seven jogged my elbow."

On which Seven looked up and said " That's right, Five ! Always lay the blame on others ! "

" *You'd* better not talk ! " said Five " I heard the Queen say only yesterday you deserved to be beheaded ! "

" What for ? " said one who had first spoken.

" That's none of *your* business, Two ! " said Seven.

" Yes, it *is* his business ! " said Five. " And I'll tell him— it was for bringing the cook tulip-roots instead of onions."

Seven flung down his brush, and had just begun, " Well, of all the unjust things——" when his eye chanced to fall upon Alice, as she stood watching them, and he checked himself suddenly : the others looked round also, and all of them bowed low.

" Would you tell me," said Alice, a little timidly " why you are painting those roses."

Five and Seven said nothing, but looked at Two. Two began in a low voice, " Why, the fact is, you see, Miss, this here ought to have been a *red* rose-tree, and we put a white one in by mistake ; and if the Queen was to find out, we should all have our heads cut off, you know. So you see, Miss, we're doing our best afore she comes, to——" At this moment, Five, who had been anxiously looking across the garden, called out " The Queen ! The Queen ! " and the three gardeners instantly threw themselves flat upon their faces. There was a sound of many footsteps, and Alice looked round eager to see the Queen.

First came ten soldiers carrying clubs ; these were all shaped like the three gardeners oblong and flat, with their hands and feet at the corners : next the ten courtiers ; these were ornamented all over with diamonds, and walked two and two, as the soldiers did. After these came the royal children ; there were ten of them, and the little dears came jumping merrily along hand in hand, in couples ; they were all ornamented with hearts. Next came the guests, mostly Kings and Queens, and among them Alice recognised the White Rabbit : it was talking in a hurried, nervous manner, smiling at everything that was said, and went by without noticing her. Then followed the Knave of Hearts, carrying the King's crown on a crimson velvet cushion ; and, last of all this grand procession, came THE KING AND QUEEN OF HEARTS.

Alice was rather doubtful whether she ought not to lie down on her face like the three gardeners, but she could not remember ever having heard of such a rule at processions ; " and besides, what would be the use of a procession," thought she, " if people had all to lie down upon their faces, so that they couldn't see it ? " So she stood still where she was, and waited.

When the procession came opposite to Alice, they all stopped and looked at her, and the Queen said severely, " Who is this ? " She said it to the Knave of Hearts, who only bowed and smiled in reply.

" Idiot ! " said the Queen, tossing her head impatiently ; and, turning to Alice, she went on, " What's your name, child ? "

" My name is Alice, so please your Majesty," said Alice very politely ; but she added, to herself, " Why, they're only a pack of cards, after all. I needn't be afraid of them ! "

" And who are *these* ? " said the Queen, pointing to the three gardeners who were lying round the rose-tree ; for, you see, as they were lying on their faces, and the pattern on their backs was the same as the rest of the pack, she could not tell whether they were gardeners, or soldiers, or courtiers, or three of her own children.

" How should *I* know ? " said Alice surprised at her own courage. " It's no business of *mine*."

The Queen turned crimson with fury, and, after glaring at her for a moment like a wild beast, screamed " Off with her head ! Off——"

" Nonsense ! " said Alice, very loudly and decidedly, and the Queen was silent.

The King laid his hand upon her arm, and timidly said " Consider, my dear : she is only a child ! "

The Queen turned angrily away from him, and said to the Knave, " Turn them over ! "

The Knave did so, very carefully, with one foot.

" Get up ! " said the Queen, in a shrill, loud voice, and the three gardeners instantly jumped up, and began bowing to the King, the Queen, the royal children, and everybody else.

" Leave off that ! " screamed the Queen. " You make me giddy." And then, turning to the rose-tree, she went on, " What *have* you been doing here ? "

" May it please your Majesty," said Two, in a very humble tone, going down on one knee as he spoke, " we were trying——"

" *I* see ! " said the Queen, who had meanwhile been examining the roses. " Off with their heads ! " and the procession moved on, three of the soldiers remaining behind to execute the unfortunate gardeners, who ran to Alice for protection.

" You shan't be beheaded ! " said Alice, and she put them into a large flower-pot that stood near. The three soldiers wandered about for a minute or two, looking for them, and then quietly marched off after the others.

" Are their heads off ? " shouted the Queen.

" Their heads are gone, if it please your Majesty ! " the soldiers shouted in reply.

"That's right!" shouted the Queen. "Can you play croquet?"

The soldiers were silent, and looked at Alice, as the question was evidently meant for her.

"Yes!" shouted Alice.

"Come on, then!" roared the Queen, and Alice joined the procession, wondering very much what would happen next.

"It's—it's a very fine day!" said a timid voice at her side. She was walking by the White Rabbit, who was peeping anxiously into her face.

"Very," said Alice: "——where's the Duchess?"

"Hush! Hush!" said the Rabbit in a low hurried tone. He looked anxiously over his shoulder as he spoke, and then raised himself upon tiptoe, put his mouth close to her ear, and whispered "She's under sentence of execution."

"What for?" said Alice.

"Did you say, 'What a pity!'?" the Rabbit asked.

"No, I didn't," said Alice: "I don't think it's at all a pity. I said 'What for?'"

"She boxed the Queen's ears——" the Rabbit began. Alice gave a little scream of laughter. "Oh, hush!" the Rabbit whispered in a frightened tone. "The Queen will hear you! You see she came rather late, and the Queen said——"

"Get to your places!" shouted the Queen in a voice of thunder, and people began running about in all directions, tumbling up against each other; however, they got settled down in a minute or two, and the game began. Alice thought she had never seen such a curious croquet-ground in all her life; it was all ridges and furrows; the balls were live hedgehogs, the mallets live flamingoes, and the soldiers had to double themselves up and to stand upon their hands and feet, to make the arches.

The chief difficulty Alice found at first was in managing her flamingo; she succeeded in getting its body tucked away, comfortably enough, under her arm, with its legs hanging down, but generally, just as she had got its neck nicely straightened out, and was going to give the hedgehog a blow with its head, it *would* twist itself round and look up in her face, with such a puzzled expression that she could not help bursting out laughing : and when she had got its head down, and was going to begin again, it was very provoking to find that the hedgehog had unrolled itself, and was in the act of crawling away : besides all this, there was generally a ridge or a furrow in the way wherever she wanted to send the hedgehog to, and, as the doubled-up soldiers were always getting up and walking off to other parts of the ground, Alice soon came to the conclusion that it was a very difficult game indeed.

The players all played at once without waiting for turns, quarrelling all the while, and fighting for the hedgehogs ; and in a very short time the Queen was in a furious passion, and went stamping about, and shouting, " Off with his head ! " or " Off with her head ! " about once in a minute.

Alice began to feel very uneasy : to be sure she had not as yet had any dispute with the Queen, but she knew that it might happen any minute, " and then," thought she, " what would become of me ? They're dreadfully fond of beheading people here : the great wonder is that there's any one left alive ! "

She was looking about for some way of escape, and wondering whether she could get away without being seen, when she noticed a curious appearance in the air : it puzzled her very much at first, but, after watching it a minute or two, she made it out to be a grin, and she said to herself, " It's the Cheshire Cat : now I shall have somebody to talk to."

" How are you getting on ? " said the Cat, as soon as there was mouth enough for it to speak with.

Alice waited till the eyes appeared, and then nodded. " It's no use speaking to it," she thought, " till its ears have come, or at least one of them." In another minute the whole head appeared, and then Alice put down her flamingo, and began an account of the game, feeling very glad she had some one to listen to her. The Cat seemed to think that there was enough of it now in sight, and no more of it appeared.

" I don't think they play at all fairly," Alice began, in rather a complaining tone, " and they all quarrel so dreadfully one can't hear oneself speak—and they don't seem to have any rules in particular ; at least, if there are, nobody attends to them—and you've no idea how confusing it is all the things being alive ; for instance, there's the arch I've got to go through next walking about at the other end of the ground—and I should have croqueted the Queen's hedgehog just now, only it ran away when it saw mine coming ! "

" How do you like the Queen ? " said the Cat in a low voice.

" Not at all," said Alice : " she's so extremely——" Just then she noticed that the Queen was close behind her listening : so she went on, " ——likely to win, that it's hardly worth while finishing the game."

The Queen smiled and passed on.

" Who *are* you talking to ? " said the King, coming up to Alice, and looking at the Cat's head with great curiosity.

" It's a friend of mine—a Cheshire Cat," said Alice : " allow me to introduce it."

" I don't like the look of it at all," said the King : " however, it may kiss my hand if it likes."

" I'd rather not," the Cat remarked.

" Don't be impertinent," said the King, " and don't look at me like that ! " He got behind Alice as he spoke.

" A cat may look at a king," said Alice. " I've read that in some book, but I don't remember where."

" Well, it must be removed," said the King very decidedly, and he called to the Queen, who was passing at the moment, " My dear ! I wish you would have this cat removed ! "

The Queen had only one way of settling all difficulties great or small. " Off with his head ! " she said, without even looking round.

"I'll fetch the executioner myself," said the King eagerly, and he hurried off.

Alice thought she might as well go back and see how the game was going on, as she heard the Queen's voice in the distance, screaming with passion. She had already heard her sentence three of the players to be executed for having missed their turns, and she did not like the look of things at all, as the game was in such confusion that she never knew whether it was her turn or not. So she went in search of her hedgehog.

The hedgehog was engaged in a fight with another hedgehog, which seemed to Alice an excellent opportunity for croqueting one of them with the other : the only difficulty was, that her flamingo was gone across to the other side of the garden, where Alice could see it trying in a helpless sort of way to fly up into one of the trees.

By the time she had caught the flamingo and brought it back, the fight was over, and both the hedgehogs were out of sight : " but it doesn't matter much," thought Alice, " as all the arches are gone from this side of the ground." So she tucked it under her arm, that it might not escape again, and went back for a little more conversation with her friend.

When she got back to the Cheshire Cat, she was surprised to find quite a large crowd collected round it : there was a dispute going on between the executioner, the King, and the Queen, who were all talking at once, while all the rest were quite silent, and looked very uncomfortable.

The moment Alice appeared, she was appealed to by all three to settle the question, and they repeated their arguments to her, though, as they all spoke at once, she found it very hard indeed to make out exactly what they said.

The executioner's argument was, that you couldn't cut off a head unless there was a body to cut it off from : that he had never had to do such a thing before, and he wasn't going to begin at *his* time of life.

The King's argument was, that anything that had a

head could be beheaded, and that you weren't to talk nonsense.

The Queen's argument was, that if something wasn't done about it in less than no time, she'd have everybody executed all round. (It was this last remark that had made the whole party look so grave and anxious.)

Alice could think of nothing else to say but " It belongs to the Duchess ; you better ask *her* about it."

" She's in prison," the Queen said to the executioner ; "fetch her here." And the executioner went off like an arrow.

The Cat's head began fading away the moment he was gone, and, by the time he had come back with the Duchess, it had entirely disappeared ; so the King and the executioner ran wildly up and down looking for it, while the rest of the party went back to the game.

CHAPTER IX

The Mock Turtle's Story

" You can't think how glad I am to see you again, you dear old thing ! " said the Duchess, as she tucked her arm affectionately into Alice's and they walked off together.

Alice was very glad to find her in such a pleasant temper, and thought to herself that perhaps it was only the pepper that had made her so savage when they met in the kitchen.

" When *I'm* a Duchess," she said to herself (not in a very hopeful tone though), " I won't have any pepper in my kitchen *at all*. Soup does very well without—Maybe it's always pepper that makes people hot-tempered," she went on, very much pleased at having found out a new kind of rule, " and vinegar that makes them sour—and camomile that makes them bitter—and—and barley-sugar and such things that make children sweet-tempered. I only wish people knew *that* : then they wouldn't be so stingy about it, you know——"

She had quite forgotten the Duchess by this time, and

was a little startled when she heard her voice close to her ear. " You're thinking about something, my dear, and that makes you forget to talk. I can't tell you just now what the moral of that is, but I shall remember it in a bit."

" Perhaps it hasn't one," Alice ventured to remark.

" Tut, tut, child ! " said the Duchess. " Every thing's got a moral, if only you can find it." And she squeezed herself up closer to Alice's side as she spoke.

Alice did not much like her keeping so close to her : first, because the Duchess was *very* ugly ; and secondly, because she was exactly the right height to rest her chin on Alice's shoulder, and it was an uncomfortably sharp chin. However, she did not like to be rude, so she bore it as well as she could. " The game's going on rather better now," she said, by way of keeping up the conversation a little.

" 'Tis so," said the Duchess : "and the moral of that is— ' Oh, 'tis love, 'tis love, that makes the world go round ! ' "

" Somebody said," Alice whispered, " that it's done by everybody minding their own business ! "

" Ah, well ! It means much the same thing," said the Duchess, digging her sharp little chin into Alice's shoulder as she added, " and the moral of *that* is—' Take care of the sense, and the sounds will take care of themselves.' "

" How fond she is of finding morals in things ! " Alice thought to herself.

" I dare say you're wondering why I don't put my arm round your waist," the Duchess said after a pause : " the reason is, that I'm doubtful about the temper of your flamingo. Shall I try the experiment ? "

" He might bite," Alice cautiously replied, not feeling at all anxious to have the experiment tried.

" Very true," said the Duchess : " flamingoes and mustard both bite. And the moral of that is—' Birds of a feather flock together.' "

" Only mustard isn't a bird," Alice remarked.

" Right, as usual," said the Duchess : " what a clear way you have of putting things ! "

"It's a mineral, I *think*," said Alice.

"Of course it is," said the Duchess, who seemed ready to agree to everything that Alice said : "there's a large mustard-mine near here. And the moral of that is—' The more there is of mine, the less there is of yours.' "

"Oh, I know ! " exclaimed Alice, who had not attended to this last remark. "It's a vegetable. It doesn't look like one, but it is."

"I quite agree with you," said the Duchess ; "and the moral of that is—' Be what you would seem to be '—or if you'd like it put more simply—' Never imagine yourself not to be otherwise than what it might appear to others that what you were or might have been was not otherwise than what you had been would have appeared to them to be otherwise.' "

"I think I should understand that better," Alice said very politely, "if I had it written down : but I can't quite follow it as you say it."

"That's nothing to what I could say if I chose," the Duchess replied, in a pleased tone.

"Pray don't trouble yourself to say it any longer than that," said Alice.

"Oh, don't talk about trouble ! " said the Duchess. "I make you a present of everything I've said as yet."

"A cheap sort of present ! " thought Alice. "I'm glad they don't give birthday presents like that ! " But she did not venture to say it out loud.

"Thinking again ? " the Duchess asked with another dig of her sharp little chin.

"I've a right to think," said Alice sharply, for she was beginning to feel a little worried.

"Just about as much right," said the Duchess, "as pigs have to fly ; and the m——"

But here, to Alice's great surprise, the Duchess's voice died away, even in the middle of her favourite word "moral," and the arm that was linked into hers began to tremble. Alice looked up, and there stood the Queen in front of them, with her arms folded, frowning like a thunderstorm.

"A fine day, your Majesty!" the Duchess began in a low, weak voice.

"Now, I give you fair warning," shouted the Queen, stamping on the ground as she spoke; "either you or your head must be off, and that in about half no time! Take your choice!"

The Duchess took her choice, and was gone in a moment.

"Let's go on with the game," the Queen said to Alice; and Alice was too much frightened to say a word, but slowly followed her back to the croquet-ground.

The other guests had taken advantage of the Queen's absence, and were resting in the shade : however, the moment they saw her, they hurried back to the game, the Queen merely remarking that a moment's delay would cost them their lives.

All the time they were playing the Queen never left off quarrelling with the other players, and shouting "Off with his head!" or "Off with her head!" Those whom she sentenced were taken into custody by the soldiers, who of course had to leave off being arches to do this, so that by the end of half an hour or so there were no arches left, and all the players, except the King, the Queen, and Alice, were in custody and under sentence of execution.

Then the Queen left off, quite out of breath, and said to Alice, "Have you seen the Mock Turtle yet?"

"No," said Alice. "I don't even know what a Mock Turtle is."

"It's the thing Mock Turtle Soup is made from," said the Queen.

"I never saw one, or heard of one," said Alice.

"Come on then," said the Queen, "and he shall tell you his history."

As they walked off together, Alice heard the King say in a low voice, to the company generally, "You are all pardoned." "Come, *that's* a good thing!" she said to herself, for she had felt quite unhappy at the number of executions the Queen had ordered.

They very soon came upon a Gryphon, lying fast asleep in the sun " Up, lazy thing ! " said the Queen, " and take this young lady to see the Mock Turtle, and to hear his history. I must go back and see after some executions I have ordered," and she walked off, leaving Alice alone with the Gryphon. Alice did not quite like the look of the creature, but on the whole she thought it would be quite as safe to stay with it as to go after that savage Queen : so she waited.

The Gryphon sat up and rubbed its eyes : then it watched the Queen till she was out of sight : then it chuckled. " What fun ! " said the Gryphon, half to itself, half to Alice.

" What *is* the fun ? " said Alice.

" Why, *she*," said the Gryphon. " It's all her fancy, that : they never executes nobody, you know. Come on ! "

" Everybody says ' come on ! ' here," thought Alice, as she went slowly after it : " I never was so ordered about in all my life, never ! "

They had not gone far before they saw the Mock Turtle in the distance, sitting sad and lonely on a little ledge of rock, and, as they came nearer, Alice could hear him sighing as if his heart would break. She pitied him deeply. " What is his sorrow ? " she asked the Gryphon, and the Gryphon answered, very nearly in the same words as before, " It's all his fancy, that : he hasn't got no sorrow, you know. Come on ! "

So they went up to the Mock Turtle, who looked at them with large eyes full of tears, but said nothing.

" This here young lady," said the Gryphon, " she wants for to know your history, she do."

" I'll tell it her," said the Mock Turtle in a deep, hollow tone ; " sit down, both of you, and don't speak a word till I've finished."

So they sat down, and nobody spoke for some minutes.

Alice thought to herself, " I don't see how he can *ever* finish, if he doesn't begin." But she waited patiently.

" Once," said the Mock Turtle at last, with a deep sigh, " I was a real Turtle."

These words were followed by a very long silence, broken only by an occasional exclamation of " Hjckrrh ! " from the Gryphon, and the constant heavy sobbing of the Mock Turtle. Alice was very nearly getting up and saying " Thank you, sir, for your interesting story," but she could not help thinking there *must* be more to come, so she sat still and said nothing.

" When we were little," the Mock Turtle went on at last, more calmly, though still sobbing a little now and then, " we went to school in the sea. The master was an old Turtle—we used to call him Tortoise——"

" Why did you call him Tortoise, if he wasn't one ? " Alice asked.

" We called him Tortoise because he taught us," said the Mock Turtle angrily : " really you are very dull ! "

" You ought to be ashamed of yourself for asking such a simple question," added the Gryphon ; and then they both sat silent and looked at poor Alice, who felt ready to sink into the earth. At last the Gryphon said to the Mock Turtle, " Drive on, old fellow ! Don't be all day about it ! " and he went on in these words :

" Yes, we went to school in the sea, though you mayn't believe it——"

" I never said I didn't ! " interrupted Alice.

" You did," said the Mock Turtle.

" Hold your tongue ! " added the Gryphon, before Alice could speak again. The Mock Turtle went on :—

" We had the best of educations—in fact, we went to school every day——"

" *I've* been to a day-school, too," said Alice ; " you needn't be so proud as all that."

" With extras ? " asked the Mock Turtle a little anxiously.

" Yes," said Alice, " we learned French and music. "

" And washing ? " said the Mock Turtle.

" Certainly not ! " said Alice indignantly.

" Ah ! then yours wasn't a really good school," said the Mock Turtle in a tone of great relief. " Now at *ours* they had at the end of the bill, ' French, music, *and washing*—extra.' "

" You couldn't have wanted it much," said Alice ; " living at the bottom of the sea."

" I couldn't afford to learn it," said the Mock Turtle with a sigh. " I only took the regular course."

" What was that ? " inquired Alice.

" Reeling and Writhing, of course, to begin with," the Mock Turtle replied ; " and then the different branches of Arithmetic—Ambition, Distraction, Uglification, and Derision."

" I never heard of ' Uglification,' " Alice ventured to say. " What is it ? "

The Gryphon lifted up both its paws in surprise. " Never heard of uglifying ! " it exclaimed. " You know what to beautify is, I suppose ? "

" Yes," said Alice doubtfully : " it means—to—make—anything—prettier."

" Well, then," the Gryphon went on, " if you don't know what to uglify is, you are a simpleton."

Alice did not feel encouraged to ask any more questions about it, so she turned to the Mock Turtle, and said " What else had you to learn ? "

" Well, there was Mystery," the Mock Turtle replied, counting off the subjects on his flappers, " —Mystery, ancient and modern, with Seaography : then Drawling—the Drawling-master was an old conger-eel, that used to come once a week : *he* taught us Drawling, Stretching, and Fainting in Coils."

" What was *that* like ? " said Alice.

" Well, I can't show it you myself," the Mock Turtle said : " I'm too stiff. And the Gryphon never learnt it."

" Hadn't time," said the Gryphon : " I went to the Classical master, though. He was an old crab, *he* was."

" I never went to him," the Mock Turtle said with a sigh :
" he taught Laughing and Grief, they used to say."

"So he did, so he did," said the Gryphon, sighing in his
turn : and both creatures hid their faces in their paws.

" And how many hours a day did you do lessons ? " said
Alice, in a hurry to change the subject.

" Ten hours the first day," said the Mock Turtle :
" nine the next, and so on."

" What a curious plan ! " exclaimed Alice.

" That's the reason they're called lessons," the Gryphon
remarked : " because they lessen from day to day."

This was quite a new idea to Alice, and she thought it
over a little before she made her next remark. " Then the
eleventh day must have been a holiday."

" Of course it was," said the Mock Turtle.

" And how did you manage on the twelfth ? " Alice
went on eagerly.

" That's enough about lessons," the Gryphon interrupted in a very decided tone : " tell her something about
the games now."

CHAPTER X

The Lobster Quadrille

THE MOCK TURTLE sighed deeply, and drew the back of
one flapper across his eyes. He looked at Alice, and tried
to speak, but, for a minute or two, sobs choked his voice.
" Same as if he had a bone in his throat," said the Gryphon:
and it set to work shaking him and punching him in the
back. At last the Mock Turtle recovered his voice, and, with
tears running down his cheeks, went on again :—

" You may not have lived much under the sea—"
(" I haven't," said Alice) " and perhaps you were never
even introduced to a lobster—" (Alice began to say " I
once tasted——" but checked herself hastily, and said " No,
never ") " —so you can have no idea what a delightful
thing a Lobster Quadrille is ! "

" No, indeed," said Alice. " What sort of a dance is it ? "

" Why," said the Gryphon, " you first form into a line along the sea-shore——"

" Two lines ! " cried the Mock Turtle. " Seals, turtles, and so on ; then, when you've cleared the jelly-fish out of the way——"

" *That* generally takes some time," interrupted the Gryphon.

" —you advance twice——"

" Each with a lobster as a partner ! " cried the Gryphon.

" Of course," the Mock Turtle said : " Advance twice, set to partners——"

"—change lobsters, and retire in same order," continued the Gryphon.

" Then, you know," the Mock Turtle went on, " you throw the——"

" The lobsters ! " shouted the Gryphon, with a bound into the air.

" —as far out to sea as you can——"

" Swim after them ! " screamed the Gryphon.

" Turn a somersault in the sea ! " cried the Mock Turtle, capering wildly about.

" Change lobsters again ! " yelled the Gryphon.

" Back to land again, and—that's all the first figure," said the Mock Turtle, suddenly dropping his voice ; and the two creatures, who had been jumping about like mad things all this time, sat down again very sadly and quietly, and looked at Alice.

" It must be a very pretty dance," said Alice, timidly.

" Would you like to see a little of it ? " said the Mock Turtle.

" Very much indeed," said Alice.

" Come, let's try the first figure ! " said the Mock Turtle to the Gryphon. " We can do it without lobsters, you know. Which shall sing ? "

" Oh, *you* sing," said the Gryphon. " I've forgotten the words."

So they began solemnly dancing round and round Alice, every now and then treading on her toes when they passed too close, and waving their forepaws to mark the time, while the Mock Turtle sang this, very slowly and sadly :—

" *Will you walk a little faster ?* " *said a whiting to a snail.*
" *There's a porpoise close behind us, and he's treading on my tail.*
See how eagerly the lobsters and the turtles all advance !
They are waiting on the shingle—will you come and join the dance ?
> *Will you, won't you, will you, won't you, will you join the dance ?*
> *Will you, won't you, will you, won't you, won't you join the dance ?*

" *You can really have no notion how delightful it will be,*
When they take us up and throw us, with the lobsters, out to sea ! "
But the snail replied " *Too far, too far !* " *and gave a look askance—*
Said he thanked the whiting kindly, but he would not join the dance.
> *Would not, could not, would not, could not, would not join the dance.*
> *Would not, could not, would not, could not, could not join the dance.*

" *What matters it how far we go ?* " *his scaly friend replied.*
" *There is another shore, you know, upon the other side.*
The further off from England the nearer is to France—
Then turn not pale, beloved snail, but come and join the dance,
> *Will you, won't you, will you, won't you, will you join the dance ?*
> *Will you, won't you, will you, won't you, won't you join the dance ?* "

" Thank you, it's a very interesting dance to watch," said Alice, feeling very glad that it was over at last : " and I do so like that curious song about the whiting ! "

" Oh, as to the whiting," said the Mock Turtle, " they —you've seen them, of course ? "

"Yes," said Alice, "I've often seen them at dinn——" she checked herself hastily.

"I don't know where Dinn may be," said the Mock Turtle, "but if you've seen them so often, of course you know what they're like."

"I believe so," Alice replied thoughtfully. "They have their tails in their mouths—and they're all over crumbs."

"You're wrong about the crumbs," said the Mock Turtle : "crumbs would all wash off in the sea. But they *have* their tails in their mouths ; and the reason is——" here the Mock Turtle yawned and shut his eyes. "Tell her about the reason and all that," he said to the Gryphon.

"The reason is," said the Gryphon, "that they *would* go with the lobsters to the dance. So they got thrown out to sea. So they had to fall a long way. So they got their tails fast in their mouths. So they couldn't get them out again. That's all."

"Thank you," said Alice, "it's very interesting. I never knew so much about a whiting before."

"I can tell you more than that, if you like," said the Gryphon. "Do you know why it's called a whiting ? "

"I never thought about it," said Alice. "Why ? "

"*It does the boots and shoes*," the Gryphon replied very solemnly.

Alice was thoroughly puzzled. "Does the boots and shoes ! " she repeated in a wondering tone.

"Why, what are *your* shoes done with ? " said the Gryphon. "I mean, what makes them so shiny ? "

Alice looked down at them, and considered a little before she gave her answer. "They're done with blacking, I believe."

"Boots and shoes under the sea," the Gryphon went on in a deep voice, "are done with whiting. Now you know."

"And what are they made of ? " Alice asked in a tone of great curiosity.

"Soles and eels, of course," the Gryphon replied rather impatiently : "any shrimp could have told you that."

" If I'd been the whiting," said Alice, whose thoughts were still running on the song, " I'd have said to the porpoise, ' Keep back, please : we don't want *you* with us ! ' "

" They were obliged to have him with them," the Mock Turtle said : " No wise fish would go anywhere without a porpoise."

" Wouldn't it really ? " said Alice in a tone of great surprise.

" Of course not," said the Mock Turtle : " Why, if a fish came to *me*, and told me he was going a journey, I should say ' with what porpoise ? ' "

" Don't you mean ' purpose ' ? " said Alice.

" I mean what I say," the Mock Turtle replied in an offended tone. And the Gryphon added " Come, let's hear some of *your* adventures."

" I could tell you my adventures—beginning from this morning," said Alice a little timidly : " But it's no use going back to yesterday, because I was a different person then."

" Explain all that," said the Mock Turtle.

" No, no ! The adventures first," said the Gryphon in an impatient tone : "explanations take such a dreadful time."

So Alice began telling them her adventures from the time when she first saw the White Rabbit. She was a little nervous about it just at first, the two creatures got so close to her, one on each side, and opened their eyes and mouths so *very* wide, but she gained courage as she went on. Her listeners were perfectly quiet till she got to the part about her repeating " *You are old, Father William*," to the Caterpillar, and the words all coming different, and then the Mock Turtle drew a long breath, and said " That's very curious."

" It's all about as curious as it can be," said the Gryphon.

" It all came different ! " the Mock Turtle repeated thoughtfully. " I should like to hear her repeat something now. Tell her to begin." He looked at the Gryphon as if he thought it had some kind of authority over Alice.

" Stand up and repeat '*Tis the voice of the sluggard,*' " said the Gryphon.

" How the creatures order one about and make one repeat lessons ! " thought Alice. " I might as well be at school at once." However, she got up, and began to repeat it, but her head was so full of the Lobster Quadrille, that she hardly knew what she was saying, and the words came very queer indeed :—

> " '*Tis the voice of the Lobster ; I heard him declare,*
> ' *You have baked me too brown, I must sugar my hair.*'
> *As a duck with its eyelids, so he with his nose*
> *Trims his belt and his buttons, and turns out his toes.*
> *When the sands are all dry, he is gay as a lark,*
> *And will talk in contemptuous tones of the Shark :*
> *But, when the tide rises and sharks are around,*
> *His voice has a timid and tremulous sound.*"

" That's different from what *I* used to say when I was a child," said the Gryphon.

" Well, *I* never heard it before," said the Mock Turtle : " but it sounds uncommon nonsense."

Alice said nothing ; she had sat down with her face in her hands, wondering if anything would *ever* happen in a natural way again.

" I should like to have it explained," said the Mock Turtle.

" She can't explain it," hastily said the Gryphon. " Go on with the next verse."

" But about his toes ? " the Mock Turtle persisted. " How *could* he turn them out with his nose, you know ? "

" It's the first position in dancing," Alice said ; but was dreadfully puzzled by the whole thing, and longed to change the subject.

" Go on with the next verse," the Gryphon repeated : " it begins ' *I passed by his garden.*' "

Alice did not dare to disobey, though she felt sure it

would all come wrong, and she went on in a trembling voice :—

> " *I passed by his garden, and marked, with one eye,*
> *How the Owl and the Panther were sharing a pie :*
> *The Panther took pie-crust, and gravy, and meat,*
> *While the Owl had the dish as its share of the treat.*
> *When the pie was all finished, the Owl, as a boon,*
> *Was kindly permitted to pocket the spoon :*
> *While the Panther received knife and fork with a growl,*
> *And concluded the banquet by——*"

" What *is* the use of repeating all that stuff," the Mock Turtle interrupted, " if you don't explain it as you go on ? It's by far the most confusing thing *I* ever heard ! "

" Yes, I think you'd better leave off," said the Gryphon : and Alice was only too glad to do so.

" Shall we try another figure of the Lobster Quadrille ? " the Gryphon went on. " Or would you like the Mock Turtle to sing you another song ? "

" Oh, a song, please, if the Mock Turtle would be so kind," Alice replied, so eagerly that the Gryphon said, in a rather offended tone, " Hm ! No accounting for tastes ! Sing her ' *Turtle Soup*,' will you, old fellow ? "

The Mock Turtle sighed deeply, and began, in a voice choked with sobs, to sing this :—

> " *Beautiful Soup, so rich and green,*
> *Waiting in a hot tureen !*
> *Who for such dainties would not stoop ?*
> *Soup of the evening, beautiful Soup !*
> *Soup of the evening, beautiful Soup !*
>   *Beau—ootiful Soo—oop !*
>   *Beau—ootiful Soo—oop !*
> *Soo—oop of the e—e—evening,*
>   *Beautiful, beautiful Soup !*

> *" Beautiful Soup ! Who cares for fish,*
> *Game, or any other dish ?*
> *Who would not give all else for two p*
> *ennyworth only of beautiful Soup !*
> *Pennyworth only of beautiful Soup ?*
>   *Beau—ootiful Soo—oop !*
>   *Beau—ootiful Soo—oop !*
> *Soo—oop of the e—e—evening,*
>   *Beautiful, beauti—FUL SOUP ! "*

" Chorus again ! " cried the Gryphon, and the Mock Turtle had just begun to repeat it, when a cry of " The trial's beginning ! " was heard in the distance.

" Come on ! " cried the Gryphon, and, taking Alice by the hand, it hurried off, without waiting for the end of the song.

" What trial is it ? " Alice panted as she ran ; but the Gryphon only answered " Come on ! " and ran the faster, while more and more faintly came, carried on the breeze that followed them, the melancholy words :—

> *" Soo—oop of the e—e—evening,*
>   *Beautiful, beautiful Soup ! "*

CHAPTER XI

Who Stole the Tarts ?

THE KING and Queen of Hearts were seated on their throne when they arrived, with a great crowd assembled about them—all sorts of little birds and beasts, as well as the whole pack of cards : the Knave was standing before them, in chains, with a soldier on each side to guard him ; and near the King was the White Rabbit, with a trumpet in one hand, and a scroll of parchment in the other. In the very middle of the court was a table, with a large dish of tarts upon it : they looked so good, that it made Alice quite hungry to look at them—" I wish they'd get the trial done," she thought, " and hand round the refreshments ! " But there seemed to be no chance of this, so she began looking about her, to pass away the time.

Alice had never been in a court of justice before, but she had read about them in books, and she was quite pleased to find that she knew the name of nearly everything there. " That's the judge," she said to herself, " because of his great wig."

The judge, by the way, was the King ; and as he wore his crown over the wig, he did not look at all comfortable, and it was certainly not becoming.

" And that's the jury-box," thought Alice, " and those twelve creatures," (she was obliged to say " creatures," you see, because some of them were animals, and some were birds,) " I suppose they are the jurors." She said this last word two or three times over to herself, being rather proud of it : for she thought, and rightly too, that very few little girls of her age knew the meaning of it at all. However, " jurymen " would have done just as well.

The twelve jurors were all writing very busily on slates. " What are they all doing ? " Alice whispered to the Gryphon. " They ca'n't have anything to put down yet, before the trial's begun."

" They're putting down their names," the Gryphon whispered in reply, " for fear they should forget them before the end of the trial."

" Stupid things ! " Alice began in a loud, indignant voice, but she stopped hastily, for the White Rabbit cried out "Silence in the court ! " and the King put on his spectacles and looked anxiously round, to see who was talking.

Alice could see, as well as if she were looking over their shoulders, that all the jurors were writing down " stupid things ! " on their slates, and she could even make out that one of them didn't know how to spell " stupid," and that he had to ask his neighbour to tell him.

" A nice muddle their slates will be in before the trial's over ! " thought Alice.

One of the jurors had a pencil that squeaked. This, of course, Alice could *not* stand, and she went round the court and got behind him, and very soon found an opportunity of taking it away. She did it so quickly that the poor little juror (it was Bill, the Lizard) could not make out at all what had become of it ; so, after hunting all about for it, he was obliged to write with one finger for the rest of the day ; and this was of very little use, as it left no mark on the slate.

" Herald, read the accusation ! " said the King.

On this the White Rabbit blew three blasts on the trumpet, and then unrolled the parchment scroll, and read as follows :—

> " *The Queen of Hearts, she made some tarts,*
> *All on a summer day :*
> *The Knave of Hearts, he stole those tarts,*
> *And took them quite away !* "

" Consider your verdict," the King said to the jury.

" Not yet, not yet ! " the Rabbit hastily interrupted. " There's a great deal to come before that ! "

" Call the first witness," said the King ; and the White Rabbit blew three blasts on the trumpet, and called out " First witness ! "

The first witness was the Hatter. He came in with a teacup in one hand and a piece of bread-and-butter in the other. " I beg your pardon, your Majesty," he began, " for bringing these in : but I hadn't quite finished my tea when I was sent for."

" You ought to have finished," said the King. " When did you begin ? "

The Hatter looked at the March Hare, who had followed him into the court, arm-in-arm with the Dormouse. " Fourteenth of March, I *think* it was," he said.

" Fifteenth," said the March Hare.

" Sixteenth," said the Dormouse.

"Write that down," the King said to the jury, and the jury eagerly wrote down all three dates on their slates, and then added them up, and reduced the answer to shillings and pence.

" Take off your hat," the King said to the Hatter.

" It isn't mine," said the Hatter.

" *Stolen !* " the King exclaimed, turning to the jury, who instantly made a memorandum of the fact.

" I keep them to sell," the Hatter added as an explanation : " I've none of my own. I'm a hatter."

Here the Queen put on her spectacles, and began staring hard at the Hatter, who turned pale and fidgeted.

" Give your evidence," said the King ; " and don't be nervous, or I'll have you executed on the spot."

This did not seem to encourage the witness at all : he kept shifting from one foot to the other, looking uneasily at the Queen, and in his confusion he bit a large piece out of his teacup instead of the bread-and-butter.

Just at this moment Alice felt a very curious sensation, which puzzled her a good deal until she made out what it was : she was beginning to grow larger again, and she thought at first she would get up and leave the court ; but on second thoughts she decided to remain where she was as long as there was room for her.

" I wish you wouldn't squeeze so," said the Dormouse, who was sitting next to her. " I can hardly breathe."

" I can't help it," said Alice very meekly : " I'm growing."

" You've no right to grow *here*," said the Dormouse.

" Don't talk nonsense," said Alice more boldly : " you know you're growing too."

" Yes, but I grow at a reasonable pace," said the Dormouse ; " not in that ridiculous fashion." And he got up very sulkily and crossed over to the other side of the court.

All this time the Queen had never left off staring at the Hatter, and just as the Dormouse crossed the court, she said to one of the officers of the court, " Bring me the list of the singers in the last concert ! " on which the wretched Hatter trembled so, that he shook off both his shoes.

" Give your evidence," the King repeated angrily, " or I'll have you executed, whether you're nervous or not."

" I'm a poor man, your Majesty," the Hatter began, in a trembling voice,—" and I hadn't begun my tea—not above a week or so—and what with the bread-and-butter getting so thin—and the twinkling of the tea——"

" The twinkling of *what* ? " said the King.

" It *began* with the tea," the Hatter replied.

" Of course twinkling *begins* with a T ! " said the King sharply. " Do you take me for a dunce ? Go on ! "

" I'm a poor man," the Hatter went on, " and most things twinkled after that—only the March Hare said——"

" I didn't ! " the March Hare interrupted in a great hurry.

" You did ! " said the Hatter.

" I deny it ! " said the March Hare.

" He denies it," said the King : " leave out that part."

" Well, at any rate, the Dormouse said——" the Hatter went on, looking anxiously round to see if he would deny it too : but the Dormouse denied nothing, being fast asleep.

" After that," continued the Hatter, " I cut some more bread-and-butter——"

" But what did the Dormouse say ? " one of the jury asked.

" That I ca'n't remember," said the Hatter.

" You *must* remember," remarked the King, " or I'll have you executed."

The miserable Hatter dropped his tea-cup and bread-and-butter, and went down on one knee. " I'm a poor man, your Majesty," he began.

" You're a *very* poor *speaker*," said the King.

Here one of the guinea-pigs cheered, and was immediately suppressed by the officers of the court. (As that is rather a hard word, I will just explain to you how it was done. They had a large canvas bag, which tied up at the mouth with strings : into this they slipped the guinea-pig, head first, and then sat upon it.)

" I'm glad I've seen that done," thought Alice. " I've so often read in the newspapers, at the end of trials, ' There was some attempt at applause, which was immediately suppressed by the officers of the court,' and I never understood what it meant till now."

" If that's all you know about it, you may stand down," continued the King.

" I ca'n't go no lower," said the Hatter : " I'm on the floor as it is."

" Then you may *sit* down," the King replied.

Here the other guinea-pig cheered, and was suppressed.

" Come, that finishes the guinea-pigs ! " thought Alice. " Now we shall get on better."

" I'd rather finish my tea," said the Hatter, with an anxious look at the Queen, who was reading the list of singers.

" You may go," said the King ; and the Hatter hurriedly left the court, without even waiting to put his shoes on.

" —and just take his head off outside," the Queen added to one of the officers ; but the Hatter was out of sight before the officer could get to the door.

" Call the next witness ! " said the King.

The next witness was the Duchess's cook. She carried the pepper-box in her hand, and Alice guessed who it was, even before she got into the court, by the way the people near the door began sneezing all at once.

" Give your evidence," said the King.

" Sha'n't," said the cook.

The King looked anxiously at the White Rabbit, who said in a low voice, "Your Majesty must cross-examine *this* witness."

" Well, if I must, I must," the King said with a melancholy air, and, after folding his arms and frowning at the cook till his eyes were nearly out of sight, he said in a deep voice, " What are tarts made of ? "

" Pepper, mostly," said the cook.

" Treacle," said a sleepy voice behind her.

" Collar that Dormouse," the Queen shrieked out. " Behead that Dormouse ! Turn that Dormouse out of court ! Suppress him ! Pinch him ! Off with his whiskers."

For some minutes the whole court was in confusion, getting the Dormouse turned out, and, by the time they had settled down again, the cook had disappeared.

" Never mind ! " said the King, with an air of great relief. " Call the next witness." And he added in an undertone to the Queen, " Really, my dear, *you* must cross-examine the next witness. It quite makes my forehead ache ! "

Alice watched the White Rabbit as he fumbled over the list, feeling very curious to see what the next witness would be like, " —for they haven't got much evidence *yet*," she said to herself. Imagine her surprise, when the White Rabbit read out, at the top of his shrill little voice, the name "Alice ! "

CHAPTER XII

Alice's Evidence

'' HERE ! '' cried Alice, quite forgetting in the flurry of the moment how large she had grown in the last few minutes, and she jumped up in such a hurry that she tipped over the jury-box with the edge of her skirt, upsetting all the jurymen on to the heads of the crowd below, and there they lay sprawling about, reminding her very much of a globe of gold-fish she had accidentally upset the week before.

" Oh, I beg your pardon ! " she exclaimed in a tone of great dismay, and began picking them up again as quickly as she could, for the accident of the gold-fish kept running in her head, and she had a vague sort of idea that they must be collected at once and put back into the jury-box or they would die.

" The trial cannot proceed," said the King in a very grave voice, " until all the jury-men are back in their proper places—*all*," he repeated with great emphasis, looking hard at Alice as he said so.

Alice looked at the jury-box, and saw that, in her haste, she had put the Lizard in head downwards, and the poor little thing was waving its tail about in a melancholy way, being quite unable to move.

She soon got it out again, and put it right ; " not that it signifies much," she said to herself ; " I should think it would be *quite* as much use in the trial one way up as the other."

As soon as the jury had a little recovered from the shock of being upset, and their slates and pencils had been found and handed back to them, they set to work very diligently to write out a history of the accident, all except the Lizard, who seemed too much overcome to do anything but sit with its mouth open gazing up into the roof of the court.

" What do you know about this business ? " the King said to Alice.

" Nothing," said Alice.

" Nothing *whatever* ? " persisted the King.

" Nothing whatever," said Alice.

" That's very important," the King said, turning to the jury. They were just beginning to write this down on their slates, when the White Rabbit interrupted : " *Un*important, your Majesty means, of course," he said in a very respectful tone, but frowning and making faces at him as he spoke.

" *Un*important, of course, I meant," the King hastily said, and went on to himself in an undertone, " important —unimportant—unimportant—important——" as if he were trying which word sounded best.

Some of the jury wrote it down " important," and some " unimportant," Alice could see this, as she was near enough to look over their slates ; " but it doesn't matter a bit," she thought to herself.

At this moment the King, who had been for some time busily writing in his notebook, called out " Silence ! " and read out from his book, " Rule Forty-two. *All persons more than a mile high to leave the court.*"

Everybody looked at Alice.

" *I'm* not a mile high," said Alice.

" You are," said the King.

" Nearly two miles high," added the Queen.

" Well, I sha'n't go, at any rate," said Alice : " besides,

that's not a regular rule : you invented it just now."

" It's the oldest rule in the book," said the King.

" Then it ought to be Number One," said Alice.

The King turned pale and shut his notebook hastily. " Consider your verdict," he said to the jury, in a low trembling voice.

" There's more evidence to come yet, please your Majesty," said the White Rabbit, jumping up in a great hurry : " This paper has just been picked up."

" What's in it ? " said the Queen.

" I haven't opened it yet," said the White Rabbit, " but it seems to be a letter, written by the prisoner to—to somebody."

" It must have been that," said the King, " unless it was written to nobody, which isn't usual, you know."

" Who is it directed to ? " said one of the jurymen.

" It isn't directed at all," said the White Rabbit ; " in fact, there's nothing written on the *outside*." He unfolded the paper as he spoke, and added " It isn't a letter, after all : it's a set of verses."

" Are they in the prisoner's handwriting ? " asked another of the jurymen.

" No, they're not," said the White Rabbit, " and that's the queerest thing about it." (The jury all looked puzzled.)

" He must have imitated somebody else's hand," said the King. (The jury all brightened up again.)

" Please your Majesty," said the Knave, " I didn't write it, and they can't prove that I did : there's no name signed at the end."

" If you didn't sign it," said the King, " that only makes the matter worse. You *must* have meant some mischief, or else you'd have signed your name like an honest man."

There was a general clapping of hands at this : it was the first really clever thing the King had said that day.

" That *proves* his guilt, of course," said the Queen : " so, off with——"

" It doesn't prove anything of the sort ! " said Alice. " Why, you don't even know what they're about ! "

" Read them," said the King.

The White Rabbit put on his spectacles. " Where shall I begin, please your Majesty ? " he asked.

" Begin at the beginning," the King said gravely, " and go on till you come to the end ; then stop."

There was dead silence in the court, whilst the White Rabbit read out these verses :—

> " *They told me you had been to her,*
> *And mentioned me to him :*
> *She gave me a good character,*
> *But said I could not swim.*
>
> *He sent them word I had not gone,*
> *(We know it to be true) :*
> *If she should push the matter on,*
> *What would become of you ?*
>
> *I gave her one, they gave him two,*
> *You gave us three or more ;*
> *They all returned from him to you,*
> *Though they were mine before.*
>
> *If I or she should chance to be*
> *Involved in this affair,*
> *He trusts to you to set them free,*
> *Exactly as we were.*
>
> *My notion was that you had been*
> *(Before she had this fit)*
> *An obstacle that came between,*
> *Him, and ourselves, and it.*
>
> *Don't let him know she liked them best,*
> *For this must ever be*
> *A secret kept from all the rest,*
> *Between yourself and me."*

" That's the most important piece of evidence we've heard yet," said the King, rubbing his hands ; " so now let the jury——"

" If any one of them can explain it," said Alice, (she had grown so large in the last few minutes that she wasn't a bit afraid of interrupting him,) " I'll give him sixpence. I don't believe there's an atom of meaning in it."

The jury all wrote down on their slates, " *She* doesn't believe there's an atom of meaning in it," but none of them attempted to explain the paper.

" If there's no meaning in it," said the King, " that saves a world of trouble, you know, as we needn't try to find any. And yet I don't know," he went on, spreading out the verses on his knee, and looking at them with one eye ; " I seem to see some meaning in them, after all. ' ——*said I could not swim*—, you can't swim, can you ? " he added turning to the Knave.

The Knave shook his head sadly. " Do I look like it ? " he said. (Which he certainly did *not*, being made entirely of cardboard.)

" All right, so far," said the King, and he went on muttering over the verses to himself : " ' *We know it to be true*—' that's the jury, of course—' *If she should push the matter on* '— that must be the Queen—' *What would become of you ?* ' What, indeed !—' *I gave her one, they gave him two*—' why, that must be what he did with the tarts, you know——"

" But it goes on ' *they all returned from him to you*,' " said Alice.

" Why, there they are ! " said the King triumphantly, pointing to the tarts on the table. " Nothing can be clearer than *that*. Then again—' *before she had this fit*— ' you never had *fits*, my dear, I think ? " he said to the Queen.

" Never ! " said the Queen furiously, throwing an ink-stand at the Lizard as she spoke. (The unfortunate little Bill had left off writing on his slate with one finger, as he found it made no mark ; but he now hastily began again, using the ink, that was trickling down his face, as long as it lasted.)

" Then the words don't *fit* you," said the King, looking round the court with a smile. There was a dead silence.

" It's a pun ! " the King added in an angry tone, and everybody laughed.

" Let the jury consider their verdict," the King said, for about the twentieth time that day.

" No, no ! " said the Queen. " Sentence first—verdict afterwards."

" Stuff and nonsense ! " said Alice loudly. " The idea of having the sentence first ! "

" Hold your tongue ! " said the Queen, turning purple.

" I won't ! " said Alice.

" Off with her head ! " the Queen shouted at the top of her voice. Nobody moved.

" Who cares for *you*? " said Alice, (she had grown to her full size by this time.) " You're nothing but a pack of cards ! "

At this the whole pack rose up into the air, and came flying down upon her : she gave a little scream, half of fright and half of anger, and tried to beat them off, and found herself lying on the bank, with her head in the lap of her sister, who was gently brushing away some dead leaves that had fluttered down from the trees upon her face.

" Wake up, Alice, dear ! " said her sister. " Why, what a long sleep you've had ! "

" Oh, I've had such a curious dream ! " said Alice, and she told her sister, as well as she could remember them, all these strange Adventures of hers that you have just been reading about ; and when she had finished, her sister kissed her and said " It *was* a curious dream, dear, certainly : but now run in to your tea ; it's getting late." So Alice got up and ran off, thinking while she ran, as well she might, what a wonderful dream it had been.

But her sister sat still just as she had left her, leaning her head on her hand, watching the setting sun, and thinking of little Alice and all her wonderful Adventures, till she too began dreaming after a fashion, and this was her dream :—

First, she dreamed of little Alice herself, and once again the tiny hands were clasped upon her knee, and the bright eager eyes were looking up into hers—she could hear the very tones of her voice, and see that queer little toss of her head to keep back the wandering hair that *would* always get into her eyes—and still as she listened, or seemed to listen, the whole place around her became alive with the strange creatures of her little sister's dream.

The long grass rustled at her feet as the White Rabbit hurried by—the frightened Mouse splashed his way through the neighbouring pool—she could hear the rattle of the teacups as the March Hare and his friends shared their never-ending meal, and the shrill voice of the Queen ordering off her unfortunate guests to execution—once more the pig-baby was sneezing on the Duchess's knee, while plates and dishes crashed around it—once more the shriek of the Gryphon, the squeaking of the Lizard's slate-pencil, and the choking of the suppressed guinea-pigs, filled the air mixed up with the distant sobs of the miserable Mock Turtle.

So she sat on with closed eyes, and half believed herself in Wonderland, though she knew she had but to open them again, and all would change to dull reality—the grass would be only rustling in the wind, and the pool rippling to the waving of the reeds—the rattling teacups would change to the tinkling sheep-bells, and the Queen's shrill cries to the voice of the shepherd boy—and the sneeze of the baby, the shriek of the Gryphon, and all the other queer noises, would change (she knew) to the confused clamour of the busy farm-yard—while the lowing of the cattle in the distance would take the place of the Mock Turtle's heavy sobs.

Lastly, she pictured to herself how this same little sister of hers would, in the aftertime, be herself a grown woman ; and how she would keep, through all her riper years, the simple and loving heart of her childhood : and how she would gather about her other little children, and make *their* eyes bright and eager with many a strange tale, perhaps even with the dream of Wonderland of long ago : and how she would feel with all their simple sorrows, and find a pleasure in all their simple joys, remembering her own child-life, and the happy summer days.